I0573873

From Men and Angels

The Deliverance Trilogy: Book One

H. L. Walsh

H. L. Walsh Books

Kansas City, Mo

Copyright © 2019 by H. L. Walsh

Third Edition

Walsh, H. L.

From Men and Angels, The Deliverance Trilogy: Book One/ H. L. Walsh/ H. L. Walsh Books, Kansas City, Missouri USA

ISBN: 978-1-7340922-0-2

Cover Design By: TheBookCoverZone

Map Design By: Najlakay

ALL RIGHTS RESERVED. NO PART OF THE PUBLICATION MAY BE REPRODUCED, STORED IN A RETRIVAL SYSTEM, OR TRANSMITTED IN ANY FORM OR BY ANY MEANS-ELECTRONIC, MECHANICAL, PHOTOCOPY, RECORDING, OR ANY OTHER-EXCEPT FOR BREIF QUOTATIONS IN PRINTED REVIEWS, WITHOUT THE PRIOR PERMISION OF THE AUTHOR/PUBLISHER.

UNRELENTING MOUNTAINS
BRIGHTWOOD
PANGOR RIVER
ANGEL TERRITORY
UNEXPLORED REGION
ANGELCROSS
THE DIVIDE
THE DIVIDE
RARGOD
RAGEWOOD FOREST
DEMON TERRITORY
RAGEWOOD
DEMON COMPOUND

List of books by H. L. Walsh

The Deliverance Trilogy

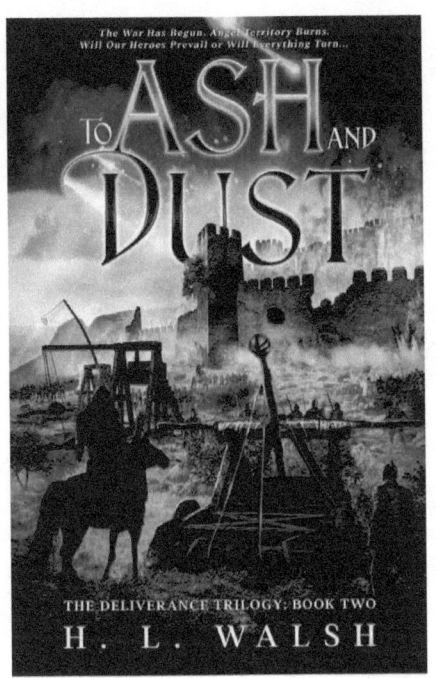

Chapter 1

Malach Tresch ran through the dense underbrush swiftly and quietly; he was in his element. It was night, and even though these woods were not the woods he grew up in, he had an idea of where he was headed. He also knew it would be easy to get turned around and lost in this forest. His legs ached from running for so long, and he was pulling in ragged gasps of breath. Something was hard on his heels and he didn't know who or what it was, but it was big. It scared him so much he didn't have the courage to even look back. He just kept running.

Something hard and metal was in his hand, and it was heavy. He looked down to see what it was. The weapon had a peculiar appearance. A short staff with two curved blades protruding from either end, so he could use either side offensively. It felt good in his hand; balanced, normal, right, like he had used it all his life. It was an extension of his body. There was only one issue. He had never seen it before. He also had his bow slung over his chest, his side quiver, and a large hunting knife on his belt. Those he recognized. However, as he ran, he realized there were no arrows in the quiver, which was probably why he was carrying the staff weapon instead of his bow, his weapon of choice.

All of this only took him seconds to process and seconds more to realize he had, in fact, gotten lost. He couldn't stop, though. He could hear the monster behind him, breathing as hard as he was and knew it would be on him at any moment. As scared as he was, he knew he would have to turn and face the creature soon. He hoped to outrun it, but that had been a mistake. Possibly a fatal one.

His mind reeled as it processed what had happened. The creature had dropped on his platoon and killed half a dozen of them in the span of a few minutes. Fully trained men. Men whom he knew and trusted. Men who had been trained from childhood lay dead, dying, or scattered like scared rabbits, all semblance of discipline lost. Malach was no exception. He had glanced back and gotten a glimpse of Daziar standing his ground with his spear and losing his head for it. Malach would never forget the sight of Daziar's head hitting the ground as his body slumped onto its side, the lifeless eyes staring out at nothing.

That one pause would probably cost Malach his life. He had been spotted by the creature at that moment. They had locked eyes, and it was going to kill him. The creature stood well over ten feet tall, mostly black, with large, bat-like wings. It stood on two legs to fight and had large, razor-sharp, clawed hands and feet with spikes sticking out of its elbows and knees. When it spotted Malach, it dropped to all fours and gave a wicked, spiked-toothed grin that made Malach's blood run cold. Malach mentally screamed at his legs to move, and after a moment that felt like an eternity, they finally responded.

Now it was almost on him. He must have run five miles, and Malach had a sinking feeling that it was playing with him. Staying just behind him to keep this sick game of cat and mouse going. But why? Whatever the reason, Malach was done with it. He wouldn't play its game anymore. He mustered his strength and reached up, grabbing a low-hanging branch. Using his momentum, he swung up onto it, climbing nimbly up a few more feet and waited for the creature to run by. He would get behind this creature to become the hunter instead of the hunted and kill this thing once and for all.

He forced his breathing to slow while he waited. He couldn't hear the creature anymore, and for a second, he thought he might have actually lost it. Then it came into view. As silent as the night. Slow, cautious, like it knew something was not right. Like it knew its quarry had changed tactics. It started toward the tree Malach was hiding in, and he held his breath. Readying his staff weapon, he prepared to leap down on top of the giant monster. He prepared for the end.

Studying the creature, he realized this monster was a demon. The bat-like wings and horns visible from the back of the demon's head were unmistakable. If the creature turned around, he would see its glowing red eyes staring back at him. His strength almost failed him at the realization. No one had seen a demon in over two thousand years. . . at least, no one he knew about. They were the stuff of legends. Something grandparents would tell their grandchildren to make them behave. Malach pulled his thoughts back to the present and the task at hand. He would be the first to kill a demon in over two thousand years, or he would die by its hand. The next few moments would decide that.

The demon was almost under him and he would have a clear path to drop onto its back and run the blade of his staff through the creature's brain. All of a sudden the demon snapped its head to the side, or rather turned it almost all the way around without moving its body, as if it heard something Malach couldn't and then took off at full speed in the way it had come with a flurry of wind from its wings. Malach didn't dare relax until the sound of its retreat had faded into the night entirely. After a few more silent moments, he sat down heavily on the branch he had been crouching on and let out a sigh of relief. He had to tell someone what he had seen. He had to get out of here before that demon came back.

He climbed down from the tree, but before sliding all the way to the ground, he peered around cautiously. Hearing and seeing nothing, he dropped soundlessly to the ground and stood upright. A roar defended him. At the same time, felt a searing pain in his chest and his feet were lifted off the ground. His eyes focused on a long black claw protruding from just under his ribcage, blood trickling from around it. The beast shook him off into the bushes like he was no more than something distasteful and stalked off into the night in search of something else to occupy its time, leaving Malach to bleed out in the unfamiliar woods.

Malach woke with a start. His eyes flitted around the room he was in. It was his room in the little cottage that had belonged to his parents. It was a simple room made of rough cut timbers. There was a bed with a wooden chest at the foot of it where he kept his clothes, two pegs in the wall where his bow hung, a square container which had several fletched arrows protruding from the top. There were also two doors, one leading out to the rest of the cottage, one leading to the washroom. He studied his chest. No wound. He tore his shirt over his head to get a good look at his bare skin. No, nothing; not even a scratch. He let out a breath he hadn't realized he was holding.

Just the dream, he thought, but he still checked his chest again. It had felt so real.

The fear.

The pain.

Even now, he could remember every detail as if it had been a recent memory, not a nightmare. Malach again checked all over his six and a half foot, muscular body for any wounds. However, he could find nothing that hadn't already been there the night before. Malach was taller than most in his village, standing a head above most men and head and shoulders above most women. With jet-black hair and a darker complexion, he stood out like a sore thumb against the fairer skin and lighter hair of most in the area.

He hated sticking out.

The kids growing up had made fun of him for being different. Until one took a swing at him. Malach had beaten the older bully and his two friends in an unfair fight. Malach didn't mind the verbal attacks. Those could be ignored; however, if someone wanted to do bodily harm to him or someone he cared about, they would be met with an unyielding defense.

Malach, in many ways, had the same childhood as most kids in the area. He had been trained for war from infancy and taught to handle several weapons proficiently. At age twenty, his body was lean and fit and even though he had a taller, lankier build than the other boys, he could best them in strength, speed, and agility. Every child was required by law to be trained in the way of combat from five years old until they were eighteen. After that, they, or more often than not their parents, could choose what they wanted to learn, and many let their fighting skills lapse. This had been set up since the fall of man to sin in The Garden of Eden, when war had come to the earth. When Satan, the lord of the demons, brought his army to earth to cut the race of men, God's creation, from the earth and the hosts of heaven had responded. Since then, demons, angels, and men have been locked in combat for thousands of years. At least, that's what they had been taught. There had been peace for more the two thousand years now, and many questioned if the war was finally, truly over.

People had a choice to make once they came of age at twenty-one; side with the Demons or side with the Angels. They were required to live in a neutral zone, an area where war was not allowed, for a minimum of two years. After that, they could make their choice if they desired or stay in that zone. This had been set up shortly after Cain made his choice and killed Abel and man joined the ranks of the demons to kill the angels and march on Heaven's Gates themselves, or so the story went. Once that choice was made, there were very few who changed their mind, and Malach wondered if the ones that did convert had ever actually chosen or if they simply said they did. They had all been taught these stories by their parents. However, for the last two thousand years, there had been no sightings of either angels or demons, and there had been relative peace, aside from the normal crimes of men.

This choice had been on Malach's mind since he turned eighteen, and the dreams had started. He was still considered a kid, and he imagined rightly so, since the average person lived to be around seven hundred years old. He was a little more than a week from turning twenty-one, and his whole world was being turned upside down. . . again.

Malach sighed, dragged his tired limbs out of bed, and went to the washroom. It was a small room with a tub and an elevated basin for a sink. He splashed the tepid water on his face to clear his mind. He had lived in this cottage for most of his life. First with his parents until they had died when he was twelve. That was the first time his world was turned upside down, and then returning when he was eighteen to live here on his own.

His father and mother were excellent parents while they lived. They had moved here from a faraway place before he was born. He didn't know where they came from, just that they had settled here to raise him. This town was all he knew. When he was younger, on his days off from training, his father would take him deep into the woods for days at a time, teaching him how to survive; hunting, trapping, herbs, shelter, and crude weaponry, you name it, and he knew it.

A week before his thirteenth birthday, he had gone to Daziar's house for the night. Daziar was his best friend and, in many ways, the brother he never had. Daziar's birthday was only a couple of days away, and they were going to celebrate their birthdays together. A large storm hit that night, and they had to take shelter with the rest of the town in the underground bunkers dug for just that purpose. He had never worried about his parents because he knew they would have done the same, but when his parents hadn't come for him, doubt crept in, which lead to fear. By the third day, Daziar's parents, Daniel and Jennari Wervine, had decided to take him back to his cottage a few miles out of town. When they arrived, the outside of the cottage was almost untouched, but the inside was a wreck. It was as if the storm had hit the inside of the house, not the outside. His parents were nowhere to be found.

He didn't understand then that something other than the storm had driven his parents from the house, though there was no evidence as to what. He had stayed the next few days with Daziar while the villagers had searched the area. They had never found his parents' bodies, assuming wild animals had taken them. They held a vigil shortly after since there was nothing to burn at the funeral pyre. The next few years were the hardest of his life. Daziar's parents took him in and treated him as their second son. Daziar had two sisters who were much younger than them. Emmeline, who was now twelve, and Marletta, who was now ten. They had become like Malach's sisters, and he watched over them.

Now Malach lived alone in his cottage, though there were few nights he slept there. Most nights he spent out in the wilderness, even in the winter, finding that more comfortable than any bed. Some of the villagers talked about how odd he was and spread wild rumors about him being part wolf, or at least was raised by them. The only basis of truth in those rumors was that his closest companion was a wolf.

Her name was Skie. He had met her the winter of his fourteenth year. She had sprung one of his traps set for a wild dog who had been taking a farmer's sheep. When he had seen her, he knew she wasn't who had been hunting in the area. She was a ragged, bloody mess. It was hard to tell she was even a wolf under all the gore coating her pelt. Malach pulled her out of the trap and took her back to his cottage. He would go up to the cottage daily, feed her by hand, and change her bandages. She nearly died.

When she was awake, he would talk with her about hunting and whatever else came to mind. She seemed to listen with some manner of interest, although he didn't know how much she understood.

He felt they bonded over that time, which was why he was a little heartbroken when he found one morning she had left in the middle of the night. Two years passed before he saw her again. He was out one evening at dusk, tracking a doe who had one of his arrows in her. He had made an excellent shot. Despite that, this doe fought on through the underbrush, staying just ahead of him. He heard a wolf howl to his right, then his left, and a third directly behind him; a hunting pattern. Either Malach or the deer were the prey. He moved then, leaving the trail of the deer, hoping they were hunting the wounded animal for an easy kill. He ran out into a clearing and into the main hunting pack. There were five of them, hackles raised, growling and snarling menacingly. He recognized the scars on the face and side of one of them and he knew it was the wolf he had saved. He had saved her just to be killed and eaten by her, hopefully in that order.

He notched an arrow. He wouldn't go down without a fight. Drawing the arrow back, he took aim at the scarred wolf. However, before he let his arrow fly, she leaped. . . onto the wolf closest to her, tearing at its jugular. The other wolves were caught off guard, and Malach loosed his arrow into a second wolf's chest as it turned to attack Skie. The arrow dropped it immediately and Malach notched a second with practiced ease. He never got the chance to fire it as the other two wolves disappeared into the brush, not wanting to end up like their companions. Malach burned the wolves' bodies, as he would have any humans, with reverence and silence while Skie watched.

Since then, she had stayed with him but was by no means *his* wolf. She was her own creature and would do as she pleased. He tried several names before she chose Skie. She was a large wolf with her head coming up past his waist. The name Skie fit her. She had almost a blue tint to her fur with silver mixed in. Three long scars, where no hair grew, started small at her snout and grew wider as they ran down her left side, finally stopping at her flank. She looked fierce and rugged, and Malach didn't blame people for being afraid of her. She was, however, quite gentle and, in fact, good with children. Malach thought often that they were much alike, and he liked the companionship she brought. She would also hunt with him, bringing most kills to him, letting him dress the animal before taking her portion. Malach always gave her the choice meat from her kills. After all, she did the work and let him take the furs to sell. This was their relationship; mutual trust, respect, and loyalty.

Malach moved back out to his room, peeled his sweaty leather breaches off, and let his legs dry. He moved out to his pantry to find something to eat. He grabbed an apple and a strip of dried meat and tore into them hungrily, taking a seat at his table. One of the traders had called the meat "jerky" and said it was all the rage in the big cities down south. Malach had been drying his meat for years. It helped it last much longer and if you seasoned it with salt and some of the edible plants in the area, it tasted rather good. It was one of his bestselling meats, and he could make it out of the lesser cuts people didn't want as much. The traders bought everything he had when they arrived in town each year. He guessed if people ever settled farther north, they use the ice and snow year round to preserve meat. As it was, Brightwood was as far north in the known world he knew of.

There was an insistent knock on the door, jarring Malach out of his thoughts. He realized he was wearing just his underwear, and he had an uninvited visitor. He jumped up from the little table he had sat down at and rushed to his room.

"Just a minute!" he called as he went.

He grabbed the first pair of pants he could find and pulled them on; they were covered in old animal blood. He winced. He looked barbaric. Realistically, though, how many new visitors did he get? It was probably only Daziar.

Too late now, he thought to himself.

He moved to the door and pulled it open. It was not Daziar. Instead, a rather fidgety man stood in front of him. Although, who wouldn't be nervous under the watchful eyes of Skie, who was laying as nonthreatening as a four-foot tall scarred wolf could. When the man saw Malach in his blood-streaked pants and chiseled upper body, his courage nearly failed him. To his credit, he didn't run; just stood up a little straighter. Malach took in the man at a glance. He was a skinny man with fair skin and a soft face. The man was tall, but not as tall as Malach. He wore a tailored suit ill-fitted for the hike he had to taken to get here. He was either a rich man or someone used to being rich. There was no chance he was from Brightwood or the surrounding area. He tried to flash a very disarming smile and broke the silence.

"Good morning, friend! How are you this brisk autumn morning?" Malach said in a purposefully cordial and proper voice. He smiled again.

"Um. . . fine. . . t-thanks!" the man managed to stutter out. There was an uncomfortable silence as each one waited for the other to talk.

Malach again was forced to break the silence. "Can I help you with something?"

"Oh! Ur, yes! Umm. . . my family and I just move into the area." His accent stood out like a sore thumb. He most definitely was not from around here. "We are starting a farm on the south side of town. I was told this was where to find the best hunter in the area. Um...is your father home?"

Malach bristled. "Sir, do you think me too young to be the best hunter in the area?" he said, echoing the man's words. He continued without letting the man speak. "I'm who you want. My late father taught me much in the short time he had, and I've only added to that knowledge since he passed."

Malach could tell the man was caught off guard once again. "They sent me to a boy?" he asked, as if Malach wasn't there.

"They sent you to a hunter!" Malach was getting angry now and a little hurt. "If you wanted someone older, you should have gone to the tavern in town! The *older* hunters will be there getting drunk off their wages! When you want someone who actually knows what they are doing, you can come back and be a little more cordial!" Malach went to slam the door, but the stranger got a boot between it and the jam, stopping it from shutting.

"Please, excuse my careless words," the stranger apologized. "I simply was told the best hunter would be here. I was not told your age. However, I trust the

word of the man who sent me, and your age will not be a problem."
Malach opened the door again, still peeved at the man. "Who sent you?"

"The general store owner. As I understand it, you have done work for him in the past and done a good job," He replied.

"I've done work for almost everyone in this area. Are you kin to anyone around here?"

"My brother has a farm on the east side of town. His name is Arjun Reybella. He has a daughter around your age. Her name is Honora."

"Oh!" Malach's brow rose. "You're Arjun's brother? You look nothing alike."

"Yes, well, he got all the muscles in the family, and he never was one to slow down," the man mused, "but where are my manners? My name is Jecrym, Jecrym Reybella, and like I said, my wife and I are settling into a farm on the south side of town. We are needing someone to come and hunt for something that has been taking our animals. We are just getting started, you know, and can't afford to lose too many."

"I'm Malach. Are you and your wife going to be managing on the farm yourselves?" Again, Malach couldn't keep the surprise out of his voice.

"Unfortunately, yes." Jecrym's shoulders dropped slightly. "Our third brother, the oldest, spent most of our wealth, and now it would seem I've almost run out as well. We must start this. . . farm so that we can live."

Malach studied the man. He said the word farm in such distaste that, personally, Malach didn't care for him at all. Although he was the brother of a good man.

"I'll take the job. I take the fur and meat of any animal caught unless you pay a fair price for it, and I charge two copper coins per animal." Malach knew he could probably ask for more, but that was the price he gave everyone else. "If you need to trade instead of paying coin, we can discuss a trade when the job is finished. Furthermore, I will not pay for any damage by any animal to your land or property." Malach put his hand out to shake on the deal.

Jecrym glanced at Malach's proffered hand and then back up at him.

"You don't want anything in writing?" he asked.

"A man's word is his bond around here." Malach warned him. "If you break that trust, word spreads fast in a small town. People will be less likely to deal with you. I will meet you tomorrow morning at your farm."

"Duly noted." Jecrym took Malach's hand, and they shook on it. "Do you know where my farm is?"

"As I said, word spreads fast in a small town. And I already know where the old farm south of town is." Malach pulled his hand back. "Now I must begin my day. Too much daylight has been burned already."

Jecrym appeared confused for a moment, then took a step back from the door. "Very well, tomorrow morning. Good day." He turned, startled at the sight of Skie again, and hurried off almost at a run as she loosed a playful growl at him.

"Skie," Malach reprimanded, "I know you have to give off your dangerous persona, but you don't have to scare *all* of my customers."

She plodded over to him, and he squatted a little to be eye level with her. She licked him once in the face.

"Alright, alright, I forgive you," Malach chuckled and scratched behind her ears. "I have to get dressed now. Have you eaten breakfast?"

He peered around her to see the remnants of an animal she had killed and eaten. "I guess so, and you didn't even leave any for me." He pushed her head to the side playfully.

She excitedly growled and nipped at him in response.

Malach chuckled and walked inside to change into a fresh pair of pants and a brown wool shirt. He grabbed the belt with his knife and quiver still attached and put it on. Some archers preferred their quiver to be attached to a sash on their back, however, Malach much preferred it by his side. When the quiver was attached at the back, it required a half quiver, or one could never pull the arrows. Unfortunately, that meant if they had to run, they were more likely to lose their arrows. No, the side quiver was the way to go. The draw was more fluid and without the danger of losing them if he had to change locations.

After he strapped on his belt, he moved to the wall where his bow hung, strung it, and set it against the wall next to the arrow container. He selected three arrows from their wooden holder and put them into his quiver. He snatched the rest of his uneaten breakfast on the way out of the cottage, pulling the door shut behind him. Skie was waiting, and Malach could swear she had an impatient look on her face. Skie didn't like going in any building, even for a few minutes, though she would make exceptions sometimes. Malach never tried to make her either. It was against her nature. She had a cave she slept in when the weather wasn't to her liking.

"Alright girl, I'm ready." He told her and she fell into step with him. Today was Malach's day for a supply run into town. He headed for his cart. It wasn't big; just a small, simple thing that used manpower. He didn't have a horse or mule, just his own two legs. Skie would never stand to be hooked up to it and he had never tried to make her. Going down into the valley wasn't the hard part. However, getting back up to the cottage with all the supplies he needed? *That* would be the challenge.

The path was a worn, winding trail with a few potholes in it, but Malach made sure they never got too large. He had been slowly making the trail straighter. As he needed firewood, he would select the next tree that was in the way and fell it with his saw. He would cut it into small pieces and haul it back up to his house to use. It was a bit of work, but he hadn't found one that he couldn't cut down yet.

As Malach arrived at the cart, he threw his pack and bow into the back, and started down the hill. The cart had four short, wooden walls to it with one side that slid in on grooves for easy loading. Skie jumped in the back and laid down. Placing her head between her legs, she looked at him.

He feigned exasperation with her, "Really, first you make haul the cart, and now you're going to make me carry you too! You've gone too far this time." He wagged a finger at her nose. "I have a mind to turn this cart around, young lady." She just snorted at him and closed her eyes.

"Fine. You just stay there and see if you get any of Mr. Reybella's honeycomb candy."

At this, Skie's ears perked up, and she opened one eye at him.

"That's right, you heard me. We're headed to the Reybella's farm. If you aren't nice to me, I won't buy you any candy. This will be the last batch of the season, you know. It will be too cold for his bees soon, if it isn't already."

Skie growled menacingly at him as if to say, "You wouldn't dare."

Malach continued, undaunted by what would sound to most people as anger in the wolf's growl. "Oh yes! You must remember who is holding the coin purse around here, but," he let that last word hang in the air for a second for dramatic effect, "I guess you can stay in there on the trip down. Just not on the way back; you're getting too fat for that."

Skie jumped to her feet in indignation and barked once in his ear.

"Alright, alright, I meant muscular. Don't get your tail in a knot." Malach chuckled.

Skie huffed once more and flopped down, jarring the cart.

Malach plodded along in silence, leaving him to his own thoughts and plans for the day. As they came out of the trees onto the open, they could see the town down in the valley about a mile away; they could even see tiny people moving around within the wooden walls.

This was Brightwood. There were too many people for Malach's liking, even though this was just a small town. With a population of around two hundred people residing within the walls, it was one of the smallest towns in Angel Territory. Around Brightwood, there was a wooden wall, maybe three times Malach's height. They had catwalks on the inside of the walls for guards. Although they hadn't seen a guard on them in well over a thousand years. Mostly, lovers and children traversed them, taking a leisurely romantic walk under the starlight or used in some game, respectively.

Malach lived on the Angel side of The Great Divide. The Divide was a large valley between the Demon and Angel Territory. It was where the first battle between angels and demons was said to have been fought. This valley formed a V toward the Western side of the continent and had a land mass in the middle. This natural formation of the land was where a neutral city formed. Those who had yet to choose a side, or those who didn't want to fight at all.

Malach caught sight of movement ahead, which pulled him from his thoughts. There was something else on the road, something unseen by those in the city. Three bandits waylaid some poor traveler. Malach immediately backed into the brush and set down his cart.

Skie lifted her head at the sudden jostling.

Malach put a finger to his lips and pointed along the road. He held up three fingers in front of her face and whispered, "Highwaymen."

Skie's hackles raised. She was genuinely upset this time.

He stopped her from charging in and motioned for her to follow as he grabbed his bow. There were some bushes along the side of the road. He used them for cover, pushing his quiver around his belt so that it rested on top of his butt as he crawled low on his stomach. He worked his way forward until voices reached his ears and chanced a peek between two of the bushes.

There were definitely three of them. Big, burly men, all armed with a number of weapons, but Malach didn't see an archer among them. He could probably make a decent shot from here, but he wanted to be a little closer in case things went south. He continued crawling to the end of the bushes. Their voices were raised and angry; probably whoever they had waylaid was not cooperating. Which was good and bad. Good, because it took them longer to steal whatever they were after. He could line his shot up. Bad because the highwaymen were angry, and they didn't think particularly well when they were angry. Although, to be fair, they generally didn't think very well at anytime. He might be forced to kill one, maybe even two, for them to survive the encounter. It also put the innocent man at risk when things got serious.

Malach peered through the bushes as he notched an arrow and judged the distance to the highwayman who had his back turned to Malach. Then one of them drew their sword.

So much for getting to line my shot up, Malach thought ruefully. He stood up, drew back his arrow, and let it fly. The arrow zipped through the air, just grazing the ear of the thug standing with his back to Malach and embedded itself in the shoulder of the man who had drawn his sword. It caught everyone by surprise and stopped the man's attack cold. All four men turned to look at Malach, the two uninjured highwaymen drawing their swords. He already had a second arrow notched, and the bow drawn.

"Now, I could have killed any one of you, but I took a wounding shot," Malach called to them.

Skie growled next to him for extra emphasis.

He continued, "I could easily change my mind and put both of you down before you could make it to me."

The highwaymen glanced at each other.

"I suggest you sheath your weapons, drop those belts, and walk away," Malach called.

The two uninjured bandits were more than happy to oblige and started backing up.

"Wait!" the third bellowed at them and they paused in their retreat. He was obviously the leader. "This git can't stop us all. Why you backin' down?" He spun the traveler around and put the sword to his throat. "Now, you drop *your* weapon and back off."

The traveler was, in fact, Jecrym, and he lowered his bow slightly. The bandit took his eyes off Malach for a second to look triumphantly to his comrades, who had stopped moving. He snapped the bow back into place, drew and released the arrow with one fluid motion. The arrow flew, and as the bandit returned his focus to Malach, it pierced through his left eye.

The man screamed. The sword fell from his grasp as his hands flew to cluch the arrow and he dropped to his knees.

Malach notched his third and final arrow, but it was a needless action as the two uninjured bandits ran for it. The third one got up and started running as well, but he had a harder time seeing where he was going and stumbled several times as he ran. Malach put the arrow away and moved forward to the shaken Jecrym.

"Are you alright?" Malach asked, not looking at Jecrym, but examining the weapons and belts that had been left behind.

Jecrym didn't respond.

Nothing spectacular, though there were a few silver coins in one purse still attached to the belt. He collected those and put them away in his own coin purse. He picked up the best of the swords and tossed it at the still stunned Jecrym. It landed at his feet, bounced once, and smacked into his shin. That seemed to snap him out of his silence

"Wha. . . you. . . shot him," he stammered.

"Yep," Malach replied calmly. "Didn't give me much of a choice, did he?"

"You could have killed me!" Jecrym raised his voice, suddenly shouting. Anger boiled in Malach's stomach, but he pushed it down, opting for the calmer response. "A simple thank you would suffice."

"Thank you? If you ever point that. . . thing at me again, I'll go to the local authorities and report you!"

Malach stood and advanced on the hapless man, who seemed to shrink. "I saved your life, technically twice, in the span of a few moments. Next time I'll just leave you to them. Oh, and good luck finding the local *authorities*. The only people keeping the peace around here is you and me." He motioned to the sword still on the ground at Jecrym's feet. "You would be smart to take that sword and get someone to re-train you to use it."

Who does this guy think he is? A king? Malach thought in disgust.

Malach collected the rest of the discarded items and headed back toward his cart.

Skie fell into step with him, shooting a venomous look toward Jecrym.

Jecrym quickly picked up the sword and ran to catch up. "You're not just going to leave me out here alone, are you?"

"I don't make it a habit to keep cowards as company," Malach retorted. He arrived at the cart and Skie jumped back in the back but didn't lie down. Instead, she stared Jecrym down.

"What if they come back?" He stopped short of the cart, watching Skie.

Malach said nothing.

"I apologize for what I said earlier." Jecrym tried, seeming to calm down a bit.

There he goes, apologizing again, Malach thought.

"I was scared, and it was rude of me. Let me pay you for your trouble." Jecrym reached for his coin purse, which jingled loudly. It was full of coins.

"I don't want your money. That's what made you a target in the first place," He really didn't want any of Jecrym's money. "Don't you know only to carry a small amount of coin with you?"

"I. . ." Jecrym started to say something, but the words died in his mouth. He let his breath out and inhaled again. His voice was better under control when he spoke again. "To tell you the truth, I don't know much about the rules of this land. I am used to living in a city with men whose job is to keep the peace. Please, let me at least replace the arrows you lost when that brute fled?"

"Fine," Malach replied. He still wasn't happy, but let the matter drop. "If that's what you wish, I'll accept, though I make my own shafts and fletching. All I need are the arrowheads."

"Then you will have half a dozen of the best heads the blacksmith makes," Jecrym beamed at him as if they were the best of friends.

Malach sighed and pulled the cart out from where he had hidden it before. Skie laid down so she wouldn't have to balance on the moving cart. However, she was not as relaxed as before. He could tell she really didn't trust their new traveling companion.

They walked almost half the distance to the city before Jecrym couldn't take the silence anymore. "So, may I ask you a question?" he asked warily.

"I can't stop you," Malach replied tersely. He hoped the man wasn't going to pry into his past. He didn't have a hard time talking about it; he just didn't want to get into it with Jecrym in particular. "I don't promise an answer, though."

"That's fair," Jecrym replied and looked over at him curiously. "Why didn't you kill the bandit?"

"What would that have accomplished?" Malach asked.

"Well," he started, "for one, there would be one less bandit in the world, but I think it would have just been a more strategically sound action."

Malach thought about what he should say and decided to make him squirm a little. "I would have had to bury him if I killed him," he stated flatly. "Or at the least drag him from the road."

Jecrym's jaw dropped, and he openly gaped at Malach.

"What did you think I was going to say? 'Everyone deserves a second chance' or 'I couldn't take another man's life'?" Malach rolled his eyes.

"As a matter of fact, yes!" He was still shocked.

"I'm not sure if he deserved another chance," Malach explained. "He had his chance to leave, and he didn't take it when the other two did. They will think twice before they try something like that again. Besides, not many men change their ways once they are set."

"So, your reason for not killing the man was truly so you would not have to deal with a body?"

"The truth is, I don't take a life unless there's a need. I knew he wouldn't kill you once he had enough incentive not to. He was a coward." Malach set the cart down and turned to look the man in the eyes. "His kind prey on the weak. Projecting strength by making his prey cower under his presumed power. He, in fact, is weaker than the men he preys on. I saw it in his eyes. When someone comes along who stands up to him, he will hide behind someone else. You can't trust anyone to protect you. Willing or otherwise. There is always a way around them."

Malach flexed his hands before picking up the cart, and they started moving toward the city. "Once they see they aren't as safe as they perceive they are, they will flee. Although, while we're being honest, I missed. I had intended to scare him, which is what happened, but I intended to scare him by taking a small chunk out of his ear."

This drew a small, shocked look from Jecrym and he opened his mouth to object, but shut it without any sound coming out.

Good, the man is learning to think before he speaks, Malach thought, and then continued. "Lucky for him I didn't pull my full draw, or we *would* be burying a body,"

They walked for a while in silence once again, Jecrym obviously mulling over what was said.

When they had gotten to within a stone's throw of the main gate, Jecrym spoke again; this time a bit more curious. "How is someone your age so full of wisdom?"

Malach didn't reply. He didn't want to explain his past. His parents had taught him the value of a life. However, he had done a lot of growing up in the years he was on his own. He supposed he had grown up more than many his age.

They passed through the gates in silence. Jecrym, it seemed, had dropped the subject. He turned toward the blacksmith's shop, even though that was not originally going to be his first stop. He wanted to be rid of Jecrym and his questions.

As they approached the blacksmith's shop, Jecrym tried to pry once again. "So, where are your parents?"

"Dead," Malach replied shortly and refused to say anything else to the man's many questions that followed.

Chapter 2

Malach and Jecrym arrived at the blacksmith's shop none too soon for Malach, and they went inside. The blacksmith was a big, burly man with a large, jet-black beard and a bald head. Togan Ravenbard, had been a good friend to Malach for a long time. Malach thought it was because he had lost his wife and son a couple of hundred years ago to a fire. He always said Malach reminded him of his son, and he had taken to the boy. Malach visited the gruff man every time he was in town, even if he didn't need anything from him.

Togan Lifted his gaze from the blade he had been sharpening to regard Malach and Jecrym. He stood menacingly, brandishing the weapon. He glanced from Malach to Jecrym and back to Malach.

"Everythin' alright here, Malach?" he asked, eyeing Jecrym again. "This man botherin' you?"

"Yes,"

Jecrym gave a startled squeak.

Malach amended his statement. "But I'm here to do business, nothing else, Togan."

Togan sat, picking up the whetstone to hone the blade in his hands again.

Malach continued, "Togan, this is Jecrym Reybel, Arjun's brother. I came upon him with a couple of *friends* on the road into town. I seem to have lost two of my good arrows in them, if you know what I mean. Jecrym wish to return the favor and replace my arrowheads for me."

Togan nodded, but still didn't say anything. He didn't even take his eyes off his work.

Jecrym spoke up now with a little annoyance edging his voice. "Could I get a half dozen of your best arrowheads?"

"Uh, just my normal heads, please, Togan," Malach corrected quickly and turned to Jecrym to explain. "If I get the different heads, I have to adjust my aim and make of the shafts. They make the arrow act differently."

Togan pulled out three arrowheads and set them on the counter. "I only have three now. You can pay for all six, and Malach can pick 'em up next time he's in town."

Jecrym turn to Malach for confirmation

He nodded. "That's fair."

Jecrym pulled out two gold coins from his purse and placed them on the counter.

Togan raised one eyebrow at him. "They're two silvers each, so you're short two."

"Oh, sorry my good man." He reached into his purse again and proffered two more gold coins. "You can keep the change."

Togan's eyebrow went up again, and he glanced at Malach, who shrugged in response. Togan slid the four coins off his counter and put them behind it. He sat back down. Malach and Jecrym turned and left the building.
When the door had shut behind them, Jecrym spoke, "Cheery fellow, isn't he?" It was a rhetorical question.

"He'll warm up a little once you get to know him, but yes, to most, he doesn't talk much." Malach explained. "Well, this is where we part ways, I think. I will see you in the morning at your farm."

Malach again offered his hand as a parting gesture and Jecrym took it and then turned and walked away. He watched Jecrym until he was out of sight, then turned and went back inside the blacksmith's shop.

Togan had his feet propped up on the counter now, obviously finished sharpening the sword he had out just moments ago, "How'd you end up saddled with 'im?" he asked.

"He asked for my services hunting out at his new farm. Since he was kin to Arjun, I agreed." Malach walked around the other side of the counter and sat in a chair opposite Togan. "Could you believe he didn't think I was a hunter?"

"Malach, you're still young." Togan took a fatherly tone with him. "You're not even twenty-one yet."

"What's your point? I'm the best hunter this side of the Pangor River, and you know it," he objected.

"You know better than t' be prideful," Togan admonished. "People outside the valley don't know a thing about you. You're a great hunter, but just a hunter, and you've never been out of this area. He's new to the valley. Cut him some slack."

"You're right," Malach conceded. "I just wish I didn't have to leave the valley. I mean, it's all I know. Can I count on you to check on my parent's cottage here and there? Make sure it's standing when I get back?"

"Of course, but I thought you had the Reybellas and Wervines watchin' over it," Togan asked, confused.

"I do, I just thought they might not have enough time to check on it, and a third person with eyes on it would be a good idea," He replied.

"Malach, you're too worried about leavin'," Togan shook his head, and a chuckle rumbled through his chest, low and warm. "You're not gonna miss much, and nothin's gonna change while you're gone. In fact, you'll probably meet new friends and have a good time in the Neutral Territory. You might even meet a girl who could put up with you for more than five minutes."

Togan slugged him in the shoulder and guffawed loudly at the look of dejection on Malach's face, and Malach couldn't help but smile at the man's laughter. Then he had a mischievous thought.

"What about you? I mean, you've been making eyes at Marena for almost a year now. When are you going to start doing something about that?" Malach grinned.

"Oh, you're talkin' 'bout the waitress at the tavern? Humph." Togan crossed his arms. "I haven't been makin' eyes at her. Just think she's pretty, that's all."

"Well, you better make a move before someone else does."

"Git out of here, you little whelp!" Togan took a playful swing at him and Malach easily ducked out of the way and hopped out of the chair.

"You're getting slow, old man," He laughed again and vaulted the counter.

"Eh, you're not worth chasin'," Togan got up slowly and put both hands on the counter. "Did ya need anythin' else before you go?"

"Yeah. Do you happen to have any whetstones for sale?" he asked with his hand on the door.

"Nah, the only ones I got are the ones I use." Togan held up the one that was in his hand. "But I heard the general store got a shipment in a week ago. You might check there and see if they got any left."

"Alright, thanks, Togan. Oh! One more thing," Malach whirled, jogged back out to his cart, picked up the two swords and carried them back inside. "Do you recognize these swords?" He set the two swords on the counter and the big blacksmith picked the one up that wasn't sheathed.

"This is not of my makin'." He flipped it over and looked the other side over. "I don't see any touch marks identifyin' what blacksmith crafted it, but it's not well made. I can tell you that."

He looked it over one last time and then set it back down on the counter. "My guess is it's from a different town, crafted by an apprentice blacksmith. I can give you two coppers for each for the metal, but they aren't worth wieldin' or repairin'."

"Deal. I don't want them."

Togan handed him four copper coins.

"Also, do you have any hunting knives made at the moment? I need to get one for Daziar's birthday. He's turning twenty-one after all."

"You know I do. He's had his eye on that ten inch one with the redwood handle. It's one of my best." Togan pulled out a wooden box and handed it to Malach. "Since it's one of my best, I'll part with it for the meat from the next deer you get."

"That's overkill and you know it!" Malach exclaimed, pretending to be upset with the deal as he turned the knife over in his hands. It *was* one of his best, almost as good as the one hanging from Malach's own belt. "Half the meat of the deer."

"Fine, half of everythin' else but the whole rump," Togan bargained.

"Togan." Malach paused their bargaining by holding a hand up. "You know I might not be able to bring down a deer before I leave, right?"

"Then you'll pay me when you get back," Togan said simply. "Business is good, and it won't hurt me any to wait."

"Fine," Malach agreed. "Then we have a deal."

They shook on it, and Malach picked up the box that held the knife.

"You know, your love for venison will drive you out of business." He turned and walked outside, bidding farewell to the blacksmith.

The knife hanging off his belt was an early birthday gift from the blacksmith. He had given it to Malach early as he ended up snapping his other one in half when he was facing down a wild boar. When he had taken it to the blacksmith to get it repaired, Togan had handed him this new knife and told him he had intended it to be Malach's birthday present, but didn't mind giving it to him early.

Malach stuffed the box into his pack so Daziar wouldn't see it when he got to the Wervine's house. Daziar's birthday was in two days, and the day after, he would start his journey to the Neutral Territory to live and learn there for two years. They had planned to meet up at Newaught and possibly live together. Newaught was the only city in the Neutral Territory. Unfortunately for Malach, he would have to get used to the big city.

Malach glanced at Skie. To anyone passing by, she would have appeared half asleep, not paying much attention. To Malach, however, she was tense and nervous. She didn't like the town, but she always went with Malach, anyway. He knew she was poised and would spring into action if the occasion demanded. She had never attacked humans unless provoked, but sometimes Malach worried about her doing something when they were in town because of how on edge she always was.

He picked up the cart and headed toward the general store. There, he acquired the few things he needed, including the whetstones, paying for them with the money taken out of the highwayman's purse. After that, he started off toward Daziar's house, which was on the opposite end of town from the gate he'd entered from earlier. It didn't take him long to cross town, however, and when he arrived, Daziar opened the door before Malach could set the cart down.

Daziar was a big man, muscular and tall. He was the only one in the area close to Malach's height and one of the few boys during training who could take Malach one-on-one. Daziar charged toward Malach, but Skie intercepted him, jumping on Daziar and knocking him flat on his back.

He bear-hugged the dog and laughed, "Malach, get your vicious beast in check. She nearly killed me!"

"She was simply defending me. I should just let her tear you to sheds." Malach pushed Skie to the side and took Daziar's hand. He pulled his friend to his feet and into an embrace. "How've you been?"

"Good! You know, just getting ready for my journey. Mom and Dad have been helping me pack things I'm going to need. I just wish I could get that hunting knife Togan has in his shop. The one with the redwood handle." Daziar looked a little disappointed. "Mom said they didn't have the money to buy it or anything to trade for it. Dad said he would have enough a week from now, but I will already be gone by then. Dad's overseeing the building of the new farm south of town. Or should I say rebuilding? That derelict house needed to be demolished and built from the ground up. Have you heard? Arjun's brother is building down that way." Daziar rambled a little when he was excited, or nervous, or worried… or just about any other time.

"Slow down, Daz!" Malach held up his hands as if to physically slow Daziar down. "I know about the new Reybellas' farm. Jecrym, Arjun's brother, came to me this morning looking to get my help hunting something taking his animals." Malach related the events from that morning, including the highwaymen, and how he had saved Jecrym.

Daziar let out a low whistle. "Wow, you really messed them up, didn't you?"

"Just the one guy, and I didn't mean to put the arrow in his eye. I'm just glad I didn't pull a full draw." Malach grabbed his pack, and they headed for the door of the house. "Don't tell your mom about the highwaymen business, or she'll worry about us for the whole two years we are gone."

"At least worry more than she does now," Daziar corrected, and they walked into the house.

The house was simple, made of wood inside and out. The dining room was directly to the right inside the front door and contained a small table that would seat four people comfortably, six if you packed in. To the left was the kitchen, separated by the counter that was waist level to Malach. Ahead and to the left around the wall was the living space and to the right was a hall which led to three rooms. One was the girls' room for Daziar's two sisters. Another was Daziar's room, which Malach had shared while he lived with them, and the last was Daniel and Jennari's room. Malach announced he had arrived and Jennari, Daziar's mother, came out of the kitchen and gave him a death grip of a hug around his waist. Just when Malach thought he might pass out, she released him.

She took his face between her two hands, turning his head to the right and then the left, taking stock of him. "Ugh, I wish you would live with us where it's safer and not up there in the cottage, all alone." She smiled then and let his face go. "I'm glad you made it down safely. Did you have any issues on the way? There have been rumors of bad men around lately, and there were a couple of people robbed in the last week." Jennari turned and went back into the kitchen, so she didn't see the look that passed between Daziar and Malach.

"Everything went fine on the way down." Malach only halfway lied. He didn't have any problems, because he took care of his problem.

Jennari was a slight woman, short and skinny, contrasting her son, and she barely came up to Malach's chest. Daniel, Daziar's father, was also not very tall, but heftily built, like Daziar. Malach didn't know where Daziar's height came from, but they always joked he had simply been trying to keep up with Malach as they grew up together. Daniel walked in from one of the back rooms with Daziar's two sisters on his heels. They were almost twins, though they were a couple of years apart. The biggest difference was their hair. Emiline, the elder sister, had shockingly blond hair that flowed down almost to her waist. Marletta, on the other hand, cut hers short and had brown hair. They both had the build of their mother and probably wouldn't get much taller.

"Mal!" they both shouted and ran around their dad to hug Malach. Malach hugged them both, one in each arm, and then lifted them off their feet, turning it into a bear-hug. He set them down after a couple of moments. They were growing in to young women so fast.

Too fast, Malach decided.

"Malach," Daniel said in his gravelly voice. "It's been too long."

They clasped each other's arms in greeting.

"I can't stay long," he said, drawing a disappointed groan from the girls. "I just came by to bid Daz a safe journey and give him his present for his birthday. I won't be able to see him again until I get to Newaught."

Malach pulled the box with the hunting knife out of his bag and handed it to Daziar. He took it and looked at his family excitedly, then back to Malach.

"You know you didn't have to get me anything, right?" Daziar said, though Malach knew he was saying it to be cordial.

"Oh," Malach said with a mischievous grin. "In that case, I'll just return it and get my money back. Open it, knucklehead."

"Fine, fine, you don't have to be rude about it." Daziar pulled the box to his chest as if Malach was going to try to take it from him.

He set in on the table to open it. Once he saw what was in the box, he looked up with wide-eyed excitement.

"Well, what is it Daz?" Marletta asked, almost as excited and he was.

"It's the knife I wanted from Togan's shop!" he almost shouted with excitement. "Thanks, Mal!"

"It must have cost you an arm and a leg," Jennari said in her normally concerned tone. "How did you ever pay for it?"

"It cost me an arm and two legs to be exact," Malach stated. "You know how Togan likes his venison."

"Mal, you are the best brother I never had!" Daziar clasped his arm and pulled him close.

When he pulled back, Malach said, "Well, I have to keep moving. I'm already behind, and if I want to get back to the cottage before nightfall, I need to go."

"Let me make you a sandwich for the road," Jennari said and hurried into the kitchen.

"That's really not necessary," Malach protested.

"Nonsense," Jennari said, not even pausing in her efforts. When she was finished, she poured him a flask of water and put the sandwich into a small brown sack before handing it to him. "Here you are, Malach."

"Thanks, Jennari. I really appreciate that," Malach responded.
He bid all of them farewell and gave Emmeline, Marletta, and Jennari each another hug. He was sad he had to leave, because he didn't know when he would see them again, but he didn't want to be late. Those bandits might be waiting for him to get revenge, and he wanted to see them coming.

His last and longest stop for the day was the Reybella's farm. Arjun's farm, that was. South of the city and a couple of miles. He would be pushing it just to make it in time and get the things he needed.

His trip to the farm was uneventful, and as he approached, he marveled once again at the size, thinking to himself, *how much land does one man need?*

Arjun Reybella was a rich man with a large belly. He was kind, but hard. He would help someone who would put the work in to help themselves, and he employed many people. Unlike his brothers, he didn't squander his money. Instead, he used it, and coupled with hard work, he multiplied it. He had built the largest farm in the valley and he continued to expand.

Malach wondered what it must be like to be that rich and thought that it could easily make a man stumble. Money seemed to make men do evil things or become afraid and paranoid. He concluded he would probably be happier living the way he did, having enough for what he needed and maybe a little extra here and there.

The sun was low in the sky and had already turned orange. It gave the farm a very peaceful look. The hired hands had already gone in to clean up for dinner, which would be served within the hour. In fact, the only person who Malach could see was Honora Reybella. She was out in the field, riding her horse. Even from this distance, he could tell it was her. Malach smiled to himself. She rode that horse of hers any chance she got. She was a day older than Malach and a week younger than Daziar.

Honora would start the same journey as Daziar, but a week from now and Malach would follow just a day later. Arjun had asked Malach to find her and keep her safe on the journey to Newaught. In return, he had told Malach he would provide food for both of them.

Malach didn't mind. He enjoyed Honora's company and, though she wasn't much for fighting, she could hold her own. He wouldn't have to worry too much about her. She had been trained like the rest of them until they were eighteen and preferred a bo staff over any other weapon.

As Malach trudged closer, she spotted him and steered her horse in his direction, waving. He couldn't wave back without setting the cart down, so he kept walking. It took her only moments to cross the distance on her horse. As she got closer, he could tell she had been riding pretty hard. The horse was covered in sweat and breathing hard.

"You're really working the poor girl, aren't you?" Malach remarked.

"Eh, she'll be fine. It's good for her, and besides, she enjoys running," Honora said in response and reined in her horse to walk next to him.

"She does, or you do?" Malach quipped, knowing the response.

"We both do!" Honora said defensively. She always got so heated about her horse that Malach couldn't help but poke a little fun at her. She caught sight of his grin and realized what he was doing. "Cretin! Just for that, I won't let you ride back to the farm with me."

"Not like I could, anyway. I have to pull the cart to the house one way or another."

"Fine," she sighed. "Have it your way. I'll tell Father you're coming." She kicked her horse into a gallop and raced toward the house.

The truth was, Malach didn't care for riding. He had had a few lessons, but he didn't enjoy it in the least. He figured it was because of the lack of control. It's true, he might have some control over the horse, but if it decided it really wanted to go somewhere, he wouldn't be able to get it to stop. At least not easily. So, he mostly left the riding to other people. Not that there were many horses in the area, anyway. The Reybellas were one of the few families to have a horse and were the only family to own more than one.

Honora was an only child, and they pampered her a bit. She had her own room, her own horse, and she even had what people called a mirror. Malach thought it strange to have such an expensive thing just to look at your reflection in. Why not just go to a lake, or pond, or even a little puddle right after it had rained?

Even though Honora was spoiled, she was not stuck up. That always impressed him. Even when they were in training, she would share some of her food with him and Daziar at lunch or she would let them, mostly Daziar, ride her horse whenever they wanted, and so on. She didn't look down on anyone and was always putting others above herself.

She might be as close as someone got to an angel these days, Malach mused.

When he reached the farm, the sun was starting to set. He couldn't stay long. He might have just long enough to collect, load, and pay for what he came for. The Reybellas grew food and raised animals, and they even had an orchard. They produced most of the vegetables and fruit for the entire valley. There were a few other, smaller farms that provided a few certain things, but the Reybellas had a little of everything; at least that's how it seemed to Malach. He always tried to buy from them when he needed anything. Since the apple he ate this morning was the last of his produce, that's what he was here for.

He set his cart down just outside the barn where he would have to load the produce, hoisted his bag over his shoulder, and whistled for Skie. She fell into step with him as they made their way to the house. Arjun came out of the house and waited for them to arrive.

When they arrived at the house, Arjun clasped Malach's arm and hauled him close. "How ya been, boy?" he asked in his gruff but not unpleasant voice. "You been taking care of this mutt of yours?" He knelt and ruffled Skie's ears. She gave a playful growl in response, and he chuckled.

"Surviving," Malach replied. "It's been good hunting so far this season. I got a boar a couple of weeks ago, a few squirrels, and a raccoon just the other night."

"A raccoon, eh?" Arjun asked, looking around Malach to see if he could see it on the cart.

"Don't worry. I promised you the next raccoon I got, and you promised me some honey."

Arjun chuckled again, "That I did, that I did. I have some in the house." Malach pulled the packed meat out of his bag and followed the man inside. Arjun still chatting as they went. Malach could see a small resemblance to his bother, and they both liked to chatter nonstop. The difference was Arjun's conversations were about the harvest, hunting, or things Malach could and wanted to talk about. Arjun left the personal questions out of his speech. He understood Malach valued his privacy and respected that, not to mention he already knew most of it.

"...since the harvest is over, don't you think?" Arjun finished, but Malach had not been paying attention.

"What was that last thing?" Malach asked. "Sorry I missed it."

"You need to get your ears looked at, boy!" Arjun laughed. "That'll cost you your life in the woods. I was saying that things were going to slow down here, and you might think about taking one of my workers to help you hunt, since the harvest is over."

"Arjun, you know I can't afford to pay someone. The only thing I have in abundance this time of the year is meat. And because of the Journey, I can't take anyone with me."

"I know, I know, it's that time in your life. Maybe one of my men wouldn't mind going with you and Honora if paid?" Arjun fell silent, knowing the answer to his question.

"I know you're worried about Honora as we make the Journey, but you have already offered your men more than I could ever pay them and none of them are willing to leave the valley just before winter." Malach reasoned with him.

"Malach," Arjun turned around, suddenly very serious. Malach knew what came next. It was a conversation they'd had many times in the last couple of months. "You protect her. She's my life. If anything were to hap-"

"Yes, Arjun. I know you and your wife would be devastated. And you already have had me swear four times that I will do everything in my power to keep her safe. I don't intend to break my word. You know that."

"Yes, yes, I'm sorry ma' boy," Arjun's facade dropped, worry making his face appear much older. "It's just, I'm her father. I'm supposed to worry about her."

"I understand," Malach nodded. He wanted to reach out and put a hand on the mans should but instead said. "Nothing is going to happen. We will spend two years in Newaught, and then we will be back here. Before you know it, you'll have her riding around the farm again and home for dinner every night."

"I pray you're right, though I'm afraid she will want to stay in the city," Arjun said, but a little life returned to him, anyway. He stood up straighter and turned back around, barging through the doors to the kitchen. "How many jars do I owe ya?"

"Does four sound fair?" That was too steep a price, but Arjun always enjoyed a good barter.

"Four jars!" Arjun was almost shouting, but with a smile all over his face. His wife rushed in to see what the commotion was all about and smiled when she saw Malach.

"Mrs. Reyb-" Malach started to greet her.

"This boy is trying to get four jars of honey from me for one raccoon, Zahra!" Arjun interrupted.

Zahra's smiled only grew a little wider, and she said, "Well, darling, if that's too outrageous of a price, you should kick him and his raccoon out."

Arjun's face was a picture of shock, but he gained his composure quickly. "Well, don't be too hasty. That raccoon is a pretty big one." He turned toward Malach again, chewing on his cheek as if he were thinking hard. "I'll give you two jars of honey for it."

It was Malach's turn to play the indignant part. "Only two jars? I've put a lot of work into that animal, and if you're going to swindle me like that, I'll take my business elsewhere."

Malach made to walk around Arjun, but the man got in his way, "Fine, fine. You're a hard man to deal with, but I'll give you two jars and," he paused for dramatic effect, "I'll throw in some of the Honey Comb Candy I made from it."

This was the outcome Malach had intended to reach. It was fair, and both parties had a good time getting to this point of agreement.

"Deal." Malach put out his hand and Arjun took it without hesitation. "I'll go get the honey out of the pantry." He turned and started walking away, still giving directions as he went. "Give the meat to Zahra and she will put it away." His voice was distant now, but could still be heard. "I assume it's already preserved?"

"Yes! With my blend of seasonings as well," Malach called in answer, handing the package to Zahra.

"Someday you are going to have to tell me what you put on that meat to make it so good," Arjun called again from the pantry.

"Oh no, I don't. That's my blend that I've come up with, and a herd of wild horses couldn't pull it out of me!" Malach shouted back, winking at Zahra who smiled back, amused with her husband.

"Fine," Arjun conceded. "I guess I will just have to continue to do business with you."

Malach looked out the window and noticed the last vestiges of the sun's light casting long shadows across the fields. He turned back to Arjun as he came back in with the honey.

"I also need these." Malach handed him a list of items that he needed to buy from him. "And if you have any chicken feathers, I need to make some more arrows."

"No problem." Arjun called for one of the hired hands and handed him the list, telling him about the addition. "Johm will go get the things you require. That'll be five silver coins."

Malach handed him the equivalent of five silvers and looked out the window again. He might have half the light he needed for the trip home. "Well, I must be off. The sun is setting, and I have to get home soon. The woods aren't the safest place to be after dark, so the earlier I leave, the better."

"Are you sure that you will be safe by yourself?" Zahra asked, worried. "You're right, it's dangerous out there. You could just stay here with us and head back in the morning."

"No, no. I wouldn't want to intrude, and besides, I have a few things to square away before the morning," Malach politely declined as he took the honey from Arjun. "I will be hunting at your brother's farm in the morning. Thank you for your kind offer, though, and I always have Skie to protect me."

"My brother?" Arjun asked. "What's he got you doing?"

"He's had a few animals taken," Malach explained. "I've got to find out what's taking them and kill it."

"Huh," Arjun grunted. "I wonder why he didn't ask me. Well, no matter. Be patient with my brother; he is used to the easy life and being on top. He won't take kindly to bein' ordered around. To tell you the truth, he is a little rude at times."

"Really? I hadn't noticed," Malach retorted dryly.

"You've spent some time with him?" Arjun raised a brow.

"I saved him from a couple of bandits on the road and walked to town with him," Malach explained. "Would you believe that he yelled at me after I saved his life?"

"I'd believe it," Arjun said, but Zahra looked shocked. "Though, it was probably because he was more scared and powerless than anything. How can I repay you for saving my bother?"

"Oh, not you too!" Malach lamented. "Your bother practically wanted to buy me a whole store in town! I would have done the same for anyone, and I don't want any payment for it."

"Alright, fine," Arjun said, holding up his hand in surrender. "Well, let me get you a third jar of honey, at least. I know how much trouble my bother can be."

"Fine," Malach conceded. "But you don't owe me anything, alright?"

"Well, just take it as an early birthday present," Zahra said, and then her tone turned to one of warning. "And you be careful. I don't want to find out in a few days you were killed by those highwaymen."

"They might be looking for payback." Arjun agreed.

"Don't worry, I will." Malach put the third jar of honey in his sack and said his goodbyes.

He walked out the door just as Honora was walking up to the front porch. Skie was lying to Malach's right, lazily looking between them, not bothering to raise her head.

"Leaving so soon?" Honora asked in surprise.
Malach briefly recounted the story of the bandits as his reason for leaving. "I don't want to be out too late or they will have more cover to ambush me, if that is their plan."

"Fine," Honora looked disappointed, "I just wish you would stay through dinner at least."

"I have to be up early tomorrow to help your uncle track, and hopefully kill, whatever has been plaguing him," he replied. "Or I might have stayed."

"Be careful, alright? I don't want you getting hurt before we head out on the Journey."

"Don't worry. I haven't met anything yet I can't handle."

Honora's face turned from worried to playfully aghast in the blink of an eye. She shoved him and started berating him. "Malach Tresch, you're getting too big of a head. Soon you'll think you can take on a demon and win!"

"You never know, maybe I can!" Malach gave her a playful shove back.

"You boys and your egos. Well, fine then, get out of here. And you better come back in one piece to see me off!"

"I guess I *might* be able to make it to that, but you know that I'll be making that trip with you not a day later, right?"

Honora rolled her eyes. "Yeah, I remember. Those are going to be an insufferable two weeks, to be sure."

"I agree, since I'll be protecting this innocent little damsel who seems to enjoy whining." With that, Honora took a swing at him and missed, as he had already turned and bounded off the front porch.

"Malach! Come back here and take your medicine!" she yelled after him as he and Skie ran to the cart.

He arrived at the cart just as Johm was setting a second large bag on his cart. Johm had worked for the Reybellas for as long as Malach could remember. He was practically a part of the family, even taking meals with them at their table. The man didn't say much, but Malach liked him. The first of the two bags that Johm had set on the cart would be flour and the second would be the fruit and vegetables for his week. He still had plenty of oil at the house. That seemed to run out a lot slower, especially since he could substitute it with some of the fat from the animals he killed.

"Thanks!" He shook the man's hand and headed out. Skie now walked beside him. The road forked not far out from the Reybella's farm and he took the right branch that would to cut through the country toward his cottage, bypassing Brightwood. This would shave off about a half hour and the trouble of getting them to open the gates after dark. As he headed up the hill to his cottage, the sun had fully gone behind the tree and darkness was falling fast.

The effort of keeping a good pace had him sweating despite the chill that blew through the trees. Eventually, he was forced to slow from the grade of the hill. With the wind rustling the leave and breaking of dead twigs and branches, he couldn't rely on his hearing to detect any danger. The tree line loomed ahead of him like a giant wall. There was no telling who or what was lurking under the cover of those tall pines.

As he passed under the first trees, he stopped to let his eyes adjust to that darkness. It wouldn't do to stumble right into the highwaymen that might be waiting. Night had fallen fully and under the canopy, the moon and stars were snuffed out as well.

He took a drink of water from the flask Jennari gave him. The sandwich was long gone by now and his stomach protested how distant that meal was. However, all his senses were on high alert for any signs of danger. Skie was sitting next to him and was on high alert as well, though she hadn't made a sound, which was a good sign. He gave her a drink of water, then picked up the cart to move on. They walked for a way without a sound, save for the crunching of Malach's boots, the silent padding of Skie's paws, and the creaking of the cart as it rolled along behind them.

As they neared the cottage, his ears caught a sound on the wind. A few steps closer and he recognized the sound as muffled voices. Skie's hackles raised and a low growl emitted from deep in her throat. Malach put his hand out to his side in front of her, letting her know to wait. He set the cart down as quietly as he could. He came around a bend to see the outline of the cottage. There were torches flickering in the windows. He stayed close to the trees, hoping to hide his presence until he was at the cottage. As he got closer, he could see the cottage door was ajar, but he still couldn't see anyone. He almost laughed when he realized whoever was in his home had not bothered to leave a lookout.

As he reached the cottage, Skie beside him, he could see the shutters to the main living space and kitchen were open. He snuck around the clearing until he was under the window. Peeking over the sill, he spotted one of the three highwaymen from earlier that day. He was digging through Malach's cupboards. He pilfered the container of jerky and tore open the lid. Strips of meat with all over the floor but he managed to keep a hold of one. He sniffed it and then tore at it with his teeth.

"Hey, guys!" he shouted, turning around abruptly.

Malach ducked quickly to not be seen.

"I found some food. Good stuff too! Dried meat!"

Malach could hear the man's heavy foot falls stomp out of the kitchen. He realized only now he had left his bow on the cart. He silently berated himself for his lack of foresight. A thought stuck him. His father's old sword was still in the chest at the end of his bed. He would have to make his way to it. That would give him the best chance of fighting these brigands.

He peeked over the sill once again, and, seeing no one, he vaulted through the window into his kitchen. Skie followed, as quiet as the night breeze. Malach peered around the house again, still no one in sight. He moved out of the kitchen and into the sitting room. His room was off to his left and his parents' old room, which he had turned into a workroom, was straight ahead. Both doors were open, with light flickering in each one. If he could get to his room and get his father's sword, he could take them.

"Hey, Bray!" a man called from the workroom, and Malach's heart nearly jumped out of his chest. "Come here and look what we found!"

The man who had been in the kitchen stepped out from Malach's room and spotted him. Malach acted quickly, more on instinct than anything. He moved across the room with as much speed as he could muster, pulling his knife as he went, holding it in a reverse grip. He swung his knife hand up and pulled the blade across the man's throat. Simultaneously, he put his hand over Bray's mouth before he could make a noise. Bray collapsed with a small gurgle. Malach caught his body and pulled him back into his room.

"Bray?" the voice shouted again.

Malach could hear the two men moving out of the workroom, heading his way. He tore open the chest, not worrying about the noise. He dug around furiously, trying to find the sword.

Where was it?

It wasn't here.

"Hey!"

Malach spun to see one of the men fill the door. He had just run out of time. He snapped his knife up and crouched into a defensive position. His quiver slapped against his leg and he remembered still had one arrow in his quiver. The man drew a sword, and Malach realized it was the sword he had been looking for. The man grinned wickedly, and the flickering light in the man's one eye only made it look worse. Malach heard a bark and yell as the second man found out how untamed Skie was. For a split second, the man's smile left his face, but it returned as he heard his companion was still up and fighting. He took a menacing step forward.

"You are outmatched, boy," he spat. "You'll pay for taking my eye." Malach was poised to meet the man's first attack when a deafening roar shook the house. It was like time had stopped. No one moved an inch. Everyone listened for any clue to where the roar came from and what had made it. Malach thought that there was something familiar about the sound but couldn't place it. After almost a minute, they didn't hear anything, and the man advanced another step. The roar came again, and this time, it sounded like it was right outside of the cottage.

Malach moved, using the man's distraction to his advantage. Rushing forward, he pulled the last arrow from his quiver and stuck it into the man's good shoulder. Malach sidestepped around him but held onto the arrow as he did. Once behind him, Malach levered the arrow up, causing the man to scream in pain and drop his sword. It thumped onto the floor, gouging a furrow into the wood. He put his knife to the man's throat and turned him around, steering him by pulling on the arrow. He hollowed again, but Malach silenced him by digging the knife into his throat, drawing a trickle of blood.

He took the man into the sitting room and found that if he had moved any slower, Skie would have been killed. The second man had gotten the upper hand and was standing over Skie's unconscious body, about to plunge his knife into her side.

"Drop the knife!" Malach commanded. The second thief looked up before he finished his blow. He saw Malach and the knife at his leader's throat and dropped his weapon.

The door to the cottage blew inward with such force it was ripped free of its hinges and slammed into the table. Malach capitalized on the distraction by pushing the man toward the door and running to Skie. He kicked the second man in the face as he sheathed his knife and hoisted her onto his shoulders. What was happening, he didn't know, but he wasn't going to stick around to find out. He ran through the workroom and kicked open the shutters. Screams sounded from behind him, which only bolstered his need to keep moving. He climbed through the window and ran to his right, moving toward the road and the front of the house.

As he rounded the corner, his feet stuck fast where he stood, and he froze as fear gripped him. He couldn't move! All he could do was watch as the demon from his dreams stood, pulling the one-eyed man out of the cottage, clutching his body in its claw.

Chapter 3

Amara crouched behind a cart in the alley, waiting for her chance to strike. She had a small knife on her, However she didn't plan to use it. She watched the man on the other side of the street as he sold food from his stall. He was her target. A group of people approached his cart. This would be her best chance. She stood up and as they passed the alley and fell in behind them.

As they walked up to the vendor's cart, she pushed up into the middle of the group. Someone protested, but she ignored them. Instead, while everyone was busy talking with the vendor and each other, she snatched an apple and slipped it into her bag. She pretended to study the oranges, picking one or two of them up before pilfering one of those as well. Just as the crowd was starting to disperse, she spied the man's coin purse. He had left it unguarded and was talking with another customer on the far side of the cart. She cautiously peered around to make sure no one had noticed her and slipped the purse into her bag as well. She turned and started walking away with what was left of the group she had walked up with.

"Hey!"

Amara forced herself not to look back or bolt. She had to appear calm. She might still get away. The merchant didn't know who had taken the purse. A hand fell on her shoulder and spun her around.

It was the merchant.

"Girl! Did you steal my purse?" he said heatedly.

"No!" Amara replied a little too quickly. "I didn't steal nothin'!" She tried to look shocked and confused, but ended up looking startled and guilty.

"We'll see about that!" The merchant was not going to let her get away.

"I didn't!" she exclaimed again, thinking quickly. "But there's someone stealing it now!" She pointed at the empty stall behind him.

When he turned, she kicked him hard in the shin and took off. She could hear the man's angry shouts behind her, but she could outrun him. He was fat and slow. She only hoped the city guard wasn't around. She just had to make it to the guild, but if she was being chased by the guard, she would have to lose them first.

She chanced a glance behind her, and didn't see anyone.

I'm free! She thought as she grabbed a storm drain and shimmied up to the rooftop.

She hopped along the rooftops until she was above the entrance to the Shadows of the Earth's lair. Shadows for short. She climbed down from the roof and opened the cover to the sewers. Instead of landing in filth, however, her feet smacked dry stone. This part of the sewer still smelled like a sewer, but you didn't have to slog through waste to get around. Whoever had come up with the plan was smart. Instead of just damming up the sewers, they rerouted and diverted all the lines away from this area, and then set up a series of pipes to take the waste from each house. It all emptied into the sea.

The short run had her sweating, and she slipped off the rags she had on over her head. It was warm outside, as it was most of the year in Caister. Under the rags, she wore a small, black, tight-fitting shirt and shorts, like most of the women of the Shadows wore. They were easy to move in and covered all the important parts, while allowing the most ventilation. She had worn them ever since she could remember.

She wore the rags over them to sell her street kid look. Sometimes she would get coins or food from passersby just by begging. Most of the time, she had to steal.

Amara moved toward the main chambers of the Shadows. She had a good haul today, which meant she would get to eat. This was the first time she had stolen money, so she didn't know what her cut would be. If there were enough coins in the purse, she might even get to eat tomorrow, too. She found her handler, Lawdel, and walked over to him, pulling out the fruit and coin purse. He studied her and arched an eyebrow.

"What do we have here?" He asked, a smile playing across his lips. "You going big on us? Started stealing more than just food?"

"It was there and open, so I took it. That's all." Amara didn't meet his gaze.

"Calm down, little one," Lawdel chuckled. He had a warm smile and a kind face. He was taller than her, but most people were.

Amara stood around five feet tall and with a slight build. She had lived with the Shadows her entire life. They found her in the street in the dead of winter. They told her when they found her, her extremities were already turning blue, even though she had been wrapped in a blanket. Lawdel had taken pity on her and took her into the sewers to live with them. Since then, she had been under his charge. They had said she was only a few months old when they found her.

The Shadows had just started the chapter in the town of Caister back then and had little, but they made sure she stayed alive. Since she could walk, they had been training her to steal and the art of the Shadows. She had better agility than most of the thieves in the guild, and she was just learning to pickpocket, which she found much easier than she had assumed. She was almost eighteen and was still learning when and what to steal. Stealing never bothered her. The guild always gave its members a cut of what was stolen, but that didn't always mean she have food every day. She was very thin and fit, but everyone in the Shadows was that way. Except Dros. He was their bruiser. If there were any problems needing muscle, he always took care of it.

Lawdel poured out the coins onto the table in front of him. There were a couple of gold coins, but most were silver or copper. Lawdel whistled low. "Girly, you hit the big one! I think it's time for me to teach you about the money system."

Amara huffed and plopped moodily into a chair across the table from him as he put one of each; copper, silver, and gold coin in front of her. "Do I have to do this now? I need to get back out there. I want a full stomach tonight."

Lawdel raised an eyebrow. "Guild standard for an apprentice is twenty-five percent of coins brought in and half of the food. If you knew what money was worth and how much you could buy, you would know that you have the money to eat for three or four days just from this haul."

Amara's mouth dropped open.

"So, do I have your attention now?" He continued before Amara could answer. "Now, you see the little copper coin?"

She nodded.

Lawdel taught her about the money system. How it took ten copper to equal a silver and five silvers for a gold. She still had a hard time listening until he told her she could buy a whole loaf of bread for only five copper. Then it started to make sense to her.

"Now I want you to count out your coins and I'll help you find out how much is yours. Do you still remember how to do percentages?"

"Yes, Lawdel," she said, exasperated that he thought she might have forgotten. In the pile of coins there were fifteen copper coins, six silver, and three gold.

"This will usually be done by your handler, me in this case." Lawdel explained. "But I want you to know how this process works so you can know when someone isn't dealing straight with you." Lawdel handed her sixteen copper coins and four silver coins.

"Why didn't you give me one gold and six copper?" Amara asked curiously.

"Because you aren't going to buy anything worth more than a silver," Lawdel patiently explained. "You don't want to carry that many coins on you. I wouldn't carry more than a silver and five copper unless you have something specific you want. You don't want to make the same mistake as this guy and leave all your money in one purse. He got all of his money stolen."

She nodded in understanding. "But where do I keep the rest? I don't have one purse, much less two. And if I leave it in my room, there is no guarantee that someone won't steal it."

"That is a good point."

He handed her the now-empty purse she had stolen and walked to the room where extra equipment was kept. She followed as she slid her coins into her new purse. He opened a crate and revealed a pile of purses.

"We keep all the extra purses and sell them with the rest of the things we pinch," he told her. "Pick one."

She dug through them. Some were thin and wouldn't last long, and some were so gaudy they would be stolen faster than she could tie it to her belt. She picked a medium quality one with good stitching and a beautiful rose etching on the leather. A nice quality purse that wouldn't stand out.

"Good pick." Lawdel smiled down at her.

She poured the coins out into her hand, picked out a silver and five copper, and put them into the one with the rose on it. Replacing the rest of the coin in the first purse, she put both purses on her belt and followed Lawdel back to the table.

"Now you have to figure out where you will keep your money and what to do with all of your extra time," Lawdel again smiled at her.

"I think, with my extra time, I will find where to put my purse. I don't trust some of the thieves here." She stood and grabbed the apple for her half of the food.

"Good girl!" Lawdel stood with her. "Glad you haven't forgotten all of my lessons. It's still early, and you don't have any reason to, but there is a job tonight that would be ideal for your first. If you want it, we would need to go over the details this afternoon."

Amara thought about it for a long moment, taking a bite out of the apple. "What's the job? I won't kill anyone." She warned.

"Lord of hell girl, we aren't assassins!" Lawdel exclaimed. "The number one rule of the guild is 'kill only in defense,' and that's as a last option. You should know the rules, girl."

"I know, I know. Sorry, I wasn't thinking." Amara hung her head. *How could she have forgotten?*

"Tell me the other rules of the guild," Lawdel demanded.

Amara sighed but had known this was coming, "Rule one: don't hurt or kill unless your own life is at risk. Rule two: don't put your brothers and sisters of the guild in danger or interfere with a job unless it is to protect the party involved. Rule three: get in and get out without being seen or leaving any evidence you were there, unless the job requires it." Amara recited these from memory. They had been drilled into her head since she was a child. She couldn't believe she had, even momentarily, forgotten one of them.

"Good," Lawdel said. "Now, if you complete a job successfully, you get fifty percent of what the customer paid. If you can steal more, the guild keeps the items you steal for the job. Then you get twenty-five percent of what we sell it for, if it sells. I will keep track of your items for you. As for the job, you would break into the mayor's house and stealing a ledger that will be in his desk. The manor has little security, and there will be a ball his entire family will attend tonight. There will be no one in the office, so you should have plenty of time, and if you miss the timing on the guard rotation, you will be fine to wait for the next one."

"Sounds like it still could be dangerous." Amara put her hands on her hips. "Why would I take this job after I got enough to live for a few days?"

"This heist is going to be one of the easiest to start on, and we might have to wait months for another one this straightforward," Lawdel insisted.

"And it probably will be more dangerous. However, you're right. This one isn't without its risk. If you're picked up in the mayor's office or leaving with the items, you will be jailed for no more than a month since you have no priors. If you're caught getting in, then the punishment with be less than a week in jail. But a lot of other jobs you would be killed on sight or hanged if caught."

"So, you think I should take it?" she asked.

She always trusted Lawdel. He had never led her wrong and had been more of a father to her than anyone, even though he hadn't known how to be one. He had taught her everything.

"Yes," he said flatly.

She liked that about him, too. No beating around the bush. Just facts and short opinions.

"Fine, I'll take it. I have to go stash my extra coin and get something to eat, and then I'll be back to go over the plan."

"That's my girl!" Lawdel awkwardly hugged her, or maybe it was just awkward for her. "I already picked it up from the board." He produced the papers from inside his cloak.

"You rogue!" Amara punched him in the shoulder. "How did you know I would take the job?"

Lawdel rubbed his shoulder, wincing. "I know you better than you think, girl. One last thing before you go. I got these for when you took your first, proper job." He moved to a sack sitting beside the table and pulled out a rolled-up piece of black leather. She could see metal rods sticking out of it, but had no idea what it was. He handed it to her. She gave him a quizzical look.

"What is it?" she asked.

"Unwrap it, and find out," Lawdel responded.

She started unwrapping it. It appeared to be a corset, but it had four ornate metal handles sticking out on each side. The handles angled up slightly and laid almost flush with the leather.

"What in the world is this torture device?" she enquired, holding up the thing.

"It's a hard leather-armored piece with the ability to hold sixteen six-inch throwing daggers," Lawdel said excitedly. "Unfortunately, I could only afford eight daggers." Lawdel's face drooped a little.

"Oh!" Amara exclaimed and re-examined the leather with newfound appreciation. She had never had anything so nice. She pulled out a dagger and tested the balance. It was almost perfect, and she knew this present had cost Lawdel a great deal. Maybe everything he had.

"This is so nice! I can't accept this." She tried to hand it back.

"Oh no, you don't. I won't accept a no for an answer." Lawdel pushed the leather piece back toward her. "Besides, I can't take it back. I bought it a year ago off a sneak that pinched it from a leather shop."

"But this cost you so much!" she pressed.

"Not as much as you would think. It's your first job, and it's bad luck to go without a present. I know how well you like your throwing daggers."

"Fine," she said. She really *did* want to keep it, and she loved the filigree on the handles. *She* hugged him this time. It wasn't even awkward for her. She was so excited.

"Let me help you into it." Lawdel took the leather from her and walked around behind her. He helped her lace it up and showed her how to do it herself for the next time. She went over to the clean well in the center of the room and looked at her reflection in the water. When the leather was properly laced, the daggers laid almost flat against her sides. It would be hard to detect it under a cloak.

"A cloak!" She exclaimed. "Do I have enough money for one?"

"Don't worry," Lawdel said. "The guild gives you one for your first job, but you will have to pay it back. They will take it out of your jobs. It will only take you one or two good hauls to pay it back."

He saw the disbelief on her face and guessed what she was thinking. "Welcome to the middle class, where you work for everything you own, but you get to eat every day." He chuckled as she smiled at him.

Amara left the Shadows with her head held high and excitement in her heart. She Had already gone to the market with her new money and then back to the lair for a rundown of the job while she ate the food she had purchased. Purchased, not stolen. True, she had purchased the food with stolen money, but she didn't care. I felt good either way.

She had played tonight's job out in her head dozens of times already. She was ready for her first job and the benefits that it would bring. The large clock tower at the center of the city showed she still had a few hours until at the manor, but she wanted to make sure the guard rotation hadn't changed. Her new leather armor fit her perfectly. She felt amazing in it. It accentuated her form without limiting her movements. Between the black leather and blacked knife hilts, nothing would shine in the moonlight. It made her a little sad to rub the black soot on the ornate hilts, but it couldn't be helped.

She ascended to the rooftops on the last leg of her journey. As she approached the manor, that was a story taller than all the buildings around it and decided to scout around to confirm their intel. The location of the office would most likely be correct, but there might be a better direction of ingress and egress.

The three-story building that wasn't overly gaudy, but was too big for any one man, in her opinion. It was more or less square, with a large lawn and a stone wall some fifty yards away from the building. There were two gates set into the wall that provided easy access to the manor. One was a simple iron-barred gate, the other was a massive wooden gate which rose higher than the rest of the wall, making the stone rise over the wooden door. This gate was for show and vanity only, and she was disgusted.

I'm glad we are stealing from this pompous idiot tonight, she thought to herself.

She had heard the mayor was arrogant. She didn't think he was evil; he just didn't have his priorities straight, though there *were* rumors of corruption. She thought he was the perfect mark since he wouldn't be able to admit that he had been stolen from. It would make him look weak, and he treasured status among all else.

On the ground floor were several entrances. There was a small servant's entrance at the back of the building. Another, on the side of the manor for the family to get to the grounds, where there were chairs and tables for their use.

The final entrance was the front door, in some ways, as gaudy as the front gate. It wasn't as massive, but it had a set of double doors trimmed in gold with gold handles. She doubted the mayor would actually have paid for solid gold handles, but they were polished and gave the appearance of wealth.

She settled down in the crook of a roof to watch the window selected for her to enter through. It was on the side of the manor that didn't have a door. The guard's rotation would take them by this side less often. There was a gutter attached to the wall she was promised would hold her weight.

She settled in and pulled out the bread and cheese. The cheese tasted so good she almost forgot about the bread entirely. It's not like she had ever truly been starving, but having a full belly and rich food was glorious. She sat there for about an hour, watching the guards move. She noted only twice during that time where the guards passed by, and they were only ten minutes apart. There was almost forty minutes where there were no guards within sight of the window. It was perfect.

Amara erred on the side of caution and move to the opposite side of the manor. She found a place to sit and watch that side to use up the last of her daylight. It didn't take her long to realize the first side was the obvious choice. There were guards everywhere comparatively.

The only missing information was the guard's movements inside the building. That was the only wild card for the night. Lawdel told her the guards didn't patrol the halls as often on the inside of buildings. However, it was something to keep in mind. She moved back to the side with the window she would enter from and again settled in to wait for her time to move. She needed to wait until darkness would mask her movement and just before the guards changed shifts.

Amara climbed down from her hiding spot. It was time to start her first heist. She had timed it just right, and pride in her prowess swelled in her chest. She had waited for one of the last rotations of the shift and there were no guards in sight. Quelling that feeling until a more appropriate time, she ran across the street, pumping her legs to get the momentum she needed. Just before reaching the wall, she made a jump and caught the top of it. Her fingers latched onto the edge of the wall and she pulled herself up and over before anyone on the street could see her. She landed behind some bushes that lined the wall and checked around before she moved on. There was no reason to be reckless.

She had a thirty-minute window to get in, fifteen minutes inside the building, and another twenty to get out. Even if it took her longer to find the ledger, all she would have to do was wait for the next guard rotation. This was a straightforward job as far as thievery was concerned. All she had to do was get in, get the ledger, and get out.

There was no one in sight, so she made a dash toward the wall. Again, she jumped as high as she could and grabbed the storm drain. She made sure she had a firm grip and then started pulling herself up, hand over hand, her feet braced against the wall for support.

When she reached the window's ledge, she leaned over to look inside and cursed. The shutters were drawn, and she had no way of telling if anyone was just inside the window or not. This window opened to a hall and there could be anyone walking by at any time. An idea blossomed in her mind and she leaned a little closer, putting her ear against the window and listened. She heard nothing, but that didn't mean much. She could open the window and run right into a guard stationed there.

Well, I can't sit on this ledge all night, she thought. She pulled one of her blacked knives out of its sheath, slipped the knife in under the window, and flipped the latch.

Too easy, she thought. *They really need to make these windows latches more secure.*

She pulled the window open and nearly lost her balance as it popped loose. Her knife slipped from her hand and she watched it fall to the grass. She cursed under her breath.

The knife had luckily fallen point down and sunk into the earth up to the hilt. Indecision froze her in place. It would cost her time if she retrieved the knife, and it wasn't sticking too far out of the ground. Nobody would notice it.

She decided to press on and recover it on her way out. She mentally kicked herself for being so careless, but it seemed to turn out fine.

Pulling the curtains aside, and she peered in. The hall was dark, and the lamps on the wall were not lit. She was at a turn in the hallway. To her left, the corridor continued along the outside wall with several doors on the right. Straight ahead, it went for about twenty feet and stopped at another junction, then turned to the right and left. There was no one in sight.

She slipped in the window, pushed it most of the way closed, and crouched down. She peered around more intently. Still nothing. She moved straight ahead to the junction and peeked around the corner to the left. Nothing. She turned to the right and nearly screamed. She clamped her hand over her mouth and froze. There was a figure standing at the end of the hall, staring directly at her. The figure didn't move an inch. She stood there, frozen, for what felt like a lifetime. Neither she nor the figure moved. Studying it closer, she wondered if there was any way the guard hadn't seen her. She slowly, inch by inch, moved back around the corner. Once she was out of sight of the figure, she leaned against the wall and let her heart settle. He was guarding the most direct route to the mayor's office. She worked up the courage to peek around the corner. He was still standing there in the exact same position.

No one stands that still, she thought, looking closer. She felt extremely foolish. What she thought was a person was simply a suit of armor. *Who puts a suit of armor in a hallway?*

She strode up to the suit, careful to make sure there was one else around, still feeling a little paranoid. *The mayor must think this makes him look important or rich because he could never fit in this, much less carry it.*

She knocked on the breastplate and a hollow, metallic sound emanated from it. It was time to get moving, though. She couldn't stand there playing with a suit of armor all night.

She made her way down the hall to the left and up the stairs to the next floor. There were no windows on this floor, which is why she had to enter the mansion from the floor below. This floor housed the Mayor's personal office as well as a sitting room and conference room. The Mayor believed that having windows in the place of work distracted from work, which she thought was a most absurd belief. This also made for an extremely hot work environment. Because of that, the ceilings and floors had vents in them to allow the air to flow from the floors above and below it. As she walked up the stairs, the air became stifling and stagnant. The vents didn't seem to help too much, though the cool night air would soon find its way into the house.

She had to be careful about any sound as it would carry through the vents and bring the guards down on top of her. Keeping her steps as light as possible, she moved through the hall and to the door they said would be the mayor's office. She tested the handle. Locked. She pulled out her lock pick set and set to work.

She couldn't recall how many locks she had picked with this same pick. It had been her first set of picks that Lawdel taught her with. Her first lock took her more than an hour to pick, but Lawdel said she had a gift for it. She didn't believe him until he had told her his first lock had taken him nearly twenty-four hours. She had asked some of the other guild members and found similar stories. From there, her skills had only grown.

It only took her a few moments before the door emitted a soft click and swung out on well-oiled hinges. She opened the door slowly to find the cleaning closet. I took her a long moment before she realized she must just have the wrong room. She must have been told wrong. She shut the door and move down the hall to the next door and picked its lock. This time, the door opened to reveal the actual mayor's office. She let out a sigh of relief and closed the door softly behind her.

Who keeps the door to a cleaning closet locked, anyway?

She peered around the room and took stock of everything. The mayor had a huge wooden desk that wrapped around the room and took up most of the space. It went from the back-right corner to the opposite corner, up the left wall, and jutted out just before the door. She couldn't believe her eyes. The desk was made of some dark, imported wood and must have cost a small fortune. There were papers stacked on most of the desk's surfaces, but a small workspace remained clear and a chair sat in front of it. That's where she'd start.

There were two sets of drawers to either side of the workspace, and both had a lock set into them. She had never seen a lock like it before. There was only one lock, but all three drawers were stuck shut.

She hoped it was the same principle as the other locks she had picked and set to work on the right set of drawers. It was just like the normal tumbler locks set in the doors, and she opened it with no issues. The top drawer held all manner of writing paraphernalia: paper, charcoal, inkwells, and a wooden cylinder; which had a sharp metal end on it. There were no quills, so she assumed it was for writing with. She put that into her bag. She wanted to take a closer look at it later; it might be worth something.

She moved the second drawer, but when she opened it, she couldn't believe her eyes. It wasn't the ledger, but it was something she wanted, nonetheless. Two bags of coins were sitting there in the drawer. She slipped those into her bag.

When she pulled the third drawer open, there were just papers in it. No doubt important ones for them to be locked up, but it wasn't what she was looking for, and she didn't know enough to know which papers would be useful.

Amara moved over to the second set of drawers and picked the lock on that set. She opened each one of those, not finding anything useful in the first two. She opened the bottom drawer and found the ledger. Picking it up, she quickly thumbed through it to confirm it to be the ledger. She stuffed it into her bag, but as she shut the drawer, she noticed something odd. The bottom of the drawer on the inside was higher than the bottom of the draw on the outside by almost half the height. It was a false bottom.

She moved her hand around the inside of the drawer and found a latch holding the false bottom in place. She moved the latch and pushed on the back. The whole bottom swiveled up and revealed a second ledger and ten more sacks of coins. She almost gasped. She had never seen so many coins in one place, and she almost missed it, almost went back with the wrong ledger. The one in her pack must be a fake to throw off any would-be thief. It nearly worked.

She grabbed the coin purses and the second ledger, but before she could put the first ledger back, she heard a pair of footsteps coming down the hall. She shut the drawer just as the footsteps reached the door. The knob turned slowly. She glanced around for a hiding spot, but the only place was under the desk. She all but dove for it, trying to keep the coin ladened bag from making too much noise.

She heard the door open, and she heard whispers between two people, but couldn't make out any words. Then she heard a giggle.

That's strange. What would a girl be doing up here? Amara thought. Footsteps rushed in and the door shut behind the pair.

"Dain, what are we doing up here? This is my father's office," the girl said. "If he catches us here, he will have you hung."

"Your father isn't here. There is no way he'll ever know," the voice that must have belonged to Dain said. "Besides, it wouldn't be fun if there wasn't a little danger."

At that point, Amara heard the couple kissing and wanted to throw up. It was hard to deduce where this was going, and she had no way of knowing how long or how far their lovemaking would go. She really didn't want to be a witness to it. Instead, she pulled her pack off her shoulder and stood up.

"What in the world is going on here?" she barked as if she were the one in charge.

Her plan was a little risky, but she couldn't wait for someone to find the couple and search the office. She picked up the boy's shirt that had been discarded on the desk and started swinging it at the two, shouting about telling the girl's father and how much trouble they would be in. She shooed them out of the room and threw the shirt at the boy. The couple tore off down the hall without even a glance back.

Amara moved back to the desk and grabbed her bag from underneath it. She had to get out of the manor before the couple realized they had been duped and called the guards. She ran as quietly as she could with her bag full of clinking coins and arrived back at the window in about a minute.

She opened the window and peered out. Her stomach just about dropped to the floor. A guard was standing directly under the window holding her dropped knife in his hand. She ducked back in the window as he looked up, but there was no way she had time to close it. He would soon see the open window and call the other guards. She was panicking now. She was caught and there was nothing she could think of to get out.

Calm down and think! She told herself and forced her breathing to slow.

She stuck her head out the window cautiously, but the guard was gone. She glanced to her left and glimpsed him moving around the corner at a normal pace. To her right, there were no guards in sight. She breathed a sigh of relief and thanked whatever god or demon helping her.

She sat down on the windowsill and swung her leg into the open space, pulling her bag out along with her. She was careful not to let herself get off balance by the heavy load. Grabbing the storm drain with her left hand, she scooted herself off the ledge. For a second, the weight of her bag drug her down, but she caught the storm drain with her second hand and slowed her fall. She felt a sharp pain in her left palm but couldn't stop to look now.

She let herself drop the last five feet and landed in a crouch. Thoughts of her knife sprung to her mind, and she vowed to never make the mistake of dropping one again. Her hand was now throbbing. She noticed a cut that ran the width of her palm and was bleeding badly. No time to bandage that. She would have to leave it for now and clean it later.

She sprinted for the outer wall, and just as she was pulling herself over, she heard the ringing of the alarm. Leaping from the wall, She disappeared into shadows in the alley across the street.

Amara jumped down into the sewers and bounced into the Shadows' main chamber with all the pride and excitement of a two-year-old who just acquired a cookie without being caught. Lawdel was waiting for her and the relief was evident on his face. He would never admit it, but she knew he had been worried about her.

All he said was, "Did you get the item?"

She pulled out the ledger in response. He took it from her and thumbed through it.

"Any trouble?" Lawdel asked, turning and walking away without waiting for a response. He seemed a lot more professional than usual. Not as warm toward her.

"No, Lawdel," Amara jogged to catch-up and then fell into step with Lawdel. "I mean, there were a couple of minor issues, but nothing I couldn't handle."

"I hear the alarm was sounded at the mayor's mansion?" He questioned her, still walking across the main chamber.

"Yes, but…"

"But nothing," Lawdel cut her off. "We've heard reports of two eyewitnesses who said they saw you, and there was one of your knives found at the manor."

"I know but…"

"But nothing!" Lawdel said again. He turned to look at her, this time stopping her in her tracks. "If the job had gone any more wrong, you would have been caught. You're lucky the eyewitnesses were young and couldn't remember you very well, and you're lucky the guard didn't look up when you had the windows wide open gawking at him." Lawdel began to walk again. "That guard would have looked up, but for some reason, he thought someone was calling for him."

"Why would he have thought that?" Amara was confused.

"Because yours truly made him think that," Lawdel leveled an eyebrow at her. "Some quick thinking on my part, if I do say so myself."

"So, you were out there watching me?" Amara said, getting a little frustrated.

"Of course I was!" Lawdel sounded appalled. "What kind of handler would I be if I just let you run solo your first mission? My point is, you need to be more careful. You don't want to have a theft go wrong like it nearly did twice tonight. After you're caught once, you are in the system and the guards will know your face. It could limit what jobs you can take."

Amara smiled. Lawdel was more worried about her than he let on. He was trying to covering it by acting like he only cared about her career. They got to the meeting room, and Amara went in first. She was shocked to see the Shadows' leader sitting at the table. She froze in the doorway and Lawdel ran into her, knocking her off balance.

"For goodness' sakes, girl…" Lawdel's voice trailed off as he saw the master.

He was smaller than people would expect and, most of the time, wore baggy robes with his hood up. Amara had only seen him once in her life, and he looked the same then as he did now. She couldn't see much under the robes, not even around his neck. The other thieves told stories about how he had narrowly escaped a fire but had nasty scars. That's why he always wore the robes, even in the dead heat of the summer. The last time Amara had seen him, he watched her train when Lawdel was teaching her to throw knives, and he had a kind, soft voice. She liked him then, and he seemed to be a good leader. They said he could steal the pants off the Captain of the Guard.

"Please come in and sit with me, Amara," he said. His voice was smooth, calm, and gentle.

Amara moved to the table and sat down. "Thank you," Amara said, and then added quickly "sir."

Lawdel took a seat to her left.

"No need for the formalities," the master replied. "We are going to be talking about your bright future as one of our members."

Amara was not sure what was going on and she didn't even have the benefit of reading the master's face to find out. Although she doubted his face would tell her anything, anyway.

"Amara," the master was looking right at her, "I watched you during this first job that you pulled."

Lawdel and Amara looked at each other, and Amara could tell that Lawdel didn't have a clue that he had been there.

"I'm very impressed." He continued. "You were a little careless with this knife, though." He pulled the knife that she had dropped out of one of his sleeves and put it down on the table. "And also, you should have waited to leave the room until the young couple had finished their business or discovered you on their own. However, making them think you were supposed to be there when they weren't, had been a decent idea. Unfortunately, they were able to piece together a passable likeness of your face."

He pulled out a rolled-up piece of parchment from the other sleeve and opened it on the table. It had a drawing of her face. It wasn't a perfect likeness, but it was close enough the guards recognize her.

"Luckily, the guard will lose this drawing somewhere and won't be able to find it. He won't want to admit the mistake, but sooner or later, he will have to tell the Captain and they will have a new one drawn. Time will have passed and memory fades. You know how that will go."

She did. The guard would only get about half the account right and the other half make up. The new drawing of her would look nothing like her at all. She was amazed at how quickly the master had moved to swipe both these items and still make it to the Shadows' lair to meet with her after the theft. But, she guessed, that's why they called him a master.

"So, let talk about your final failure." Both Amara and Lawdel looked at each other, confused, as the master continued. "In your hurry to get out without being caught, you left the window open and a bloody trail down the storm drain. I could not both clean up after you and take the items which would put you at risk. If we ever need to get to the mayor's office again, it will most likely not be possible to use the same entry point. It will be more difficult and dangerous. You have inadvertently put your brothers and sisters in the Shadows at risk."

"Now hold on a minute," Lawdel said, leaning forward in his chair. Amara cut his outburst short. "It's true."

Amara was ashamed. She hadn't even thought of it then. All she thought of was getting out. She had put future heists at risk. She had nothing to say against his accusations, so her only course of action was to face it head-on.

"I *did* do that. I should have taken the few seconds to close the window and safely make the descent," She held out the hand that she had cut. She had taken the time to clean and bandage it before coming back to the guild. Lawdel gaped at her for a moment, then let out a sigh and flopped back into his chair. "Girl, what have I told you time and time again?"

"Slow down, even when leaving with the loot." Amara recited. "And I know that's what happened. I made a mistake." She turned to the master. "I promise it won't happen again."

"I think that, in the end, it was a small price to pay, but I appreciate the honesty. It's hard to come by in a thief. Please, show us the goods you managed to obtain." The Master gestured toward her bag, sitting on the table.

Amara undid the leather thong that held the flap down and upended the bag onto the table.

Lawdel let out a low whistle. "Now that's a lot of coins. How much is in there?"

His question sounded more like he was talking to himself, but Amara answered him anyway. "I'm not sure. I haven't had the chance to open them yet."

Now that she was in the light, she could see a difference between the two coin purses. The two purses from the first draw were well worn and very thin in a couple of places. The ten purses from the false bottom drawer appeared to have been bought recently. She reached for one of the new purses.
"Hold on, young one," the master said. "Why do you think the purses look different? And why do you think the mayor would have all of his purses in the false drawer and not the treasury?"

Amara thought for a moment, "The purses from the first drawer could simply be older, but I think they're worn from being handled more. Maybe those two are the coins the mayor is legally allowed to use in office. As for the newer purses, I would think they wouldn't be in the treasury and not as worn for the same reason. These are the coins he has gained illegally. He couldn't take them to the treasury because he would be questioned, and he didn't take them out often because he didn't want anyone to know they were there."

"Very good deduction, I think you are correct," the master agreed. "Now you can open them and find out how much you have acquired."

Amara took the first worn purse and dumped out the coins.

They were all silver. The second of the worn purses held all copper, and eight of the ten new looking purses were gold coins. The other two new purses held silver and copper, respectively. Amara's head was spinning as she and Lawdel counted the coins. She was rich. She could do anything with these coins. She couldn't believe it. Not only did she get her cut of the coins but also her cut of the job's profit. She couldn't fathom being that rich. In a day she went from hardly able to feed herself to being able to pay for just about anything she wanted.

Lawdel and Amara counted to coins under the watchful eye of the master. There were twenty gold coins in each bag, and thirty silver and fifty copper in each of the other bags, respectively. They totaled it up to be one hundred and sixty gold coins, sixty silver, and one hundred copper. So, her cut was forty gold pieces, fifteen silver, and twenty-five copper.

The master stood and picked up the two ledgers. "Your outfit will be paid in full by your payment for the job. If I can get double for the job like I think I can, you should get a cut of that as well. I will let Lawdel know through the normal channels. Oh, and from this day on, you are no longer an apprentice. Farwell, Journeyman Amara."

The master walked out the door.

Amara looked at Lawdel and squealed, "I'm a journeyman now!"

"Not just a journeyman," Lawdel corrected, "the youngest journeyman in the history of our guild. Now you receive thirty percent of the gold taken in." She hugged him, grabbed her three purses off the table, and ran out the door. She had to put her money in a safe place. Her life changed so much in just one day.

"Wait!" Lawdel called just as she went around the corner.

She turned around and popped her head back around the corner. "What?"

He held out his hand. In his open palm were her knife and a few more coins. "The extra five percent for your job since you are a journeyman and your knife."

She snatched the knife and coins from Lawdel. "Thanks!" She ran back out of the room.

She headed for the watchtower, where she kept all of her important things. The watchtower was a part of the old city wall and wasn't used anymore. As the city expanded, a new wall was built and the old wall left to crumble. At the top of the tower, there was a landing that was open to the elements. It had a trapdoor that led to the stairs that would take her to ground level. The door on the ground level was always locked.

She went there often just to look at the stars. On warm nights, she would sometimes sleep there on the roof. There was a stone under the awning that was loose, and she hid her few belongings there.

She scaled the tower and peeked over the wall of the landing. No one was there, like normal. She pulled herself up onto the wall that rimmed the landing. She stood up and, holding onto to roof so she didn't fall, leaned out, using one hand to pull a stone out of its housing. The tower's roof was hollow, and she kept three things in there other than her coins. First was the blanket that she was wrapped in when the thieves found her, the second was a pouch of her first set of throwing knives, and the third was an amulet which she assumed had been her mother's. She would have worn it wherever she went, but she lived with thieves, so she learned to take precautions.

She pulled out the amulet and hung it around her neck. Then she put the new purses full of coins in the hole. Pulling two gold coins and adding them to the few she had left in her purse. She replaced the stone, climbed down, and walked into the town market as the sun rose.

Chapter 4

It was the demon.

The demon from his dream. Malach stood frozen in fear, Skie still draped across his shoulders. It bit off the highwayman's head and tossed the rest away like he was the unwanted rind of fruit. Its gaze landed on Malach and took a step toward him. Malach still couldn't move.

He could feel his heart beating out of his chest, hear the blood pulsing through his ears, but he couldn't get his feet to move. It was like they were rooted to the ground. He was saved when the final highwayman ran screaming from the front door the demon had just passed. It spun, spearing the man in the chest with one of its talons.

Malach finally got his feet to listen, and, taking a few unsteady steps, he started running. His mind had shut down, and he was running on base instinct. A tree branch scratched his face as he passed, and the pain seemed to kick his brain back into gear. He realized he was running nearing in the opposite direction of town. He made a right turn, knowing if he couldn't get to town, he was dead.

As he ran, the underbrush grabbed at his legs as if it were trying to pull him down and hold him for the demon. Soon, any exposed skin was cut and bleeding and there were several tears in his clothing. He didn't dare look back, though. Even when he heard the demon crashing through the woods behind him, he didn't look. This time, he would *not* stop. He had no chance of fighting this monster, and he knew it. He burst through the underbrush and out into the open valley. The earth fell away suddenly, and he stumbled with the change. He was forced to slow to gain his footing, but quickly picked up speed as he ran down the hill. Skie's body bounced on his shoulders, his spine protesting her weight. Even though he didn't know how long he could keep up this speed, he didn't dare slow down from his breakneck flight down to the town.

He finally chanced a look behind him and did not see the demon. It seemed it didn't want to come out of the trees into the opening. If he had learned anything from his dreams, it was that this creature wanted him dead, and it was cunning. Malach was still running at an all-out sprint when the light from the moon suddenly disappeared. He looked up to see a shadow soar over him. His heart skipped a beat, and he skidded to a stop on the loose rock, not knowing what to do now. However, the demon didn't land in front of him; in fact, it didn't land anywhere. It flew over the town and past the tree line on the other side of the valley.

I didn't know it could fly, Malach thought.

His knees were shaking, and his legs felt like noodles. Even though the demon flew out behind the tree line, he still didn't feel safe. He wouldn't until he was in town. He started jogging again, scanning the sky, and ignoring the burning in his muscles.

He was out in the open and he felt vulnerable, but he could also see in all directions in case the demon attacked again. A fast moving shadow caught his eye and his head snapped to look. The shadow sped along the valley floor toward him. The demon had doubled back.

A boulder rose up ahead of him that might give him some cover from the demon's attack. He broke into a sprint again, make sure to track the demon's progress toward him. It seemed to speed up realizing where Malach was heading and its red eyes narrowed on the outside edges almost as if…

It's smiling, Malach realized with a stab of fear. It was playing with him, enjoying the challenge.

Malach reached the boulder and dove into cover, dropping Skie. He hit the ground hard enough to knock the wind out of his lungs, but the demon would have had him had he been any slower. Half of the large rock he had taken cover behind split and fell over, sheared in half by the demon. Malach saw something in the demon's claw as it flew past him and banked right to swing around for another attack. It was a sword.

"These things fight with swords, too?" Malach shouted, even though he was pretty sure no one could hear him. "Come on!"

He hefted Skie back up onto his back and took off for the town again. It wasn't far now, but he wouldn't make it before the demon attacked him again. He would not leave Skie, but he didn't know how he would make it with her on his back. The demon had turned around and was coming back at him with its massive black sword held out to the side in one claw.

Malach ran faster, pushing his legs harder than he thought possible. He would not make it. He pulled up and set Skie on the ground and moved away from her.

What am I thinking?

Everything within Malach screamed for him to run, but that wouldn't do any good. He pulled his knife from its sheath and readied himself for the attack. He didn't think he would be able to do much to the demon, but he would rather go down fighting than running like prey.

As it bore down on him again, he rolled to the side at the last moment and plunged his knife up into the demon's belly. The impact ripped the knife from his hand, sent it flying. It also pulled his shoulder free of its socket with a wet popping noise and his feet free of the earth. He and the demon roared with pain as they both hit the ground.

Good. Malach grinned despite the pain.

This thing could be hurt, and he had hurt it. He rolled over onto his stomach and looked around to find the demon. This time it didn't turn around, but leaped back in the air and headed back down the valley toward Jecrym's farm. He felt a sharp pain in his side, and he looked down. His shirt and skin were separated and, as if the act of looking at it caused his body to realize its existence, blood welled up and poured out. The paint hit him in full force as well, and his body convulsed involuntarily. He hadn't quite made it out of the demon's attack unscathed. It must have got him somehow. His vision started to blur and go dark on the edges. The last thing he heard were shouts coming from

Brightwood. As he fell, he hoped they would get here in time. Then everything went black.

Malach woke with a start and reached for his dagger. It wasn't on his belt. He started to open his eyes and his whole body sent him messages of pain. Three things hurt much more than anything else. His shoulder, his side, and his head.

The memories of the fight came back to him. He took stock of his shoulder and found that it was back in joint, but tightly wrapped with a cloth. His side had been bandaged, and he imagined there would be some stitches under there. He lifted his good arm and felt the back of his head. There were bandages around his head, too. He must have hit his head when he hit the ground. Someone had patched him up.

He glanced around the room and found it very familiar. He was at the Wervine's house in what used to be his old room. Now there was only one bed and Daziar was usually the one who slept in it. Malach couldn't remember how he got here, but he was safe. He started to lie back down and then remembered he had left Skie in the field and bolted back upright, causing new waves of pain to erupt. The room swam, but he fought through it and turned his head to the side. Skie was laying there with bandages of her own, sleeping in the room's corner. He laid gingerly back down, a groan escaping as he did so.

Jennari rushed in and, thinking he was trying to get up, she protested. "Don't try to move. You've been beaten up pretty badly." She helped him lie back down.

"I was actually trying to lie back down. I had to make sure Skie was alright. She let you bandage her up?" Malach asked.

"No," Jennari said, frustrated. "She wouldn't let me touch her for even a second. She just about bit off my hand."

Jennari saw the confused look on Malach's face and continued explaining.

"I had Daziar try, and she just about killed him, too. I finally had Daziar run out to the Reybella's farm and get Honora. She's the only person that wolf would let touch her and not get killed for it."

Malach smiled and laid his head back.

Jennari was right. Malach had never seen Skie warm up to anyone as much as Honora, barring himself, that was. Skie would let him do just about anything to her and not complain. He was glad Honora had come last night to help. If she hadn't, Skie would still be in rough shape, and he would have had to get out of bed for it. His body ached too much to do that.

"You need to rest," Jennari said. "You took some bad hits from those bandits."

"It wasn't the bandits that did this," Malach said, suddenly realizing no one was safe with a demon on the loose. "There was a demon at my house last night. It killed the bandits and then came after me. I injured it and it flew off. Didn't you see it?"

"Malach, the only person who saw anything was the town drunk, and you had a head injury. I don't think you saw what you think you saw," Jennari replied, touching his arm comfortingly.

"I saw it," Malach insisted, not believing what he was hearing. "Jennari, I watched that monster kill two bandits and chase me through the woods long before I hit my head. It chased us into the valley and tried to kill me."

"No more talk," Jennari said, with a dismissing wave of her hand. "You need to rest. The Elders will want to talk to you soon and you need to be clearheaded when you do."

"But-"

"But nothing, young man," Jennari cut him off. "Rest, and you can tell me all about it after you have talked to the elders. Despite the talk of demons, there is no evidence of any around now."

Malach laid back down and realized he was extremely tired.

Jennari wouldn't listen to him, and obviously the town hadn't been attacked last night. He probably had some time to sleep before people would be in danger again. As soon as his head touched the pillow, he fell asleep.

When Malach woke again, it was just getting dark out. He must have slept through the whole day. His side still burned, and his shoulder throbbed, but his head was starting to feel better. He didn't have as bad of a headache as before. He slowly sat up and propped himself upright with his back to the wall. Skie was lying on his lower half and let out a slow huff as his movement disturbed her.

"Oh, calm down. I need to sit up," he huffed back at her.

"You're up," a voice said, and he nearly jumped out of the bed.

All his muscles tensed, and he reached under his pillow for his knife, which wasn't there. He just about lost consciousness as all of his members screamed in pain at the sudden movement. His vision went dark at the edges, and he had to fight back an urge to vomit.

When his vision cleared, he saw Honora sitting in front of him, concern painted on her face. "Sorry, I didn't mean to startle you. Are you alright?"

"Fine," Malach croaked, his throat was dry and raw. "Water?"

Honora grabbed a pitcher next to the bed and poured water into the cup that was sitting next to it. She handed it to Malach. He gulped it down.

"Slow down, there's plenty more," Honora told him, smiling. "Skie woke up a little while before you and wouldn't leave your side. I had to change her bandages as she laid on top of you. She's a loyal friend."

"How long have I been asleep?" he asked, sipping the next cup of water she handed him.

"Just under two days," she said, and he just about choked on his water. "Careful."

"Then I missed seeing Daz off?" Malach asked, alarmed.

"No, Jennari wouldn't allow Daziar to leave yet and got permission from the Elders to postpone his journey. There is talk of demons," Honora explained. "Do you know anything?"

So Jennari had listened to him after all. She might have dismissed his concern to his face, but she had kept Daziar from leaving.

Malach studied Honora. Worry knitted her brow and fear shone in her eyes. He didn't know whether to comfort her or tell her the truth. "I'll explain once I've talked to the Elders about what I saw."

She silently accepted that answer and helped him out of bed. She helped him down the hall and sat him at the dining table. He was out of breath when he arrived. Daziar and his sisters were already waiting for him. They had a myriad of questions and bombarded him with them all at once.

"Quiet!" Honora shouted over the others, then softer, "Can't you see he has just woken up and doesn't have the energy for your questions? Once he has eaten, then you can question him *if* he is up to it."

Malach gave her a grateful look, and she went to the kitchen.

She returned with some potato and beef soup. He practically inhaled it. It had been over two days since he'd last eaten, and Honora kept his bowl refilled until he had had his fill. When he had finished, he was feeling more like himself.

"I promise I will answer all of your questions when I get back, but right now, I need to talk to the Elders, immediately," He told them. "Daz, can I get you to help me to the Elder's Hall?"

Daziar got up to help Malach. He took him under the arm on his good side and helped him to the door. Honora jumped up and opened the door for the pair and walked out behind them.

"Malach, are you sure you should be moving around?" Honora asked. "Jennari said the stitches could come loose if you moved too much."

"I appreciate your concern, Honora, but this is news that can't wait. It should have been presented to the Elders as soon as I was awake the first time," Malach replied through gritted teeth.

It hurt to move, but he had to push through the pain and get to the elders. They had to know there was a demon in the valley. Malach wondered why it hadn't struck yet. It had to know it had been seen, and it had the power to wipe out the town if it wanted.

There had to be other witnesses. The guards, for one, would have seen it, but there should have been some of the town's people up and about at that hour. There had to be someone else who had reported the demon. With this thought, he almost had Daziar turn him around and take him back. If someone else had seen the demon, the Elders would already know, and his so-called important news would already be common knowledge.

"Honora," Malach turned his head to ask, "You said you have heard people talking about a demon in the valley?"

"Yes," Daziar answered eagerly before Honora could. "Mostly that drunkard, Durvain. He's been going on and on about a demon that tore into you in the field. He says you were running away from it with Skie and then fought it. Although, he was near to passing from wine at the time. No one else claims to have seen anything. We all heard it, though. Nobody wanted to go outside until they heard you yell."

"Fine, then I still need to go to the elders. They need to hear what I've seen," Malach replied and continued moving down the street with Daziar's help.

When they reached the Elder's council building, there was a town guard posted outside the door, and he held up a hand to stop them.

"State your business," he drawled, barely glancing their way.

"We need to see the Elders about the recent attack on Malach's cottage," Honora said, stepping up in front of Daziar and Malach.

"Wait here," the guard grunted and went inside.

"I thought you were against me coming here?" Malach asked Honora after the guard had left.

"I am." she crossed her arms and glared at him. "But I know better than to tell you *not* to do something, so I thought I ought to help instead."

The guard returned and waved them in. They passed through the door and into a hallway that would lead them to the elders. The hall was tall and made of dark wood. Torches set in sconces every few feet lit their way. The hall wasn't very long, and it didn't take them long to pass through. At the end of the hall, a set of doors was slightly ajar. The three could hear hushed voices coming from inside, and they paused before going through, not wanting to interrupt. The

Elders could be a little grumpy, as elders are inclined to be. They weren't there for more than a minute when a voice called out to them clearly.

"Please, children, come in."

They push through the doors, and Honora shut them behind the trio. She then joined them on Malach's other side. He had only been in here one other time, and it had been when his parents died, and they were deciding what to do with him. Jennari and Daniel were with him then, and they had done all the talking. Now he felt a bit out of place, standing in front of the Elders.

He took in the room. It was circular, and there was an elevated platform which wrapped around about half of the room. There were four elders spaced out around the platform, and they were all looking at him. The Elders were the four oldest surviving members of the town and none of them were under six hundred years old. The newest elder, Elder Bartholemu, celebrated his six hundredth birthday six years prior. He took the elder's chair last winter when the oldest elder fell ill and passed. Bartholemu was sitting on Malach's far right. The oldest elder now, Elder Enziarel, was sitting on the far left and looked to like he might be asleep in his chair. Who could blame him, though? He was more than eight hundred years old. Elder Maria sat on the chair in the middle, right next to Bartholemu. She had a reputation of being in the middle of everything that happened in Brightwood, whether she was welcome or not. The second oldest elder, Elder Reymold, sat in the middle on the left. He was the one to speak first.

"Malach, we hear tell of a battle of epic proportions that you fought three nights ago in our very valley," Elder Raymold's tone was patronizing and mocking. "What do you have to say about this? We heard from Durvain you survived a demon attack no one else witnessed."

Malach saw Daziar's fist clench beside him.

"Elder Reymold," Malach started politely, "while it is true, Durvain is not the most reliable witness. He is, this time, telling the truth. The demon-"

The elder directly to the left of Bartholemu, Elder Maria, laughed hotly, cutting Malach short. "You're telling us there is a real demon that attacked you? There hasn't been a demon or angel sighting for more than two thousand years, *and* you would have us believe that it was this deep into Angel Territory? I think not."

"Please, Maria," Bartholemu chided gently, "let the boy finish, and then we can judge his words."

"Fine, but I've already made up my mind on this matter." She crossed her arms and glared at Malach.

"What's got her underwear in a bunch?" Daziar whispered to Malach. Malach ignored him.

"Thank you, Elder Bartholemu." Malach nodded politely toward him. "Let me take you through the events of the day leading up to the attack."

Malach told them how he had saved Jecrym from the highwaymen and how they had waited for him to come home that night. They all agreed Malach had been right to defend himself and Skie against them, but when he got to the part about the demon, the elders' expressions turned from politely interested to skeptical. Most of them tried to hide it, but Elder Maria made no such effort. Elder Enzariel never woke up, although he stirred several times, changing positions in his chair.

When he finished, Elder Reymold spoke, "Malach, you say there were three bandits, and Jecrym's account confirmed that, but when we sent men up there to investigate, they only found two bodies. One in the house, killed as you said, and the other outside in two pieces, cleaved in half as if by a sword. I understand you believe what you are saying to be true, but it wouldn't be the first time a young man has had to kill and his mind was broken by the trauma."

"It's hardly the first time I've had to kill to defend myself," Malach responded.

"And what about the ground shaking roars we heard? What about the guards on watch? They must have seen something," Daziar almost shouted. Malach put a hand on his shoulder to calm him.

"He's right. The guards had to have seen something. What were their accounts?" Malach asked.

"The guards tell that they spotted you stumbling out of the woods already blooded," Maria said with the same tone as before.

"They said you were stumbling badly, and they thought you were drunk at first. When they heard you yelling, they, of course, ran to help. They state they didn't see any demon or battle going on," Elder Reymold explained calmly.

"Then what about the noises?" Malach challenged. "How do you explain that?"

"For all we know, there could have been a storm that night just out of sight of the town. Thunder could explain the sounds we heard," Reymold countered again.

"So, you are calling me a liar?" Malach snapped back.

"No, I'm simply saying your mind broke at the sudden violence. You believe you fought a demon, but in all reality, you killed two bandits in self-defense and were wounded in the process." Reymold folded his arms and studied Malach, watching for his reaction.

Malach couldn't believe what he was hearing. They didn't want to believe him, and they weren't going to do anything about this threat. The demon wasn't just a threat to the town, but to the territory. If one demon could make it this far, there could be demons all across Angel Territory.

"Elders, with all due respect to you and the guards who were on watch, I didn't make this up. My mind didn't snap. I fought a demon. You can't just ignore the facts," Malach pleaded. "No storm could have made the noises you heard last night, and if you try to explain this away, you are fooling yourselves and doing a disservice to this town." Malach thought he might have gone a little too far with his last statement, and he was right.

Elder Maria jumped to her feet and let out an enraged squeak. "How dare you tell us how to do our duty to this town. Most of us have sat on the council for longer than you have been alive, boy. You are simply a spoiled brat, desperate for attention. I, for one, will be glad when you are gone. And if, for some reason, you are right about this demon you dreamt up, I hope it comes back and eats you." With that, she stormed out the back exit behind the platform.

Elder Reymold watched her leave and then turned his attention back to Malach. "Son, you need to leave the running of this town to us." He stood as well. "You and a drunkard are the only people who claim to have seen this so-called demon, and I don't need widespread panic. I have to two people who hadn't been on the bottle or in a stressful situation that testify against your claim. Our ruling is that there is no demon, so you'd better come to terms with yourself about that."

Elder Reymold turned and walked out the same door as Elder Maria. Elder Bartholemu stood and followed him without a word to Malach. The final elder stayed in his spot, but his head was now laying on the table in front of him.

Daziar turned to Malach, a venomous look in his eyes. Malach could practically see the steam rising off of him. "I can't believe they would dismiss this so flippantly. They practically called you a liar to your face. I'm so glad I'm leaving this town of self-righteous bigots who can't see past their own noses!"

"Daziar," Honora soothed, "don't take it so personally. They have it on the word of two guards that there was no demon, and they are right about Malach going through a traumatic experience. It doesn't help that the town drunk is the only one who will corroborate the story."

"Honora." Daziar was shocked. "How could you take their side and not Malach's? You know as well as I do he didn't make the whole thing up."

"I'm not taking their side," she argued. "I'm simply saying the evidence they have is against Malach and they have to follow the evidence. I don't think he made it up either, but why would the guards lie?"

"Because they were asleep at their post," a voice boomed and all three jumped.

The three whirled toward the platform to see the fourth elder standing there. Elder Enziarel hadn't said a word since the three entered the council room. However, now he was on his feet, peering down at them with a hard look in his eyes.

"I thought he was asleep," Daziar whispered out of the side of his mouth.

"Not asleep, Daziar, just listening and thinking." Elder Enziarel turned to Malach. "The guards lied because they were asleep. The easiest way to get out of trouble is to say what they think we want to hear. With only you and the drunkard contradicting them, they were safe to bear false witness against you."

"But how could they do that? They're putting this town at risk." Malach was dumbfounded that they could lie about such an important thing. They needed to warn everyone. People in the area, other towns, even the angels if they could get a message to them.

"Correct, but perhaps they truly believe that there was no demon," Elder Enziarel mused. "Perhaps they are simply scared, much like the Council."

"You mean the Council is scared? That's why they won't believe Malach?" Honora asked.

"Correct again. I think what you said is true, and there is a demon on the loose in Angel Territory. I can't say anything when there is a three to one vote, however. They came into this hall knowing what they would vote before they even heard the first words out of your mouth. Maria was the only one who didn't hide that fact. They all know there is a demon out there, but they refuse to believe it because it would mean war is on the horizon. It would mean the time of peace is coming to a close."

Malach, Daziar, and Honora stood there in silence, each of them thinking about the implications of those statements.

"Malach Tresch." Malach's gaze snapped back up to Elder Enziarel. "You are the one that can decide the fate of the war. You have seen it coming and you will play a key part in this. The friends and enemies you make will influence you, and the coming war, more than you think. You will be the tipping point, and whichever way you tip is up to you. Make sure you make good choices in Newaught. Some will lead you to destruction, others will lift you to glory." Elder Enziarel turned to leave but turned around again. "Oh, and Malach, I think your parents would be proud." He walked out of the room through the back entrance, leaving the three stunned young people standing there gaping.

"That wasn't odd at all." Daziar broke the silence first. "Did that mean anything to you, Mal?"

"I think so," Malach said slowly. "At least some of it, but it didn't make anything any clearer."

"Well, alright then," Honora clapped her hands. "Let's head back to the Wervine's house and get you back in bed."

"No," Malach replied. "I think I need to head out of town and check on my cottage. Start cleaning up and repairing things."

The three turned to walk out, but Honora wasn't having any of his plans. "No, Malach, you need to get back in bed and heal. If you keep moving around and doing all this work, the stitches *will* pull out, and it will take longer for you to heal. You still have to escort me to Newaught, remember?"

"Yes, yes, I remember," Malach replied. "But I also can't leave my parents' cottage in shambles, with no door for any animal to walk in and make it their home."

"One more night and then you can go up there and start cleaning, but give your side one more night to heal," Honora compromised.

"Fine," Malach reluctantly agreed. "But first thing tomorrow morning, I'm hiking up there."

"Alright, I will have Johm head up there with you to help with the cleanup."

"And I'll go too." Daziar said. "I'm going to try to get the elders to let me wait to leave for Newaught until we can all go together. That would give me time to help you with the cottage and then get ready to go."

"Well, let's get back to the house," Honora said as they stepped through the door onto the street. Jecrym was standing there, waiting for them.

"Malach, my friend!" Jecrym greeted him warmly, and Malach groaned internally. "Is it true that the bandits attacked you again?"

"Yes, it is," Malach replied. "All three of them are dead now, so you won't have to worry about them again."

"That's wonderful!" Jecrym exclaimed and then quickly added. "That we won't have to deal with them again, not that they attacked you. That was a terrible business. Anyway, I feel like I still owe you since you never would have had this issue if you hadn't saved me in the first place. Can I do anything to help you with the cleanup?"

"No-"

"Yes!" Honora pushed in front of him, cutting him off. "Yes, Uncle, you can help. If you could send some men up to Malach's cottage and help clean up tomorrow, that would be wonderful!"

Jecrym thought for a second and then said, "I think I can spare someone tomorrow. They will meet you up there two hours after dawn if that's alright."

"That would be great! Thank you, Uncle!" Honora hugged him.

"I could never say no to my favorite niece," Jecrym chuckled.

"I'm your only niece, Uncle," Honora reminded him fondly, and with that, the three walked back toward the Wervine's house.

When the three arrived at the Wervine's house, Daziar helped Malach to his bed. They talked for a bit about what the elders had said, but couldn't come up with a way to change their minds. They decided it would be best to keep their thoughts to themselves for now. The elders would just tell the town people Malach had been hysterical and he would only confirm that if he went around shouting about a demon. When they left Malach, he had decided he would wait for a bit and sneak out to look for evidence of the demon before it got dark, but he quickly slipped off to sleep before he could act on his plans.

Malach woke with a start for the fourth time that night. He couldn't sleep. Every time he closed his eyes, he saw the demon bearing down on him with the black sword, a wicked smile on its face as it came in for the kill.

He imaged what the look on its face had been when he had plunged the knife up and into the creature's chest. That made him smile. He had lost the knife, but he didn't mind the loss, knowing he had done some damage to the creature. He would have done it again and again to save himself and Skie. It would have to be replaced, however. Maybe Togan would have a suitable replacement he could buy until he got to Newaught. He would have to sell most of his meat for it, but he wouldn't need much to get him through the next few days until he left. Then he still had the job to do for Jecrym. That hopefully would pay his way to Newaught.

Malach sat up in bed and glanced over at the sheath of his knife. It was still attached to his belt when they found him. He caught Skie studying him through the darkness of the room. The moon outside was bright enough to illuminate her and set her eyes to glowing. He swung his legs off the bed and stood up. She stood too.

"Not this time, girl. You won't be able to make it over the wall." Malach whispered.

Skie emitted a low growl but laid back down, anyway.

As he stood, there was a small twinge of pain in his side, but it wasn't nearly as bad as the day before. He had always healed quickly. His father had told him to keep that hidden, but he didn't know why at the time. The need for the stitches would be gone in another day, and the scab, gone a day after that. He put his shirt and pants on and fastened his belt. The knife's sheath hung lightly on his belt. He would leave it there until he could get a replacement as a reminder of the danger that was out there.

He didn't want to wake anyone, so he went out the window. The stairs that led to the top of the wall creaked loud enough in the silent night to wake the dead. He hoped no one heard them as he took them three at a time. However, the guards would either be asleep or at the front gate, so he wasn't too concerned about being caught. Besides, even if the guards were awake, they were watching for people coming in, not going out. He descended the wall easily enough, although it hurt his side a little. He pulled up his shirt and he could see a small amount of blood soaking through the bandage, but it didn't seem to be growing, so he moved on.

He moved away from the town and then circled around. Luckily, there was some cloud cover, which hid the moon and shrouded him in shadows so he could move without being seen from the front gate. When he got to the rock shorn in half by the demon's sword, he traced his steps back to the spot where he had fought it and searched the area. He immediately spotted a set of grooves in the ground near where he would have fallen. Maybe the demon's claws had made these? There was another set about ten feet past it and a little to the right. He noticed the silhouette of something sticking up out of the ground. It was almost as tall as he was and very slender. It seemed to have a cross at the top of it. Malach crept forward to get a better look.

It was the demon's black sword. He moved to it and carefully touched the hilt. Nothing happened. He wrapped his hand around it and pulled it from the ground. It was so large and heavy he almost couldn't lift it. All of a sudden, he had a stabbing pain in his head, as if someone was driving a spike into it. At the same time, to his shock and horror, the sword started to shrink in front of his eyes. He tried to let go, to throw the writhing sword away, to even move a finger, but he couldn't. It was as if his hand wasn't his and he had no control over it: it had gone completely numb. It shrunk down to the size of a hand and a half sword before it stopped. Suddenly, he had a feeling in his hand again. He dropped the sword to the ground and jumped back from it, staring at it, baffled. There was no way he just saw what he thought he just saw, no way had his hand had gone numb. It was just not possible. He stared at the sword for a solid minute, watching for it to do something else. Attack him, go back to the size it was, jump up and sprout legs. At this point, he wouldn't put anything past it. If it could change size, what else could it do? Did it have to stay a sword, or could it become anything?

Gathering his courage, Malach slowly moved forward and picked up the sword, ready to pry it out of his numb hand at the first sign of movement. It didn't do anything, however. Maybe he really did have a head injury affecting what he saw. But no, he could feel a slight vibration in his hands. A sort of humming that was emanating from the sword. He decided he would keep it for now, but he knew that it would be too conspicuous if he went back to town with a sword he didn't have when he left. He couldn't hide it at his house either, with the crew of people coming to help clean up.

He hiked up the hill a little way and found a small ditch where the water had eroded the earth. He cut a few small shrubs with the sword to cover it and hide it from anyone passing by. It felt good to swing the sword. He almost couldn't feel his injured shoulder anymore and the few swings stretched his muscles, leaving him feeling a little more refreshed. He reluctantly put the sword in the ditch and covered it with the brush. Tomorrow, he would retrieve it after everyone had left his cottage.

He left it and headed up the road toward his house. When he got there, the cart was right where he had left it, although his bag of produce had been ripped open and the contents picked clean. The honey was still there in its jars and the flour was mostly unpillaged. He pulled the cart up to the front door. He checked his bow, still on the cart. It had been strung the whole time, which wasn't the best for it, but it seemed fine. He unstrung it and turned to go inside.

The door had been ripped off its hinges when the demon attacked, and someone had propped it up against the frame, mostly closing off the house to the wild. He was grateful for whoever had done that. Moving the door to the side, he went in. The kitchen was still a wreck where the bandits had sacked it, and now some detritus littered the floor from outside. He picked up the items that weren't broken and found his broom. Once he was done sweeping the bits of broken things and dirt out the door, he moved to the living room. He could tell where the bandit's bodies had been dragged out of the house. There were still pools and trails of dried blood marring the wood floor. He passed over those. He would have to get some water from the stream and clean that up later, although the stains would never come out. Moving into his room, he hung his bow on its pegs and set his quiver in its corner. Not much had been disturbed here, although some of his clothes were lying around the floor. He moved into each room and put it back together.

By the time he was done, he had an idea of all the materials he would need to fix the things that were broken. He felt better having seen everything and cleaned up a little. He moved the remaining items on the cart into the house and put them away.

He propped the door back up against its frame and headed back toward town with the cart in tow. By the time he arrived, the sun's first light out was just becoming visible over the mountains. He left the cart outside the wall between two outcroppings of rock, where it could be retrieved in the morning. Climbing back over the wall was most of a challenge than climbing down, but he managed. He crept through town, although if anyone was awake they hadn't left their house, and snuck back in the window at the Wervine's house. He closed it, holding the latch so only a whisper of the shutter against the frame was heard.

"Where have you been all night, mister?" Honora might as well have shouted in the quiet morning.

"Holy Angel's wings, Honora, you scared me half to death," Malach said, holding his chest.

"Well, I might beat you the other half of the way and call it a day," Honora said, staring daggers at him. "Malach Tresch, why in the world did you leave the house last night?"

"Well…"

"Well, nothing. I can't believe you. Let me see your side. I need to make sure you didn't pull any stitches out." Honora reached for Malach's side.

"I didn't do anything strenuous. There is no need for that." Malach pulled away from her.

"Malach, I'm going to look at that, and you are going to stand there and let me." She said it with such finality Malach knew he didn't have a choice.

"Fine," Malach said, worried the commotion of putting up a fight would bring more people in and then he would have to tell his secret to everyone. Malach pulled up his shirt and started unwrapping the bandage. When he was done, he looked up to see.

Honora gawking at him, slack-jawed.

"That can't be right," she said slowly. "How…" Her voice trailed off.

"I don't know. It's been like this all my life," Malach explained, and in a way, it felt good to tell someone. "I heal at an alarming rate. Scrapes and bruises are gone in a day or less, and wounds that should take weeks are healed in just a few days. My father was the same way, faster even."

"But how?" Honora asked again.

"I don't know. I asked my mom about it once, and she told me she would explain when I was older. But before they could…well, you know."

"I need to tell Jennari," she said, heading for the door.

"No," Malach said quickly. "You can't tell anyone."

"Why not?" Honora asked.

"I'm afraid she will want to tell the Elders, and I don't know what they'll do. You know as well as I do that only angels and demons have the powers to heal. Angels don't consort with humans. It's against their code."

Honora let out a small gasp, "Malach, are you saying…" Her voice trailed off again.

"Somewhere in my family line, I have demon blood. I don't know how or who, but that's the only thing that makes sense." Malach stared at the floor, ashamed. "I would assume it was on my father's side of the family."

Honora sat hard on the bed.

"I'm still the same person, Honora. I'm still Malach." He tried to look her in the eyes to show his sincerity, but she averted her gaze quickly.

"I… I don't…" she stammered. "I have to go." She stood and fled the room.

"Honora, wait," Malach called, but she was already out the door. He moved to the door and was met by Daziar. "What did you do to her?" he asked, a hard look in his eyes.

Daziar already knew his secret, and Malach pulled him into the room and shut the door to explain. Once he had, Daziar calmed down.

"Well, we knew you were going to have to tell her eventually. If you remember, I advised you to tell her sooner. You remember, several *years* ago?"

"I know, I just wasn't ready for anyone else to know." Malach studied his feet.

"Well, now she knows, and it's not just the shock that has upset her, but the secret you have been hiding from her." Daziar sat on the bed next to Malach.

"You think she will tell anyone?" he asked, looking at Daziar.

"I don't know, but I would bet not," he replied. "Regardless, you need to apologize to her when you get the chance."

"Yeah," Malach said glumly. "I will, but now she will be mad at me for the whole trip to Newaught."

"Well, that's what you get for keeping secrets from your friends." Daziar walked out of the room. "You ought to learn from this. True friends will accept you for who you are, not who you descended from."

Malach put the bandage back on, pulled on his shirt, and gathered the rest of his belongings. He joined the Wervines for breakfast and announced he was heading back up to his cottage to start the cleanup process. Jennari didn't like it, but she gave her blessing reluctantly.

He said his goodbyes and walked out of the city not long after. The cart was just where he left is and he pulled it up to the general store. After promising a few pounds of dried meat for the items he needed, he met with Daziar and they headed up the hill. When he got to the cottage, Johm was waiting for him, and to his surprise, so was Jecrym.

Malach greeted them and then said to Jecrym, "I expected a couple of your men, not you personally." And then added quickly, "Not that I'm ungrateful for your help. I'm just curious why."

"No, that's alright. I've had to swallow a lot of pride in the past few days." Jecrym deflated visibly. "It turns out people don't take too kindly to being promised pay in the future for work they have done today. I can't find anyone who will work for me until I get some coin. I can't get some coin until I take my stock to market, and I can't take my stock to market until I kill whatever is taking my livestock. I can't pay you, but I would be in your debt if you would find and kill that thing before you leave."

"I think we can work something out. Let's get this done, and I will call it payment for the hunt," Malach said, clapping Jecrym on the shoulder. The man seemed to cheer up a bit.

"Thank you, Malach. I really appreciate that."

Malach put them to work. Now that it was light out, he could see the roof was damaged. He sent Jecrym to get the door back on its hinges. Daziar went to fetch water from the stream nearby, and he and Johm headed for the roof. There were four large claw marks that had scraped off the pitch sealing the roof. The middle claw mark went all the way through to the inside of the house. They got the pitch out and repaired the hole. When they finished, they found Jecrym had hung the door and was almost finished with two of the shutters which had been broken off. There was a third shutter in splinters which would need to be rebuilt. That would have to wait until he could get some wood from the carpenter.

When they were finished with the outside damage, they moved inside. Several of the shelf supports were broken, as well as one of the table's legs from where Skie and the bandit fought. Johm set to work on the shelves with a few boards, and Malach picked up the pieces of the broken table leg. It would have to be remade by the carpenter as well. Until then, he measured the length of the leg and cut a board roughly the same length, putting a nail in to hold it for now. It was a little wobbly, but it would do. While he and Johm were working on the wood repairs, Jecrym and Daziar scrubbed the floor as clean as they could get it.

I can't believe how much Jecrym has changed in just a few days, Malach thought as he watched the man work.

Through the whole thing, Johm didn't say a word, although Jecrym made up for Johm's silence with a steady stream of chatter. Two very different men, but Malach would count both as a friend from here out. Even though Johm was ordered to come up here, Malach suspected the man volunteered. They broke for lunch, having repaired and cleaned everything they could. Johm, Daziar, and Jecrym went their own ways.

Malach hiked down to where he had hidden the demon's sword and pulled the brush off the ditch. It was still there, to his relief. Only then did he realize he had been worried about someone else finding the sword before he could get back to it. Not because it might be dangerous, because he was curious. He picked it up and started the climb up to the cottage.

As he walked, he thought about his knife he had lost and how he would have to pay for another. Togan would believe him about the demon and would offer to give him a new knife for free, but he didn't like doing that. He felt dishonest taking the man's hard work without paying for it. He realized he could hardly feel the weight of the sword anymore. His eye snapped to the sword in his hand. Only there was not a sword anymore. There, in his hand, was a knife the same black color as the sword and with the same hilt, although much smaller and without the cross guard. In fact, the knife looked to be the same size and shape as his old one. He slipped it into the sheath and it fit snuggly, as if the leather was molded around this knife, not the one he previously owned. He couldn't believe it. The sword seemed to change to the size and shape of the knife he was thinking about. He needed to talk with Togan about it. He might know more about this mysterious blade.

On a whim, Malach whipped the knife out and flung it at the nearest tree. He realized too late; he had thrown it from the wrong side for it to hit point-first into the tree. The knife should have bounced off on the hilt. Instead, it landed point in and sunk into the trunk up to the hilt. Malach again stood there staring, amazed at the blade's ability. He walked up to the tree and pulled the blade free almost effortlessly. He tucked the knife into its sheath and examined the tree. Where the blade had gone in, there were small scorch marks, and the inside of the hole it had made was burned black. The blade hadn't just cut the tree; it had burned it. He pulled the knife out of its sheath again and carefully touched the blade in case it was still hot, but it was quite cool. There was no evidence of the heat that, just a couple minutes ago, had scorched a hole in the tree.

He put it back into its sheath and continued down the path. He wondered about the blade and all it could do. However, he had things to do more pressing things to deal with. Namely, Jecrym's farm. He arrived at the cottage and went inside. He picked up his bow and had a thought. What if the demon's "sword" could turn into any weapon? He excitedly pulled it from its sheath and thought hard about his bow.

Nothing.

It didn't even shudder. Maybe he was doing something wrong. He thought about the hand and a half sword it had turned into and it started to grow almost instantly until it resembled the image he had in his head. He imagined the knife again and watched it shrink back down.

So, it can't turn into any weapon, only sword-like weapons, maybe anything with a blade, he mused.

He tried a few more abstract blade weapons. Any type of knife or throwing blade worked, but it would not turn into an arrow or a bo staff. He thought of his old knife, and when the weapon shrunk down to the correct size, he put it away. He would have to continue to test different weapons later. Right now, he needed to get to Jecrym's farm.

He picked up his bow again and put his last two arrows in his quiver. He really needed to make some more arrows. These definitely weren't his best. He started to head out, but noticed Skie had followed him inside the house. She was curled in the corner of his room, sleeping. She had been sleeping in the corner of his room for the last few nights, which he thought was odd.

She never goes inside a house unless there's something wrong, he thought, looking at her sleeping form.

He figured her wounds didn't heal as fast as his, and she probably just needed sleep. Knowing the house was a relatively safe place, she opted to sleep there. He walked outside and grabbed the cart, in case he got whatever it was taking the cows.

He started walking to Jecrym's farm but almost missed the path branching off since it hadn't been beaten down enough yet to call it a road. The path was rough and not well-maintained. The cart's wheels got stuck a few times, and he had to work to get it out.

"Next time, I'll take the long way around," he grumbled to himself when his wheel got stuck in a hole for the third time.

He came around a bend in the path and beheld the "new" farm. It was a wreck. The roof was sagging in several places, a lot of the fences were missing rungs, and most of the animals were looking a little thin. There was a middle-aged woman sitting on the porch. She was looking a little gaunt herself. Malach walked up to the porch, but the lady seemed to be asleep.

"Ma'am?" Malach said gently, to not startle her.

"Are you looking for my lazy, no good, deadbeat husband?" she asked without opening her eyes or lifting her head.

"Umm, yes?" Malach said warily.

"He's on the roof, *trying* to fix it," she said shortly.

Malach decided it was best if he just walked away. He didn't want to get in the middle of an argument. He walked around the house to the back and found Jecrym just where she said he would be.

"Ho, Jecrym!" Malach hailed him.

"Malach, my friend, one moment and I'll be down there," Jecrym climbed down from the roof and clasped hands with Malach. "How did lunch treat you?"

"Good! Not to be rude, but how are you holding up here? Things look a little wrecked." Malach raised a brow, motioning around them as he did.

"Yes, well, when we bought the property, we knew there was a building here but never inquired as to the state of it." Jecrym shrugged with a sheepish grin. "I've been having to do most of the work myself, and I'm just not as handy as I always thought myself to be."

"Uh-huh," Malach grunted. "Was that your wife on the porch?"

"I see you've met Kath!" Jecrym said enthusiastically.

"I'm not sure 'met' is the best word, but yes, I spoke with her," Malach replied.

"Ah, well, she's not been in the best of moods lately. I think she's mostly upset because I didn't talk to her about our financial situation until it was too late. We bought this pretty quickly as a last-ditch effort, and I'm afraid if this fails, so will our marriage," Through his explanation, Jecrym began to look more and more defeated, and Malach couldn't help but want to aid the man.

"Cheer up! I'm sure you can get things ship-shape around here soon and you both can be happy again." Malach wished he could stay around to help, but he only had a few days and plenty to occupy his time.

Jecrym brightened a bit, and they went to look at where the latest attack had happened. Malach could tell almost immediately that this was a bear attack, and after examining the tracks, he knew for sure it was one of the large grizzlies that frequented the area. By the size of the tracks, he could tell this one was massive. He was going to have to be extremely careful with this one or he would end up as the next meal. It didn't help the bear had been eating meat, which made it more aggressive. It was most likely fattening itself up for the coming winter.

Malach let out a low whistle. "Well, Jecrym, I'd say you have encroached on a grizzly bear's hunting grounds. The good news is their territory is very large, so you may be less likely to see it often, the bad news is since it's been coming back regularly, it might have decided to stay for a bit since food is easy to find."

"Great," Jecrym said, lack luster. "So, what can we do?"

"Kill it, but I'll need a different weapon."

Chapter 5

Malach walked through the front gates of Brightwood and started in the direction of Togan's forge. As he walked down the street, a few guards were sitting around playing cards. One guard noticed him walking by and nudged his buddy.

He sneered at Malach, "See any demons today, Malach?"

Malach ignored him and kept moving. He was going to get a lot of those comments until he left. As he walked, he thought about the problem at hand. He didn't know if he could get a bear spear in time for this hunt before he had to leave. He may have to hand this over to one of the other hunters. Unfortunately, there was only a handful that stood a chance of coming out alive. He was the best one for the job, but if Togan didn't have a spear in stock, then he would have to make one, and that would take too long.

Well, there is nothing I can do but ask, Malach thought to himself. *I'll have to cross that bridge when I get to it.*

Malach had fought bears before, and no mistaking it for a hunt. It was a fight. However, all the bears he had fought in the past were of the smaller, black bear variety. This bear was at least twice the size of those, judging by the tracks, and most likely, it was a grizzly. He tried to stay out of their way, as they were much more aggressive than black bears. Now he was about to face off with one, and he needed the reach of a spear and the power of its thrust to get to the heart. This bear would take a lot of skill and force to kill. This was going to be very dangerous, and he was now doing it without pay. At least he would be able to pay for the spear with the meat.

He walked into Togan's shop front, and the big man was sitting behind the counter. Malach walked up to the counter and waited for him to finish with the little animal he was carving from wood.

"Malach!" Togan greeted him when he was at a stopping point. "Did you need a new knife? I notice you didn't have yours when they brought you in. You left it in that demon so he could remember you, didn't ya?"

"Ha! Something like that, Togan, but no, I need a bear spear. Do you have one in stock?"

"No, not much need for it. I can have one made for you in a week, but that won't help you much when you're leavin' in two days."

"Alright, well, thanks anyway. I may still have you make one if I can get another hunter to take the job. I'll talk to them and let you know." Malach turned to go.

"Malach," Togan reached out and grasped his shoulder. "Where'd you get that knife?"

"What do you mean?" Malach stalled, trying the think of a good lie. "I found it when I went out to the field after I healed. It must have fallen out of the demon after I let go."

"That is my sheath, but that ain't my knife," Togan said, warning in his tone.

Malach considered lying again. He wasn't sure he wanted to have this conversation now, but there was no point. Togan knew each of his creations intimately, and there was no fooling him. He told Togan about the demon sword and about his realization that it could change to any blade. Togan remained silent through the recounting, but his face became still and his mood dark. When Malach finished, Togan still didn't say anything, but just stared at Malach, brow furrowed with a frown on his face.

"What?" Malach said after a long, uncomfortable pause.

"You picked up the demon's blade?" Togan roared so suddenly, Malach jumped back.

"Why boy? You know those monsters have killed countless millions!"

"Yes," Malach said, defiance creeping into his voice. "But haven't the angels killed just as many?"

"Yeah, but they only kill when it is necessary. I've heard of more than one givin' his life for a human. You won't find demons doin' that." Togan took a deep breath and lowered his voice back to his normal volume. "But that's not really the point. The point is, you have no idea what that blade will do to you. It's evil, Malach, just like the bearer you stole it from."

"Togan, it's a tool, just like any other weapon. It doesn't have the ability to do anything you don't want it to," Malach reasoned.

"Then let me ask you this; how do you control how to change the size and shape?"

"I just think about it and..." Malach trailed off, realizing the point Togan was making.

"That means, at a minimum, that it can see what you're thinkin'. You don't know that it can't affect you in other ways, do ya?" Togan stared Malach down again, daring him to refute the evidence he had just given.

"Fine, however, right now I'm not going to give it up. I see your point though, and I will keep it in mind," Malach said.

"Fine, boy, but I think you're makin' a big mistake. Mark my words, you're goin' to regret it," the big man warned.

Malach turned and started to walk out, but whipped around at the door. His demeanor had changed to all business. "I will let you know if another hunter needs to have you make the bear spear."

"Malach..." but Togan's voice trailed off.

"Have a good day, Togan," Malach turned again and walked out.

Malach didn't know why Togan had to be so narrow-minded. Togan wouldn't say anything about the blade to anyone else, but he hated being at odds with the big blacksmith. Maybe he should give up the blade and work with regular weapons as Togan wanted. Maybe he was right, and the blade was evil.

He pushed the thoughts aside. How could a tool be evil? It didn't have a mind of its own. It was just like anything else, just like a regular sword. The deeds it did were dependent on the bearer.

In the midst of his thoughts about the demon blade, his mind turned to the spear. The head was a blade. Maybe the demon blade could morph into that. He ducked into an alley to get out of sight of anyone on the street. Pulling the blade from its sheath, he closed his eyes and held the image of the spear in his head. He felt the blade handle get heavier. To his surprise, the blade hadn't just changed into the head, but the whole spear, just as he had thought of it. It was all metal and black. It had a long pole, and the head was about ten inches in length. The sides curved out from the point making the blade, and at its broadest point, it was about four inches wide. There was a cross guard at the bottom that was about an inch wider on both sides to hold the bear off of the wielder if needed.

The blade must be able to turn into anything that is fully metal. It couldn't change into the bow because it is wood and string, Malach thought, astonished.

He quickly thought of the knife again, and it returned to its former shape. He sheathed it and walked out of the alley, back toward the main gates. The guards once again peppered him with insults, which he ignored. He had a quarter of his day left to get back to the farm and track the bear. If he didn't find it today, he would only have one more day or he would have to give it up to another hunter.

When Malach was a few hundred yards away from Jecrym's farm, he changed the knife into the bear spear. He still had his bow and arrows, but he didn't think they would be of much use. Kath was still napping on the porch.

How could someone be so tired? Malach thought. *She seems to have slept most of the day.*

He passed her without a word and move to the back of the house. Jecrym was on the roof again and Malach hailed him.

"Malach!" Jecrym called down. "I see you got what you needed."

"I did. Time to start this hunt." Malach said, his adrenaline starting to pulse.

After a pause, Jecrym asked nervously, "Did you want me to go with you?"

Malach laughed, "No, Jecrym. No offense, but I don't want to worry about you *and* the bear."

Jecrym sighed with relief. "Alright, well, let me know if I can help in any way."

"If I don't come back by nightfall, look for my body in the morning," Malach said seriously.

Jecrym laughed nervously but stopped halfway through. "You're serious?"

Malach nodded. "A regular black bear is dangerous, but this one will be much worse."

"Do you think you can best him?"

"If I didn't think I could, I wouldn't be going out there," Malach reassured him and then explained. "I should be back before nightfall, with or without our bear. If I don't get him tonight, I'll go back out tomorrow. After that, I will have to hand this hunt to another hunter. You will, most likely, have to pay them. I doubt they will honor our agreement."

"I understand," Jecrym said. "Good luck, my friend."

Malach turned and headed to the field where the last attack occurred.

The bear's trail was almost as large as the trail that led to the farm, though much more traversed. From the farm, there had been a small, winding game trail, but Malach came across the bear's main path about a half mile from the farm. That meant this bear had been here for a while. He didn't want to stumble across it without warning, so he stayed about ten feet off the path and followed it north. Up here, it seemed a lot of animals made their dens and beds north of their hunting grounds. Possibly because of direction of the prevailing winds. He would follow the path until he found the bear's den or the end of the trail. Although, sometimes these trails made a large circle. In that case, he would find the den no matter which way he went.

He followed the trail for another half mile, seeing the bear's marks on the trees, but they were all old marks. Nothing new. He turned a corner on the trail and spotted a meadow coming up. There was something brown moving in the meadow, but he couldn't tell what.

Creeping forward, he found it was only a few deer. There was a good size doe with her broadside toward him and he couldn't resist. He notched an arrow. With practiced ease, he brought it up to his check and let the arrow loose. It hit the deer and knocked her over. The deer tried to rise but fell again. He ran up and slide the spearhead into the animal's side to end her suffering. He left the deer in the clearing, just out of the way. It would be there when the hunt was over.

He followed the path until the sun was almost behind the mountains. He decided he'd better turn back while he could make it out before dark. It could be dangerous, tracking a predator after dark or to even be in a bear's territory, for that matter. He made it back to the cabin with the deer across his shoulders just after darkness had fully fallen. The deer carcass thumped on the porch as he relieved himself of its weight. To be polite, he knocked on the door, although they probably heard the noise. He heard some shuffling, and Jecrym jerked the door open.

"Malach! I was starting to get worried. Glad you made it back in one piece," Jecrym greeted him. "Please come in."

Jecrym stepped back out of the doorway and let Malach in.

"Any sign of the bear?" he asked, motioning Malach to a chair in the common room.

Malach propped the spear, bow, and quiver in the corner and gratefully took the seat.

Jecrym sat in a chair which looked as if it wouldn't hold the weight of a child, much less a full grown man. However, through some miracle, it held.

"Not hide, nor hair," Malach frowned. "Do you have any water?"

Jecrym jumped up. "Oh, of course. I should have thought of that." He grabbed a pitcher of water and poured Malach a cup.

Malach took it and gulped it down before holding it out for a second. Jecrym obliged, and Malach drank the second much slower. He had run out of water in his water skin about halfway back.

"I could have simply walked the wrong way on the trail. I'll try again tomorrow and walk the other way. Though I suspect it goes in a big circle," Malach explained. "How often have the attacks been happening?"

"About every three days," Jecrym informed him. "The last attack was three nights ago. We are due for one anytime now."

Malach grunted in response. "I need to get back to my cottage for the night." He started to get up, but Jecrym held up his hands to stop him.

"Please stay for dinner. It's the least I can do for all the work you have done and plan to do tomorrow."

"I guess I could stay through dinner," Malach said. He really didn't want to, but he couldn't find a reason to refuse at this point.

Just a few minutes later, Malach was sitting at the table with Jecrym and Kath. An awkward silence hung over the table like a fog. The food was good, though. It was pork in some kind of sauce.

Malach broke the silence first. "This is excellent pork, Mrs. Reybella."

"Jecrym prepared it," Kath replied shortly.

"Thank you, Malach. I appreciate the kind words." Jecrym shot a warning look at Kath.

Malach pretended not to notice and tried again. "Well, you are wearing a very pretty dress. I'm sure something like that could only have been bought in the city. Is that correct?"

Kath perked up a moment, but then gave Malach a look of suspicion. "What would a peasant know about dresses?" Kath's voice had turned haughty, looking down her nose at him as if he were in a lower class.

Maybe she is used to being a higher class, Malach thought, and he checked his temper before he said anything.

"Kath!" Jecrym exclaimed. "Don't take that tone with a guest."

Kath opened her mouth to protest but Malach cut off the would-be argument, "No, that's alright." He turned toward Kath, making sure his tone was polite and calm. "Mrs. Reybella, I'm sure you are used to more sophisticated company, but the fact is, you're correct."

That surprised her, and she sat back in her chair.

Malach continued, "I don't know much about dresses or fashion. However, I don't believe that you need to have intimate knowledge of something to give a compliment to the owner. I simply thought it was a nice dress and that it accented your own beauty well." Malach went back to his food, and there was another long, awkward silence.

"I am sorry, Malach," to Malach and Jecrym's surprise, Kath had spoken. "I forget to show common courtesy sometimes. I should have graciously accepted the compliment for what it was. To be honest, I *am* used to more sophisticated company. Everything here is so much simpler and laid back. I'm working to adapt to how you all live. I come from a place where we would never talk. The men deal in business and the ladies talk to each other at social gatherings. When we lost our money, we lost our status, and people I thought were my friends stabbed me in the back. We had to relocate to. . ." she gestured around her, "here. And I don't know how to act. It is easy for me to be bitter and reclusive. But you don't deserve that."

Jecrym was staring at her with his mouth wide open, and Malach, too, was at a loss for words.

"What? Don't stare at me like that, Jecrym. You should have known this would be a hard transition for me," she stated.

"Mrs. Reybella," Malach started.

"Please, call me Kath. The valley people don't seem to stand on formalities with each other, and, whether I like it or not, we are now valley people," Kath said.

"Kath," Malach started again. "I can understand your feelings of being alone. I understand you may see our customs and lives as strange. Might I suggest you spend some time with the ladies in the town? They meet often to talk and gossip. Many of them sew or do other hobbies while they talk. You may find they will be truer friends than your former ones, if I may be so forward."

"You may, and I appreciate the suggestion," Kath was smiling now. It was the first time Malach had seen her smile and her laugh lines seem to fall into place, as if greeting an old friend.

Before anything else could be said, there was a commotion outside. Something was upsetting the cows. Malach jumped up from the table, toppling his chair.

"What is it?" Jecrym asked, standing up as well, although his chair remained on all four legs.

"I'm not sure. Stay here and I'll check it out." Malach ran for his spear, grabbed it out of the corner, and flew out the door, closing it behind him.

The moon was just starting to wane, but it was still mostly full and it provided enough light for Malach to see once his eyes adjusted. He spotted the cows huddled in a corner of the field but he didn't see what cause the commotion. He scanned the field. There was one dark lump on the ground not far from the fence-line. He started toward it being aware of his surroundings. Getting ambushed by a grizzly bear was the last thing he wanted.

He neared the lump on the ground and as he came close enough to see more detail, he could see it wasn't just a cow, but a mass of brown fur about a quarter the size or less of the cow it was munching on. It was a cub. A rumbling growl sounded behind him, turning into a roar. Malach cursed loudly and turned to face the large female bear charging directly at him. He leaped to the side at the last minute, using the butt of the spear as leverage to push himself farther to the right. He whirled around and ducked, as claws narrowly missed beheading him.

An arrow slammed into the side of the bear, burying itself a quarter of the way up the shaft in the bear's shoulder. It might have gone farther in if it had hit behind the shoulder, but it was most likely stopped when it hit the bone. The bear roared and reared back, standing up on two paws. It was still coming after

Malach and he couldn't worry about who shot the arrow or much else other than saving his own life.

He acted quickly, moving his hands to the middle and end of the spear shaft and, taking a step forward, he ran the spear up for the bear's throat. The bear moved to the side, and he cut the side of its neck. Blood pulsed out of the wound and the bear roared again. Malach had hit the vein, but now he had to survive an angry bear until it bled out.

Malach rolled off to the side again as the bear tried to bring both claws down on him. He regained his feet, planting the spear butt into the ground and letting the bear run onto it. It raked its claws across his chest and left four furrows in his skin. Malach let out a guttural cry and pushed the spear up and back, using the leverage to push the bear far enough away that it couldn't reach him. The bear backed off, leaving another hole for it to bleed from. Malach didn't know how much longer he could survive. He circled the bear, starting to get a little lightheaded. The bear wasn't doing any better. It was starting to stumble around. It finally fell to the ground and Malach rushed it. He put the spear through its throat and then brought the weapon down a second time, piercing it through the temple. The bear was dead.

Malach left the spear embedded in the bear's skull and flopped to the ground on his butt. He was sweating and bleeding. He checked the claw marks on his chest, and they wouldn't require stitches. They would be gone in a couple of days, leaving four scars for him to remember the bear by. To Malach's surprise, Kath showed up at his side before Jecrym, with his bow and last arrow in hand.

"Malach, you are insane," she said with a big smile. "How bad are the scratches?"

"Not bad. Just like that shot. I thought you were prim and proper. Who taught you to shoot?" Malach responded, taking the hand that was offered to him.

"My father did, a long time ago. I used to enter tournaments when I was a girl. I'm afraid I'm not as good as I used to be."

Jecrym made it to them at that point, clapping Malach on the shoulder and breathing rather hard from the short run. "That was worthy of songs, my friend! That was amazing!"

Movement caught their attention and Jecrym grabbed the spear, pulling it free of the bear's head. He headed for the cub with the spear at the ready.

"Wait!" Malach called, running ahead of Jecrym. "Hold on. Don't kill the cub."

"Why not?" Jecrym asked incredulously. "It killed one of my cows!"

Malach saw something in his eyes, something that hadn't been there before. There was something different about his face. It was tight and angry.

"No, the mother killed your cow. It was just eating your cow." Malach jerked the spear out of Jecrym's hand. "Just run this one off. If it comes back, you can deal with it then."

Jecrym's face changed back to normal, "Alright, yeah…that makes sense." He looked a little confused, but turned on his heel and started to walk away.

Malach was concerned by the change in Jecrym when he had grabbed the weapon. Maybe there *was* something about the weapon that was evil. He needed to figure it out before he used it too often. Maybe Togan was right.

"Where are you going?" Malach asked, putting the thoughts of the blade out of his mind.

"Inside," Jecrym responded. "Why?"

"Well, when I do a job, I usually get paid. In this case, I'll have to take my pay out of you in the form of work."

Jecrym still looked confused.

"Well, this bear isn't going to skin, gut, and quarter itself."

Jecrym's face fell and Malach laughed.

They ran the cub off and rolled the bear over. Kath went and retrieved a knife from the house to Malach's relief. He didn't want to have to change his spear to a knife in front of them. She had also changed out of her dress into a simple shirt and pants. He showed them how to dress the bear so they could drag it over and get it hung up to butcher. To his surprise, Kath was more than willing to be hands on.

"It's kind of fun to get your hands dirty, isn't it?" Kath said after Malach showed her where the different cuts of meat were and how to remove each one.

Malach turned to Jecrym, "Watch out, next thing you know, she will be eating the raw heart out of all her kills."

"Do people actually do that?" Kath asked, aghast.

"They do in some circles," Malach replied, shrugging. "They say you take the power of the animal you kill if you eat the heart. But only if you eat it raw and right after you cut it from its chest."

"That's barbaric!" Kath said, the haughty tone returning to her voice.

"You would have thought this barbaric not too long ago, Kath," Jecrym responded. "Now look at you."

Kath was covered in blood. There was even some on her face.

They laughed and shared a loving look. They were on the mend and that was good.

Malach showed them how to build a smoking rack to smoke and dry the meat. They built several racks. He got them started on drying the meat, and he prepared the skin to be tanned and sinew to dry. Once he was done with that, they had all the meat cut and hung up on the smoking racks. He went and grabbed the cart, pulling it up to their work area. He loaded the skin and sinew. They had also salvaged what they could off the cow and dressed the deer. Around half of the hide and meat were able to be saved from the cow. Malach told them he would take the hide and sell it for them when he went into town the next day and bring back what he got from it. However, Jecrym wouldn't have any of it and had told him to keep it for his pay.

"I'll have to come back for the meat, since it will take a few more hours to smoke," Malach told them. "I need to get up to the cottage and check on Skie."

"Understandable," Jecrym replied. "We will take turns tending the fires for the racks."

They cleaned the blood off of themselves and Jecrym thanked him again for helping him out. Malach picked up his cart and walked away with it. He couldn't shake the thought of Jecrym's face. Was it because he had lost another cow? No, even when the man was talking about his lost livestock before that he didn't have that look. The only difference was, he was holding the spear. Could the spear have influenced him in some way? He continued to think about this as he walked toward his cottage.

When he was out of sight of the farm, he changed the spear back to a knife and sheathed it. He decided he wanted a regular knife, anyway. That way, he didn't have to change the demon blade and draw attention to himself. Also, he needed more time to sort out what the demon weapon might be doing to him. By the time he made it to his cottage, it was midway through the night. He would only get a small amount of sleep tonight. He pulled the cart up and opened the door.

Skie burst through it, knocked him over, landing on him and licking his face.

"Alright, I get it; you were worried," Malach said, pushing her off and getting up.

He picked up the scrap and things most people didn't want to eat and threw them to her. She tore at them ravenously and they were gone in a few brief moments. She looked up at him and whined.

"I don't have any more raw meat. You will have to go hunt that yourself," he told her.

She came over and put her head in his hand as a farewell and then stalked off into the night. Or was it early morning? Malach covered the cart and went inside. He doubted anything would get at it in the little time he would be sleeping, and he didn't want to waste any time unloading it and then reloading it. He took his ripped shirt and bloodied pants off and dropped them in the corner. There would be time to clean and repair them later. He cleaned and bandaged the scratches on his chest and wiped the blood from his hands. He dropped into the comfort of his own bed and was out before his head hit the pillow.

As Malach wheeled the cart down the mountain trail, the sun was just coming up and he could see the guards in the distance opening the gates. Skie walked beside him this time, as the cart was full of things to sell. He had stopped by Jecrym and Kath's farm house and picked up the rest of his portion of meat.

Malach rolled the cart through the gates and turned toward Togan's shop. Once there, he set his cart down and walked in. Togan wasn't at the counter. He must be back in the forge. Malach walked around the counter and into the forge. He opened a heavy door and a blast of hot air greeted him. The big man was standing there, working a piece of metal.

"Hey, Togan," Malach said cautiously.

"Malach, I knew you'd be back," Togan said without turning around. "Did you need somethin'?"

Malach ground his teeth together. "I came to apologize for the other day and to ask you for a new knife. I still don't agree with you, but I am willing to wait to use the demon weapon until I know how it will affect me."

"I accept your apology and agree that your plan is acceptable," he said stiffly. "I'll make you a knife to use until then. Did ya still need the bear spear?"

"No, I used the demon weapon to kill the bear," he stated, wincing a bit as he knew how that would sound to the man.

Togan let out an unimpressed grunt. "What bear was it?"

"A big female; brown with grey tips on the fur."

Togan finally turned around and Malach could see that he was already working on a new knife roughly the shape of his old one. "That bear's killed hunters before."

"Well, it won't be killing anything ever again. It had a cub with it, though. I think there may be a male in the area," Malach mused. "Another hunter may need a spear soon. I didn't see any signs of him though, so he might hunt a different area."

"Maybe. I'll have your knife to you by tomorrow," Togan said.

"How much do I owe you? I've got two hundred and fifty pounds of dried smoked bear on the cart. And the deer I owe you, I started the salting process, but you will have to finish it."

"Give me about twenty-five pounds and we are even," Togan said, grinning. "But you know I would get you a knife, no charge, if you asked. It wasn't your fault you lost my last one in a demon's hide."

"I know, but I can't accept that," Malach said. "And I have the meat to trade."

Malach turned to walk back into the shop side of the building, sweat already starting to run down his back. "I'll just leave it on the counter, and I'll see you tomorrow at the send-off. I've got a few things to do before I leave."

Togan grunted an affirmation and turn back to his work, "Oh, Malach. The other arrowheads Jecrym paid for are finished. They are sitting on one of the shelves behind the counter."

Malach piled about thirty pounds of meat, and the deer, on the counter for Togan, making sure there was more meat than they had settled on since he didn't have anything to weigh it with. He checked behind the counter for the arrowheads and smiled as he pulled out seven of the metal tips. Togan didn't take charity, so he had made what Jecrym's coins were worth. That meant he would soon have ten new arrows in total.

Malach purchased everything he thought he would need for the trip and sold the half of cowhide for a few coins. He settled up what he owed the general store for the repairs on his house and traded some of the meat for coins. He still had about a hundred pounds of meat left. Twenty pounds of bear went to the Wervine's for payment for housing him and fixing him up. He would give another twenty to Arjun, mostly because he didn't want to carry that much with them on the journey. That would leave about sixty for Honora, Daziar, and himself for the journey. He would tan the bear and deer hides along the way and sell it once they were in Newaught, which should fetch him a good price and buy him some time to find work.

Malach made his way back to his cottage, pulling his cart up the hill. He made it to the tree line and slowed to a crawl. Heading back to his home gave him pause now. The demon had to know he had its weapon, and it obviously knew where he lived. At least he would be going away for a few years. He would miss the place, though. He pushed on, still keeping an eye out just in case, but he didn't think that the demon would attack in broad daylight. Skie padded off into the woods toward her cave when they arrived at the cottage. She would probably go hunting and then bed down for a few hours.

Malach got to work on making his new arrows and getting ready for the journey the next day. He didn't have to worry about food now or coin for the first few weeks. But he would have to make sure they were safe on the road and that they had shelter. He cleaned his soiled clothes and repaired the damaged ones. He made sure his pack for the road was in good shape and the things he would need were in it. They would have a wagon, so he didn't worry about how much weight was in his pack. He loaded the rest of his things in the trunk at the base of his bed, then packed the hides and packed meat into his trunk as well. He placed his father's sword on the top of it all, making sure it was wrapped tightly against any moisture that could harm it. The demon blade was wrapped in the same manner, however, he didn't believe it would be subject to the same tarnish. He set the trunk and his pack out by the door so it would be ready in the morning when Honora came to pick him up.

Suddenly, he heard something scratching at the door and jumped. He moved cautiously to his front door and opened it a few inches. Skie pushed inside, knocking him a little off balance. She walked past him and disappeared into his room as if that was the most normal thing for her to do. He followed her, dumbfounded. She had never gone into a house willingly, unless there was something wrong.

"Skie?" Malach asked as he walked into his room to see the wolf laying on his bed. "What's wrong?"

She lifted her head groggily, then flopped it back down onto the bed. He rushed over to her, but she was already asleep.

He felt her nose and checked her ears. Her nose was wet and her ears weren't hot.

She wasn't sick. Could she be exhausted from her wounds? She rolled onto her back with her legs up in the air. He smiled. She was making herself comfortable.

Good, Malach thought. *She's going to have to learn to sleep indoors in Newaught, anyway.*

Malach closed up the house with the sun only a sliver peeking above the mountain and slipped into bed. He had to work his legs around Skie since she took up the middle of his bed. He fell asleep with her head laying on his leg, happy and content for the moment.

Chapter 6

Amara sat in a jail cell.

How could I have been so stupid? She thought.

She messed up big time, and now she was stuck in a jail cell. Caught by the same vendor she had stolen from the day before, and this time, she hadn't gotten away. At least, until the Shadows got wind of what had happened. Then they would come to pay the bail and get her out. She got nicked for a minor crime, so it wouldn't cost much, but it would come out of her pay. What was worse was she was in the system now. They had a sketch artist draw up her face and now it was filed away. She would have to come back and steal it to make sure they didn't copy it and send it around.

Just as she predicted, the door opened and Lawdel walked in. He looked angry, but gave Amara a wink. The guard stood up from where he was sitting.

Lawdel turned to address the guard. "What has that no-good daughter of mine done now?"

The guard looked at him, confused, and started to answer, but Lawdel cut him off.

"She's always in some kind of trouble, and now she's gone and gotten herself locked up."

The hapless guard looked at Amara for help and she just shrugged, a look of boredom carefully masking her delight.

Lawdel continued, "I have a mind to just leave her in there and let her serve her time. But I guess I'll pay the bail." Lawdel deflated and looked at the guard. The guard didn't know what to say. "Well, how much is the fine?"

"Um, well, uh," the guard stammered.

"How much is it?" Lawdel demanded again.

"Uh, well sir, um, it hasn't been posted yet," the guard didn't meet.

"Oh." Lawdel gave the guard a confused look to sell his part. "Hmm, then I'll give you one gold coin to bail her. That should be more than enough for the fine, and you can keep whatever is left for yourself."

The guard looked at him dumbfounded, "Um, yeah, I guess, since it's her first time, and it wasn't that big of a crime that should cover it."

"Of course it should cover it. So, open the door and let her out," Lawdel demanded.

The guard unhooked the ring of keys from his belt and walked over to the holding cell. He started trying the keys in the cell door, but he obviously didn't know which one went to the cell. Though, in his defense, they all looked that same. He finally found the right one and unlocked the door. He pulled Amara out, roughly, by her arm. She wrenched her arm out of his grasp and glared at him.

"She's a fighter," the guard warned. "You sure you want her out early? We could send her to the prison for a few days. Teach her a lesson."

"No, that won't be necessary," Lawdel said calmly. "I can handle her. I'll make her cook in the kitchens and clean all the dishes every night for two weeks to pay me back for the trouble she's caused. That should straighten her out."

"Alright," the guard said, letting Lawdel take her and push her out the door. "Have a good day, sir. And keep her out of trouble." The guard called after him.

Once they were out of earshot Amara whispered, "What was that about? The posted bail would have been less than half of what you paid that guard and you know it."

"Quiet, girl. We caught wind they were going to send you to Newaught or execute you. Apparently, they know you were the one who broke into the mayor's house last night. Since we would rather not lose you to the Newaught chapter and we really don't want you dead, I came to get you out before that guard got his orders. One of the boys is running interference with the courier, but that guard is going to get them any moment. They will tell him he can't post any bail for you," Lawdel explained under his breath.

As if conjured by Lawdel's words, the guard came bursting around the corner. They had just turned. "Stop!" he shouted.

"Run!" Lawdel cried, and they bolted.

Lawdel turned to the left, down an alley, and Amara tore straight down the street. She passed a set of guards who gave chase, having heard the command from the first. She took a quick left and ran right into the chest of the Captain of the Guard. His hands clamped down on her arms, pinning them to her sides and, try as she might, she couldn't wriggle free of his grip. He was a hulk of a man and he simply picked her up off the ground. Her legs swinging underneath her. She tried to kick him, but couldn't get her legs out far enough.

Stupid, short legs, she thought bitterly. Why did she have to be so short? The captain held her there until the guards chasing her caught up. They clamped shackles on her ankles and wrist and escorted her back to the jailhouse without a word.

Once they had her back in the cell with the door locked, the captain spoke, "Well, you almost made it out, thanks to this idiot." The captain shot a look at the young guard.

"Sir, sorry, sir. It won't happen again, sir," the guard said smartly, still standing at attention.

"No, I suppose it won't." the captain turned back to her. "What do you think would be a fitting punishment?"

Amara was taken aback. "You're asking me?" she asked.

"Yes, I believe I was addressing you when I asked the question. It's only fitting he would be punished, and I am curious how your kind would punish such a failure." The captain glanced from her to the young guard, back to her again. The guard had started sweating, and she could tell he thought his punishment was going to be very severe.

Amara met the captain's eyes and decided the ruse was up. "We don't have to punish failure in the streets. Usually, when you fail, you get caught, go hungry, or die. The price of *failure* is enough punishment in most cases."

"Very interesting." The captain turned to his man. "I believe I have decided your punishment."

"Yes, sir," the guard still looked worried.

The captain turned to Amara again. "Now, what to do about you?"

"You still only have me for the theft of an apple. I'm sure I will not do a lot of time for that," Amara replied, feigning confidence.

The captain bust out in a roar of laughter, "You are good, aren't you? If I truly believed that, I would be as foolish as my guard." His face turned serious suddenly. "You just told me that you were living on the streets, but I suspect you are actually a member of the Shadows."

Amara could have kicked herself for her careless words, though there was no way he had proof of her association with the Shadows.

"I don't believe this is your first offense at all," the captain mused, "only the first time you've been caught. I think you were the one who robbed the mayor."

Amara opened her mouth to speak and thought better of it and closed it.

The captain watched with interest and then continued, "The mayor wants your head on a plate. He thinks if there is even a chance you were stealing from him, you should die. He won't let this go to a trail." The captain linked his fingers behind his back and started pacing in the small space in front of the cell. "The question is, what do I do with you? I would be in a bad position politically if I let you live, but it goes against my personal code to kill someone who isn't proven guilty."

"Sir, I promise, I had nothing to do with the robbery at the mayor's mansion," Amara lied. Her chest felt tight and she could feel the panic start to rise. She would have said just about anything to get out of this cell at the moment. She didn't want to die.

"The mansion? I don't think I said anything about the mansion," the captain said coolly, turning to the young guard. "Did I say anything about the mansion?"

"Sir, no, sir," the guard replied.

"I didn't think so," the captain turned back to Amara. "So, if I didn't say anything about it how did you know that the robbery occurred at the mansion?"

Amara wanted to crawl under a rock. *How could I have been tricked so easily? Think, Amara, think.*

"I heard the alarm last night. I was near the mayor's mansion, out for a stroll, and I heard the alarm go up from the guards. When you said he had been robbed, I just put two and two together." She didn't even let herself sigh in her head in case her body betrayed her. It *was* a good lie. She covered for her mistake and gave herself a way out. Her plan was forming in her head.

"Were you now? Can anyone vouch for your whereabouts?" the captain asked.

"Yes, my father was with me," she said quickly, already anticipating the question.

"Oh, the man that came to bail you out?" he asked.

She nodded.

"The one who ran when your cover was blown?"

She gulped. She hadn't seen that one coming.

"Tell me, why would your father run like that? He had just paid bail. He would have thought you were free to go. Unless you are both guilty. Is he even your father?"

"He's the only father I have ever had," Amara almost shouted, and that was the truth.

"But you are both members of the Shadows," the captain stated, as if he had known all along. "Why would he risk his life for you? There's no honor among thieves, right?"

Amara's plan was quickly fragmenting in front of her, and she didn't know what to say. She was going to end up hanged for the theft last night, and she didn't know how to get out of it.

She heard herself say, "You have no proof that I am a member of that den of thieves. You are fishing for information. I won't say another word."

The captain stopped pacing and turned to her. "You're right, I have no proof." He moved up to the bars and peered in at her. "So here is what I am going to do. I am going to transfer you to Newaught, away from the mayor. I knew one day he would put me in this position. If I send you away, I don't have to lose face with the mayor and my men, *and* I don't accidentally kill an innocent."

Amara couldn't believe what she was hearing. "But I'm not twenty-one yet!" she objected.

What are you thinking? She mentally berated herself. *The alternative is getting hanged. Let them send you away.*

"Do you even know how old you are?" the captain asked.

Amara thought for a second. "Eighteen, maybe nineteen." She replied defiantly, but her words lacked conviction.

"We don't have any record of you as a citizen. Do you have proof to back up that claim?"

Amara hung her head. She didn't have any proof.

"Then we will make some up."

"Huh?" She was really confused now.

"We are going to make you a citizen and all your papers will say you are twenty-one years of age. Then send you on the journey to Newaught. I will give you the private here as an escort," he nodded to the young guard.

The guard's face fell for just a moment, and then he stiffened once more.

"And he will make sure you get *all* the way to Newaught, safe and sound. Once there, you are free to live however you want." The captain turned around with a stack of papers in his hands. "But I will warn you. If you come back here, I will have no choice but to hang you."

Amara's head was swimming. Things were happening so fast. She didn't know what to do. Her life was over here, and she couldn't change it. One simple mistake and she had to start her life over again. This time, no one would be there to help her like Lawdel had all her life. She was going to be alone.

"Amara?" the Captain asked, as if she had missed a question that he was waiting on.
She gave him a blank look.

"I know that this is a lot all at once, but it's the only way I can get you out of here and not put you in the ground," he told her. "I have a limited window of time to get you out, or I will have to hang you, regardless. So, what is your last name?"

"I . . . I don't have one," she mumbled.

"Oh, do you have a preference?" he asked.

"No."

"Well, you were apprehended in the West Bay district, so we will just put Westbay on the papers." He scribbled something on his paper and thumbed through the pages quickly. "I think that was all I needed to finish your papers. You're lucky that I prepared these a while ago, in case the mayor put me in such a position. Happy birthday, Amara Westbay. I hope your journey goes well. You will spend the majority of it in shackles in the back of a cart. The private here will provide you with protection and any essentials. Once at Newaught, you will be given everything we found on you. Hopefully, that will give you a chance to start a new life. Maybe you will choose a more. . ." the captain seemed to search for a word, "honorable profession."

The captain handed the papers to the private and told him something under his breath. Amara only heard a few words, but it was something about an unseen escort. The captain was using her as a trap for the Shadows; she realized.

How could she warn them? She had to think or her fellow Shadows would be killed.

She looked up, and the private was coming her way. He unlocked the door for the second time that day and grabbed her arm. She was still in the shackles, so she shuffled forward. He pulled her so hard she almost fell. He seemed to realize he was pulling her too fast, however, and slowed. Out behind the jailhouse, a wagon waited. Someone had already harnessed a singular horse to it. The private took off the ankle shackles so she could climb in. Once in, he clamped them down again and ran an extra length of chain attached to her shackles through a loop bolted to the cart and locked it in place. She was locked to the cart for better or worse.

The cart was not covered, but the walls of the cart were high enough she could barely see out. For most people, it would provide cover from any enemy archers while still allowing them to see where the attack was coming from. For her, though, the wall was almost too high to see out.

The cart started rattling forward with a jolt. Just as the captain had said, the private was the only one with her in the cart. The Shadows would think that getting her back without casualties would be easy. They would go for the bait without a second thought.

She peered over the top edge of the cart, straining to get a good look at the streets. There was a crowd waiting for them to come out of the jailhouse stables. The commotion of the attempted escape and the promise to get to jeer at a prisoner had drawn them. By now, the transfer would have been leaked and spread around the general population. That's how Lawdel had heard they might send her to Newaught. She peeked out at the crowd, searching for any of the Shadows. The crowd was shouting and jeering at her, calling her all sorts of names and words she didn't want to think about. She blocked them out, continuing to search the crowd for any familiar faces. She spotted him, one of the Shadows. He was looking directly at her. She shook her head firmly twice. He nodded solemnly and vanished into the crowd. Amara hoped Lawdel wouldn't try anything stupid. The message was received and all she could do was wait and hope.

A rotten fruit slammed into the side of the cart and she ducked down quickly, sinking below the wall. A few more pieces of produce slammed into the side of the cart before the guard shouted for the crowd to stop and move on. They did as they were told, and the cart slowly left them behind. They passed under the arch of the main gate and didn't slow down. Her life was changing forever. Either she would be on the run every day of her life if she stayed in Caister or she would start over in Newaught. Tears streamed down her face. She dropped her head into her hands as the cart continued to rattle down the road.

Malach stood on the back of the wagon with the bearskin stretched upright on a makeshift rack. He painted a mixture on the fur to tan it. This process would take a while, but it was worth it. The mixture smelled awful, but the wind was blowing almost directly at them, sending the smell back the way they'd come. Malach felt sorry for Honora's horse, Celewen. She was tied up behind the cart, plodding along with it. She didn't seem to care too much, but she would let out a snort every once in a while.

"Malach, do you have to do that now?" Honora asked. "It smells and looks disgusting." She wrinkled her nose at him.

Malach put the lid on the mixture and turned around. Honora and Daziar were sitting on the bench at the front of the wagon. Daziar was holding the reins of the two mules that pulled the wagon.

"It's not *that* bad, and no, it can't wait. If I wait too long, it will start to rot, and then I'll lose the whole fur. This will fetch a good price in Newaught, and I'll need that money to live long enough to get a job," Malach explained as he sat down just behind the front bench, his back facing the outside of the cart.

They left Brightwood early that morning, and even though it was before dawn, most of the town had come out to see them off. Since they were a small town, it wasn't often someone left for the journey. This was the first time three had left, at the same time. They were given some gifts and a grand send-off. Togan gave Malach the knife he had made. It was the spitting image of the one he had lost in the fight with the demon. He had thanked the man and offered his hand, but was caught off guard when the big man pulled him into a hug. Malach swore he could see tears in Togan's eyes.

Since then, they had been taking turns holding the reins of the cart and making sure the mules stayed on track. The road was pretty straightforward. There were small roads leading off the main road, but most of these went to small homesteads or the like. Most were little more than a game trail. They had a map to keep them on the right road if they had any question of which way to go.

Even though Brightwood was in a valley in the middle of the mountains, they would have to descend even farther down onto the plains and foothills before climbing again once they arrived at Newaught. They had a long road ahead of them that wasn't without its perils. If they made a wrong move on the side of one of the switchbacks, they could fall down the mountain, ending their trip quickly. There were also highwaymen that robbed smaller parties. Hopefully, their wagon would overtake a merchant caravan and travel with them most of the way, giving them protection, but there was no guarantee of that happening.

They were lucky the snows were late this year, or they would be making the trip on foot. They would have to wear snowshoes to walk on top of the snow. Although even with the shoes, it was like walking in sand and would add a week or more to their trip. They had the shoes with them just in case, but so far, they hadn't seen any sign of the snow though the temperature was dropping daily. It wouldn't be long before the snows came.

Malach was told they wouldn't have to worry about the snow as much down in Newaught, but he couldn't imagine a winter without a couple of feet of snow. Apparently, the city only saw a few inches once or twice a year. They wouldn't need the snowshoes or their heavy cloaks and furs if was the truth. A merchant told him some towns in Demon Territory never got snow, as it was warm all year round. So warm, in fact, that no one wore anything heavier than short pants and a light tunic.

"What jobs do you think they will give us?" Honora asked, breaking the silence and Malach's train of thought.

"I'm not sure," Malach said. "I think they would give us one that would suit our strengths."

"You mean we don't get to pick?" Daziar asked incredulously.

"Really, Daziar?" Honora said. "Don't you remember anything from training?" Honora sighed when Daziar shook his head. "They told us on one of the last days of our training that when you get to Newaught, you are given a skills test, and then they put you where you are most needed. That's the only fair way to handle the large number of people that make the Journey throughout the year. Either that, or they would be short-staffed in some areas and over-staffed in others."

"So, we don't get any say in what we do?" Daziar said, dismayed.

"They *do* take into account what you want to do, and sometimes people are given a choice between two professions," Malach clarified, trying to make Daziar feel better. "But for the most part, no, they just give you a job. But they would be crazy if they didn't make you a city guard. They would be wasting your potential, and I'm sure they won't want to waste anyone's potential."

"I've been training to be a city guard in Newaught all my life," Daziar said confidently. "And not like our slacking city guards. I want to be the kind who will rise through the ranks and one day become Captain of the Guard." Malach chucked, "I'm sure you will be. I just want to be a lowly hunter. Just be left in peace to hunt and enjoy my life with Skie."

Skie raised her head at the sound of her name. She had been sleeping under the overhang right behind the front bench. Malach ruffled her ears, and she gave him a sleepy and contented smile and laid her head back down.

They pulled off the road at dusk into a clearing they could set camp up in. It seemed like a lot of the merchants that passed this way used the clearing, and it was well-packed and clear of debris. With only a small amount of work, they had it cleared and their camp set up. They lit a fire and Honora made a stew with the supplies they had brought. Malach put in the seasonings he had brought with him. It was delicious. By the time they were done with dinner, night had fully fallen. Malach stood and inspected the bearskin. It had almost dried, and Malach was out of the solution. He worked the skin a little, stretching it so it would be soft. Satisfied, he left it alone and went back to the fire.

"So, Honora, Mal and I have said what we want to do when we get to Newaught. What do you want to do?" Daziar asked.

Honora thought about it for a minute. "I would love to train the horses. But I might have to work my way up to that."

"Once they see what you can do with a horse, they will move you right up there, though," Malach said. "Just like with Daz; they won't waste your skills and talent with horses."

"I hope you're right. I don't want to be mucking out stalls for the rest of my life," she laughed. "Malach, what would you do if they don't let you hunt?"

"I'm not sure," he said, looking at the fire. "I haven't thought much about it. I guess I don't have much of a preference."

"I'll tell you one thing: you could be a guard, easy," Daziar said.

"Why do you say that?" Honora asked.

"He knows how to use a lot of weapons, and even though he's not anywhere close to my size, he beats me in strength, hands down," Daziar said and then added, "always has."

"Really? How is that possible?" Honora asked, sizing up Malach and then Daziar. Then it dawned on her. "Oh. . ."

An uncomfortable silence hung over the group for a long time.

Honora broke it first. "Malach, how come you didn't tell me sooner?" She quickly added. "I understand why you didn't want people to know, and I promise I won't ever tell anyone. It's just. . . well, it hurt that you didn't trust me."

"Honora, it's not that I didn't trust you. I just spent my whole life hiding it. My father told me to *never* tell anyone. Ever." Malach again turned his gaze to the fire. "Daz only knew 'cause we shared a room after my parents. . ." Malach trailed off. It still hurt to think of that night.

"Malach. . ." Honora said, but Malach cut her off by holding up a hand.

"My father had the same curse." Malach's voice was almost bitter. "The only time we didn't have to worry about it was in the woods. That's one reason I enjoyed our hunting trips so much. When I'm out in the woods, I don't have to worry about revealing my curse to anyone." Malach looked up at Honora. "I'm sorry I never told you. I do trust you, and I know you wouldn't tell anyone, but I don't openly share with anyone."

"I understand. It must be awful having to hide it, knowing if someone found out you would never be looked at the same again," Honora said sympathetically. "Is that why your parents moved to the valley?"

"They never told me why they moved. I just know my mother was carrying me at the time," Malach said. "I think it was for other reasons, though. They didn't talk about their life before the valley often, and when they did, it was carefully. Not giving away too many details, not even to me. I think they might have told me when I got older but. . ." Malach trailed off.

"Malach," Honora asked carefully. "Do you mind if I ask what other powers come with your lineage?"

"I don't mind. I can heal quickly, but not instantly. It still took me five days to fully heal from the demon attack, but for most men, that would have been a week and a half to two-week injury, easily."

"If not longer," Daziar added.

"Right," Malach agreed. "I also have more strength than most men."

He saw the excitement blossom on Honora's face.

"Don't get too excited. I can't pull a tree up by its roots or anything. I can, however, best most normal men. Daz isn't far behind me, though, so I assume there are some men out there that could best me."

"That's still amazing!" Honora exclaimed, her excitement bubbling over. "So even though you don't train as much as, say, a trained soldier, you could beat him in a fight?"

"I won't say that. A soldier trains much more than I do, and fighting isn't just about strength; it's about outmaneuvering your opponent. My strength would help, but a better trained opponent would most likely still best me." Malach explained.

"I understand," Honora said thoughtfully. "So faster healing and better strength, anything else?"

"Well, I can see better in the dark than most people, but that might not be part of the lineage thing, and I think I can hear better, but again, that might not be related. But with the strength comes better endurance. I don't get winded or tired as fast. I can run for miles, but it's nothing a regular human can't do with a bit of hard work."

They talked for a while longer and then put out the fire and retired to their respective tents, Honora to hers and the boys to theirs. Skie stayed in the open, laying just outside of Malach's tent, and they all were asleep within a few minutes.

Amara was awoken by the private, who was unshackling her from the cart. She studied him for the first time. He was young, probably close to her own age. He had a strong jaw but a kind face. She thought in another life they might have been friends. Here, however, he was the man who was taking her away from everything she knew. She glared daggers at him as he finished unhooking the chain from the ring, and when he looked up, he jumped, not expecting her to be watching him.

"You're awake." His eyes were wide with surprise.

"Well, with you rattling the chains like that, the dead would be awake," she retorted, putting as much venom in her voice as she could.

"I thought you might want to come down to the camp with me and sit by the fire. I'll let your hands loose so you can eat and relieve yourself," he offered, giving her a genuine smile.

"Fine," she said shortly, and followed him off the cart.

True to his word, he let her hands loose, and she shuffled a little way into the woods to get some privacy. Just before she disrobed, she heard something rustling in the woods. She froze. Was it a wild animal? Should she run? Should she call out to the private? Just before she made up her mind to run, she heard a whisper. She turned back to where the rustling was coming from.

She heard it again, more clearly. "Amara."

"Lawdel, is that you?" she whispered back.

Lawdel came out of the bushes with a small bundle in his hands. "Shh," he whispered. "I don't have a lot of time, but I went and got your things from on top of that blasted tower."

Amara smiled.

"Why did you have to hide it all the way up there?" he complained. "Don't you know it's hard for an old lard like me to climb that high?"

She hugged him and then pulled back, brow knitting with worry, "Lawdel, you know it's too dangerous for you to be out here."

"I know. Those guards are in a tight circle around you. It was a bit hard for me to get through them, but I managed." He smirked at her. He appeared to be rather enjoying himself.

"Lawdel, you must go. They could see you at any time, and then you would be caught, too. You are a wanted man. They won't let you off with just a warning and move you to another city." Amara was genuinely worried for him.

"I know, I know." He put his hands up in surrender. "But I couldn't just let you go without a goodbye. I assume by your message to our man that you are going to let them take you to Newaught?"

She could tell he was trying to keep his voice natural, but she could hear the sadness in it.

"Lawdel," she said softly, "you have been like a father to me, and that won't change. But I'm wanted by the mayor. This is my only chance to stay free. It's hard for me to leave and start over, but I think it would be worse for me to stay. Besides, it's not like it's forever. I'll still sneak in and visit here and there."

"Well, you have your money and your things now. We sent word ahead of you to the local chapter of the Shadows, letting them know you are on the way and should look for them. There is a coded map in that bundle. Make sure the guards don't get their grubby paws on it."

"Thanks, Lawdel; you're always looking out for me," she said and hugged him again. When she pulled away, she could see tears in his eyes.

"Bloody pollen, always making my eyes leak," he said, his voice heavy with emotion.

"It's time to go, Lawdel," she said solemnly. "I have to get back or they will come looking for me."

"Well, don't let them mistreat you. And don't let your new handler talk you into anything too dangerous. Oh, and make sure he doesn't take more than his share." He turned to leave and then turned around again. "And make-"

"Lawdel, go," she said sternly. "I'll be fine, you old fusspot."

"Goodbye, Amara. You are the daughter I never had."

"And you are the father I've always had." She smiled through her own tears.

She watched as he disappeared into the darkness. Wiping her eyes, she stood up straight. She would see him again. She vowed to herself that she would come back and visit after the heat cooled off. Her papers would disappear from the guard's post, and she would have a clean slate again soon, but the Captain and the few guards who had seen her would need a year or more for the memory of her face to dim in their minds. Once that happened, she could return home and things would go back to normal. She just had to survive a year or two in Newaught first.

She did her business and walked back to the fire. The private was just starting to get up to come locate her when she came out of the woods. She had stashed the map in a hidden pocket next to her breast, and had stowed the bundle under the cart, wedging it between a metal bar that was coming loose and the floor of the cart. It seemed like it would stay until she could find her chance to get away. "Don't worry. I didn't run away. Besides, your friends in the woods wouldn't let me, anyway."

"What friends?" The private's eye widened and his words were a little too quick to spring to his lips. "There's no one out here but us."

"Ha!" Amara barked out a bitter laugh. "There is a score of armed guards that have been following us since we left Caister, and I know you know about them."

"There are no guards following us," he said again and crossed his arms, as if repeating himself would convince her.

"If telling me that helps you sleep at night, then, by all means, believe it," Amara said noncommittally. "I smell food and I'm starving. I haven't eaten since breakfast."

The private, still nervous and distracted, picked up the pot of meat and potatoes he had been cooking and came over to sit beside her. He spooned it out of the pot and handed her a plate. They sat and ate in silence for a while. The private still seemed to be lost in thought.

"So, were you really a member of The Shadows of the Earth?" he finally asked.

"I'm not going to tell you," Amara said indignantly, shocked that he would ask that question so blatantly.

"Why not?" He seemed genuinely confused.

"Cause if I tell you I wasn't, you won't believe me, and if I tell you I was, then you will haul my butt right back to your captain and have me hung." Amara explained.

"Oh, I hadn't thought of that." The private looked disappointed and embarrassed. "Well, I just thought it would be interesting to get to say I've met someone who was a member of the Shadows."

There was an uncomfortable silence and Amara decided to finish eating before the private asked any more questions.

"I've read all the reports on any case they think had to deal with the Shadows," the private remarked. His excitement was starting to return. "I think it amazing how they can sneak in and out without raising an alarm or killing anyone." He glanced at her, but turned his eyes back toward the fire quickly.

She didn't meet his gaze but kept on eating.

"I really respect the Shadows for that," he continued. "I mean, they seem to have some sort of code forbidding them from killing."

Amara paused for a second, but again said nothing.

"Every time they raise the alarm or are caught, they only disarm or injure their opponent. There has only been one case in the past ten years that a suspected Shadow killed someone. And it wasn't even confirmed it was a Shadow who did it." He looked at her again, this time his gaze lingering. "I know you can't say if you are a Shadow, but can you tell me if they have that code?"

Amara chewed on the bite of meat she had in her mouth thoughtfully. "I think you already have the answer to that. It seems, given the evidence you just stated, they *do* have a code against killing."

The private waited for more, but Amara just took another bite.

"Well, that's good to know. At least I won't have to worry about you killing me in my sleep." The private started eating and a few moments passed wherein neither of them spoke.

"What would you do to me if I were a Shadow?" Amara asked curiously.

It was the private's turn to chew thoughtfully. "I'm not sure. At first, I would just have a lot of questions. After that, I have my orders to take you to Newaught. I don't think the Captain wants to hang you either way, so I don't think it would be in my best interest to take you back. I could still report you to the Captain at Newaught and let him decide. But then I would make my captain a liar, since he said you would be free in Newaught and forged your papers. So, to tell you the truth, I don't think I would do anything different, other than ask you about the Shadows." He took another bite.

Amara remained silent. *Maybe he really is just curious, but I don't think I can trust him to let me go once we reach Newaught if he knows I'm a Shadow,* she thought. *I might not even be able to trust him, even if he doesn't know.*

A thought dawned on her. He might have standing orders to turn her in at Newaught, even if the captain told her she would be free. He had already tried to use her as bait. Turning her in at Newaught or following her once she got there so they could find out more about the Shadows wouldn't be too far out of the question. She had to escape before reaching Newaught.

"Well, I'm going to get some sleep. I set up one tent for you and one for me. Unfortunately, I will have to bind your hands again. Protocol and all." The private said, getting up and walking over to his pack.

He cleaned up a bit and put his pack into his tent. Then came back with the key to her shackles and fastened them onto her wrists, which were just beginning to stop hurting. He helped her over to her tent and then inside. He was surprisingly gentle, but she couldn't help feeling a bit of animosity toward him. After all, he was keeping her prisoner. He let the flap fall behind her and left her in the dark. She found the bedroll he had made for her and laid down.

She waited a bit for the private to fall asleep. By the snoring that soon came from the direction of his tent, she figured it was safe. Then she carefully felt around the hem of her breeches for the hidden pocket. They hadn't found her lock pick yet, and she used it to open the shackles on her wrist and then the ones on her ankles. She carefully set them aside, making as little noise as she could, and got up.

She peered out through the tent flap. The guards in the woods would be watching the camp. She slipped under the back of the lean-to and into the shadows. She moved to the private's tent and slipped in unnoticed. Once inside, she looked down at his sleeping form.

Oh, to be so innocent again, she thought.

Had she ever been *that* innocent? She moved to the saddlebags full of supplies and the tack for the horses piled next to him. She picked up what she needed and pushed it out of the back of the tent. It was going to be hard, moving around with all this stuff without being spotted. She carefully exited, searching around to see if she had been spotted yet. No one was shouting or running at her, so she assumed she hadn't. She hung all the tack and supplies over her shoulders and crept around the camp.

She retrieved the bundle she had hidden and moved to where the horses were tied. She picked the horse farthest from the fire that was now burning low and slung the saddlebags onto it. The horse accepted the bit, and she slipped the bridle over its head. There were no saddles, not that she could have lugged it over to the horse without being spotted, anyway, so she would have to ride bareback.

How hard could it be? She thought.

The second horse stamped its foot and snorted at her, as if it knew she was taking its companion. She untied the second horse, an idea forming in her head. Hopping onto the horse she'd just put her gear on, she turn to the second, newly freed, steed. A shout came from her left. She slapped the loose horse hard on the rump, and it took off in a random direction. Then she kicked her horse into movement and off they flew into the dark woods. It would take them some time to find the runaway horse and she should have a good lead by the time they did.

She had slept a good portion of the day, not having anything else to do, and she would travel most of the night tonight. The private would have to go back to the captain with his tail between his legs and admit he had failed. She felt a pang of guilt about that, but didn't turn around. The poor young man would be doing a year of night watches to make up for this.

She steered the horse back in the direction of Newaught, and as it turned, she nearly slipped from its back. She didn't have anything to hold on to, so she grabbed a handful of the horse's mane and clamped her legs down so she wouldn't fall. A tree zoomed past in a blur so close to her head that some strands of her hair ripped from her head as they were caught in its bark. With effort, she pulled herself back upright on the horse.

Too close.

She had a two-week trip to Newaught if she was on foot or in the cart, but with the horse, she should be able to cut that in half. She would travel all night and the rest of that day to make sure she had enough distance between her and the guards so that they couldn't follow her. Then, she would ride all the way to Newaught and start her new life.

Chapter 7

Malach woke up screaming, his throat raw. He had the dream again, but this time it was different. Oh, he was still killed alright, but he hadn't run this time. He had the demon's blade in his hand, though it was still in the shape of that strange double-bladed pole weapon.

When the demon descended on his troop, he stood his ground and fought it. He had done well, taking off a horn and one of its hands at the wrist, but in the end, he had died all the same.

He was drenched in sweat despite the chill in the air. The sun wasn't up yet. He looked to his right, and Daziar wasn't on his bedroll. Malach got up and left the tent. He found Daziar and Honora staring at him from the other side of the fire.

"I woke you up, huh?" Malach asked, his voice still scratchy. He headed over to the water barrel in the back of the cart and poured himself a drink.

"Mal?" Daziar asked. "Are you alright?"

"Just a nightmare," Malach replied, hoping not to talk about it. "Sorry I woke you up.
He heard Daziar whisper a "see" and heard an "oomph" as Honora elbowed him in the ribs.

"Malach, that seemed a little more intense than a simple nightmare," Honora said in a sweet voice. He could tell she was trying to get him to open up, but didn't want to offend him. "Do you want to talk about it?"

Malach opened his pack sitting on the cart. He dug down to the bottom and pulled the demon blade from under his things just to confirm it was still there. He put it back, but he couldn't help but think that somehow, it was connected to his dreams.

"Not really," Malach said honestly, turning back to look at the pair. "Thanks for the offer, though. How long have you both been up?"

"About an hour for me, but that wasn't because of you," Honora said. "Daziar got up when you started shouting, so maybe a quarter of an hour now."

"Honora, you know we don't know how that time thing works," Malach chided. "Only your family owns one of those weird things with the hands."

"You two need to learn," Honora shot back. "And it's called a clock. Newaught will have several clock towers and most people there will own one in their homes. You need to learn so you can be on time for things."

"Fine, but you will have to teach us when we get there unless you brought one with you," Malach replied.

"No, I didn't. My family only owns one, and it was too big to bring, but I will teach you when we get there," Honora conceded.

"You were in a war or something, man, shouting, and cursing the name of a demon and everything," Daziar change the subject back to the dream.

Malach winced. "Sorry, Daz. If you want to go back to sleep until sunrise, I'm not going to get any more sleep tonight."

"I think I might just do that," Daziar said, standing up and walking to the tent.

Malach and Honora sat in silence for a while, not wanting to keep Daziar up. Once they heard him snoring loudly, Honora broke the silence. "You've had this dream before?"

Malach looked at her and sighed. He knew he wasn't getting out of talking about it now unless he gave her something.

"Yes," he said shortly. He really didn't want to tell anyone.

Honora waited for a minute for him to elaborate, but when it became clear he wasn't going to, she prodded with another question. "So, what happens in the dream?"

Malach sighed again, "I am with a small troop of soldiers or guards in the wood, and we are attacked by a demon. When that happens, most are killed or flee."

"Do you think this is because you were attacked by a demon back in Brightwood?" she asked. She seemed genuinely concerned about him.

"No," he said matter-of-factly, "I've had the dream since I was eighteen. Every night. You'd think I'd be used to it by now. I always die in the dream. Come to think of it, though, this was the first night since the demon attack I've had the dream. And this time it was different." He didn't know why he said so much, but it felt good to talk about it to someone.

"Do you think it's a vision of the future?" she said it so nonchalantly, like it was the most normal thing in the world.

"Why would you think that? I mean, it's not like visions are commonplace," Malach said. "Besides, I really hope it isn't, because I die every time."

"Well, you're right, but if it is the future, you have changed it since the demon attack, right? So maybe it's not set in stone," she laughed at herself. "I just heard what I was saying, and it sounds ridiculous. How could it be a vision?" She chuckled to herself again.

"Right. How could it be? I'm probably just going insane. Pretty soon you'll be spoon feeding me after my mind breaks, and I lose all control," he said, laughing.

"I'll leave that to Daziar," she said, playfully punching him on the arm. Then she got serious all of a sudden. "Malach? If you need to talk about anything, I'm always here." She put a hand on his shoulder.

"I know," he said. "Thanks."

And he meant it. Her friendship was something he truly cherished. He didn't have many friends, but those he had, he would die to protect. They sat in silence for a while, staring at the fire, and then watched as the sun peeked over the mountains in the distance.

Daziar emerged from the tent without his shirt on, stretching his muscles as he did. His muscles weren't unimpressive. Though he still had a layer of fat on his body, which softened some of the definition. If he went into the guard, he would lose a lot of that, since they did drills every week. Although Malach had seen some guards with a belly, so maybe not if Daziar didn't apply himself. But if he didn't apply himself, he would never reach the captain's seat. Malach guessed he would find out in the next few years.

"Show off," Honora said playfully.

"What's he showin' off? All that flab of his?" Malach joked, standing up and giving his friend a little jab to the stomach.

Daziar tackled him to the ground, and they scuffled. They stopped a moment later, both panting and grinning at each other. They faced off again, but Honora got in between them.

"If you two are done being two-year-olds," she gave them each a pointed look, "then you can help me get some breakfast so we can get on the road. We have a lot of ground to cover."

Malach chuckled and brushed the dirt off his pants. "Fine, but I would have beaten you, eventually."

"No, you wouldn't have. I would have put you in the dirt, little man," Daziar shot back.

"Little man? I'm taller than you and stronger." Malach pulled the food sack out of the tree they had hung it in.

"Stronger? You only wish," Daziar caught the bag of food that was hurled at him. It knocked the wind out of him with an "Oomph".

"You admitted it last night," Malach said triumphantly.

"You weren't supposed to remember that." Daziar shot back.

"Boys. . ." Honora sighed and took the bag from Daziar, which ended their banter.

Malach grabbed the cooking supplies from the cart as Daziar got the fire going again. Soon, they had a few eggs and some ham cooking over the fire. Once they finished breakfast, they packed up everything in the cart, and Daziar took the first shift driving. Malach checked on the bear fur and found that it had stiffened a little, so he started working the stiffness out of it. Skie trotted out of the woods and caught up to the cart. She had two large rabbits in her mouth, and she jumped up on the cart with them.

"Hey, girl! What did you bring us?" Malach took the rabbits from her and turned to the other two. "Look what's for lunch!"

They turned around and Honora look revolted. "Why would you show us the dead animals?"

"Where do you think meat comes from, Honora?" Malach asked incredulously.

"I know where it comes from, but I don't want to see the fresh kills," she explained.

Daziar looked at Malach and shrugged. "Girls."

Honora punched his arm.

Malach took out his new knife and processed the two rabbits.

He cut out what they would want to eat and handed the rest to Skie, who ate it happily. He put the meat out of the sun so it would last the hour or so to lunch. Then he dealt with the furs so he could sell them in Newaught. They wouldn't fetch a good price. They had too many teeth holes in the fur, but it would be something.

About the time he was finishing with that, they broke for lunch. He cooked, since he didn't take a turn driving that morning. Daziar and Honora rested in the shade. Once they were done with lunch, they got back underway. Skie fell asleep quickly in the back of the cart. She had most likely been out hunting all night and seemed to be exhausted. Malach took his turn driving the cart.

"Hey, you two feel like we are being watched?" Daziar asked a while later, careful to keep his voice down.

Malach looked as if taking in the surrounding sights. He hadn't seen anyone, but he had been having the same feeling as Daziar. "I do, but I don't see anyone, and Skie hasn't woken up yet. Usually, she is up and alert if there is any danger."

He glanced back at Skie and saw the fur on her back raise. She opened an eye and growled low.

"You mean like that?" Daziar asked.

"Yep. Honora, if you could get my bow and arrows ready and hand me the small bundle in my trunk, I would appreciate it," Malach said and then added. "But don't make it look like you are in a hurry or that anything is out of the ordinary."

Honora leaned down and started rummaging through the things in the back of the cart as if she were looking for something. "Why would highwaymen be out this far into the wilds? There are no merchants this way until after the snows. Brightwood is pretty much on its own for the rest of the winter."

"I'm not sure," Malach replied. "It doesn't make sense for them to be this far out unless they are a smaller band, but they wouldn't attack a group if they were. Even a group as small as ours."

As he said that, they turned a corner in the road and saw a tree fallen on the road.

"Scratch that. Get that bow ready fast as you can." Malach halted the mules and tied off the reins quickly, rolling off the seat just as an arrow whizzed out of the woods and stuck in the bench where he was sitting. He grabbed the bow from Honora and notched an arrow as she took cover. Spinning, he trained the bow on the treeline where the arrow had come from. He couldn't see anyone. He heard a hiss and ducked as the arrow passed over him, missing his head by inches. Celewen pulled at her rope, flaring her nostrils in fright.

Honora grabbed her head and quickly calmed her down.

Malach had noted where that arrow came from and put one of his own on a return trajectory. He was rewarded by a scream and a man fell from a tree.

The highwaymen weren't just on the ground in the cover of the trees; they were actually *in* the trees.

Malach scanned the trees themselves and loosed two more of his arrows in quick succession. Two more men fell. One was dead before he hit the ground. Daziar drew his sword and hopped out of the cart, drawing Malach's attention. Honora had her bo staff out and held in a ready stance, but seemed to be frozen in place. Malach tackled her to the cart floor as an arrow flew past them.

"Honora!" Malach shouted at her and slapped her roughly on the cheek.

The fall or the slap snapped her out of her stupor, and she returned his open hand strike with interested.

He grinned and pulled her up.

She hopped out of the cart.

He had to keep the archers trained on him and kill them before they managed to land an arrow. Daziar and Honora's job would be to protect him while he took out the archers. They had been trained for these situations but had never been tested in the real world. They fell into the stance and flow of battle easily. The problem was, the highwaymen would be similarly trained. They would have to see who had the better skill.

Malach pinpointed another archer and let loose his last arrow.

He had only been able to make a few along the way. He pulled the arrow from the seat and checked it. It seemed sound, so he notched it and continued scanning the trees. He turned when he heard a hiss and an arrow cut his face.

That was too close.

He had seen the area the arrow had come from and lowered his bow, readying himself. The arrow came out of the tree, and Malach sidestepped and loosed his arrow. It caught the man in the shoulder, and he lost his balance. The mans cry of pain and fear was cut short as his head hit the ground first. Malach was far away, but he could still hear the 'whomp' of the body landing.

A stabbing pain in his thigh drew his attention down to see an arrow protruding from it. He hadn't been fast enough. However, there was no time to dwell on his injury. He spotted an assailant heading for Honora's blind side.

Gritting his teeth, he pulled the arrow from his leg and nocked it, putting it through the heart of the man attacking Honora. He watched Skie rip out the throat of another man who had mistakenly thought she was not a threat. There were only three highwaymen left, and they weren't faring well. Daziar was dueling with two of them while Honora only had one now.

Malach pulled his knife and hurled it at Honora's attacker. It struck him in the neck, and he crumpled like a wet rag. Malach turned to see Daziar decapitate one man with his backswing and the other man decided he didn't want to stay and fight anymore. Malach jumped down from the cart and his injured hip gave way. He landed in a heap, pain ripping through his leg. He saw Daziar pull the knife from his own belt and hurl it at the retreating man. It fell a little short of the mark and got him in his right calf. He put his hands out to stop his fall, and Malach heard a pop as something broke in the man's wrist.

Daziar helped Malach up, and they walked to the fallen highwayman. Daziar pulled the knife out of his calf roughly, causing him to gasp and curse in pain.

"Are there any more of you out there?" Malach demanded.

The man shook his head with a whimper.

"What are you doing this far from a city on a road that has few travelers?" Malach asked.

"We were told that you three would be coming down this road today carrying something extremely valuable. The one who hired us said he would pay one hundred gold coins for the cart and your heads. When we saw you were youths, we thought it would be an easy job." The man started sobbing. "Are you going to kill me, too?"

"Why would someone pay one hundred gold coins for a bear fur?" Honora asked, ignoring the man. "That's the most valuable thing we have with us. Maybe my hand-held mirror?"

The demon blade, Malach thought, but didn't say anything out loud. "I think I'll leave you for the wild animals."

Skie growled for emphasis. The man cowered away from her and then clawed his way off into the woods as fast as he could. They lined the bodies up on one side of the road. Malach sat down as his friends retrieved his arrows. They took the highwaymen's arrows off of them too; they wouldn't need them anymore, and anything else they could use or was of value and left the bodies for the scavengers.

Malach ended up with about thirty arrows. Most were of good quality, but some needed a bit of work. He didn't think he would keep many of them, though. After Honora dressed Malach's wound, he and Daziar, mostly Daziar, were able to pick up the tree enough to slide it out of the road, and they went on their way. They were only a couple of days from the town of Whiteshade, where they would be able to get a healer to check on Malach's leg.

Malach couldn't get the thought of the demon blade out of his head. That many people were dead because the demon wanted this blade back. Maybe he should leave it somewhere. Or maybe he should have given it to the man they let go. He didn't know what to do with the blade, but it was clear the demon wouldn't stop until he got it back.

"Malach, are you alright?" Daziar asked.

"Yeah," Malach said, glancing at his friend. "Yeah, I'm fine."

"You know we didn't have a choice but to kill them, right?" Daziar said, misinterpreting his friend's mood. "They would have killed us for whatever they thought we had. It was self-defense."

"Yeah, I know," Malach said and then thought to himself. *That not what's bothering me.*

Honora hadn't said a word since they left and suddenly burst into tears. Malach moved over to her and put an arm around her shoulders. Malach didn't think she had actually killed any of the highwaymen, but the experience was still traumatizing.

Malach had been in so many life-threatening situations, it didn't faze him as much. He had shed tears over his first brush with death and had sobbed for days after he killed a man trying to murder him for his coin pouch. Honora, he was pretty sure, had never had to hit someone outside of sparing practice, let alone fight for her life.

"Sorry, I slapped you," he said quietly. "I just knew you wouldn't have moved without something shocking you back to reality."

She didn't say anything.

"It's alright to be upset. Just remember, there was nothing else you could have done," he tried again. "They would have killed us if we didn't fight back."

"I know," she said through her tears.

"I know that doesn't make it easier."

"I'm not upset about the fight," she said, and Malach looked down at her face, confused. "I couldn't finish it."

That didn't help Malach's confusion at all.

"Finish what?" Malach asked.

"I couldn't kill him." She started sobbing again. "You and Daziar were so brave, and I couldn't even kill one man. I was useless."

"That's nothing to be ashamed of," Malach said, pulling her close again. "There isn't anything wrong with not being able to kill a man. In fact, I would say that is a good virtue to have. Once you have killed, you can't go back. But you *weren't* useless."

Honora pulled away to peer up at him. "You held a man at bay long enough for Daz and me to survive and help. If you haven't held him off, Daz would have been facing too many enemies for him to survive. I would have been too busy with the archers to help and one, both, or all three of us, could be dead right now. I'm glad you were there."

"Really?"

"Really!" Daziar cut in, having heard most of what had been said. "I've sparred with three opponents before, but without much success. And four would have overwhelmed me quickly if they were any good. You did well, Honora."

"Alright," she said in a small voice, sounding a little more convinced. "I guess I did fine for my first battle." She smiled at the boys. "Thanks for cheering me up."

"Anytime," Daziar said, turning back to the road. Malach took his arm back and scooted to the other side of the cart, facing her.

They sat in silence for a while and then Daziar stopped the cart. "Well, I'm hungry, and we need to get cleaned up."

Malach snapped out of his thoughts and realized he could hear running water. Daziar had parked the cart by the Pangor River, where they could wash the gore off themselves and their clothes. They got out and let Honora wash first, giving her privacy.

While they waited, they started the fire and got the meat cooking. When Honora returned, she was in a fresh set of clothes and was shivering slightly. She warmed herself by the fire, wringing the water out of her hair. She said she would take over the cooking, and the two boys went to the stream to wash off. When they got back, the three ate in silence and packed up the things they had pulled out. They hung their wet clothes on the side of the cart to dry.

The rest of the day they spent in silence. Each one left to their own thoughts, taking turns driving. Malach kept thinking about what to do with the demon blade. He went to sleep that night with the blade under his pillow, still unsure of what he should do with it.

Amara awoke, still bouncing along on the horse. She had gotten a good look at the horse once the sun had come up and found that he was a gelding. She decided his name would be Shasta. He was a beautiful mixture of black and white. His coat was like spun black silk with a beautiful blanket of white dappling across his rump. He had a white blaze between his eyes on his otherwise black face. Even his fetlocks and forelock were a beautiful blend of black and white.

She'd always loved horses, even though she had little experience with them. She thought they were beautiful and majestic. A couple of years ago, Lawdel had taught her the basics of riding. Since then, however, she hadn't been up on a horse. She never realized how bad hours of riding could hurt. Everything hurt; her chest, her butt, her legs. Everything. Shasta seemed so smooth when she first started riding him, but as the long hours wore on, every little movement the horse made under her hurt.

She had ridden through the night and all day. Now the sun was falling, and she needed to get a shelter started. She had never been out of the city, so she wasn't really sure how to do that. She slowed the horse to a walk until she found a clearing.

She slid down from Shasta, but as soon as her weight hit her legs, they collapsed under her and she crumped into a heap. Forcing her body to move, she picked herself up off the ground and trudged over to the flattest spot in the clearing. She put her bed roll there and tied up the horse just a little way off. She tried to set up a lean-to but couldn't get it to stay upright. Finally, she got the main support sticks to stay, but whenever she put branches on them, they would cave in. After what felt like the hundredth attempt, she gave up and used the wood to make a fire. She cooked, ate, and laid down on her bedroll. Despite her body throbbing, she fell asleep within seconds of laying down.

She was awakened by the rain. It was already pouring, and she was soaked and shivering. With no shelter and the fire already out, she moved her bedding and the food sacks close to a tree to keep them as dry as possible. She sat down next to them, where she passed the rest of the night. She passed out from sheer exhaustion just before dawn, but the rain still hadn't let up.

When she woke again, the rain had slowed, but there was still a steady drizzle coming down. She put the saddlebags back on Shasta and laid the wet bedding over the animal. Taking a running leap, she managed to pull herself up onto the horse's back. She started to follow the road again, but only a few hours later, she passed out once again on the back of her horse.

She woke up hours later, but she couldn't really tell just how long she had been asleep. Shasta was off the road a little way, in a clearing, grazing, and they didn't seem to be much farther down the road than when she had fallen asleep. She directed the horse back on to the road. A breeze from the north cut through her wet clothes like ice stabbing her heart. She pulled her cloak out and put it on, but it didn't help much as it, too, was dripping. It kept some of the wind off of her skin, nonetheless, and the violence of her shivers lessened. The weather was turning colder the farther she traveled away from the sea. She had never felt this cold before and she didn't have any clothes that would keep her warm. That would be her first purchase in Newaught. Warm clothes.

Days passed in the same way: riding, eating, sleeping, and hurting. She had to get off the horse a lot due to the chafing of her legs. She was afraid if she rode much more, she would start bleeding.

More than a week passed, and she had no clue how close she was to Newaught. All she knew was everything hurt, and she was running out of food. She dismounted to let her body rest, but instead of a controlled slide, she slipped off due to her stiff muscles. She landed hard on her back and she laid there for a little while, catching her breath.

Luckily, she had landed on a bed of moss, which cushioned her fall somewhat. She was still on the road, but it had descended into a marshy area without her realizing it. The road seemed to be well traveled, but the moss was battling to take it over. To her left, there were still trees, but they were more sparse than only a half mile back. To her right was the road descended into a bog. Fog hung just above the water there, and the trees that were growing out of the water had wide bases. It looked like their root system was showing just above the water. Some of those roots looked like legs, and others were so close together they more resembled a skirt around the tree. It was a little eerie, and she kept the horse between her and the marsh.

She walked like that for a while, letting her body rest from the constant bumping and rubbing. Just as she was about to jump back on Shasta when she heard a splash come from the marsh. She peered around the horse to see if she could locate where the disturbance came from. She couldn't see anything in the water, but the ripples betrayed whatever had caused them. Whatever it was, it had been real. She hadn't just imagined it.

Probably just a fish, she thought to herself and then said aloud, "Amara, you're being ridiculous. There is nothing out there to be afraid of and you are jumping at nothing."
The bog exploded and showered her and Shasta with gallons of the cold, putrid water. She looked up at a monster emerging from the bog. It was many times her height in length, with rows of sharp teeth in a snout that tapered to a point. It could almost swallow her whole if it wanted to, and the horse would have

made a good meal for it. She had heard about these monsters. They grew until they died, and some people had claimed to see one larger than buildings.

She tried to get up on Shasta and failed. The monster lunged at them on its four stubby legs. Although the legs were short and stout for its body, it was surprisingly agile on them. She lost her hold on the reins as the horse bolted for safety. She watched the horse take off at a gallop, and he would soon be lost to her.

She turned to see the monster bearing down on her, mouth agape. Ignoring her body's protests, she dove to the side, rolling out of the way just as the beast's jaws closed. She ran despite the pain, staying just ahead of the monster, but only just. It would be on her in a couple more seconds and she would be ripped to shreds by those teeth. She reached up for a low hanging tree branch and let her momentum carry her into the tree.

She climbed as quickly as she could, but almost lost her footing when the thing slammed into the tree. She heard a large crack from the somewhat small tree trunk, but it held, for now. Regaining her balance, she continued her climb to safety. The tree shook violently as the beast rammed into the tree again.

She got her first look full look at the monster from above. Scales ran the length of its body and she could barely tell where head turned into body and body into tail. The tail itself could have bludgeoned her to death. As thick as a log, it looked powerful enough to send her flying if she found herself in its path. There was no weak point in its scaly armor that she could see.

It stopped backing up and charged again. The tree fractured with the impact and it began to lean. One more hit and it would fall. She spun, eye searching wildly for someway out. The tree was about thirty feet tall and she was almost at the top. The closest tree was about twenty feet away. There was no way she would be able to jump that far. The beast was backing up for a final run. When it charged forward, she timed her jump and leapt into thin air. The alligator hit the tree, and it started to topple, but Amara had landed on its back. She drove one of her knives down as she landed, and the force of her weight snapped it at the hilt. The blade bounced off the beast's armored skin and didn't even leave a discernable scratch.

The beast bucked and spun, trying to throw her off. She held on for dear life, not knowing what else to do. Soon this thing would shake her off and eat her alive, and there wasn't anything she could do about it.

A memory hit her. The two thieves were talking while she was practicing her eavesdropping. She had listened intently as if they were saying extremely important things so that she could return to Lawdel and tell him what she had heard.

They had been talking about this thing, hadn't they? She searched the memory, trying to come up with some weakness. Someone had been eaten? No, they had suspected the report of the giant beast was just the cover for another thief killing him. However, they had said something about this thing she needed to remember. Something on its head?

"You know how they say you have to kill one of those creatures, right?" the one had asked.

"No, I wasn't sure you could kill one," the other replied.

"There is one spot on their head that is softer than the rest,"

Amara snapped back to reality. Her trip into her memory had taken only moments. She prayed with all her being to anything who might listen that they had been correct in their musings. She started climbing up the beast's back. Inch by inch, careful not to lose her grip, for that would mean certain death, she made it to the base of the creature's skull and pushed around on its head until she felt a small give where there was no bone. She took out a second knife and waited for the beast to pause in its thrashing. After what seemed like an eternity, it did, and she plunged the knife as hard as she could into its head. The knife went in to the hilt.

The beast roared and rolled, crushing Amara into the earth that had been churned to mud under its claws. It came up and stumbled. It took a step toward her and then crashed down right in front of her. She pulled herself from the sucking mud and scrambled back on all fours, putting as much distance between her and the creature as she could. Afraid it would get back up and come after her, she only stopped when her back hit a tree trunk.

A few silent, still moments passed. The monster didn't move.

She stood, covered in mud, using the tree to support her still shaking legs. She wobbled over to the beast, ready to run if it so much as twitched. A limb from the fallen tree stuck out of the mud not far from the beast and she picked it up. She poked the creature's scales, no movement. Emboldened by its lack of reaction, she jammed it into the beast's eye, which was still open but not moving. No response. It was dead.

Her legs gave out on her and she collapsed, drained of any energy. She laughed. She laughed so hard her already aching lungs felt like they would split. The kind of laugh only extreme relief produced. She didn't know why she was laughing but, she couldn't help it.

After a few moments of laying there, she caught her breath. Sitting up, she turned toward the beast again. She had killed this enormous monster. Sure, she had a few bruises and scrapes, but she had killed it. With effort, she climbed to her feet and moved to the beast. The top of its head was high enough she couldn't get a good look and the place the place would have entered. She climbed up on the monster and it didn't take her long to find the wound still oozing blood lethargically. Something glint in the wound. She pulled the small puncture apart and managed to fit her hand into it. Her fingers curled around the handle of her knife and she pulled it free.

I didn't kill it, she realized in a moment of sober clarity. She had stabbed it, but not deep enough. When the monster rolled, it must have driven the knife in farther. Dumb luck had saved her.

She slid down off the creature and decided she was going to take a trophy. She worked at pulling a tooth out of the creature's mouth and, after using her knife and a couple of stout sticks, she managed to pull one free. It was almost as large as her entire hand.

She took stock of her surroundings and realized the rest of her things were on Shasta, who had bolted at the first sight of the monster. She sighed and walked in the direction she last spotted the horse running away. It took her the rest of the day to track and find him. She wasn't a very good tracker and lost the trail often, but he seemed to mostly follow the road. The gelding wandered off of it here and there but always would return to the road, eventually. She finally found him off the road a little way in a meadow, grazing. He lifted his head and almost took off again when he caught sight of her. His nostrils flared and the whites of his eyes were noticeable at their edges. She was still covered in the creature's blood, and the smell was upsetting him. She found a small stream and washed off the blood. Only then did Shasta allow her to come close to him.

Once she had caught him and mounted, he calmed down and allowed her to steer him back toward the road. She rode another few miles until she was clear of the bog and found a spot to camp. After another few hours, she had successfully created a lean-to shelter and had a fire going. She had learned a lot on her journey so far, but she hoped it was coming to an end. She wasn't sure she could last much longer in these conditions. Her dwindling supplies spoke to how little time she had until she would be in trouble. She would need to ration her food until she made it to Newaught. It had been a whole day since she had eaten. She still wasn't used to having all the food she needed, so rationing it didn't bother her too much.

Even though she was exhausted, and had managed to build some semblance of a shelter, she couldn't fall asleep for several hours. She kept hearing the sounds of the night and couldn't help but wonder what other monsters were out there waiting to take their chance to kill and eat her. The uneasy feeling of being watched also never left her. She told herself she was just being jumpy because of the attack earlier that day, but it didn't do much to soothe her nerves.

Finally, after many hours, she fell into a fitful sleep. She tossed and turned most of the night, dreaming of a large, misshapen creature raising from the swamp and dragging her back in with it. Just before the sun came up, she woke to a man sitting at the edge of her campfire. He had lit it and was warming himself by it. He seemed larger than most, and his back had the appearance of a permanent hunch, but he didn't appear to have any weapons on him, and she didn't think he meant her any harm outright. Besides, if he had wanted to hurt her, he could have done that easily while she was asleep. The man was wearing a thick cloak that covered most of his features, with the hood drawn up to obscure his face. Most likely, the man was a hermit of some type, just in need of a little warmth and maybe some food. She sat up on her bedroll and the hermit spoke.

"Good, you are awake," The man had a deep, gravelly voice. His voice was quiet now, but she could tell this man's voice could boom and echo if he wished it.

"Yes, I am," she said cautiously. "Could I ask who you are?"

"I saw you kill that monster yesterday," he said, ignoring her question. "Impressive."

"Thank you. What do you want?" she asked bluntly, still wary of the stranger.

"You, my dear," he said, his voice rumbling. "I need someone like you in Newaught. I need someone smart and cunning and strong. And *you* are that person."

"That doesn't answer my question," she said. Her gut twisted. This man was not to be trusted. "What exactly do you want me to do in Newaught?"

"All I want is information," he said innocently, almost like he was hurt that she wouldn't trust him. "I just need some information about people in the city and some of the inner workings of certain government bodies. I thought you might be able to help, since you are a member of The Shadows. Usually, people like you pick up information quite valuable to the right person."

"I think you better speak to the Master in Newaught. He would be able to get you the information you need. He'd have more people to gain information from and he would make you a fair deal for it," she replied.

She didn't like this man. Also, she didn't want to overstep her authority in the Shadows. That could jeopardize her position before she even started.

"A very good idea, but..." he let the word hang in the air for a second. "I don't want just anyone getting the information. There are too many hands in the pot if I did it your way. I just need one skilled person to find out what I want. Think of it as a side job. Something you would do for me outside of the Shadows. I would pay handsomely for it."

"What does an old hermit like you want with that kind of information? Newaught is days from here." She couldn't think of how to get out if this. She didn't want to work for this man. He put her on edge and made her stomach twist uncomfortably.

"Dear, little Amara," the man purred.

She shivered. He knew her name.

"You are closer to your journey's end than you think," he told her and then continued.

"I am not always in one spot. I have many things I must do, and such information would be of great value to me. Do not think me a shut-in just because we did not meet on the bustling streets of Caister. Do we have a deal?"

"I will have to talk with the Master at Newaught. I won't leave him out of the loop," she said defiantly.

"Then I have no need of you." From underneath his cloak, he produced a sword. The blade was black and seemed to grow longer, even as he held it up. He was up and closed the distance faster than she could blink. Then her feet were off the ground. One hand clamped down on her throat, holding her against a tree and the other holding the sword up to her throat.

"Last chance, little one," he growled, his voice turning rough and menacing. "You get paid for discreet information or you can die in the woods alone, and I'll find someone else."

Amara's heart was pounding, and she couldn't breathe. She tried to speak, and only a small gurgle passed her lips. She was sure she was going to die, and no one would ever find her. Staring into the man's eyes, she only saw pure evil reflected there. They were bright, almost glowing red. She was going to die by the hand of the devil himself. The man let her down, and she gasped for air, but he didn't let her go. The sword was still against her throat.

"So, what is it going to be?" he asked.

"I'll do it," she gasped. She couldn't get the words out fast enough. "Whatever you want me to find out, I will."

"Good." He let go of her throat and her knees buckled under her. "Here is your first payment." He tossed a small coin purse down beside her. "Thirty pieces of silver. There will be much more in it for you later. You may not see me for a while, but I will be watching. And I shouldn't have to warn you about double-crossing me. You won't like the outcome."

She watched the man's feet walk away. Just outside the firelight, he seemed to disappear into the trees. The last thing Amara remembered was the world going sideways before the darkness closed in on her.

Chapter 8

The rest of the trip to Newaught had gone by without any more problems. Malach's thigh was all but healed under Honora's watchful eye. The three were now looking at the outer walls of the city of Newaught. They were still a way away, but they could already see the massive city and its walls. They could see people going in and out of the main gate, and they looked like ants. The doors themselves, however, looked almost big enough for them to walk through now.

"Do you see how big the city is?" Honora asked, excitement evident in her voice. "Can you imagine all the people living here?" She squealed, and all but jumped up and down in her seat.

"Can you imagine the things we are going to experience?" Daziar was right there with her. "The new weapons we haven't seen and the new technology they might have come up with? I heard they had running water in their homes and an outhouse *in* the house. And when you pull a rope, it sends the waste out of the house, so you don't have to smell it!"

Malach glanced at Skie, and they traded a nervous look. Both of them lacked enthusiasm for the bustling metropolis. They preferred the wilderness. Malach only hoped he could still hunt with Skie, and they could at least be away from the city for most of the day. Malach thought he might go insane if he had to spend his whole day in the large crowds.

As they got closer, the sheer size of the walls and gates staggered him. He had to crane his neck up to see the top of them. They fell in line with the other carts waiting to enter the city and after what seemed like an eternity to Honora and Daziar, but only a few moments to Malach, they were at the gate. One guard came up to the cart. He looked bored and tired.

"Papers." He held out his hand, not even looking at them.

Honora looked at Daziar, confused. "Papers?" she whispered to him. He just shrugged.

The guard finally took stock of them. "Papers, please," he repeated, giving them a questioning look.

"We don't have any papers, sir," Malach explained from the back. "We are on our journey from Brightwood."

"Oh, very well," the guard said. "You will have to take your cart over there and walk into the guardhouse. There is a secretary there that will help you with your papers. Take a number and sit down. She will give you more instructions once you are finished with that."

"Thank you, sir," Malach said politely. Skie sat up next to Malach and the guard jumped back in fright, pulling his sword. That caused the rest of the guards to draw their weapons and advance.

"You have a wolf in your cart!" The first guard exclaimed and one of the other guards took aim with his crossbow.

"Wait!" Malach shouted. "She's trained! She's tame!"

Skie raised her hackles and jumped to her feet, ready to throw herself at the guards were threatening her. Malach popped her on the nose and she looked at him, confused and maybe a little hurt.

"No!" He said sternly. She cocked her head at him but sat back down in the cart. Malach turned to the guards. "See, she wouldn't hurt anyone. I promise. I've had her since I was sixteen."

The guards didn't budge, but the one with the crossbow shifted his finger off the trigger. "That's a wolf, son. They can't be trained to follow anyone or to be anything but what they are. One day, that thing is going to turn on you or someone else and kill them."

"I've had her for five years and she has never hurt anyone. In fact, she has saved my life more times than I can count. She won't hurt anyone that doesn't try to hurt her," Malach defended Skie. He put his hand on her head and ruffled her ears. "This wolf is tame. Please come up and pet her. See for yourself."

The guard warily inched forward and put his hand out to touch Skie. When his hand got close, she licked it, causing the guard to jump back again. The other guards laughed uproariously, and the first guard turned red. He marched back up to the cart and put out his hand again, petting Skie. She let him, and then licked him in the face.

"Fine, but you need a permit for her since she is. . ." the guard paused and then corrected himself, "was a wild animal. You can get it at the same place you get your papers."

The guards put away their weapons and motioned the cart to the side. Daziar pulled it over where he had indicated and they all piled out. Malach and Honora went inside and picked up three cards that had numbers on them. The cards were well worn, and one was falling apart. Malach could barely tell which number it was anymore. They took their seats and Daziar joined them after he had taken care of the two mules and Honora's horse. They waited for what felt like an eternity. As It turned out, this was the place everyone outside of the city came if they needed any permits for anything, and there were many people in front of them.

Malach tapped on a man's shoulder that was sitting in front of him. "Does this normally take this long?"

"Yep," the man responded. "In fact, it's a slow day. Usually, there are a lot more people here. But this is the smallest office in the whole city. You would have been better off going into the city and sitting there. Though, with travel included, it still sometimes takes just as long, but at least you're moving for part of it."

"They wouldn't let us in the city since we don't have papers, so I guess we are stuck," Malach explained.

The man just shrugged and turned back around.

Malach slumped back in his seat and sighed. After another hour, Daziar's number was called. He walked up to the counter and went through the process of getting his papers, then Honora, and finally, it was Malach's turn. He and Skie got up and moved to the front, and the receptionist peered down at Skie over the counter. Malach watched her throat constricted tightly, the muscles tensing as her Adam's apple bobbed up and down a couple times.

"Don't worry; she's tame," Malach reassured her.

"She's beautiful," the lady coughed and took a drink of water from a cup on the counter. "And huge."

"Thank you," Malach said politely. "I guess I need papers for me and a permit to have her?" He motioned to Skie. "They told me I could do both here."

"Oh, yes, yes!" The woman finally pried her eyes off of Skie.

She went through a series of questions which Malach answered to the best of his knowledge, although he had no idea what hour he had been born or things of that nature. Once they were done with his papers, they moved on to Skie.

"How old is she?" The lady asked.

"I'm not sure. I found her in the woods and nursed her to health, but she was already fully grown by that time," He answered.

"Alright, how long have you had her?" She asked.

"About five years."

"So, if you have to guess, would you say she is over or under ten years old?"

Malach thought about that for a moment. "Just under. She might have been three or four when I found her, but I have no way of knowing."

"Alright, to your knowledge, has she. . ." the receptionist lowered her voice and glanced at Skie, "killed anyone?"

"Yes, she has." It was Malach's turn to be nervous. He was afraid that they wouldn't let Skie in if they knew, but he didn't want to lie. "But it was only in self-defense or in my defense," he added quickly.

The lady looked at Malach. "I can't let her into the city if she has. . ." the receptionist paused again, not wanting to say the word killed, "done things like that."

She must have lived her whole life in a city. Maybe even this one, Malach thought. She probably has never had to kill or even hurt anyone.

The receptionist looked at Malach pointedly. "So, I will ask again. Has she ever killed anyone?"

"Um, no?" Malach said, still a little unsure if she wanted him to lie or not.

"Good," she replied and picked up the stack of forms she had been filling out before Malach could change his mind. "Then I will sign the permit for her to live with you in the city." The receptionist signed her name and made Malach sign his and handed him the papers. "Now, since you are on your journey, you need to report to the city square. There is a building there that will give you the test to tell you what job you will have. It's too late tonight to take the test. The facility will be closed. I would suggest you get a room at one of the inns closer to the center of town. They are a little more expensive, but a lot less dangerous."

"Alright, thanks for the information and the tip," Malach took his papers and walked out to the cart. The sun was just going down and Honora and Daziar were waiting by Celewen and the mules.

"Did you have any trouble getting a permit for Skie?" Honora asked.

"None, but that was because the receptionist was very understanding. It could have been a lot harder," Malach told her. "She told me we don't have time to test for our jobs today and that we ought to get an inn closer to the center of town."

"She told us the same," Daziar agreed, but shuffled his feet and didn't look at either of them. "I will admit, I have very little money right now. The only money I have has to be for food for the next week."

"I've already told you I would take care of it," Honora said. "You know, just because I'm a woman doesn't mean I can't take care of you."

"I just don't want to be in debt to you," Daziar said.

"But you don't mind being in debt to Malach?" Honora asked.

"Well, I know I will see him every day so I can pay him back easier," Daziar lied. Malach knew he really didn't like taking money from anyone, but especially not Honora. He had had a crush on her for a long time, and he hated taking anything from her. Something about his code.

Malach moved in between the two. "Daz has a point. I can cover his room for the night, and we can find out our job and housing situation tomorrow. From there, we can figure it out."

"Malach, do *you* have enough money to cover that?" Honora asked. "I know you have been working most of your life, but you aren't rich either."

"Don't worry, I have plenty of money for the next few days, and by then I can sell the furs I have and make enough money until I get my first payment," Malach explained, and he did have enough.

With the money he would get from the bear fur, he probably could pay for him and Daziar for two or three weeks, if the prices were the same as Brightwood.

"Fine." She leaned around Malach and wagged a finger at Daziar. "One of these days you will let me pay for you when you need it."

"Not if I can help it," he countered.

"Alright you two, let's get going before they close the gate," Malach mediated again. "I'm sure that will be happening soon, and we need to get a room for the night."

Malach was right. Before they were out of sight of the gate, the guards started closing them. The massive doors took almost a full minute to swing shut. They closed with a boom that could be heard throughout the city. There were several more muffled booms from different directions, which must have been the other gates closing. It took them almost a full hour, by the clock tower, to move through the city to the town square and they had to stop several times to ask for direction to make sure they were still on track. Honora took that time to educate Malach and Daziar on how to tell time by the clock and many more useless facts about how a clock worked. Skie was on edge the whole time, and

Malach couldn't blame her. She hated going into Brightwood and that was a fraction of the size of Newaught. They could get lost here and not find their way out for days.

The buildings got taller and taller as they moved toward the center of the city. This was probably because the closer they got to the center, the richer the people got. Also, it proved to be a good tactical advantage if an army got past the gates. The archers could line the roofs and shoot down on the enemies without worrying about their own men getting in the way.

They made it to the town square and located the building they would need to go to in the morning. Then they worked their way back a few blocks and found a nice, lively inn. Malach and Honora went in while Daziar stayed with the cart.

They opened the inn door and were greeted by raucous laughter. The atmosphere of the inn was excited and full of energy. It seemed clean, and the patrons were well-dressed. Even though everyone was drinking and there was a lot of activity, no one was mad or brawling. Malach liked the place even though he didn't enjoy crowds. They walked up to the counter, and the innkeeper came up to them, polishing a wooden tankard.

"Hello, friends!" he boomed over the sounds of everything else. "Do you need food and lodging for the night?"

"Yes, please," Malach said and started to ask for two rooms, but the big man cut him off.

"One room and a table coming right up!" The man hustled off.

Malach looked at Honora. She was blushing fiercely, and he laughed. "I believe he thinks we are a couple." Malach could swear her cheeks got even redder.

When the innkeeper came back, Malach explained their situation and got the misunderstanding straightened out. The innkeeper sent a stable hand out to get the animals and cart and take care of them. They paid a silver coin each for the rooms, meal, and the animals to be taken care of, which Malach thought was a fair deal. The innkeeper was reluctant to let Skie in at first, but when Malach showed him the permit, he allowed it, though he still didn't like the idea.

They stayed in the common room for their meal, listening to the music and watching the cards being played from a distance. They didn't recognize any of the games, but a few of the songs they knew from Brightwood. After a while, they retired to their rooms. Malach and Daziar shared one while Honora got her own.

There was only one bed in the boys' room, and Daziar volunteered to take the floor. The bed probably wasn't much better, however. The mattress was so flat, Malach was practically sleeping on the board, but with his bedroll down, it wasn't the worst he had slept on. All of their things had been brought up to the rooms for them, and Malach pulled out the bundle that had the demon blade in it and used it as a pillow. He had been sleeping on it since the highwaymen had attacked them on the road. He didn't want anyone getting to it before he had figured out what to do with the thing. At least that's what he told himself. Really, he liked having it close by. It gave him a sense of security. Also, when it was near, he didn't have the nightmares. Maybe there was something more to the blade, like Togan had said. He didn't think it was evil, however. If it were evil, wouldn't it cause him to have worse dreams? Maybe it was just a tool. The demons were once angels, right? So, what was the difference between an angel blade and a demon blade, except the one who wielded it?

Malach thought about all these things for what felt like the hundredth time, but he still couldn't fully convince himself his argument was the right one. If only he had someone to guide him, someone who would know. Like an actual angel. If only they were still around, he could seek one of them out and get answers.

That's just wishful thinking, he thought to himself, rolling onto his side. *The demons and angels probably killed each other off and there is only the one demon left who won. If God is real, that demon might have killed him too, for all we know. Even if God's still around, he doesn't seem to care about any of us. He would have stopped the war long ago if he did.* And with that thought, Malach fell asleep.

He woke up suddenly. It felt like no time had passed. It was still dark, and he couldn't see anything in the room at the inn. Strangely, though, he didn't hear any of the noises of the city.

It must be early morning, he thought.

He realized he was not lying in the bed in the inn. But it didn't feel like the wood floor either. He put his hand down on the surface but couldn't really make out what he was feeling. It was something solid, but also felt like nothing. He looked behind him and lying on the "not floor" was the demon blade, unwrapped and naked. It almost glowed, but with a darkness that didn't look like anything Malach had ever seen. He started to pick it up, and it pulsed red, starting at the bottom of the hilt and traveling up to the tip of the blade. He jumped back, scrambling away on all fours.

"Malach!" a voice boomed. It sounded like it was coming from all around him and it echoed as if they were in a large cavern. It was deafening and made him wince. He felt a headache coming on.

What is going on? Malach wondered. *Who is calling my name and where am I?*

"Malach," the same voice called, but much quieter. It didn't echo as much, and Malach pinpointed a direction the voice was coming from. It was the blade! No, not the blade. The voice came from the opposite side of the blade. A man materialized out of the darkness and walked up to the blade. He was tall and gaunt, like he hadn't eaten in a while. Scars marred his face, arms, and bare chest. It appeared as if he had wounds from many years of torture. His face was so thin that his eyes were sunken, and his cheekbones looked like they might push through his skin if too much pressure was applied. The man didn't reach out or pick up the blade. But just gazed down at it for a moment. Then the man looked up and focused on Malach.

"Malach," he said politely. He had a pleasant voice, rich and deep. It was in stark contrast to the way he looked.

"You are Malach, correct?"

"Y-yes," Malach stammered.

He thought he was in pitch darkness, but he could see the man clearly. He looked down at himself and he could see himself clearly; he could see the blade clearly. Nothing made sense to him.

"Where am I?" he asked, looking back up at the man.

"The inn where you purchased a room for the night. You haven't moved more than a few inches from when you fell asleep, and I believe that's because you were getting more comfortable," the man said calmly.

"Obviously we are not at the inn." Malach gestured to their surroundings. "But we can move on to the next question. Who are you?"

"You know who I am," the man stated cryptically. "I've been with you for some time now."

"God?" Malach asked skeptically.

"Of course not," the man chuckled. "I'm a little more tangible than that." The man motioned to the blade sitting on the "not floor" between them.

"You are the demon's blade?" Malach exclaimed.

"Got it on the second guess," the man said. "I'm impressed. Now I have a question for you. Who are you that you can wield me?"

Malach was confused. "What do you mean? Anyone can pick up a sword and swing it. It doesn't take anyone special."

"You are correct, but most people can't change my form." The man narrowed his eyes and added. "But you can. So, who are you?"

Malach decided the truth was probably the best policy when stranded in an unknown place with a blade that had taken the shape of a man.

"I'm not sure. I've guessed by now I have demon blood in me, but I don't know my lineage. My parents died when I was young."

"I see. Well, I would say you were a close descendent of one then," the man said thoughtfully.

"Why would you think that?" Malach asked, a little alarmed.

"Because you can wield me so effortlessly," the man answered, as if it were obvious. "You have to be at least third generation, if not second. Even then, some second generations couldn't wield a blade like myself as effortlessly as you do. But I'm thinking out loud. We ought to get to know one another since we hopefully will be spending many battles together." The man sat down in front of the blade, crossing his legs and motioning for Malach to do that same.

"Wait just a minute. You're saying that I don't just have demon blood in me, but that either one of my parents or grandparents was the demon?" Malach asked incredulously.

He couldn't believe that. His parents would have told him. His father would have told him. His father told him everything. Except for his past. Malach more fell than sat, his knees buckling from the realization that his grandfather or grandmother was a demon. Maybe even the demon that tried to kill him.

"That's correct," the man said, still sitting there, looking at Malach curiously. "Are you alright? You look white as a sheet."

"Fine," Malach said, preoccupied with his thoughts. "So, where are we at the moment?"

"I told you, the same place you have always been," the man said cryptically.

"But what is this place?" Malach asked again, starting to get frustrated with the man and gesturing to the surrounding darkness.

"Oh, you mean this?" the man said, raising both arms and looking around them. "This is your mind!" The man seemed to be excited. "And what a great mind it is, I might add. Though right now it is a bit boring since you're asleep and not dreaming anything. Although, you might consider this a dream, since you're seeing things while you're asleep. But I digress."

"My mind?" Malach exclaimed in alarm. "Then that means you can read my mind?"

"Yes," the man said matter-of-factly, letting his arms drop. "I can read it as long as I am in close proximity to you. But don't worry, I can't take control of your actions or change your thoughts or anything crazy like that."

"So, what can you do?" Malach asked cautiously. He was already considering how to rid himself of the blade in case it turned out it was evil. Sink it in a lake? Bury it somewhere on the ground? Then the thought occurred to him the blade might be hearing his thoughts even now, and he tried to wipe them away.

But if the blade was hearing him, he made no indication of it. Instead, he answered Malach's spoken question. "I can talk to you. Like this, or in your mind when you are awake. Though, I thought this might be a better first meeting than just talking to you in your head. I've heard some people have thought they were going crazy when that had been tried in the past."

He seems to like to talk a lot, but doesn't seem to say much, Malach thought.

"Well, when you haven't talked to anyone but a demon in more than four hundred years, you would want to talk a lot, too." The man said, obviously hearing what Malach was thinking.

"Sorry," Malach apologized. "Four hundred years?"

"Yes, before that I was owned by Ariel, the angel who was, at the time, charged by God with dominion over the earth. He was defeated by the demon who has owned me until you took me from him, though I don't believe Ariel died at that time. The demon was a dreadful monster and wielded me against many righteous men and angels. I am ashamed of what I was made to do." The man hung his head. "I am sorry for that nasty cut I gave you as well. I'm glad you are not hurt anymore and that you have liberated me from that monster. I can see there is righteousness in your heart, even though you still are undecided what side you will fight for."

"Umm, apology accepted, you're welcome, and no I haven't, but I'm not sure it matters since there has been peace for just under two thousand years. The demon I fought was the first demon or angel to be seen recently." Malach's head was spinning with the information and implications thrown his way in such a short time. The demon blade was not a demon blade at all. It was an angel blade. It could talk through the wielder's mind any time it wanted. It could read the wielder's thoughts anytime it wanted. Too many things to think about.

"That's simply not true!" the man exclaimed, aghast. "The war has been raging even more fiercely the past two thousand years than ever before. Many angels have lost their lives and many demons have been slain. I hear tell one of the archangels has been captured, though I don't know which one. As for the sightings, do you think anyone will hear about your sighting? How many others do you think have seen demons or angels and reported it only to get laughed at or mocked? Any reports have been swept under the rug, and if the bearer of the news persisted, they were cast aside as well." The man stopped, out of breath.

Could you really get out of breath in my mind? Malach wondered briefly.

"I hadn't thought of that," Malach realized out loud. "There could be many more sightings, but the leaders could have been too scared or too proud to allow the news to get out."

"Exactly!" the man said. "The war is still raging. Though, you are right, most of it has been in the shadows. The demons want it that way to lull you humans into indecision and the angels aren't strong enough to fight a full-blown war, but it's coming again, and these years are the most important in our history. Just look at Newaught. It is the largest city in the known earth. That means that there are more undecided people than people on the two sides of this war. Whoever can sway this city will win the war."

"How do you know all of this?" Malach asked. "I mean, I can't image the demon who wielded you would let you in on this information knowing you were still loyal to the angels."

The man sighed, "No, he didn't, and I paid for every bit of information I gleaned from him." The man gestured to his scars. "I didn't use to look like this." The man looked down, sadness in his voice. "I used to be proud and magnificent. That demon pried my armor off, starved me, and beat me down. But I survived. Thank you again for taking me from him. I don't know how much longer I would have lasted."

"So, did you want me to get you back to the angels?" Malach asked, not knowing what else to say. "I mean, I don't know how to find one, but I'm willing to try, if you want."

"A kind offer, but I don't know if they would take me back. Many of my kind turned when the angels fell, and many more over the years. They would put me in quarantine for many years until they were sure that I was safe to wield again. I think I could do more good staying with you if you would have me?"

"Well, I haven't fully decided yet. You are a great weapon and have served me well so far, but I didn't know there was a mind *inside* the blade. That changes a lot. I will have to think about it," Malach said warily.

He didn't know if this blade was telling him the full truth or simply lying to gain his trust. He wouldn't put his full faith in it for now. Better to stay cautious and alive than fall into a trap and be killed.

"What is your name?" Malach asked, realizing it was never mentioned.

"Reckoning," The man responded. "The demon called me Angel Cleaver. I hated that name, though."

"Reckoning it is then," Malach said, noting that sadness that had once again crept into Reckoning's voice.

"Thank you," Reckoning said and sounded like he meant it. "For now, you have a long day tomorrow full of tests and a new job, if I'm not mistaken. And whereas you are resting in this state, you won't wake up fully restored if you stay like this all night. It would feel more like a nap than a full night's rest. We can pick up where we left off tomorrow night, or if you have any needs during the day, as long as I am with you, I am only a thought away."

"I would ask you to stay out of my thoughts for now," Malach said sternly. "It's a bit unnerving knowing someone is listening to your every thought."

"Oh yes, that's fine. I will be listening for my name only," Reckoning said, as if he hadn't thought Malach would care if he was in his mind or not. "And tomorrow night, we will start your mental training so you can block me or know when I am in your mind. That would help put you at ease, would it not?"

"Yes," Malach affirmed. "That would go a long way to helping me trust you. Thank you."

Reckoning stood, and Malach could see a fire in his eyes now. Something that hadn't been there before. Hope. Reckoning turned and walked away, his voice fading as he went. "Remember, I am always one thought away."

Chapter 9

Malach actually woke this time. Sitting up in the inn's bed, looking around the room. It was just before sunrise, but after light started creeping into the world. Malach got out of bed, careful not to wake Daziar. He was a pretty heavy sleeper, so Malach didn't have to be too careful. He strapped on Reckoning instead of his knife and walked to the door where Skie had posted herself. If anyone came or went from the room, she would know. Or perhaps it was simply the closest she could get to being outside. He placed his hand gently on Skie, and she opened her eyes. He motioned for her to be quiet and follow him. She did what he asked. Sometimes he had to remind himself that she wasn't trained but chose to obey him. They went down the stairs to the common room. He ordered a cup of tea and Skie followed him to a table. He sat down with his tea and she laid beside him.

Was last night a dream? Am I going insane? Or was it really true? He had liberated an Angel Blade, and it was now his to wield. Reckoning, if he really was real, wanted to help him. He knew a way to find out if it was just a dream.

Reckoning? Malach called out mentally, feeling a little crazy for calling someone else's name within his own thoughts.

I'm here, came the eager response in his head.

The voice was just in his head, but it made him jump and look around all the same. It was as clear as if someone was sitting right next to him at the table.

No one else was in the common room other than the staff, however, and Malach felt a little embarrassed.

Is there something you need, Malach? The voice came again.

No, I just wanted to make sure I wasn't dreaming last night, Malach thought back.

Oh, Reckoning sounded a little disappointed. *You didn't, and I'm here if you need me, or if you need to talk, or if you need advice. Or anything-*

I got it, Malach interrupted the thought. *Thanks.*

Alright, Reckoning said, starting to fade. *Good talk.*

He must have been going insane not being able to talk to anyone but that demon for more than four hundred years, Malach thought to himself. *I know I would have. He probably just needs someone to talk to.*

Even with that realization, Malach didn't engage the blade in conversation. He need some time to herself to sort things out and talking to the blade wouldn't give him that time. He sipped at his hot tea. Reckoning said the war is still being fought, and it was at a more important time than ever. A pivot point, it would seem. He said whichever way Newaught went would decide the victor. Was that really true? But what could he do? A young man from Brightwood. This city was huge, and he would be branded a lunatic if he started yelling "war is coming!" on every street corner. No, that wouldn't help him. He would have to figure out how to manipulate things from the background.

Malach shook his head. He was getting carried away. Besides, he didn't even believe in one side or the other. Why would he do all that work to change people's minds? Better to keep his own head down and not get involved. In two years, he would be able to go back to Brightwood and live out the rest of his days hunting.

Right now, he had to think about the test. He had asked people back in Brightwood about the test and none of them would tell him anything, mostly because they couldn't remember. The most he had gotten out of anyone was that it was so abstract. No one could figure out how they got what jobs they were given. He had to figure it out so he could ensure he was given a job as a hunter.

Malach spotted Daziar walking down from the rooms. He caught sight of Malach and walked over to him. He sat down at the table just as the serving girl came by and they ordered some breakfast.

"Are you always up this early?" Daziar asked.

"Most days. I knew you would want to sleep longer, so I came down to get some tea," Malach responded. "How long do you think Honora will sleep in?"

"Long enough. You know her; she doesn't get up when she doesn't have to. Remember when we did our wilderness training? Someone would have to go get her up each morning and make her get out of her tent." Malach chuckled and nodded in agreement. "Think we can make it to the market and back?"

"Maybe, but don't you think she would want to come too?" Daziar asked.

"Do you want to be the one who gets her out of bed?"

"Not really," Daziar admitted.

"Then we will see if she wakes up before we are ready to go," Malach reasoned. "If she's not, we go without her. I need to sell my furs and get some money to live."

"Sounds fair," Daziar agreed.

The food made it to the table, and they dug in. By the time they finished, Honora still hadn't come down. Malach and Daziar went back up to their room and gathered the things they would need for the market. Daziar strapped on his sword, and Malach strung his bow and grabbed a quiver of five arrows. They didn't expect trouble, but would be ready if they found it. Once they got their things, they headed back down and out the front door. They froze with the door still open. Even this early in the morning, the streets were crowded.

Malach and Daziar looked at each other, and Skie whined at them.

Malach looked down at her.

She didn't take her eyes off the crowd but just sat down, as if to say, "I'm not going out there."

"Well, if you don't like it you can stay here with Honora,"

That was all she needed to hear. Skie stood up, turned around, and plodded back inside.

Malach and Daziar glanced at each other again, and Malach shrugged. "I guess we are on our own."

Reckoning? Malach called, a sudden thought dawning on him.

Yes, Malach? The hopeful reply came back in his head.

Can you see things? I mean, you don't have eyes, but I just wanted to know if you could look around in some way. Malach didn't like the idea of not having Skie to watch his back, and he wanted another pair of eyes to watch for any danger while they were in the market.

I can look through your eyes if you allow me to, and I might be able to spot things you don't, but I cannot look around on my own. Only see what you see, Reckoning explained.

Fine, I want you to do that. But only that. I don't want you reading my thoughts still. The only time you have permission to contact me is if you see something that you don't like, Malach said, trying to carefully outline the permission he was giving the blade so there would be no loopholes. Although, if the blade was evil, he didn't think any amount of rules would stop it.

Understood, Reckoning replied, and Malach got an impression of the man saluting.

Daziar waded into the crowd, and Malach followed in his wake.

They fought their way through the crowd toward the market. They had asked the innkeeper, and he gave them the general direction it was in. Even so, they had to stop and ask for directions a couple of different times, and they were surprised how unhelpful people were. Some were almost hostile. Both times, they managed to find someone who hurriedly gave them a few directions and then turn back to whatever they were doing.

"People are in such a hurry around here," Daziar commented, ducking into an empty alley after talking to the second person.

"Yes, they are," Malach agreed. "It's very different from Brightwood. You could ask anyone, and they would give you directions, and make sure you understood them before going back to their business."

"Do you think we are getting close?" Daziar asked.

"Well, this last person we asked just gave us three turns instead of the first one who gave us six, so either they didn't have time to finish the directions, or we are halfway there." Malach reasoned.

Daziar nodded and pushed his way back into the crowd. They followed the instructions given to them, and when they turned the final corner, the road in front of them opened much wider than the previous roads. On both sides of the street were booths that had been set up for vendors to buy and sell. Almost all the carts were occupied with things. Some booths had the same things as others, each vendor shouting that they had the best prices for their respective items. Malach and Daziar stood there for a moment, not knowing where to go first. There were just as many people moving around, but with the wider streets, they were spread out so Malach and Daziar wouldn't have as hard of a time getting through the crowd.

Malach moved to the first fur trader he saw and started haggling with him for some of the smaller furs. He did that with several vendors, selling the smaller furs that weren't worth as much getting a feel for the prices he got at each vendor. Finally, he sold the bear fur. The vendor he traded it to had looked at the fur with longing the whole time Malach haggled with him. He almost didn't look at Malach at all.

He wondered how often the vendor actually saw a fur like this.

He was able to get the price much higher than he thought it was worth, but the vendor seemed to feel like he got a great deal on it. Both of them walked away, happy with what they got. He sold all the arrows he had picked up off the highwaymen as well, although most of them weren't well made, so he didn't get much for them.

With his business completed, he started looking around for Daziar. He looked at the booth where he had last seen Daziar, but couldn't find him. Malach still stood head and shoulders above most of the people in the market, and he used his height to his advantage, but still, there was no sign of Daziar.

Reckoning, Malach thought. *Do you see Daziar anywhere? Am I just missing him in the crowd?*

I haven't seen him since he was over at the leather workers' booth across from the fur trader's booth you traded the pair of fox furs to, Reckoning replied.

"Fine, I'll head that way, and we will check there," Malach replied, forgetting to just think it back to the blade.

A passerby looked at him like he was a little crazy, but kept moving.

"Malach!" he heard Daziar's voice above the din of the crowd. It had a tone of danger to it. Malach pulled his bow off his back and nocked an arrow. The crowd parted like water going around a stone in a stream. People shouted in alarm, and a few of the women let out small screams. Malach rushed toward where he thought Daziar had called from. As the crowd parted in front of him, and he spotted Daziar. He ran to his friend.

"What? What's wrong?" Malach said, looking around wildly for the trouble that would be coming.

"Nothing," Daziar said, looking confused. "I just wanted to show you something." He looked at the bow in Malach's hand and added. "Put that down, Malach. No one is in any danger."

Malach let the bow out and put the arrow away. "You were calling me. I thought something was wrong."
He glanced around at the crowd that had gathered in a circle around them. They were all staring at him as if he were insane. "Umm, sorry, everyone!" he called out to the crowd. "I, uh, overreacted a bit. Sorry."

"What's going on here?" a guard shouted, pushing his way through the people.

No one answered him, so he walked up to Malach and Daziar. A second guard entered the circle shortly after the first.

"What's going on here?" The first asked again, looking pointedly at the two well-armed young men.

"Nothing, sir," Daziar answered respectfully. "Just a small misunderstanding."

"It looks like you two might be causing trouble here to me," the second guard said, stepping forward, his spear leveled at Malach.

The spear tip was inches from Malach's face. The second guard was much younger than the first and seemed to be a little hot-headed.

Malach raised an eyebrow at him, challenging him to do something.

"No, no trouble," Daziar said, trying again to defuse the situation. "My friend here thought I was in danger and rushed to my aid." Then he added. "But there was no trouble. We are new in town and a bit on edge, that's all."

"Fine," the older guard conceded, pushing the younger guard's spear away from Malach. "But if it happens again, we will have to confiscate your weapons and put you in jail for the night."

"I think we need to make an example of them now," the younger one said, raising his spear again.
The older guard slapped the spear aside again and forcefully turned the guard around, looking him in the eyes,

"We will do nothing of the sort. The major has put me in charge over you, and you will listen to me."

The younger guard ground his teeth and glared at the older guard. Malach could tell he was contemplating picking a fight, anyway.

"Fine," the younger guard conceded and turned back toward Malach. "But if I see you again, I will put you down, cur."

With that, he stormed off, shoving past some onlookers. Daziar put a hand on Malach's arm. His hand had instinctively moved to Reckoning's handle on his belt without him realizing it.

"Sorry about him," the older guard apologized. "He's a hot-headed recruit. He will learn soon enough." The older guard turned and walked away from them.

"Well, that was eventful," Daziar commented as they watched the guard leave. "Can I show you something now, or do you want to start shooting your bow at nothing again?"

"I never shot the bow, just nocked an arrow and drew it," Malach said in his defense.

"'Cause that's so much better." Daziar rolled his eyes and turned back toward the vendor. "You know how Honora was complaining that she needed a new set of saddlebags?"

"Yeah?" Malach said. "I think I remember her mentioning something on the way here."

"Well, look at these!" Daziar pulled a set off the rack it was hanging on and showing them to Malach. "Do you think she will like these?"

It was a stunning set of saddlebags. The top flap was tooled leather with a pattern that looked almost like small leaves and the main part of the bag had been tooled with a vine-like design. All of the leather had been dyed teal, one of Honora's favorite colors. It was well made and would last a long time, if taken care of. Honora would absolutely adore it.

"What money do you plan on using to buy this?" Malach put his hands on his hips. "You owe me half a silver already and you may owe more by the time you get your first pay."

"I know, but you got gold coins off of the bear fur and I know that will be more than enough to make it through the next week, and I can work at paying you back," Daziar pleaded. "I was hoping to buy this for Honora and ask again for her hand in courtship."

Malach just shook his head. "You know she won't say yes."

This would be the sixth time Daziar had asked in half as many years.

"I know," Daziar said, growing melancholy. "But I can't help myself. I love her."

"I know, but you ought to lay off for a bit," Malach advised. "She knows you want to court her. But she probably wants to see what her options are. Find out what is available to her. Not everyone finds the person they want to spend the rest of their life with so quickly."

"But I don't want her to see what her options are," Daziar protested.

"I understand, but you aren't going to be able to stop her, and being aggressive like this will just push her away." Malach reasoned with him. "If she finds someone else, that means it wasn't meant to be, and you will find someone who makes you happy as well. If not, she will come back to you, and all you have to do is give her a little room."

"Fine," Daziar said, looking at his boots. He knew Malach was right, but he didn't have to like it. "She likes you, you know," Daziar said abruptly.

"Ha!" Malach barked. He didn't mean to, but it came out suddenly. "Why would you say that?"

"She told me," Daziar said, as if it wasn't a big deal. "Three years ago, before I asked her to court me the first time."

"That was three years ago," Malach scoffed. "I'm sure she has no interest in me now."

"I've seen the way she looks at you," Daziar said.

"You are thinking about this too much," Malach replied.

"Well, you should get these for her," he said, holding up the saddlebags again.

"Why? Wouldn't you be disappointed if we courted?" Malach was confused and really didn't want to talk about this anymore.

"Yes, but better you than some man that won't treat her right," Daziar said. "Besides, it doesn't have to be a courting gift. You know, you didn't get her anything for her birthday."

"Dung! You're right!" Malach exclaimed. "I didn't even think about it."

"So, you better get something really good, and these would be something she would really like." Daziar shoved the bags into his hands.

"Fine," Malach walked up to the vendor and haggled for the price of the bags. He ended up getting them for a gold and a half. More than he thought it was worth, but the lady wouldn't go any lower, claiming she wouldn't get any profit if she did. Malach paid her and the two of them set off for the inn.

Malach looked at the sun and realized that it was mid-morning. The market trip had taken longer than he had thought it would. They would be getting back only a little before the mid-day meal.

The crowd seemed to have died down on the way back, and they made much better time. They only had to stop and ask directions once, and they asked a nice, elderly lady that had to be in her seven-hundreds.

She had patiently explained where they needed to go and they thanked her, moving on. When they got to the inn, they found Honora sitting at a table in the common room, reading one of the few books that had been in the valley. She loved books and would read often, even though she had read all the books in the valley three or four times over each.

"Good morning, Honora," Daziar hailed her when they got close enough that she could hear them.

She turned around and Malach braced himself. He could see the storm raging behind her eyes.

"Where have you two been?" she asked, shutting the book with a clap.

"Mal had to sell his furs, so we went to the market," Daziar said defensively.

Obviously, he hadn't seen the same thing in Honora's eyes that Malach had, and he was taken off guard by her frustration.

"And you couldn't bother to let me know?" Honora asked, standing and putting her hands on her hips, her glare moving between the two boys.

"Sorry, Honora," Malach said. "I thought it would be best to let you sleep. It's my fault we didn't come to get you."

"Well, Malach, I appreciate you taking responsibility, but I think you both can and will be blamed," she said. "But while you two were out gallivanting around town, I finished my test. I was told my results would be in after mid-day."

Malach realized he was still holding the saddlebags behind his back. He was going to surprise her but got sidetracked trying to defend Daziar and himself. He pulled them out and extended them out to Honora. "Happy late birthday!" He exclaimed. "Perhaps this will make up a little for us, leaving you out of the trip to the market."

"Oh my, these are gorgeous!" She squealed a little, obviously excited. "Thank you, Malach. How did you know?"

"That credit goes to Daz," Malach told her. "He remembered that you were in need of new saddlebags, and we felt that you would like these the best."

"Well, thank you both," she replied. Then, remembering she was supposed to be cross with them, added. "I guess it makes up for leaving me behind." She sat back down, gesturing for the boys to join her.

They did and then waved down the serving girl. They ordered the mid-day meal and talked and laughed for a bit while they ate. After they had eaten, their conversation turned to the test.

"So, Honora," Malach started. "Was the test as abstract as everyone says?"

"Absolutely, maybe even more-so," she said. "It asked scenario questions that didn't seem to have anything to do with anything. I have no idea what job it will say I need, but I've guaranteed the job I want."

"Really?" Daziar asked. "How did you do that? Did you cheat?"

"No!" she said, a little offended that he would suggest that. "I have other ways of getting what I want," she replied, flipping her hair back with one hand.

"So, are these ways that we can use to get the jobs we want?" Malach prodded.

"No," she said shortly. "You'll see."

She wouldn't say anything else, even though Malach and Daziar pressed. They finished their meal, and Malach and Honora put their things up in their rooms while Daziar talked to the innkeeper. He arranged for them to leave their things in the room for the day even though they might not need to rooms for the night.

Malach and Honora came down the stair, Skie trailing after them as they descended. Daziar relayed the information from the innkeeper as they walked to the testing facility. The crowd seemed to have lessened even more as the day went on. They were able to move through the streets without pushing through all the bodies.

They got to the facility quickly, and Malach paused outside the door to take a steadying breath.

"Well, the rest of our lives await," Daziar said next to him.

"So dramatic," Honora said, rolling her eyes. She took a step forward and pulled open the door. "Would you two quit lollygagging and get inside?"

"Yes, ma'am." Daziar mock saluted and walked inside, Malach following him.

Malach walked in and looked around. There were almost no windows inside, and those were covered. The whole place was quiet and draped in shadows. There were a few lanterns, but it looked like night had fallen early in the building. There was one man sitting at a small table.

He glanced up as they walked in, looking bored. Honora walked in and his mood brightened immediately.

"Honora! You've come back to me so soon!" he said, smiling devilishly.

"Broak! Sweetie, I just couldn't stay away for long," she replied over-exuberantly.

Malach studied at Honora, confused, then glanced at Daziar, whose jaw had fallen so low Malach thought it might have broken.

When Malach turned back, Honora was already up to the table sitting on it, looking at the man who seemed to be named Broak.

"Who are your friends, honey?" he asked.

"This is Malach and Daziar. We grew up together and made the Journey here together," she told him. "They need to take the test as well."

"Great!" Broak said. "Let me get two tests ready, and we can spend some time together while they are back there. Get to know each other a little better." He stood up and turned around.

Daziar brushed past Malach, heading for Broak, murder in his eyes. Malach caught his elbow and pulled him around.

"Don't," Malach said, putting his finger in Daziar's face for effect.

"Mal, he's bad news," Daziar growled under his breath. "And I'm not going to let him get anywhere close to Honora."

"I'm sure she knows what she's doing," Malach tried to reason with him. "But if she doesn't, beating the guy up is just going to get you thrown in jail, and it won't solve anything."

Luckily, Broak and Honora hadn't seen what transpired behind them, so when they turned back around, it was almost like nothing had happened. It was about that time that Broak caught sight of Skie sitting behind Malach.

"Lord above! Is that a wolf?" he shrieked and jumped behind Honora. She rolled her eyes and shot a disgusted look at Malach.

Although, he realized, her ire wasn't directed at him and Skie, but Broak. She didn't like him at all. He must be the way she was going to get the job she wanted.

Clever, though a little low, Malach thought. "Don't worry, she only attacks when she smells fear."

As if on cue, Skie stood, sniffed the air and growled. Broak let out a small whimper from behind Honora, eliciting another eye roll. Although this time, Malach wasn't sure if it was because of Skie, him, or how Broak responded.

"I'm just kidding," Malach said. "She doesn't hurt anyone that doesn't need hurting. You're safe, for the moment."

Broak peeked over Honora's shoulder and then stood up abruptly. "Yes, well, I wasn't too worried. You would have to have papers for her to be in the city, which would mean she's tame." He feigned bravado.

"Oh, she far from tame," Honora commented, and Broak's eyes went wide again.

"Well, um, yes," he stammered, "I have your tests here. If you will follow me, then I will let you take them. And Honora, your results should be out anytime now."

He led them to the door behind his desk and ushered them through, shuddering slightly as Skie brushed past his hip. Malach and Daziar found themselves in a hall that had three doors running down the left side of the hall.

At the end, it made a right turn, but a sign on the wall read "Proctors Only" just before the turn. Malach assumed that's where they checked the test and determined what job people would get. Broak motioned to the doors on the left.

"One of you in each of the first two rooms. You will have as much time as you want to take the test. Don't rush, but give the most honest answers, or you might find yourself in a job you're not suited for," Broak instructed.

Malach took the first room and Skie followed him, heading over to the corner in front of the small table and chair. The rooms were just big enough to move around in. The small table and chair took up most of the square room, but Malach had enough room to be comfortable and Skie just enough room to lie down. Skie looked up at the door and Malach realized he didn't shut the door. He turned to look and found Daziar standing there. Broak had left, the door to the main room latching behind him.

"Do you need something?" Malach asked him.

"I need to wring that sleazy coward's little neck," Daziar said through gritted teeth.

"Daz, I think you are missing some vital information here," Malach chuckled. "Honora doesn't like the guy. I guess you were too busy glaring at him to see the look on her face."

"Really?" Daziar's rage was replaced by confusion. "Then why is she acting like that? Letting him call her pet names."

"I suspect *he* is the way she is going to get the job she wants," Malach told him.

Understanding dawned on his face. "Oh, so she doesn't really like him?"

"I don't think so," Malach said. "Now, I need to start this test, so please close the door on your way out."

"Fine," Daziar said, but a smile had returned to his face.

Malach looked at his test. He studied the questions, but none of them had anything to do with jobs or skills. They were all scenarios, and he was instructed to answer them as if he were a certain person in the scenario. He finally answered them and walked out of the test room. Still unsure of what any of it meant or what it would tell the people who grade them. Daziar was waiting for him in the hall.

"What took you so long?" he asked.

"I was trying to figure out what each of the questions would say to the proctors and how to answer them to get the results I wanted," Malach responded in a hushed tone.

Daziar lowered his voice to match Malach's. "Did you find something?"

"No," Malach said disappointedly.

"Oh," Daziar sounded just as disappointed. "Well, I guess we will just have to wait for the results, then."

"Yeah, I guess so," Malach said. They turned and walked out of the door into the main room. Honora ran up to them excitedly.

"My test result came back while you two were taking the test!" She exclaimed. "I got a job tending the mayor's horses!" She bounced up and down in front of them. "And better yet, when I am not tending the mayor's horses, I get to look after the city's horses, which include the guards' horses. So, if you," she looked at Daziar, "get the job with the guard, we might see each other here and there."

"That's wonderful, Honora!" Daziar said. "That would be amazing. Maybe have lunch here and there in the stables."

Malach took Daziar's test from him while he and Honora talked. He took both tests over to Broak, who appropriated them from Malach, and went to the back. He came back out in a couple of minutes, and he had more papers in his hands.

"Are those our results?" Daziar asked hopefully.

"Ha," Broak scoffed. "No, they won't be out for a few hours. Honora told me the three of you would like adjacent apartments and that the two of you," he pointed to Malach and Daziar, "would like to room together to save some money. So, I have your apartments here, and it's not too far from where Honora's job will be."

"Great!" Malach said and then thought. Honora's flirting is coming in handy for us.

After they had signed the paperwork, Broak asked. "Honora, would you want to stay here and spend more time with me?"

"I think that we need to get moved in, and if we don't get out of the inn, we are going to get charged," Malach said, giving Honora an easy out.

"Well, I will bring your paperwork with your job assignments on them when I come to get her," Broak told them.

"Thank you," Malach said politely. "We would really appreciate that."

Honora turned to Broak and took his hands. "We will just have to wait 'til tonight to be together, honey."

Broak smiled at her. "Until tonight, my beautiful flower."

Daziar made a gagging sound, which earned him a glare from Honora.

The three of them walked out of the testing facility and Honora slugged Daziar in the shoulder.

"Hey!" Daziar objected. "It's not like you actually like him."

"But you don't have to be such a cretin," she shot back. "You could at least be polite."

"I'm sure he knows you are putting on to get the job you want," Daziar said. "You laid it on way too thick for there to be any real interest. Besides, he only has one thing on his mind for the night, and a nice dinner, isn't it."

"Daziar Wervine!" Honora said, aghast.

"You know what he wants just as well as I do," Daziar replied.

"Malach," Honora turned to him. He had been trying to look like he wasn't listening or interested. "Are you even listening? You need to talk some sense into your friend."

"I'm not getting in the middle of this," Malach replied, holding up his hand defensively.

"Fine," Honora turned back to Daziar. "I know what Broak wants, but he isn't getting it, so there's no reason to bring it up. Besides, it's not proper."

"Fine, but if he touches you, I'll kill him," Daziar said, and Malach believed him.

"And I would let you," she said, and that was the end of it.

They finished the walk back to the inn in silence. Malach and Daziar loaded all of their things into the cart while Skie and Honora waited in the barn. Once everything was loaded, they settled with the innkeeper and got directions to the apartments. The innkeeper told them the best route to a take a cart, and they headed out.

He was right. The route that was given to them followed the outer wall around the city, but they didn't have to stop once because of pedestrians. Daziar decided he would drive them there, and Honora and Malach were in the back.

So much had changed for Malach in the last two weeks. Being attack by a demon, finding Reckoning, the Journey, the possibility of a new war, and soon, a new job. So many things to figure out, so many possible paths to take, and so many things that could go wrong. It was overwhelming. Why did he have to bear all of it? Why was he the one who had to know war was coming again?

"Malach?" Honora asked. She had been watching him and he didn't realize it until now. "Are you alright?"

"Yeah, just a lot to think about," he answered honestly. "A lot has changed in a couple of weeks, and a lot could still change in the next few hours."

"I'm sure you will get the job as a hunter," she tried to reassure him, but it didn't help much.

"I guess I'll find out in a few hours," he said noncommittally.

"Malach, there's no sense worrying about it," she told him. "You can't change anything now."

"I know. I just don't like change," Malach complained. "If I had a choice, I would just have stayed in Brightwood and hunted for the rest of my life."

"No one likes change," she said. "But change is a part of life."

"You and Daz seem to like the change to Newaught," Malach pointed out.

"Yes, but I miss my family, and I'm nervous about the new job tomorrow," she told him. "I would have sooner stayed in Brightwood with my family if I had the choice, but I am making the most of it since I didn't have a choice."

"Yes, fine," Malach conceded. "I'll try to quit worrying about the job."

"Good," Honora said. "So, what do you think our new apartment is going to be like?"

"Probably plain and drab," he guessed.

"Malach, what did you say about not worrying?" she scolded.

"I'm not," he protested, holding up his hands. "I'm just stating a thought. Think about it. If they have to make all of these buildings for anyone who is on the Journey to live in, they are going to make them cheaply and without a lot of variety."

"I guess," she said, "but I believe they will be better than you think."

It wasn't long before they turned down the road that their apartments were supposed to be on and found a line of buildings that all looked the same on both sides of the street. They were pushed right up next to each other. There was only a small gap, maybe big enough for two people, between them. Through the alleys, Malach could see another set of the same buildings. The buildings were two stories tall, and very plain on the outside. They were made of stone and not very large. They pulled up to the two buildings, which corresponded to the numbers they were given, and tied up the mules. Malach and Daziar started pulling their stuff out of the cart, and Honora hopped down and ran inside her apartment. Before Malach and Daziar could get their packs on their backs, she ran back out.

"They aren't furnished!" she exclaimed, distraught.

Malach looked at Daziar, and Daziar carefully said, "Did you expect them to be?"

"Well, yes," Honora looked a little sheepish. "But I guess I shouldn't have."

"No, I think we will have to buy some things along the way to make our new homes more comfortable," Malach said, equally careful.

"I need to go by the market then," she said. "I just assumed we would have a few things, or I would have brought more with me."

"Nobody enjoys change, right?" Malach winked at her.

"Oh, shut up," she retorted and grabbed her pack from the cart before storming inside.

She wasn't really angry, Malach knew, so he didn't worry too much, but he would probably pay for that comment one way or another. He grabbed her trunk out of the back of the cart and carried it inside for her. She was right. When he got in and his eyes adjusted to the low light, he could see that there were only four plain walls and a stone floor. To his right, about halfway down the wall, was a stove that could be used for both warmth and cooking. The room was empty otherwise. There was a staircase to get up to the second floor at the back of the room, with a plain metal railing set into the stone. The only light in the room was from the two windows set in the front wall on either side of the door.

Malach set the trunk down and went over to the windows. There were no shutters, and he was curious as to how they could be sealed against the cold and bugs. He was amazed when he found they had a glass pane set in them that was already sealed. Brightwood had some glass, but nothing like this. Small glass containers were easy enough to come by, but if someone wanted glass windows, they would pay a fortune to have them brought out and installed. Most of the glass he had seen wasn't as perfect as this either. It usually distorted whatever was behind it. Some of the cheap glass wasn't even clear enough to see anything through, though it would let in some light. Through this glass, however, he could see everything clearly. It was amazing. Then he realized everyone would be able to see him through them as well, and he would have to come up with some way of blocking their view. He looked up and there was a rod set in the stone. He realized that the rod must be for that very purpose.

"Are you alright, Malach?" Honora asked from behind him.

"Yeah. Have you seen this glass?" he asked, still unable to take his eyes off the window.

"Yes?" she said questioningly. "Haven't you seen the window in my room back in Brightwood? It has the same clear glass window."

"It does?" He turned and looked at her. "How come you never showed me?"

"I didn't think it was that spectacular," she replied, shrugging.

Malach's jaw dropped. "Not that spectacular? I've never seen glass so clear. It's beautiful."

"I guess I take my window for granted," she said, chuckling. "Father had it put in when I was a child, so I've always had it. It's commonplace for me. I guess if you have never seen it, though, it is pretty amazing."

"Yeah. I can't wait to show it to Daz," Malach said excitedly. He rushed out of her door and into his house. Daziar was already staring at the window in much the same way Malach had.

"This is breathtaking!" he exclaimed. "Have you seen this, Mal?"

Malach laughed, "I saw it at Honora's. I'm sure I had the same awed expression you have now."

"Have you been upstairs?" Daziar asked, finally taking his eyes off the windows. "There are two more windows and we have the stove down here so we can cook and stay warm. We will need wood or charcoal, though."

Malach headed to the stairs at the back of the room, but just before mounting them, he spotted a door set into the back wall underneath the stairs. He went over to it and opened it.

"Daz!" he called to his friend.

"What?" Daziar saw what Malach was looking at. "The rumors were right! They have indoor outhouses!"

Malach pulled a lever that was just over the seat and water spiraled out and around the bowl and disappeared down the hole at the bottom.

Malach and Daziar looked at each other wide-eyed. They had never seen anything like this before. No more cold trips to the outhouse in the middle of the night.

Malach decided to check out the upstairs and mounted the stairs, taking them two at a time. With his height, though, it was more natural to take two steps than just one. He turned to look at the upstairs room. Sure enough, there was a door that led out to the deck overlooking the street and two more windows. They would need something to block the windows and firewood, at the least. They brought all of their pots and dishes with them, so they wouldn't have to purchase those. Malach went back down to the first floor and retrieved his pack.

"What are you doing?" Daziar asked.

"I'm going to set up my bedroll near the stove, so we don't have to burn as much wood tonight. Then we need to go to the market again and get some things to survive the night. Also, it might be nice to eat something other than dried meat." Malach responded.

Once he got his bedding set down, he propped his pack against the wall and set down his quiver. He would have to find something to hang his bow on so that it wouldn't warp.

Daziar set up his bedding, and they both went outside to find Honora. They walked over to her house, and the door was shut. Daziar knocked, and they heard a crash come from behind the door.

Chapter 10

Malach and Daziar shared a glance, worry creasing both of their faces, but just as they were about to go inside to check on Honora, the door opened. She was standing in the door, but just behind her, her trunk was tipped on its side.

"Are you alright?" Daziar asked.

"Yes, but you scared me half to death," she scolded, hands resting on her hips.

"I just knocked," Daziar said incredulously.

"Well, what do you want?" she asked, perturbed.

"We were going to head to the market to get firewood and something to cover the windows," Malach said quickly, trying to dispel the small argument about to ensue. "I thought we might ask you since you didn't get to go last time."

"Yes, I would," she said, still a little ruffled. "However, I need to get some of my things put away before we do, so you two will just have to wait." Before Malach could say anything else, she shut the door.

"Well, you really made her mad," Malach said to Daziar.

"All I did was knock," Daziar said, throwing up his hands in defense.

"I know that, and you know that," Malach said, starting to walk toward the cart. "But she doesn't believe that."

Daziar sighed and followed.

They decided to take the mules and Celewen out to the stables, leaving the cart parked in front of their new homes. There were stables for those who lived in the apartments to use. They got the animals to the stables and found several stalls that were marked with their apartment numbers on them. They put each in a respective stall and then used one of the empty ones for the equipment. Honora would eventually sell the mules, as Arjun had told her to. Arjun figured it would cost more money to keep them for two years than it would to buy them back when they wanted to leave. Once they had finished with the horse and mules and left feed and water for them, they went back to the front of the apartments to wait.

Honora had apparently gone to the washhouse to bathe before going back out into public. As they were sitting down on the cart, they saw her returning. She finally came out after what seemed like forever.

Daziar nudged Malach, and he looked up, realizing that Honora was walking around the cart.

"Alright, I'm ready," Honora announced.

"Well, you might have to carry me since I grew so old waiting," Malach retorted.

"Ha, ha," Honora said in mock laughter. "You think you're so funny, Malach."

Malach grinned at her and then hopped down from the cart, stretching his stiff muscles.

Daziar got down off the cart as well, and they headed toward the market. Their apartments were located closer to the market than the inn was, and it didn't take them long to reach it. Malach and Daziar bought some material. It was folded over at the top with a row of stitches in it, which made one long loop the rod would fit through. The merchant they bought it from said they were called curtains. Malach thought it was just a new way to charge more for a piece of cloth. There was nothing special about them. He ended up spending a whole two silver coins for the four pieces of material, and he wasn't happy about it. He then got two bundles of wood, one for each house. Those were more reasonably priced. He planned to chop his own wood throughout the winter, but this would get them started.

Honora bought curtains as well and some food. She also shopped for a mattress, but didn't buy one yet. She said she could deal with sleeping on the floor for a week to make sure she had enough money until she got paid. Malach didn't know how much her father had given her, but he assumed it would be enough for her to live on for a month or more. She probably would have plenty for the week, even if bought half the furniture she wanted. Especially once she sold the mules..

They hauled their new things back to the houses, stowed them in their appropriate places, and cooked at Malach's and Daziar's house for the night. Dusk had settled, and they had to light the lanterns they had brought with them to see. They were in the middle of cooking the food when there was a knock at the downstairs door.

"That will be Broak," Honora sighed.

"You know, you already got the job," Daziar said. "You don't have to go with him tonight."

"But I gave him my word that I would go," Honora pointed out. "And I won't go back on that. Besides, it's only for a few hours and then I never have to see him again. It's worth it."

Honora walked to the door, and Malach heard it open.

Malach heard the muted voices of Honora and *two* others. He puzzled over that. Did Broak bring someone with him? He turned around but couldn't see who was standing outside.

"Watch the food." He told Daziar. "I'll go find out what is going on."

Daziar got up to tend the food without questioning him and Malach headed to the door, checking that Reckoning was still at his side. To his surprise, Honora ushered a young couple into the house; neither of them were Broak.

"Malach," Honora said, seeing him coming toward her. "This is Auron and Prinna Barclay; they are our neighbors."

Malach stopped beside Honora and extended a hand to Auron and then to Prinna. "Good to meet you, I'm Malach," he positioned himself next to Honora, in case there was any trouble.

Paranoid, Reckoning's voice said in his head.

Am not, and I told you to stay out of my head. Malach defended himself and chided the blade at the same time.

I am not in your head, came the response. *I'm simply noticing where you have placed yourself.*

Malach was about to think a rebuttal to the blade, but realized a question had been asked of him. "What was that? Sorry, it's been a long day. My mind is already starting to shut down."

"I just asked if this was your first day in the city," Auron repeated his question.

"First full day," Malach replied. "We made it in yesterday evening but had to stay at an inn."

"Well, Prinna and I would like to welcome you anyway," Auron said. "We brought a couple of meat pies and a bundle of wood as housewarming gifts."

Malach realized for the first time that Auron was carrying wood and Prinna had two pies in her gloved hands that were still steaming.

"Here, let me take that wood off your hands and we can share the pies," he said, moving forward to take the wood.

"Well, thank you!" Prinna said. "We just remembered our first week in the city. We were newlyweds, and we barely had enough money to make the Journey. Once we got here, we didn't have enough money to get any firewood and barely enough to eat for the week."

"Yeah," Auron agreed. "We still don't have a lot, but we thought we could help you out a bit with what we had."

Malach continued listening as he stacked the wood with the small pile they had bought earlier. As he did, Daziar introduced himself to the newcomers from where he was standing at the stove.

"The vegetables are almost done, and then we just need to heat up the last of the meat," Daziar announced.

"It looks like you three are a little better off than we were for our first week in town," Auron said.

"I was able to sell some of my furs at the market today and turned a fair profit," Malach explained. "But we still appreciate the food and wood. It will help."

Malach and Honora gestured for the couple to come and sit, and they continued talking as they did.

"So, have you gotten your job assignments?" Prinna asked.

"I have, but the boys are still waiting on theirs," Honora answered.

"What job did you get?" Prinna asked politely.

"I get to take care of the Mayor's and city's horses!" She almost squealed, but held that back.

"I guess that is something you really wanted," Prinna said, noting her glee.

"Yes!" Honora exclaimed. "I have my own horse. She's the dappled gray out in the stables. Her name is Celewen. It means 'silver maiden.'"

"She sounds beautiful," Prinna cooed.

"So, do you hunt?" Auron asked Malach, changing the subject. "Your clothes are made from skins."

"All my life," Malach answered. "My father taught me before he passed. It's my first love."

"What do you hunt?" Prinna asked.

"Mostly whatever is bothering the farmers," Malach explained. "They hire me, and I kill what they need, but I hunt other things on my own. I leave out traps for smaller animals and stalk and shoot the larger ones."

"Interesting. I might have you teach me some time," Auron said. "I've always wanted to hunt, but I never had the chance."

"Um, sure," Malach said hesitantly. He didn't know if he really wanted to teach someone. He liked it better when it was just him and Skie, but he figured taking Auron once or twice would be fine.

"So, what was the hardest thing that you have ever hunted?" Prinna asked.

"Probably Skie," Malach laughed. Honora and Daziar laughed with him, knowing on that hunt, Skie had saved him even though he thought he was going to have to kill her.

"Who's Skie?" Prinna asked, confused. "I thought you two were married or betrothed. Is Skie your wife?"

Daziar choked on the piece of food he was sampling and then laughed so hard he had to sit down.

"Honora and I aren't married or betrothed," Malach said, looking at Honora. Her cheeks were red, and Malach felt he must be as well. "And Skie isn't my wife either. She's my hunting partner. I found her almost dead in the woods and saved her. She returned the favor on one of my hunting trips. She turned against her own pack to save my life." He whistled and Skie came down the stairs. She walked over to the platter of food Daziar had in his hands and grabbed a slab of bear meat.

Prinna gasped, and Auron jumped to his feet.

"She's a wolf!" Auron exclaimed at the same time Prinna said, "She's gorgeous!"

Skie plodded over to Prinna, snapping up the bear meat as she walked, and sniffed her. "Is she safe?"

"Not in the slightest," Malach responded, and then added. "But she won't hurt you."

Prinna's hands were raised while she let Skie sniff her, and Skie put the top of her head in Prinna's hand as if to say. "It's alright. I won't bite." Prinna patted Skie's head carefully. Skie then plodded over to Auron. He wasn't as trusting, but let her sniff him, anyway. Once she was satisfied, she went over to Malach's side and laid down next to him. He casually put a hand on her flank, petting her side.

"She goes hunting with you?" Auron asked.

"Yep," Malach said. "She has saved my life many times over."

Daziar finally got up off the floor with the platter of food and started serving everyone. He put a little of the meat pies, a little of their bear meat, and a small pile of veggies onto each plate and passed it around.

"What kind of meat is this?" Prinna asked. "I work in the mayor's kitchens, and I have never tasted something like this."

"Bear," Malach said through a mouth full of food.

"Really?" Auron asked. "Did you kill this yourself?"

Malach shrugged, but Honora spoke for him, "Yeah, he killed it for my uncle!" she told the account third-hand, which meant it had a few exaggerations to it, which Malach corrected and Auron and Prinna stared at Malach like he was God himself.

"You mean to tell me that you killed a bear with a spear?" Auron asked. "There's no way I would do that!"

"It's more reliable than bows." Malach shook his head. "The bows we have just don't have the power to reliably peirce a bear's heart. Most just make it angry, and then you would have to use a spear, anyway. Unless it's one of the smaller black bears. Then you could use a bow and most likely kill it."

"Well, promise me we won't go hunting a bear on our first hunt together," Auron said, chuckling, but Malach knew he was a little afraid.

"I promise," Malach grinned back.

"Can I see that scar from the claws?" Auron asked.

"Auron!" Prinna scolded.

"What?" he asked.

"It's fine," Malach chuckled and pulled up his shirt. "They were only shallow cuts. They healed quickly."
Auron let out a low whistle, and Prinna, a small gasp. Malach put down his shirt and picked up his plate again.

"Are all those scars from animals you have hunted?" Prinna asked.

"Most," Malach responded.

Prinna turned to look at Auron, "You are not going hunting, ever."

"Prinna," Auron almost pleaded, "don't be like that."

"Prinna, it can be dangerous out there, but I would never put anyone in danger on purpose," Malach assured her. "I would make sure we hunted safe game if Auron comes with me. Nothing that would harm him."

"Fine," she said reluctantly. "But at least wait until the spring. I don't want you caught out there in the cold."

"Deal," Auron promised.

"Honora," Prinna said, realizing Honora didn't have a plate in her hands. "Why aren't you eating?"

"I have, well, I have a date and we are supposed to go to a local kitchen for dinner," she told them reluctantly.

"You don't sound excited," Prinna commented. "Are you just nervous?"

"Well, I am a bit nervous, but really, this was a deal with someone to get the job I wanted," Honora halfway explained. "I just have to go with him for one night, and then I never have to see him again. He gets on my nerves."

"Just be careful," Auron warned. "They say that there is a new powder someone can put in people's drinks, and it's nearly tasteless, but it will knock you out. They say people have been doing this to young women and then raping them."

"Oh my," Honora gasped.

"You're not going with him!" Daziar raised his voice almost to a shout and jumped up, upsetting his plate.

"I'm sure he wouldn't do that. He doesn't seem like that kind of person," Honora said.

"I don't want you going with him tonight," Daziar said again.

"Maybe you should rethink having a chaperone," Malach said, much calmer than Daziar.

"No, I can take care of myself, and I don't need one of you glaring at him all night," she turned to Auron. "Thank you for the warning. I will make sure that I keep an eye on my food and drink."

A knock sounded at the door for the second time that night.

"Speak of the devil," Daziar muttered, but Malach knew he was secretly waiting for that knock so he could find out what job he was assigned.

Malach stood this time and went to the door. He opened it and there stood Broak, dressed in nicer clothes than he had had on earlier that day.

Broak looked a little confused as he tried to see in past Malach without looking like he was trying to see in past Malach. "Is Honora here?" he asked, looking back at Malach. "I knocked on her door, but there was no answer, and I couldn't see any lights on."

"Maybe she is," Malach said noncommittally. "Let me talk to you for a second."

He stepped outside with Broak, pulling the door closed behind him.

"Her father put me in charge of her safety while we were on the Journey. As far as I'm concerned, that protection will extend to her as long as I am around." Malach stared him directly in the eyes. "I'm putting you in charge of her safety tonight. I am willing to trust you because she does." That wasn't strictly true, but Malach didn't mind letting him think that. "If anything happens to her while under your care and you don't protect her with your own life, your life will be forfeit. No matter how long it takes me to track you down."

"Hold on one second. What makes you think you have the right to speak to me like that?" Broak said, feigning bravado.

Malach could see in his eyes, however, he was unnerved.

"And what makes you think you could kill me?"

Malach didn't touch the man, though he knew with Broak's size, he could easily lift him with one hand from the ground. Instead, he said, "I've hunted with wolves, which means I'm faster than you. I've killed bears with a spear, which means I'm stronger than you. I've put an arrow in a man's heart from two hundred paces, which means you won't even see it coming. But that's only if Daziar doesn't find you first. I don't think he will kill you as fast as I will."

Broak's face had gone white as a sheet.

"So, I will say for the last time. You are in charge of Honora's safety tonight. If she is hurt in any way, I will kill you. Do we have an understanding?"

Broak just nodded, and Malach heard him swallow.

"Good!" Malach said cheerfully, purposefully changing his demeanor. "Did you happen to bring our papers with you?"

Broak just nodded again, holding out the papers to Malach.

Malach took them and then opened the door and ushered the still shaken Broak inside. Daziar was waiting by the door and plucked the papers from Malach's hands before he could do anything to stop him. He took them over to one of the lanterns and started looking through them.

"Why are these damp?" Daziar asked.

"Someone must have some sweaty hands," Malach commented, looking at Broak. He was still white as a sheet and wouldn't meet Malach's eyes.

"I got it!" Daziar shouted, making Honora and Prinna jump a little. "I got the Guard job!" He read a little more of the page. "I am to report to the main barracks first thing in the morning."

"That's great!" Honora said. "I knew you would get what you wanted. What about you, Malach?"

"I don't know," he said. "Sticky fingers here didn't let me look at them before he took them from me."

Daziar handed the second set of papers over sheepishly. "Sorry Mal, I just got excited."

Malach took the papers from him, feigning frustration, and then smiled to let him know he wasn't serious. He scanned over his name, height, weight, and all the other things about him. Finally, he got to the information about his new job. His chest tightened. He hadn't gotten the job he wanted. He dropped the papers and walked over to the stair to sit down. Skie stood from where she was cleaning up the food Daziar had dropped and followed. She always seemed to know what mood he was in. She sat down with head in his lap, trying to comfort him.

"What's wrong?" Daziar asked, first to break the uncomfortable silence.

Malach didn't say anything. He really needed to sort out his life before he talked with anyone. He stood up. "I didn't get the job. I just need time to think." With that, he walked up the stairs, Skie still following him.

He heard Auron and Prinna bid good night to everyone and leave.

Then he heard Broak speak, "Um, we need to be going as well."

"No, I need to go up and check on Malach." Honora protested.

"If we don't leave right away, the kitchen we are going to eat at will be filled up. It's one of the best in town." Broak insisted.

I silence ensued where Malach could all but see Honora struggling between her promise and her friend.

"I'll check on him." Daziar told her. "You go and try to make the best of the night."

"I...make sure he...I'll be back soon." Honora obviously didn't know what to say.

"I know. He'll be ok Honora." Daziar assured her.

Finally, she conceded, and they left. He heard Daziar come up the stairs and sit down on the floor beside him.

"Honora would have come up, but Broak wouldn't let her," Daziar said bitterly.

"I know, I heard," Malach replied.

A moment of silence passed.

"Do you want to talk about the job?" Daziar asked.

"No," Malach said simply.

Daziar just sat there then. Not saying anything else and Malach was finally able to start sorting out his thoughts. He had to leave his home to go to a new city. He had to take a stupid test to tell him what job he would do. Now he was expected to show up and do that job whether he wanted to or not. It wasn't fair. On top of all that, he had been attacked by a demon and Reckoning wanted him to help fight in a war he wanted no part of, nor had he taken sides in.

He sighed.

No doubt the blade would see this new job as a way to hone his skills to fight. He sat thinking like that until the last bit of sun had gone behind the wall. There was still light, but it would be dark soon.

"I didn't get the hunter's job, Daz," Malach finally said.

"I figured that much out," Daziar said.

"You didn't look at the papers?" Malach asked, looking at him surprised.

"No, I knew you would tell me," Daziar said.

"Well, I think you will like the news," Malach told him. "I'm supposed to report to the main barracks in the morning. I will start my guard training tomorrow with you."

"Really?" Daziar said, but it sounded more like an exclamation than a question. "That's great!"

"Yeah, all sunshine and roses," Malach said sarcastically.

"Mal, I know you wanted to be a hunter, but this might be a good thing. And you can still go hunting on your time off," Daziar said, his excitement was still evident in his voice.

"I know," Malach said, looking down. "It's just that now we are going to have to stand guard for hours or wait at the gate while we check in carts and farmers. We will probably never see any real action, and our days will be filled with the same old boring thing every day. Is that really what you want?"

"Well, no," Daziar said, as if just now thinking about it. "But it's not going to be all guard duty. I mean, there are the Shadows to catch."

"Do you really think that, in the two years we are here, we will get put on the Shadows' case?" Malach asked. "And even if we did, do you really think we could solve it when so many others haven't?"

"Well, I mean, fresh eyes and all. Right?" Daziar said, sounding like he might be trying to convince himself instead of Malach. "Well, maybe we will be on the same squad."

"More likely we will be split up after training," Malach countered sourly. "They will want to put us where we are most needed."

"Fine, but there's always a chance," Daziar said weakly. "Come on, let's not worry about it tonight. We will find out more in the morning when we report for training."

"Fine." Malach conceded. "Daz?"

"Yes?" Daziar asked.

"There's something else I need to tell you." Malach said cryptically. He wasn't sure he wanted to tell him about Reckoning or if he was even supposed to, but he was tired of keeping secrets from his friends. He would have to tell Honora another time.

"What is it, Mal?" Daziar prompted.

Malach realized he had been quiet for a long moment. "Sorry, I wanted to show you why the highwaymen attacked us on the Journey from Brightwood."

Malach pulled Reckoning out of his sheath and decided he would change Reckoning's form to show Daziar, then explain everything else from there. He thought of the bear spear he had used in Brightwood, but nothing happened. The knife stayed a knife. It didn't even shudder. Malach thought at first that he had mixed Reckoning up with the knife Togan had given him, but after a quick glance at it, he knew Reckoning was in his hands.

"The knife you got from Togan?" Daziar asked skeptically. "Malach, I don't think they would have attacked us just for that."

"No, it's not the knife from Togan," Malach said, exasperated. "It's the demon's sword that I picked up after he dropped it."

"Mal?" Daziar said warily. "I think you might have bumped your head a little too hard somewhere along the way."

But Malach wasn't listening. Instead, he was trying to work out why the blade hadn't changed.

Reckoning? Malach called for the blade.

Yes? Came the polite but eager response.

Why can't I change your form? He asked, frustration starting to become evident, even in his thoughts.

If you will remember, you banished me from your thoughts, Reckoning reminded him. *If I can't read your thoughts, how would I know when and what you want me to do?*

Fine, Malach thought quickly. *I give you permissions to read my thoughts for the purpose of changing form only.*

He was trusting the blade quicker than he should have. It had only been a day, and he had already started giving Reckoning permission to read his thoughts again. How far would this go? Since most of this had happened in his head, not much time had passed in the real world. Daziar was still eyeing Malach warily. Malach decided making a less threatening weapon would be a better idea. He thought of a metal bo staff and watched as Reckoning slowly changed, flowing almost like water, into the image he had picked.

Daziar's mouth fell open.

"It's an angel blade," he told his awestruck friend. "I'm still learning about him, but I took him from the demon when it attacked me."

"Him?" Daziar asked, one of his eyebrows raised up questioningly.

"He can communicate through some kind of telepathic link. I just found that out last night. He can also change shape whenever I want him to into almost any weapon," Malach explained. "I'm still learning about him myself, but he is respecting my space and not invading my mind, even though I know he could whenever he wanted to."

"Mal," Daziar looked like he might have been talking to a crazy person. "Do you hear the words coming out of your mouth?"

"Umm, yes," he said slowly.

"You sound insane!" Daziar exclaimed.

He's not wrong, Reckoning chimed in.

Daziar jumped to his feet as if he had sat on a hot stone and started looking around him. "Who said that?" he questioned, squinting at the stairs in the failing light, assuming someone had come into their house.

I did, Reckoning replied calmly, and Malach realized Reckoning was talking to him and Daziar at the same time. He didn't realize that could happen.

Reckoning, I thought you said I could wield you only because I was half demon. How are you talking with Daz? Malach thought.

I can communicate with any human within a certain distance when I am being wielded by an angel or demon, he explained. Since, as you told me, you are only part-demon, my range is extremely limited. Usually, I could project to a mind from miles away, but with you, I am limited to about twenty feet.

Hmm, well next time warn me when you are going to do that, Malach scolded him. Then turned his attention to the confused, and a little stunned Daziar.

"Daz," Malach stood and pet a hand on his friend's shoulder, stopping him from looking around anymore and held his gaze. "Reckoning said that. There is no one else in the house with us. Sit back down and I will explain everything."

They sat, and Malach placed Reckoning between them. He explained everything he knew about Reckoning and everything that had happened to him since the demon attack. Daziar had a lot of questions to which Malach's answers were "I don't know" most of the time, but Malach answered the questions he could, and Reckoning helped with some of them, speaking through Malach.

"So how do you know that this isn't a huge plot to use you against all that is good in the world?" Daziar finally asked.

Malach stopped and thought about that for a moment; even though he had been thinking about that same question since Reckoning first contacted him.

"When he touches my mind, I can feel his intentions, though I can't hear his thoughts unless he wants me to," Malach finally said. "It's subtle, like a whisper or a feeling in the back of my mind."

"But how do you know that Reckoning isn't making you feel those intentions to trick you?" Daziar countered. "And for that matter, that he isn't controlling or manipulating your thoughts right now?"

"I can tell when he is in my head and when we have that kind of connection. He can't hide it from me now that I know how it feels," Malach said, but only truly realizing it as he said it.

He remembered back to the first time he picked up Reckoning and felt the searing pain in his head when they had connected. Reckoning had told him that was normal, but was it really? Or was it the start of him losing control of his mind? No, he had to trust his own thoughts or he really would go crazy. If he ever thought Reckoning was starting to control his thoughts, all he had to do was take the weapon off his belt and get it away from him.

They talked for a bit longer, walking down to the stove to lay out their bedrolls for the night until they heard Honora's muffled voice drifting in from the street. They rush up to the balcony just in time to see Honora give Broak a peck on the cheek. He seemed put out and trudged away, deflated. Honora glanced up at the balcony and the two boys ducked, not wanting her to know they had seen that moment between the pair. She walked into her own apartment, but no light turned on. She must have gone straight to bed.

Satisfied Honora was safe, Malach descended once again to his bedroll and took his belt off. He put Reckoning under his pillow and laid down. He vaguely remembered answering more of Daziar's questions and drifting off to sleep, still trying to convince Daziar that Reckoning was good.

Chapter 11

Amara steered Shasta toward the gates of Newaught. Judging by the sun, it was a little past mid-day but she would be able to see one of the city's clocks soon and know for sure. She had thought her hometown, a booming port city, was big, but it didn't even come close to the size of Newaught. She had gotten a glimpse of the size of it coming down the hill into the valley. The walls were so high she could barely see over them and she could barely see the other side of the city. She would have never found the Shadows had she not had the map Lawdel had given her. It was now tucked down her shirt in the hidden pocket next to her breast. It would most likely be safe there if she were searched at the front gate. She found a lot of guards were good men and didn't tend to check around a woman's breasts unless they suspected something. Of course, there were always the pigs to worry about, the guards who would use their position as a means to violate a woman's privacy and not get punished for it. She hoped none of them would be at the gate. She had been told more than a few times she was a very pretty young lady, though she didn't know if she really believed them.

Shasta fell into line behind a cart, pulling the hunters who had gone out that day and the spoils from the day's hunt.

The guards inspected each cart or person entering the city and each one they let in inched her that much closer to the gate. She retrieved the papers she had stolen from the private. She had tossed the papers outlining the orders of the guard and kept all the papers that told them who she was. Hopefully, the

Captain hadn't sent word ahead in another form to let the city know to be watching for her. She didn't think that was likely, but she was ready for the possibility.

She nudged Shasta forward when the guard motioned her to and handed him her papers. She made herself appear relaxed, even though all of her muscles were tense, and she was ready to bolt at the first sign of trouble. There were three guards on the ground and two up on the wall with crossbows. She didn't think she would be able to outpace an arrow no matter how fast her reactions were, but she would have to make the first few seconds count if she were to have any chance of escape.

The guard was saying something, but she realized it too late.

She brought her focus back down to him, not sure what to do or say. She was just about to turn tail and run when he repeated himself uncertainly. "Umm. . . everything looks to be in order, Ms. Amara. Do you need directions to the testing facility so you can be placed?"

"Umm. . . yes, that would be lovely," Amara said, realizing they were going to let her through. She felt a little ridiculous that she almost ran when everything was going so smoothly. She had no intention of going to the testing facility. However, anyone else making the Journey would have asked for directions, and she didn't want to look suspicious. She only half listened to the guard as he rattled off the directions to her. They seemed a little complicated, and she was glad she didn't have to actually remember them. He handed her papers back, and she thanked him. With that, he motioned her into the city.

The first thing she saw were rows of houses, which all looked the same. In fact, she noted there were several rows of these same houses, all the same size and shape. These must be the houses they gave to the people who were actually making the Journey and starting their new life in Newaught. She wondered what it would be like to live in an actual house, having a job she went to every day, having money and not being hunted by the guard.

She shook her head at herself. That life wasn't for her. It would be too boring. She wanted adventure and she could make more money stealing it. She already realized that, when she had stolen from the mayor back in Caister.

Thanks to Lawdel, she still had a lot of that money, and she would make much more here in a larger and wealthier city.

As she rode down the main street, she saw a cart with two young men in it. They must be new arrivals, she thought, one of them handing a trunk to the other. She thought the one in the cart was very handsome; tall, a darker tone to his skin. He wore a knife on his belt. He wasn't as big as the other man, but he was taller. In fact, he was taller than anyone she had ever seen; she realized as he straightened up. She could tell he worked outside and wasn't comfortable with the big city. He kept looking around him at all the people passing by. His eyes met hers and she averted her gaze quickly, but not before noticing he had black eyes. So black, in fact, that she couldn't tell the difference in the center of his eye and the colored ring that would normally be around them. It unnerved her, and when she looked back, he had returned to handing things to his companion. As she passed the cart, she gasped involuntarily as she caught sight of the largest wolf she had ever seen. It was laying in the cart but was the furthest from sleep as it could have been. She encouraged Shasta to hurry past the cart in case the wolf decided it was tired of all the people and started killing.

She moved farther down the road until she was out of sight of the main gate and its guards. Steering Shasta into an alleyway, she shook her head to clear her thoughts of the young man with black, unnerving eyes and his huge terror of a wolf. She didn't want to run into them at night.

Glancing around to make sure no one was watching, she pulled the map out of the pocket next to her breast. She unfolded it and peered down at it. It had one red X on the map of the city over a house that she knew would have no significance whatsoever. She had studied the map many times on the trip here and had already worked out that it was coded, and she had already cracked that code. There was a message from Lawdel which hadn't seemed to mean anything either, but it mentioned a poem he had made her memorize as a young girl. It had taken her a little while to understand the message of Lawdel's actually did mean something. The poem was about a young girl that had lost her way in the woods, and it kept stating directions on every other line of the poem. If she used the X on the map as the starting point, she believed the directions in the poem would lead her from that house to the entrance to the Shadows' lair.

He had a set of numbers in the message which had the same amount of numbers as the directions in the poem. She just had to match the number with the direction in the poem and she would know how many buildings to pass and which directions to go to get to the entrance. It was a genius code, really. Anyone looking at it would think her destination was the house and that her dear father had written a message letting her know he loved her and that her aunt was expecting her. No one would realize it was actually a map to the Shadows.

She studied the map and worked it out again in her head, following the numbers and directions, moving through the map with her eyes until she landed on an old guardhouse. That had to be the entrance. She had double and triple checked it just in case. She didn't want to walk right into a real guardhouse. They wouldn't take too kindly to that and would start asking questions. This guardhouse must be abandoned, or the map was wrong on purpose to throw people off, and it wasn't really a guardhouse at all.

She turned Shasta back toward the road and merged back into the throng of people. Winding her way through the streets until she sat across the road from the old guardhouse. It was run down and falling apart. The roof sagged dangerously, and she wasn't sure if she really wanted to go into the building for fear it might collapse on her. She watched the building for a while, looking for anyone to come or go from, but no one did. In fact, it appeared just as abandoned as it should be.

She was just starting to wonder if Lawdel's information could be wrong, or just too old, when a seedy-looking man walked up, glanced around, and ducked inside the opening. She watched and waited for the man to come back out for a while, but he never did. It was time for her to go in. If the man was in there, she would just play dumb and back out before anything could happen.

She found a stable a few blocks away and gave Shasta over to their care with a few coins to take care of her horse. Eventually, she would move him to whatever stable the shadows used. She walked back to the guardhouse with the saddlebags hanging over her shoulder. She walked up to the doorway that didn't actually have a door.

She took one more look around, just as the man did. Realizing this, she felt foolish knowing that just as the man had missed her, she would inevitably not be able to see everyone who might be watching her. She finally ducked in and moved to the side of the doorway so she wasn't visible to anyone walking down the street. She let her eyes adjust to the darkness and took in her surroundings. At first glance, the building appeared just as rundown on the inside as it did outside. However, as she looked closer, she could see, though the walls and ceiling were left to appear as if they were falling and sagging, there were new beams put in place to support them. She was in the right place.

She search the small room and couldn't find any trap doors or any other hidden entrances to the Shadow's lair. As she was moving a rug that was in the middle of the room a voice called out, startling her, "as the light falls. . ."

She straightened and faced the direction that she thought the voice had come from and responded almost automatically, "the Shadows rise to steal away on the wind." She knew this code by heart. It was one of many used by the Shadows across the continent. Most of them had been drilled into her head as soon as she was old enough to speak. The rest were added shortly after.

Through the dim, dusty light of the old guardhouse, she saw something moving. She squinted to get a better look and realized it was a section of the big wall shelves against the back wall. Behind it, a strange greenish light shone as if the walls gave off the light themselves. She stared for a moment and then notice the small hunchbacked man standing in the opening. He was short, and not just because of his hunch. Even if the man was able to stand at his full height, he would still be shorter than her by a few inches, and she was always the shortest person around. The man grinned a creepy, lopsided grin that made her shudder.

"The master bringing in yet another whore," he said in a mocking tone. "The master will enjoy you, I think." His voice was raspy and full of greed. It sickened her.

"I am no whore, hunchback." She said harshly and with all the authority she could muster. "I was sent here by the Shadows of Caister."

He flinched back. "I am sorry." He cowered. "Please forgive me. I will take you to the master at once." He motioned her past him, the grin threatening to spread across his face again.

Amara had no desire to have this man at her back. "Please, show me the way. I will follow."

The man's faint grin dropped off his face. She had no doubt he would have at the least tried to steal from her and might have stabbed her in the back if he had the chance. He turned and led her down the strange green tunnel, the section of shelf sliding back noiselessly.

As they walked, she looked around at the glowing walls in amazement, but was disappointed to see they weren't actually glowing but were reflecting the light that was put off by the lanterns on the wall. The green glow was partially the rock, but the lanterns also had pieces of green, stained glass in them. It must have cost the Shadows a fortune to buy them. Unless they just stole them.

The Hunchback, as she now dubbed him in her mind, led her to another tunnel about the same size as the one they were in, but this one had two metal rails running its length, disappearing down both sides of the tunnel. On these rails was a platform with wheels. It had a leaver in the center with a set of handle on each side, one tilted up which had pushed the other down.. She thought this might be how the cart moved. When the hunchback got up on the cart and motioned her up, she hefted her pack up higher on her shoulder and did as she was bidden. The hunchback pulled a second, smaller lever off to one side of the cart and it started to move. She realized they were on a downward slope and the handles would not be necessary until the return trip. She wondered how she would ever get her horse down here.

As they moved, they slowly picked up speed until the lanterns were going by every moment now. Instead of a few moments; then she saw it. The tunnel ended. She expected that there was a tunnel off to one side or the other hidden from view until they got close. She wondered in a slight panic why the hunchback hadn't pulled the braking lever yet, and gasped when she realized the "end" of the tunnel was not the end at all. It was a sudden drop in the tracks. The "wall" was really the ceiling of the tunnel. She dropped to all fours and held on to the side of the cart as she looked over the edge of the drop for what seemed like an eternity. Then the floor fell out from under them and they were dropped at an alarming rate. She felt her stomach go up into her throat and fought the urge to throw up. The bottom of the drop came up fast, and Amara was pinned to the cart as it reached the bottom and leveled out a little. However, they were still going downhill and hadn't lost any speed. They sped through the tunnel; the lanterns flying by in a blur. Spark flew off the wheels of the cart as it skipped over the metal rails. She looked back at the drop that seemed so big. It was only a small dip.

She spotted an opening ahead, and then they were past that opening in a vast cavernous room. The sight took her breath away at the sheer enormity of the space. She could see torches well over her head, so far up that some of them looked like the stars in the night sky. Huge columns of stone flew past, and she followed one up with her eyes to see they went all the way up until they disappeared into the dark. They must be what was holding the tons of weight that would be above them in the city.

She glanced down for the first time since they entered the cavernous room and just about screamed. The two rails were there, but there didn't seem to be anything holding them up. Below the cart was nothing. Just nothing. The darkness was so deep and thick it might have only gone down for twenty feet, or it might also have been bottomless. She realized, after composing herself, there were pillars holding up the track, extended down into the pit. From what she could see of them, they appeared much like the stone pillars holding up the roof. They must have had the same architect overseeing their construction.

As she peered into the darkness, she could almost swear she spotted movement. But it must have been her imagination or the darkness playing tricks on her eyes. Nothing could be down there, and she couldn't see anything past fifteen feet or so. She still couldn't shake the feeling she was being watched and followed as they continued to glide over the expanse and to the other side.

When they finally reached the other side and a rock floor was once again under the cart, Amara breathed a sigh of relief. The hunchback pulled the lever all of a sudden and Amara was almost jolted off of the front of the cart, and she thought that she might have heard a grunting laugh from the hunchback.

Horrible man, she thought to herself.

The brakes squealed loudly, and even though they seemed to be slowing down quickly, it still took them several moments to come to a complete stop. When they did, they were only about a hundred feet from the wall of the main cavern. She could see many tunnels carved out of the wall, some on the "ground" level, some had ramps carved out of the wall allowing people to ascend along the wall up to the second, third, fourth, and so on, levels. The one thing she didn't see were people.

"Where is everyone?" she asked the Hunchback.

"Huh?" he grunted, as if surprised she was talking to him. "How should I know? I just watch the door all day." And with that, he shooed her off the cart and started pumping the handle to take back up the track.

"Wait!" she called after him, afraid of being left alone in the huge cavern. "Where do I find the master?"

"The Master's chambers are down the tunnel first cave to your left," The Hunchback called without slowing. His voice sounded farther away with every word. Then he was over the chasm and out of hailing distance.

She turned back to the wall of caves. The open the track disappeared into, she guessed, was the one that the Hunchback was talking about. She walked into the tunnel and took a left at the first opening.

It was a short tunnel which made a right turn at the end of it. She couldn't see past the turn at the tunnel and she had a hand on one of her knives hidden below her cloak when she made the turn. No one was there. She relaxed slightly, but the feeling that someone was watching her was back. That feeling seemed to be a constant companion recently.

The room she was in was a posh living space with a couch along one wall that looked like she would sink into it if she sat on it. On the opposite wall was a bed with silk covers and more pillows than Amara had ever seen in her whole life. Hung up along the back wall was a myriad of weapons. Under those were several mannequins with armor hung on them. Surprised, she realized the armor looked feminine. There were several pillars scattered across the room, which looked like scaled-down versions of the ones in the main chamber. She set her pack down at the entrance of the chamber and moved into the room to study the weapons.

Before she had a chance to get a closer look, she caught movement out of the corner of her eye. She turned just in time to see a throwing knife coming straight at her. She twisted her body to get out of its way and took a shallow cut on the arm instead of a knife to her chest. Had she not turned around, it would have most likely pierced her heart, killing her. She crouched down, ready for a fight, pulling two of her own knives from their sheaths. She didn't see anyone in the room. They were most likely using the pillars as cover, but she didn't know which one they would be behind. She moved and positioned herself where she could see all pillars at once, making sure she wouldn't be ambushed again.

She caught sight of a second knife headed her way. She was ready and easily dodged it, but she still hadn't seen where it was thrown from. Almost like it materialized directly in front of her. She waited motionless, watching the room. Then she saw the hand come out from a pillar to her left, releasing a third knife in her direction. She ran toward it, catching it on the fly, and throwing it back toward a man in black as she passed him.

His eyes widened in surprise, but he sidestepped the knife with ease and rushed her. She threw one of her knives at him to slow his advance. To her surprise, her knife hit the man, disappearing into his cloak. He let out a small pained grunt, but didn't slow down. He produced a short, curved sword with little more than a whisper of steel on leather and slashed upward toward her torso, attempting to cut her from her right hip up to her left shoulder. She stepped to the side and deflected the blade with one of her own, letting it pass by her harmlessly. The man let his blade continue through the arc and came back with a cross cut meant to take her head off at her neck. She ducked the blow, lunging in close to her attacker, attempting to render his sword useless with her proximity. She plunged her knife in, trying to dig it up under the man's ribs with her right hand and pulled another of her throwing knives with her left hand. The knife went through his light armor and into his ribs, but he jumped back quickly before it could do any serious damage.

They stood there, both painting with the exertion of battle. She had a short sword with her, but it was in her pack and not easily accessible. She would have to continue fighting with her throwing knives. Then it dawned on her. There was an entire wall full of weapons, just a few paces behind her. She would have to distract the man, or he would simply kill her before she could reach the wall and pull a weapon from it. She threw the two knives in her hands; one toward him and one to the man's right, where she thought he might move. Although, more likely, it would force him to the left, putting a pillar between them and giving her the couple of seconds she would need to gain a weapon.

She didn't wait to see which way the man would go, but turned and grabbed at the first hilt she saw. She pulled the weapon from the wall and the tip of the heavy two-handed sword hit the ground, putting her off balance. It was so heavy she could barely lift it, much less fight with it. She dropped it and looked toward where the assassin had been. One of the man's throwing knives thudded into her shoulder. Searing pain shot through her shoulder and chest. She stumbled back with the impact, but regained her feet quickly.

The pain seemed to clarify everything, bringing the battle into sharp focus. Her attacker was almost upon her, rushing toward her with his short sword. She didn't have much use of her left arm because of the knife in her shoulder. The man was coming to kill her.

His overconfidence was evident in his wide, frenzied eyes, and she realized his fatal mistake. He was timing his blow for where she was standing and already had his arm back ready for the thrust, leaving him open to her attack. She rushed forward, surprising the man and throwing off his timing. This allowed her to sidestep his thrust and ram the fourth of her throwing knives into the side of his neck. His eyes widened even farther with the pain. He stumbled back, clamping a hand to his neck, trying in vain to stop the bleeding. She had missed his throat but had cut deep into the side of his neck, and by the look of the blood shooting out along with the timing of his heartbeats, he wasn't going to last long. He dropped his sword and put his other hand on the wound. It didn't help. He pulled one of his blood-soaked hands away from the wound, reaching for what looked to be his last throwing knife. He pulled it from his belt and with a shaky hand tried to throw it. It clattered to the stone at her feet, lacking the power to make it even the short distance between them, much less do any damage.

It was over. The man collapsed forward onto the ground, hands flopping to his sides. The blood was still shooting from the wound, though not as far or as often as it had when she first opened it. She stared with morbid fixation, unable to turn away from the bloody sight.

Finally, she tore her gaze away from the gruesome scene and promptly threw up on the ground. She had never seen a real dead body. Much less one that had just been alive and one she had killed with her own hands. She fell to her knees, staring at her bloody hands, and threw the knife she was still holding away from her. It clattered to the ground next to the man's body. She started sobbing uncontrollably now, the pain in her shoulder started up again, reminding her she was wounded as well.

She heard footsteps coming from the hall, and she saw a woman turn the corner, sword in hand. Amara picked up the man's knife on the ground but didn't really have any fight left in her. The woman paused, taking in the sight.

She sheathed her weapon and started toward Amara. That was the last thing Amara remembered before the room spun in her vision and the blackness took her. Her final thought was she was going to die. After all the struggles, she was going to die.

Amara opened her eyes to see the woman who had run into the room at the end of the fight. Her survival instincts kicked in and she started to jump up, but found she was tied down to a bed. In fact, she was tied to the bed in the room she had just killed the man in. She fought against the ropes again, hoping to get away from the woman who clearly wanted to kill her.

The pain in her left shoulder stopped her. She looked over to where the knife had pierced her. It was gone and there was a bandage on it. That made her pause for a moment. Why would they patch her up if they were going to torture or kill her? Her muddled brain started working slowly at first, then seemed to catch up. She spotted the woman sitting calmly next to her.

"Who are you?" the woman asked calmly.

"Amara," Amara answered truthfully. Then it dawned on her. "You are the master?"

"You sound surprised," the master smiled. "Are you going to keep fighting if I untie you?"

"No," Amara said.

The master leaned down to untie her. "We had to tie you down to stop you from doing harm to others and yourself while my healer worked on you. They've only just left, actually." She explained. "You have a surprisingly strong right cross, young Amara."

Amara realized the master had a slight bruise on her left cheek which must have come from her, "I'm sorry, Master. I didn't... I..." she stammered, not sure what to say.

"It's quite alright. You thought you were fighting for your life," the master interrupted. "I'm glad you still had that much fight in you after killing a member of the Dark Hallow. A rather skilled one at that."

"Dark Hallow?" Amara asked, not sure what or who that was.

"Yes," the master answered, seeing her confusion. "It's an up-and-coming group of assassins. They are trying to take over our territory and jobs, but they don't have a problem with killing. In fact, most of their members seem to enjoy it."

"They sent someone to assassinate you?" Amara was starting to grasp what was really going on.

"So it would seem," the master affirmed. "But it appears you arrived at my chambers before me and the assassin attacked you instead. Thank you for taking care of him, by the way. However, I'm sorry that it happened like that." She looked genuinely sad.

"Well, I'm alive, and I've made it to safety. It shouldn't be long before I'm ready to be of use again," Amara said, trying to act tough.

What she really wanted to do was sleep for a week. All the small cuts stung, the wound on her shoulder throbbed and burned. It would stop her from lifting or climbing for weeks to come, and she still had all the sores and bruises from her long ride here. She would be useless for a while and probably wouldn't get to eat for half that time.

"Well, until then you can help me in other ways, and I will make sure you are cared for," the master said.

Amara was shocked. She had lived her whole life under the rule; if you don't work, you don't eat. "Why would you do that?" Amara heard herself say before she realized she was even saying it.

The master looked confused. "Because you, quite possibly, saved my life. Also, you will be working for it in... other ways."

Amara didn't know what to think about that, and her mind ran wild with ideas of the "other ways" she would be helping the master.

Apparently, it showed on her face because the master chuckled at her. "Not in any way you are uncomfortable with. Obviously, you have been talking to Grent," the Master assured her.

"Who?" Amara asked, perplexed.

"Grent, the doorman."

"Hunchback?" Amara asked

"Yes. He thinks I entertain working girls every other night. And I want him to keep thinking that," the master replied.

"Why?"

"Because they are my spies," the Master explained. "They come down once or twice a week and give me good intel on the rich men and women in the city. Sometimes they will even set up a distraction so we can rob one of them."

"Really? That's kind of risky for them, isn't it?"

"Not at all. They get paid just like normal and the idiots just think we noticed an opportunity and took it. They never put two and two together," the master explained. "People really only see what they want to see, and when they are with their favorite working girl and they get robbed, there is no reason to think it was her fault."

"Huh," Amara snorted. "That's pretty clever. So why are you telling me this?"

"Because Lawdel sent you," the master replied, as if that explained everything.

"So just because Lawdel sent me means you can trust me with all your secrets?" Amara asked, skeptically. "That doesn't seem right."

"It's not," the master said. "Lawdel and I go all the way back to our childhood in the streets of Caister. We grew up together there, but that's not important either. What I really need help with, and the reason I'm telling you these secrets, is I think there is a traitor in my ranks. I need you to help me find out who. Obviously, someone let the assassin in one of our entrances. I'm just not sure who did it. I need a fresh pair of eyes, one who is new to this chapter of the Shadows. Someone who can infiltrate and find out information on people that are in my own house. I trust you because Lawdel raised you. I know him, and I know he instilled good qualities in you. Also, you are new, so you can't be one of the people who has already betrayed me. In other words, you are one of the few people I can trust that the traitor might also trust."

"So, you want me to find out who the traitor is and feed you information about their movements?" Amara said flatly.

"Yes, but I would still need you to take jobs to keep suspicion off of you. However, you took care of *that* problem for a little while," the Master said, motioning to her shoulder.

"Yeah," Amara said sourly. "Do you have a plan for where to start?"

"Yes," the master stated. "But let's wait until after the evening meal to continue this discussion. Are you feeling up to going to eat or would you rather I send someone here with a tray?"

"I'm fine. Like you said, I won't be able to do much for a while, but I can still walk." Amara swung her legs to the side of the bed and sat up.

The rooms swam for a second, and she thought she was going to black out again, but then her vision returned to normal and she was able to sit up straight. She did, however, stand up a lot slower. Nothing happened, so she took a few steps without a problem. On closer inspection, she realized she was in a different room than the master's. It looked almost identical, but the wall of weapons and armor was gone, as well as the couch. Really, the only thing that was in the room was the bed itself. However, the size and the columns were the same as the master's room. She wondered if all the rooms were this grand. She probably would be given some small, out of the way room, just big enough for her to gear up and sleep in. Her pack was sitting next to the door, and she picked it up.

"You won't need that at the meal," the master told her.

"I know. I don't want to leave it here for someone to find," Amara said.

"It won't get stolen. That's strictly forbidden here," the master informed her. "I know the Shadows' chapter in Caister encourages stealing within its ranks. Here we do not. In fact, your punishment is to hang over the chasm for a night if you are caught stealing."

"Really?" Amara said. An involuntary shiver when through her body. "I don't want to do that, but I don't know that wouldn't stop everyone. It's not like you are being thrown in or anything."

"You would think that, but since the first man got caught, no one has been brave enough to steal anything," The master told her. "There's something in the chasm. No one has seen it or knows what it is, but it's not uncommon to hear it moving down in the depths. The first man we hung there overnight was never seen again. All we found was a frayed, broken rope."

"What?" Amara wasn't sure she believed the master, thinking it might just be a story to scare the new recruits. "If there is a monster down there, why do you still use the room at all? Why chance it?"

"The beast has never come out of the chasm, and you won't find anyone who claims to believe there even is a monster, but you won't find anyone stealing anything either," the master said. "There's no danger unless you venture into the chasm, and no one does that."

"So, you live on the edge of an underground chasm which holds a giant monster that could kill you all at any time? You're insane," Amara said.

"Never said I wasn't," the master chuckled. "Now leave your pack and let's go to dinner."

"Well, where will I be staying?" Amara asked, since she obviously wasn't going to be staying there. "I can swing it by there and drop it off."

"Here, of course," the master said.

Amara could have sworn her jaw hit the ground.

"You thought we would stick you in a small closet somewhere, since that's what they do in Caister, didn't you?"

Amara could only nod her head, dumbfounded, mouth agape.

"Well, they are pressed for space, and we are not," the master said. "In fact, there are still a lot of caverns to explore and map still. We have more rooms than we know what to do with it. And this is one of the smallest rooms in the known caverns."

"But the bed too?" Amara was still shocked; she had never had a bed before.

"That can hardly be considered a bed, but all the new members get them. You can buy a better bed once you have gotten a few jobs under your belt and a little coin in your purse." The master helped Amara take off her pack as she processed what she had been told and set it down next to the bed.

My bed, she thought.

The master beckoned for Amara to follow her out of the bedroom and into the hall.

They walked down a few different tunnels, turning this way and that. She didn't think she would ever find her way back. She followed the master into a large hall and, for the second time that day, was utterly shocked at what she saw. The hall was filled with close to one hundred people at tables filled with food and drink. She had never seen so much food in her entire life. The tables were stuffed with everything from potatoes to whole cooked pigs. Nobody was arguing or fighting over who got what scrap of food. She scanned the room and found no one was paying for the food, either. Everyone was just taking what they wanted.

The master turned around and looked at her, smiling. "Well, aren't you hungry?" she asked. "Pull up a chair and dig in. I'll go find your new handler and bring him to you." With that, the Master turned and disappeared into the crowd. There was an open seat at the end of one of the long tables, and she sat down. She didn't know what to do at first. She had always been taught nothing was free, but sitting right in front of her seemed to be a load of free food.

She almost had made her mind up to start taking a little of the food when a big chunk of meat plopped down onto the plate in front of her. It was followed by a plop of mashed potatoes and a pile of green beans slathered in some kind of sauce. She turned to the man who had just loaded down her plate and was met with a wall of muscle. She followed those muscles up even farther to look the man in the eyes. He was several feet taller than her and more than three times her weight in pure muscle. "T-Thanks," Amara stuttered, not sure how to react to the huge man.

"You're welcome, little one," the man said in a rich bass voice and beamed at her. "Pleased to make your acquaintance."

He stepped back and bowed lower than she thought anyone of his size could while still balancing a full platter of food. He sat on the bench seat next to her and produced a fork and knife. She realized the platter he had been carrying was really his plate. She gawked at the man as he started cutting the meat on his plate and shoveling food into his mouth.

He noticed her after a few minutes and, after swallowing the food already in his mouth, said, "If you leave your face like that for too long, you're going to start catching flies in your mouth, but if you enjoy that, then please, carry on." He still beamed from ear to ear, and Amara knew he was teasing her.

Amara closed her mouth and then said, "I've never seen so much food in my life, much less one man eating so much in one sitting. Sorry for my rudeness."

"No need to apologize, little one. All the new kids have the same expression when they see their first feast. But where are my manners? My name is Borden." He wiped his hand on his shirt and held it out to her. His hand could have fit four of her hands in it and still been able to close around them. She awkwardly put her hand in his and shook it.

"My name is Amara. I just came up from the Caister chapter," she explained to him.

"Oh, good. I knew you looked like a good sneak!" he exclaimed boisterously. "Do you have a handler?"

"The master is getting him now, but I don't know who he is."

"Well, if you find you don't like him, you let me know, and I will take you on in a heartbeat, little one." Borden patted her shoulder, and a good portion of her back, with one of his massive hands.

"You know, I'm not that little," Amara said defensively. "You are just as big as a building. Do you even fit through the tunnels without hunching over?"

Borden burst into loud guffaws. When his laughter finally subsided, he said, "Fiery little thing, aren't you?"

"Only when people are rude!" Amara said sourly, which triggered another round of guffaws from Borden and the men within earshot.

"I like you, little one. You come find me, and I will give you the good jobs." Borden said, turning back to his food. Just then, the master came back through the crowd, followed by a tall, skinny stick of a man.

He was dressed in cheap clothes, which only looked expensive to the untrained eye. Amara disliked him already. Anyone who had the money to buy expensive clothes but didn't, prized money above all else. Worse than that, in Amara's opinion, was someone who doesn't have the money but wants others to think they do. Those people would lie to your face without a second thought. The master had a look on her face like she had just tasted something foul.

When she reached Amara, she made introductions, "Demien, this is Amara. Amara, this is Demien, your new handler."

The master had said it cheerfully, but Amara could hear the undertone of disdain in her voice. She did not like Demien either, which made sense if she thought that the man was a traitor and wanted Amara to get proof. Demien didn't offer his hand to Amara, so they just stood looking at each other awkwardly for a moment.

"Pleased to meet you, Amara," Demien finally said. His voice was very proper and nasal. He peered down his nose at her as if she was a bug. She hated him already. This was going to be a hard assignment.

"Pleased to meet you as well," Amara replied stiffly, fighting to not grit her teeth. She didn't know what to do next, and Demien didn't seem to want to say or help her at all. They stood there in awkward silence for a few moments.

"Well," the master said, finally breaking the silence. "Demien, I will leave her with you so you two can talk jobs and skills." With that, she walked away quickly, abandoning Amara to her fate.

She sighed and sat back down at the table.

Borden stood up and walked away, but before he went, he leaned down and whispered in her ear, "When you get tired of this sod, come find me."

Demien sat down in the spot Borden had just vacated. He pulled a new plate from the closest stack and put food on it. He didn't seem to have heard Borden's comment.

"I hear you botched your last job, and that's why you had to come here. Is that correct?" he asked, without any preamble.

Amara wanted to punch that smug smile right off the man's face and keep punching until he couldn't smile anymore. Instead, she took a deep breath and answered, "No, the job went fine. I was pinched afterward when I was walking through the market for a different theft. The mayor was going to hang me on the mere suspicion of being involved, since the reports mentioned a female thief."

"Yes, I understand, but you never would have been under suspicion if you weren't seen in the mayor's house, which in my book means you botched the job. I expect perfection from all my fingers." Demien used one of the terms for "thief," common in the Shadows. "*You* are far from perfect. I know in Caister you are thrown to the wolves, so-to-speak, but here, we have actual training grounds where you can hone your skills as well as pick up new ones. You need more training before I send you out against the guards of Newaught. The law is not as kind here as in Caister. If you have a job, go as badly as your last one. You might as well leave the city because you will never be able to be seen in public again. The guards are trained to kill people like you, and they are trained well."

Demien paused and Amara took the moment to jump in, "Alright, fine. I get it. More training."

"You understand that if you are apprehended in Newaught, you will be tortured to find where our hideout is, right?" Demien said, taking a dainty bite of pork and following it with a sip of wine.

"I will what?" Amara said, taken aback.

"You will be tortured," Demien said again, casually. "The Shadows have long outmaneuvered the city officials, and this hideout is the only reason we have been able to prosper and grow as large as we have. If we lose this hideout, a good number of our members will be killed, which would save the rest of us from starving in the woods, but we would still live in poverty instead of the wealth you see before you. My job is to not only get you jobs but to train you so you won't get caught, and if you are, to withstand the interrogation long enough to either kill yourself or for a rescue to be mounted to extract you." Another small bite and sip of wine. "In short, if you *are* arrested, you are dead if we can't get you out quickly and doomed to live a meager life if we do, so don't get caught."

Amara's appetite quickly left her, and she set her fork down on the plate.

"Now that you see the gravity of your situation, will you submit to training under my supervision?" he asked, as if he already knew the answer.

"Yes, fine," she said reluctantly. "I will, but I will have to wait until my arm is better."

"Your arm doesn't stop you from running, does it?" Demien asked.

"No," Amara said, puzzled.

"Does it stop your brain from functioning?" he asked smugly.

"No," she said angrily, understanding his point.

"Then we start in the morning," he replied with finality. "Meet me at the chasm first thing tomorrow."

This man is infuriating! She seethed internally. *Does he have to be so smug and self-righteous?*

They finished their meals in silence, and then Amara was approached by a serving girl who told her she would take her back to her room. To her surprise, her pack and things were all still there when she returned. Maybe there was something to this cavern monster. Or at least, there was enough fear among the Shadows to stop them from stealing. She liked the security of the new place, even though the jobs would be harder and much more dangerous for her.

She laid down in bed and fell fast asleep almost instantly.

Chapter 12

Swords clashed as Malach fended off his attacker's blade. One blow after another met, and either stopped outright or deflected away from his body. He didn't have to attack, as he knew the older man would tire quicker than he would. All he had to do was wait for him to make a mistake and finish the man quickly. As good as he was with the sword, though, this was not his preferred way to fight, nor his preferred weapon. He would much rather use a pole weapon, giving him the ability to attack from either end. However, he had been trained well in the sword and would beat this man without any issues.

He and Daziar had come to the main barracks as their papers had instructed and started their testing immediately. Daziar had soundly beaten his opponent through sheer strength, even breaking the man's "practice" sword when the man tried to block but turned it the wrong way. The swords they were using were blunted but still metal and would do some damage if either scored a hit on the other. Daziar had followed through with a second strike that the man couldn't block, stopping it within inches of his neck.

Malach was taking a much more reserved approach, letting the man attacking him think he had the upper hand and tiring him out before his final strike. There was nothing like swinging a blade to tire a person out, and the man had been swinging his for the past three minutes straight. Malach could see the beads of sweat dripping from him. It wouldn't be long now.

Finally, the man stopped, taking a defensive posture, but his sword was lower than it should have been, telling Malach the man was becoming fatigued. Malach went on the offensive. He took a swing toward the man's neck to force his opponent to bring up his sword in defense. It worked. The man brought his sword up to block, but Malach changed the angle of his swing, hitting the sword just above the crossguard. Malach used the block to stop his own blade, and in the space of a heartbeat, Malach slid his blade down to the crossguard of his opponent's sword. Malach hooked the edge of his sword between his opponent's crossguard and the blade itself.

Reversing his sword, Malach wrenched his opponent's blade from his hands, disarming the man and sending the weapon flying to the side. Before his opponent could recover, Malach kicked him square in the chest, sending him sprawling. As he was struggling to his feet, Malach put the tip of the sword under his opponent's chin, signaling the victory.

He reached out his hand to the man and pulled him to his feet.

The major walked out from one of the building's overhangs onto the practice field. "Form up!" he barked, and the four of them moved to stand in a line at attention, Daziar and Malach quickly mimicking the two men they had just fought.

"Well done, you two," the major praised.

"Thank you, sir," Malach and Daziar answered in some semblance of synchronicity.

"You have been trained well," the major continued.

He dismissed the two men that they had been fighting and signaled to two others that had been waiting off the field. These two were much older. One looked like he would be retiring soon, and Malach wondered if he would be training one of them as his replacement.

"These two men will be your mentors for the next few months, teaching you what they can of the streets, the laws of the city, and your new jobs. After they are finished with you, you may be assigned to someone else or to a different post. Dismissed!"

"Yes, sir!" All four said at once, the two men saluting with their fists across their hearts, so Malach and Daziar quickly followed with the same salute.

The Major returned the salute and walked off the training field.

The two men who were to train Malach and Daziar turned without a word and walked off the field as well. They followed quickly. Once they were outside, the two men split off and went separate ways. Malach and Daziar looked at each other and Daziar shrugged quickly, following the man closest to him.

The man Malach followed didn't say a word until they were at the top of the wall facing toward the southwest. He was the older man from the market who had helped them the day before. He looked out at the planes surrounding the city. The guards posted up on the wall were more of a tradition than a need. Guards at the gate were to watch for individual infractions. Guards posted on the wall were to watch for armies marching on the city. Since there had been no war, there was really no need to keep as many guards up on the wall as they did.

"Son, do you know why we still stand guard?" the man asked Malach.

"No, sir," Malach responded crisply and honestly.

"The war, boy!" the man exclaimed. "How could you not know?"

"Sir, not to be rude, but there hasn't been war in more than two thousand years."

"Boy, you know as well as I, you fought a demon in the angel territory," the man turned to him.

"How do you know that?" Malach asked, shocked that he knew about that. He had assumed the elders would have covered everything up.

"My blade has made known to me that you are in possession of an angel blade, and they have been communicating. That is why I asked to train you," the man responded. "My name is Elzrod, and I am here to find and train an army for the angels in the coming war. Starting with you."

"Whoa, hold on." Malach's head was spinning with the revelation. "I don't want to be on a side, I don't want to be in a war. I just want to get these two years over with and go back to hunting in my small town where nothing happens and everything stays the same."

"There is much you do not know, boy," Elzrod said. "I can tell you more in time, but I need to train you. The storm is coming, and you have seen what is after you. You must know you cannot defeat it. These dreams you are having must be a warning."

"Wait, how do you know about my dream?" Malach asked, scooting farther away from the man.

"The blade boy!" Elzrod shouted. "It told me everything." The man seemed to listen to something and then took a breath, visibly calming.

"Did you ever wonder why your parents' bodies were never found?" Elzrod asked.

Malach stumbled back as if he had been shoved, leaning against the stone parapet that ringed the wall. Did he just hear what he thought he heard? This man knew of him and his parents. Hundreds of questions swam in his brain, but he was too shocked to voice any of them. "H-how. . . What?" he finally stammered out.

"Your parents are more than just a small-town couple, more than just runaway lovers that happened to settle in Brightwood." Elzrod turned to him, his face a picture of stone. "Your parents were the best soldiers in the Angel Army. They did more for the war in the final years than most angels did. We thought they were dead for years after the war ended and then they were spotted in some backwater town just getting started."

"Slow down," Malach realized after he said it that he was shouting, and lowered his voice. "None of what you say can be true. The war ended before my parents were born."

"They are much old than you think." Elzrod replied.

"Stop referring to them as if they are still alive!" Malach shouted. This man had to be crazy.

"Your parents are still alive, boy!" Elzrod almost shouted in frustration.

Malach couldn't take any more lies. He turned, rolling around the inner parapet and down the stairs that led off the wall. Elzrod was shouting for him to come back, but he didn't turn around. He didn't even look back. Why was this happening? Why him? He just wanted to be left alone in peace and live out his life hunting with Skie. Instead, he was supposed to be some hero that helped raise an army. Also, there was no way his parents were still alive. They had died so long ago. Maybe he would just go live in Demon Territory where no one knew him or his parents, so he could live in peace.

No! Reckoning's voice came through his thoughts like a bell being rung right next to his ear, sharp and resolute. Malach, you cannot live in Demon Territory even if no one knew you.

Why not? Malach thought back angrily. He was still running through the city toward the gate when Skie came running out of an alley and knocked him flat on his back with her bulk.

"Skie?" Malach said once he had his breath back.

She rumbled a deep, happy growl and licked his face.

"Good to see you too, but how did you get out? And how did you find me? I locked you in the house," Malach realized he was asking questions to her that, if she understood, she couldn't really tell him. "Well, I'm happy you're here, but would you get your fat self off my chest? You're making it hard to breathe." She huffed out a breath and got up, still wagging her tail.

"I was coming to get you, anyway. I need to get out of the city and away from people and blades," he added, "who want me to become a great hero and leader of armies?" He said the last bit with sarcasm dripping from his voice, but Reckoning remained silent this time.

Skie cocked her head to the side, looking a little confused.

"Nevermind, let's go." Malach ruffled her ears.

He threaded his way through the city, a little slower this time, leading Skie back to the house. Once there, he found the door to still be locked. Skie must have jumped from the balcony. That was a decent drop, but Malach had no doubt she had done it easily.

He opened the door with his key and went upstairs to get his bow. He grabbed it and selected five good arrows. Once he had all he needed, he replaced Reckoning with Togan's knife.

Malach, you shouldn't leave me here, you might need me, he protested, but Malach wasn't listening. He shoved the blade under his pillow. Reckoning was still protesting and telling Malach all the reasons he shouldn't leave him behind by the time Malach was out of range of their telepathic link.

Malach and Skie walked out of the city just a few minutes after he lost the link.

The guards didn't give him any trouble as he walked out. He thought Elzrod might have been waiting to stop him at the gate, but he wasn't. By now, the man most likely knew where he lived and might have been waiting to see if he would leave the city. Though, more likely, Elzrod was looking for him at the house. He turned toward the forest in the distance and started off at a jog. It didn't take him and Skie long to make it there and just a few moments more to locate a game trail.

Malach let his mind and body fall into a familiar role as he tracked an animal through the undergrowth. He found two rabbits not five minutes later and killed them both with the same arrow as it passed clean through both of their hearts. It stuck, quivering, in the root of a tree behind them. He hung them by their feet to let the blood drain from their bodies, so he got less on his clothes and sat down next to a tree to wait and his mind wandered back to what had just happened.

Elzrod said he had known Malach's parents. But he had also said that his parents fought in the last battles of the war. Which was impossible. His parents weren't more than four hundred years old when they died. The war ended just over two thousand years ago. His parents wouldn't have been born yet. No, there was no way that what Elzrod was saying was true. Maybe he got mixed up with someone else? No, that didn't make sense either. Elzrod possessed an angel blade, which meant he was probably too smart to make a mistake like that, and if he had made a mistake, his blade would have corrected him. No, Elzrod had to believe what he was telling Malach to be true.

Most likely, Elzrod subscribed to the belief that the war hadn't ended when history said it had but was still being fought, just in the dark areas of the world which hadn't been explored yet. But there was becoming less of those places now as each territory had begun spreading over the last two thousand years, exploring those unknown places.

Malach thought the angels might have left humans out of the war, but demons would never have given up any advantage. If the war was still being fought, all of Demon Territory would be fighting it. So then how could Elzrod be right? How could his parents have fought in the last days of the war if the war ended before they were born?

Skie let out a low growl snapping Malach out of his thoughts. He glanced at her, but she was looking into the woods to their right, away from the city. There was a man walking toward them slowly. He was covered head-to-toe in a black cloak, which made him look ominous and mysterious. Malach nocked an arrow, but didn't raise his bow yet.

"Stop right there," Malach said once the man was close enough to talk without shouting. "Where are you headed?" he asked

"Why, I'm looking for you," the man said with a gravelly, husky voice. "No doubt by now, you know you're important to a great many people."

"No, I'm just a hunter from a small town," Malach answered, willing it to be true with all his might.

The man chuckled unpleasantly. "Let's not play games. The creature by your side is proof enough you are no mere hunter."

"You mean Skie?" Malach asked, looking at the wolf. "I saved her, and she follows me now. That's not so uncommon."

"Is that so?" The man asked, seemingly unconvinced. "No matter. I can give you what you want, boy. Whatever you want: riches, power, women. Whatever your heart's desire."

"I just want to be left alone," Malach said, which was the truth.

He could live without all those things. He just wanted to be left alone to hunt and maybe one day, if the right girl came along, marry and settle down with a family. Teach his son how to hunt, as his father had taught him. "I don't want any part of any war on either side."

"You could have that. I would make sure that after everything was done, you would have your own country where you could hunt, live, and whatever else you wanted." the man tried again to sway him, but Malach saw through the offer.

The man would use him as a weapon, and *if* he made it through the war, maybe he would give Malach what he promised, but most likely, he would have him killed in the end.

"No deal," Malach said flatly. "I'm going back to the city. I suspect you are not allowed in since you haven't approached me before now, but if even if you can, just leave me alone." He turned to get his rabbits but kept an eye on the man.

"Very well, Malach. This was your only chance," the man said.

Malach could see movement underneath the man's robes. He turned to the man, arrow ready. Bulges pushed out the robes all over the man's body and red eyes showed from underneath the hood. Skie growled and pulled on Malach's shirt, wanting him to leave, but Malach was rooted to the spot, watching the bizarre sight before him. A single horn grew through the top of the hood, and Malach realized he had seen that type of horn before. He needed to leave. He fired his arrow at the monster's heart, and it would have struck true, but the demon's clawed hand came out of the robe and caught the arrow before it could find its target, snapping it in half.

Malach didn't stay to watch any longer. He turned and ran with Skie toward the city. They were a few miles out, but if he got within sight of the guard, he would at least have some help. He could hear crashing in the woods behind him. Luckily, this time it was in the daylight, so he would be able to spot the demon before it struck. This time, however, Skie wasn't injured. He came out onto the plains at a dead sprint, not caring about the possible holes he might step into. If he slowed, he was dead. Skie ran ahead of him, leading the way as they made their mad run toward Newaught.

They had made it almost halfway before Malach had to slow down. He was breathing heavily and, as he glanced around, he didn't see the demon anywhere. Skie seemed to realize he had slowed and circled around to stay with him. Malach slowed to a walk, looking at the sky and the plains for any sign of the demon. He still saw nothing.

Why didn't the demon chase him like at Brightwood? A deafening roar came from the forest, but it seemed to come from farther away rather than closer. He saw a black shape rise from the forest and fly away from the city toward Demon Territory.

Malach looked at Skie, and she locked eyes with him. "I'm not going back for those rabbits," he told her.
She whined at him and then let out a yip of agreement.

They turned back toward the city together. Malach couldn't help but look over his shoulder every few moments at the forest. He kept watching for the demon to come swooping over the trees to chase them down. But he never saw horn, nor scaly hide of the demon. They made it within sight of the city gate, and Malach saw Elzrod standing there waiting for him. His heart sunk. It seemed like everyone wanted him to do something about this coming war and he didn't want any part of it.

He and Skie arrived at the gate, and Elzrod was waiting, giving him a very disapproving look.

"I know," Malach said, hanging his head to not meet the man's eyes. "Demons might want to kill me."

"I was actually going to reprimand you for leaving your post," Elzrod replied with a smirk. Then he turned serious and said. "But now you see what the demons will do to you if you don't side with them. Before you say anything, I'm not asking you to decide now, but sit under my training and decide when the time comes."

"Fine. I have to do that anyway since I've been ordered to," Malach said reluctantly. "Let me go get Reckoning, and I will meet you up on the wall. But I want some answers."

"That seems fair," Elzrod nodded. "I will see you up there soon and answer all of your questions."

Malach ran off toward his house with Skie on his heels. He was finally going to learn more about his parents and their cryptic past. If the old man wasn't lying.

Amara awoke to the same light as when she fell asleep. She was used to that. She had lived underground her entire life, and at some point, she had gained a sixth sense about what time of the day it was. It was early morning sometime, maybe even before the sun had risen. She wanted to roll over and go back to sleep, but her shoulder throbbed too badly to let her.

She stood and got dressed, putting her knives on and hiding several others in various locations on her person. Her arm was a constant reminder that she could run into danger at any time, even when she thought she was safe. She walked out into one of the tunnels and caught a man passing her quickly. She asked which way the training ground was, and he quickly told her a series of turns, of which she only caught the first three or four. He sped off in the direction he was headed before she could ask for him to repeat the instructions, so she went as far as she could remember and caught one of the cooking girls passing by her. The girl told her how to get there from where she was, but this time much slower so Amara could remember it. She thanked the girl and found her way there. Demien was already there, though he didn't seem to be waiting on her.

"Good morning," she said, as she walked up to him.

"If you could call it good," he said gruffly, sipping on something hot out of a mug. "It is morning, though." He followed up with a sarcastic tone.

"Who pissed in your breakfast?" Amara asked.

"What?" Demien asked, confused. "No one. Why would a person do such a thing?"

"It was a figure of speech," Amara explained. "Never mind."

"Oh, no, I'm just not a morning person," Demien said, understanding. "I never have been. You are early though, and that's something to be happy about. Most of my new students don't get here until midmorning, or I have to go roll them out of bed. I chalk it up to being underground, though I don't let them know that." He said the last part conspiratorially.

Amara couldn't help but smile at the thought of Demien, prim and proper, rolling a young, soon-to-be thief out of the warm, comfy bed.

"Well, I'm used to being underground and my shoulder woke me up early," she told him. "Which begs the question; How do you want me to train? I obviously can't use my arm for at least a month"

Demien looked down at her, although with a more thoughtful look than condescending, unlike the night before. "I think we can do some running without it hurting you too badly. At least to keep you in shape. Then you have a lot of studying to do about the city and the inhabitants. Also, I want you to look at the layouts of some of the wealthier houses and come up with plans to get in and out in different scenarios."

Demien had obviously given some thought to her training already, and Amara decided that she might have underestimated the man.

"Very well, you look like you need a run," Amara said smugly and took off at a fast jog.

How wrong she was. She had grown up on the streets and therefore learned to run before she learned to walk and talk. Even with that, Demien could have run laps around her without breaking stride. She thought they must have run ten or more miles when Amara finally had to stop.

Demien, though sweating, wasn't anywhere close to doing. Amara retched on the side of the path and continued to suck breath greedily into her burning lungs.

Demien watched for a moment, getting his breath under control quickly, "Come now, surely you aren't done after only five miles. You wouldn't be outdone by me, someone who, how did you put it, looks like they could use a run?"

"You. . . can't be. . . serious," she said between breaths.

"Very," Demien said with what Amara would say was a sadistic grin on his face. "Come now, you've had a long enough break. We are only halfway done."

Amara glared at him but couldn't say much as he took off at the same pace they had been going. She got up and jogged after him. She finished the second half of the run, although with many more stops, and it took her more than twice as long as the first half had. When she finally passed the mark Demien had set for them to stop, she collapsed on the ground, chest heaving.

"Come now," Demien chided. "That was just our first run."

In response, Amara rolled over and dry heaved. She had long since emptied her stomach of its contents.

"Tomorrow, we will run farther. Since you think I need a run," Demien said, chuckling at the look of loathing that she sent his way. "Come, let's go have breakfast and look over what you will be studying for the day."

She arrived at the breakfast table and Demien provided breakfast for the morning and a mug of what he had been drinking earlier, as well as a pitcher of water and a couple of cups. Amara poured herself a glass of water and started gulping it down before she remembered she shouldn't, since doing so would risk stomach cramps. She sipped a little more, and Demien loaded their plates.

"I've been told since you have saved the master's life, the rest of your meals will be taken care of for you until you heal. Normally, only one meal a week is provided, though there are also occasional feasts. After you are healed, you will need to buy your meals. You can buy each meal from the cooks or the kitchens are always open for you to cook your own food if you choose. Store any food supplies in your room or you are inviting the whole of the Shadows to use them at their leisure. Same goes for anything anyone else leaves in the public kitchen. Don't take anything but dinnerware out of the kitchen and wash anything you use."

Does he ever stop talking? Amara wondered.

"Most people simply buy the meal from the cook unless they have special needs, though that tends to be a little more expensive," Demien finished. "Now eat up. You will need your strength. We have a lot of studying to do."

Amara didn't realize how much energy could be drained by sitting in one place and studying books. It was just after lunch and she was nodding off, reading a history of Newaught Demien had given her. She wasn't good at reading, and he had to help her with some of the words she didn't know. Lawdel had taught her enough she could sound out most of the words she didn't know, but interpreting the meaning of those words was sometimes hard. She had never sat down and read for hours, however, and it was testing her patience. She had tried to skim some of the book, but at lunch, Demien had looked at her place in the book and grilled her on anything she had already read. After failing miserably, he had made her start at the beginning again. This time, he gave her a pad and what he called an ink pen. It was fancier than the quill and ink well that she had learned to write with. This pen had a well in it and it let out ink when the tip was pressed into the page. She realized it was the same thing she had stolen from the mayor in Caister and still had in her room. She didn't fully understand how it worked, but after a quick lesson and demonstration of how to use it, she was able to make notes with it. Though her writing was worse than her reading.

At dinner, when Demien quizzed her about what she had read, she was able to get almost all of his questions correct. Including things like where some of the hidden tunnels were built under the city at the time of its construction. He told her she would soon learn where those were in the city in the present day. She was starting to understand how the history she was reading could help her with her jobs. Although, most of the information she was reading didn't seem to do her any good.

After dinner, Demien gave her a set of blueprints and guard rotation for a mock job and told her to study it and they would look at it in the morning after their run and breakfast. She took it back to her room, which she still had to ask for help to find. This time, the young man helping her told her it was only three turns from the main chasm and took her there first to make sure she found her way back. That helped Amara, since getting to the main chasm was easier for her than finding her one room in the middle of all the rooms. She thought she would be able to at least find her way to her room, the dining room, the training room and the room they were using to study in, but was about it so far.

As she got to her room, she realized, throughout the day, she had forgotten to try to learn any information which would implicate Demien in the assassination attempt and mentally kicked herself for her lapse in memory. That's what she was really there for, to find out if he was the traitor. She dropped her rolls of parchment that the blueprints and information for the mock job were on and ran as fast as her already sore and somewhat stiff legs would take her back to the dining room. She turned the second to last corner and ran full-on into Demien.

"Oomph," Demien let out a grunt as she ran into him. "Amara?"

Lord of Hell! She thought. *This isn't good.*

"What are you doing back?" he asked and then smiled. "If you haven't gotten enough running for the day, we can always get another one in before retiring."

What should I say? Think, Amara, think! She shouted internally at herself.

"Well?" Demien prompted.

"I was just going to ask if I could take that history book to my room to read if I got the scenario finished," The words came out in a rush and much louder than she meant them too. She could feel her cheeks growing red as Demien raised an eyebrow at her.

"Very well, if you are so confident you can look over the scenario and read the history, I supposed it couldn't hurt, but I expect you to read and be able to answer questions on the next fifty pages by the morning," Demien said and then added. "Since you are so confident."

Amara could have throttled her own neck. She was so stupid. She had gotten caught and now she would have to stay up most of the night to finish all the work given to her. This was so unfair.

"Fine. Can I take the pad for notes?" she asked. "I already have my own ink pen, though I didn't know what it was until you showed me."

"Yes." Demien handed her the pad and book of history that he had been carrying. "Have a good night, Amara," he said cordially, though she could hear the smile in his voice.

That sadist was enjoying this! She fumed.

She could almost imagine the steam coming out of her own ears. She was so frustrated with the man. As he walked away, it once again dawned on her the reason she came back was to follow him. She hurried to a table and dropped the books on it. She didn't think anyone would mess with them, and she didn't want to carry them while tailing Demien.

When she rounded the corner Demien had just disappeared around, she spotted him at the end of the hall making a left turn, away from the residences. He was up to something before retiring for the night, and she would know what it was before she could do the same. She hurried to the corner and peeked around it. He turned another left into a room her instincts told her wouldn't be a hallway. She moved to the entrance and peered in with wonder. Hundreds upon hundreds of books, large and small, were set neatly in rows on the shelves with signs to let people know what type of books they were and then smaller signs with letters on them. She assumed they were in alphabetical order, possibly by title or author.

She caught sight of Demien slipping down a row labeled romance, of all things. She stifled a giggle at the thought of him reading about two lovers. The way she saw it, he would obviously never have a lover. She moved to the row just before the one he had entered and ducked down it. Listening to him move down the row. He stopped and seemed to be perusing the books there, but just as he picked one off the shelf, she was startled by another voice.

"I was told I would find you here about this time." It was Borden, the large man, from the feast last night. "I wanted to give you one more chance."

"Borden, you know what my answer will be," Demien said. "I will not partake in such a scheme. There are too many things that could go wrong, and it is too dangerous."

Amara's ears perked up and her eyes widened. *They are talking about the assassination!* She thought. She just couldn't believe the kind, boisterous man she had met the night before would be in on it. Maybe they were talking about something else? But what?

"Besides, our own code forbids us from killing for anything short of the direst of circumstances," Demien continued, replacing the book he had pulled from the shelf.

She leaned in closer, as if that would help her listen better.

Demien didn't seem to care if they did it, but he didn't seem to want to take part in it either. Maybe he wasn't their man after all. It sounded like Borden was who she needed to investigate.

"You know I wouldn't have any moral dilemmas about taking a life, but we did swear an oath not to kill when we joined the Shadows," Demien continued. "Not to mention if the master were to find out it was you, you would be executed."

"She would just hang me over the chasm for a night," Borden said dismissively. "And that's *if* she found out it was me."

"Same outcome," Demien said indifferently, and she could almost imagine him waving his hand in the air with that sense of superiority. "Though, I note you don't believe in the chasm, monster. That's a mistake."

"Your right, I don't," Borden said, scoffing. "That's just a story they made up, and it's been told for so long everyone believes it. Back to the topic at hand; if you were to help us, our chances of success would more than double."

"Doubling such a small chance of success is still a small chance of success," Demien said and slid a second book from the shelf. "It doesn't change the fact that it's too risky, especially after the attempt on the master's life."

"They killed Runt," Borden growled low and threatening. "Or are you too high and mighty to remember that?"

A book snapped shut with an air of anger and Demien's mood changed dangerously. "Don't go there, Borden. You know, I was just as close with her as you were. But more killing will only prove to be our downfall. She made a mistake and paid for it. That's what happens in our line of work."

Boom!

The shelf between Amara and the two men shook and threatened to fall over. Amara jumped back in surprise, colliding with the bookshelf behind her. Luckily, the noise that she made was covered by a few books falling from the shelf that had been struck.

"She didn't deserve death!" Borden boomed. His voice seemed to shake the whole room, or perhaps that was just Amara's knees.

"No, she didn't," Demien agreed sadly, but then continued in a more confident voice. "But your plan will just get more people killed, possibly including yourself. Let it go, Borden."

"I can't, and the fact that you can means…" Borden's voice trailed off. "Well, it tells me a lot."

Amara heard Borden's boots scrape and stomp off away from her. She heard Demien sigh and replace the fallen books on their shelf. Moving a little to her right, she could see through the books to the other side. Demien leaned against the shelf with his back to her. He seemed to be carrying a large burden on his shoulders, sagging, although no physical weight was present. When he straightened, he again carried himself with the same confidence as before. Amara could tell now it was forced. She felt bad for the man and for what she had thought about him before. He was carrying a lot more than she had previously perceived.

Borden, on the other hand, would have to be investigated closer. He might not be her man, but if he was putting together a team willing to murder, the traitor might be among them. She had to get in with them and to find out who else would be bold enough to turn from thief to assassin. She also needed to check in with the master and tell her about what she had found.

She snuck out of the library and back to the dining room to pick up her books. She noted Borden was there, drinking from a mug. He looked defeated, and she knew he was drinking something far stronger that night than ale. She left, thinking that now was not a good time to approach the man. First things first, though. She had to get all her homework done and go to bed. She had a long day ahead of her.

Malach crested the top of the wall with Skie still by his side. She didn't seem willing to leave him since the confrontation with the demon in the woods. Elzrod was standing looking out toward the plains as he had been the first time they stood on the wall. This time, however, the sun was much higher in the sky than it was before.

Malach saw the man's angel blade in his hands in the form of a spear. He should have realized the weapon was different from the first time he laid eyes on it. The shaft was completely metal and few spears were made that way. Most would have a wooden shaft as that would be more than sufficient to stop most strikes from a blade, not to mention more cost and resource effective.

"What is his name?" Malach asked before he realized he was speaking.

"You assume it's a 'he'," Elzrod replied. "In fact, you assume they have genders at all."

"Ur, well, yes, I guess I did," Malach said sheepishly. "Reckoning speaks with a man's voice, and to tell you the truth, I don't know much about the blades at all. I didn't even know they existed until a few days ago, when Reckoning contacted me."

"My blade speaks with the voice of a young woman," Elzrod explained. "Her name is Storm Breaker. Storm for short. She was given to me about two thousand years ago when the war was said to have ended, but it was really only four hundred years ago when the war truly stopped. Now we wait, catching our breath until the demons attack again."

"Wait, you claim that the war ended only four hundred years ago?" Malach asked, confused. "But the elders of my village are much older than that and they claim it ended when the histories say. Wouldn't they know?"

"No," Elzrod said flatly. "The war continued long after most of the humans who fought on the angel side were either dead or too tired to continue. They came up with the lie that the war had ended. That left those of us loyal to

God and the angels to stay and fight a one-sided battle. That was when the first angel blades were bonded to men."

"But Reckoning said the only reason he was able to bond with me was that I am part. . . demon." Malach looked at Elzrod to judge his reaction but found the man glaring at him only in annoyance at his interruption.

"If you want answers, boy," Elzrod almost spat the word boy, "listen to my tale and don't interrupt. After I am done, you can ask questions." Elzrod turned back to look out to the horizon again. "What Reckoning told you is true, but a human can be bonded to a blade by the will of God as well. The first human to be bonded to the blade found his strength was enhanced and he could do far more than he would have been able to do on his own. Many think they were given the power of angels to do God's bidding. Twenty blades were given, one for each of the men and women who were loyal to their calling. Only five of those twenty remain. Now, we are six, since you are primarily human; although Reckoning was not in the original twenty blades. Some were destroyed by the enemy. Some, like Reckoning, were captured and made to do the bidding of the demons."

"What about my parents?" Malach blurted out before he could stop himself.

Elzrod sighed, "I was getting to that, boy. Be patient."

"Sorry," Malach murmured.

"How old do you think your parents were?" Elzrod asked, seeming to switch topics.

"Between three and four hundred, I think. I was too young to care about it at the time, but that's what I am told," Malach replied.

"How old do you think I am?" Elzrod asked.

It was Malach's turn to sigh. "Maybe five or six hundred. But that's just a guess. Though you are very fit for your age, if you don't mind me saying."

Elzrod chuckle at that, "I wish I was still that age. Or even looked that age. The fact is that when the blades were bonded, the bearers were given a much longer life than they ever wanted or anticipated. I am two thousand, four hundred and twenty-two years old as of a few weeks ago, and there doesn't seem to be any end in sight, save a valiant, violent one. Yet, I can tell even now that day is not far off."

Malach chuckled nervously after a moment of silence. "That's a good joke, Elzrod. You had me going there for a second. But no one can be that old. Can they?"

"I do not jest, Malach," Elzrod turned again to Malach and looked him directly in the eyes, and Malach knew every word was true.

"Your parents both wielded an angel blade and were much older than anyone would have realized. Your father carried the blade has been recently liberated. Your mother's blade is still out there, as far as we know, in the hands of the enemy."

Malach's knees buckled, and he was forced to sit down, hard, against the wall. He needed time to process this information, but Elzrod continued, not giving him the time he needed.

"Your father was the angel Ariel; your mother, a human, bonded to a blade. They were on a mission together for many years, trying to infiltrate a human group that was thought to be working with the demons to build the new army. They were thought to have been captured and killed. Imagine our surprise, four hundred years later, to hear about a couple matching their descriptions living in Brightwood with a young son. I was dispatched right away to find them and bring them back."

"Did you kill them?" Malach asked, his tone turning dangerous.

"Malach, why would you think that? They were two of God's most loyal. They had simply strayed from their path and I was sent to bring them, and their new son, back into the fold. But the demons must have gotten the same intel as us and beat me there. Your parents had already been taken when I got there."

"Taken?" Malach asked. "You mean killed."

"No, I mean taken," Elzrod replied firmly. "We believe your parents are still alive. At least your father. An angel's death leaves a mark and sends a kind of ripple the angels and bearers can feel. At the height of the war, it was so common to feel a ripple of an angel's death they wouldn't know who died or pinpoint the time of their death. But now that the war is fought in the shadows, a death ripple would have easily been felt and pinpointed to your father's death; however, none of us felt that and haven't felt it since. I left you in the relative safety of Brightwood when you were a boy, but only for your father's sake. I hoped to find and liberate him and bring him back to you. However, once you came of age, you were deemed a threat by the demons, and one was dispatched to kill you. The cruelest part of their plan was most likely to kill you with your father's blade and then bond it back to your father, making him watch your death over and over until it broke him."

"Wait," Malach said, realizing the full meaning of that last part. "You're telling me that Reckoning was my father's blade?"

"Yes," Elzrod replied. "I just stated that."

"And Reckoning didn't tell me before now?" Malach continued.

I did mention Ariel was my last wielder before the demon, Reckoning chimed in. *I didn't know you were Ariel's son. I only found out after talking with Storm and Elzrod this morning. If you remember, I was taken from Ariel before he and your mother left the army and settled in Brightwood. I had no knowledge of you.*

Malach finally put it all together in his head and got everything straight. He was the son of an angel, most likely the only son of an angel. His father, and possibly his mother, were still alive. He could save them and then go back to Brightwood and live happily with them. Like they were before. They would face any opposition that threatened them together, angel or demon.

Elzrod smiled at Malach albeit a bit sadly. "Luckily, and I'm not sure how, you survived the encounter and took back your father's blade. He told us where your father was being held."

"Then what are we waiting for?" Malach sprung to his feet. "Let's go get him!"

"A dispatch of angels is already on their way; they will reach the place in Demon Territory much faster than we could even prepare to leave," Elzrod told him. "If he is there, they will bring him back, and if not, they will hopefully find a clue leading them to him. As soon as we know something, I will make Reckoning aware so he can relay the information to you."

"Fine," Malach said, crossing his arms. He didn't like it, but he realized the Elzrod was right, and he wouldn't be able to do anything but wait. "But I want to know the moment they know anything!"

"That's fair," Elzrod conceded. "Malach, we need to start your training immediately. Now that they know of your identity, you *will* be hunted."

"Not if I stay in the city," Malach argued. "I may not want to fight on the demons' side, but I don't want to fight for the angels, either. If I stay here in the city, neither side can touch me. I'm sure you aren't even supposed to be here. That's why you posed as a lowly city guard instead of the mighty warrior that you are. Am I right?"

"Well, yes, technically I'm not supposed to be here, but your first assumption is wrong," Elzrod said hesitantly.

"You will only be safe here until the city falls."

"Falls?" Malach scoffed. "Have you seen this city? The demon army is not strong enough now to raze the city. And what would that accomplish?"

"They will not take it by force. They will take it by the hearts of the inhabitants. You have already seen the violence even among the city's so-called protectors. Many of the political leaders and men who are in charge of this city have already given their allegiance to the demons, though they hide it carefully. It may be another year or another hundred years before the demons take control of Newaught, but mark my words, that day is coming. I believe it will happen sooner rather than later. Malach, soon you will have to pick a side, regardless of what you want. I can start training you now. You could defend yourself and your friends much better, but only if you let me."

Malach thought about this for a long time and Elzrod waited patiently. "Fine, I will submit to your training, but I still won't pick a side." Malach stubbornly set his jaw.

Elzrod nodded and turned back to look out at the plains.

Malach watched him for a few minutes, waiting for the older man to tell him what to do. When no instructions were forthcoming, Malach thought he might have gotten distracted. "Elzrod? Are we going to start training?"
"Tonight," was the simple response.

"Well, I thought you would say something like, 'We start now' and, you know, start training me," Malach said, coming to stand by Elzrod at the edge of the wall.

"Malach, as you have pointed out, I am not supposed to be here. As such, I cannot train you as a Blade Bearer while under the guise of a common city guard. We will have to do that on our own time," Elzrod said. "We can use the training grounds at night. However, most of the training can be done in your mind while you sleep, using the link between the blades."

"But if our minds are active all night, won't we be tired during the day?" Malach asked, remembering what Reckoning had told him.

"Yes, but a few hours a night won't hurt anything, and you will still wake almost as rested as you normally would."

"Sounds like a plan. So, what do we do for the rest of the day?" Malach asked, already getting bored at staring at nothing.

"We will play a game to keep our mind occupied and still watch the plains for potential danger," Elzrod answered seriously. "Have you ever played a game called I Spy?"

Chapter 13

Malach trudged back to the house he shared with Daziar after a long, boring day of standing guard on the wall. Elzrod assured him most of their days would be spent training or playing mediator in the city, and only one day out of every two weeks would they have wall duty.

Those days are going to be torture, Malach thought.

Malach and Skie turned the corner onto their street, and the house came into view. Skie bounced along next to him. She had taken an immediate liking to Elzrod and was at ease enough to curl up and sleep. She had woken up and stretched a few times, and Elzrod and Malach had shared their lunch with her, but she hadn't had much else to do. They reached the front door, and Malach opened it, allowing Skie to walk in. He should go talk to Daziar and Honora, but all he wanted to do was crawl into bed. Although even that wouldn't give him much of a break since Elzrod, Storm, and Reckoning would be waiting to train him in his mind.

How did he get so deep into this in such a short time? Just days before, he had arrived at Newaught, thinking it would be a quick two-year journey to the rest of his life. Now it seemed like the rest of his life would be spent in hardship and fighting.

"Good evening, Malach!" Honora said excitedly. "How was your day? Mine was wonderful. I spent all day getting to know all the horses that I will be taking care of and. . . what's wrong?"

"Mal?" Daziar enquired. "Did something happen today?"

"Yeah, I found out that the man training me, Elzrod, has an angel blade and has been talking with mine behind my back for quite some time," he replied.

"Really?" Daziar asked at the same time Honora barked, "Angel what?"

I don't think that's a fair assessment of the situation, Reckoning mumbled in the back of his mind.

Malach explained the angel blade to Honora, and then what had transpired between him and Elzrod.

"Malach, that's great news!" Honora said. "Your father is alive, possibly your mother, and you're not part demon; you're part angel!"

"Remarkable," Daziar said, more muted than Honora.

Malach thought he might have grasped the full extent of the situation a little better than Honora, or maybe she was just trying to cheer him up.

"That's a lot to process in one day," Daziar continued. "My day was spent at the market trying to find the thief who stole some goods there. I think it was a member of the Shadows, but Jarsar thinks it was just street urchins. But back to the matter at hand, the angels are going to save your father and bring him back. There shouldn't be anything to worry about, and you get your dad back after all these years. And you get to be trained by probably one of the greatest fighters in the world. I'm not sure how your day could have gone any better, other than not being attacked by the demon."

Malach realized his friends didn't share in his desire for a quiet life. He sighed and stood up.

"Malach." Honora stood with him. "I know you don't want this kind of life, but you can't deny you were meant for this. Your father is an angel, your mother, blade-bonded. Now you're attacked by a demon with your father's blade and you won it back. Now you are bonded to it and you must take it up and fight."

"Honora, I don't want to fight. We have been trained our whole lives to fight, and all I want to do is live my life in peace," Malach complained. "I don't want this blade. I don't want any powers. I don't want my father to be an angel. I just want to be normal."

"You're *not* normal, Mal," Daziar said resolutely. "We are past the point where we could go back, but I can promise you won't be alone. I will follow you to battle or wherever this takes you."

"Me too!" Honora exclaimed. "I don't know how much help I would be in a fight, but I will help in any way I can."

"Thanks, you two, but I don't want to drag you into the coming war when you could avoid it," Malach told them, though in truth, he would love to have their company. He just didn't want them to get hurt.

"Hello, you're talking to the person who came to Newaught for action and adventure," Daziar laughed. "What could have more action or be a better adventure than a war and being a part of its beginning? You couldn't stop me if you tried."

"I'm not letting my two best friends go to war without me, so you can't kick me out that easy," Honora said, and even though Malach could tell it was mostly false bravado, he knew she wouldn't back down for anything.

Malach smile for the first time that day, "Thank you. You are my best friends, and I'm not sure I could ever have better."

"Of course you couldn't," Honora laughed. "Now get some food and get to bed. You look exhausted."

"Yes, ma'am," Malach chuckled and did just what she said.

Honora and Daziar talked about how their day had gone at their new jobs while he ate. Both were very excited about the direction their lives were taking them. Malach was happy for them, but he couldn't help but feel jealous their lives were going the way they wanted. That caused him to feel guilty. He didn't want to begrudge them their happiness, and it just made him feel altogether terrible.

"I'm going to call it a night. Feel free to stay up as long as you want. You won't bother me," Malach told them.

"But you've only eaten half your dinner!" Honora protested, playing the part of the mother hen.

"I'm fine. Thanks for the dinner. It was really good. I just don't have much of an appetite tonight." Malach set his plate down and walked upstairs.

He stripped off his leather armor and weapons, listening to Daziar and Honora finish their meal. He laid his bow on the floor next to the pile of armor and sat down for a moment, letting his muscles relax. After a while, he heard Daziar see Honora off and close the door. He went downstairs again and, without a word to Daziar, laid down on his bed and put Reckoning under his pillow. He laid in bed for a few moments and thought about what awaited him in his dreams.

Malach, Reckoning's voice in his head startled him and made him jump. *Sorry,* He said sheepishly. *However, Elzrod and Storm have news of your father. You must fall asleep right away for them to communicate directly with you.*

Great, Reckoning, you just ensured that I won't fall asleep anytime soon, Malach thought back. *He would never get to sleep with thoughts of his father running through his head and the anticipation of the news that was to come.*

I can put your mind into a state of rest if you will let me, Reckoning told him.

Wait, you can put me to sleep anytime you want? That thought disconcerted Malach.

No, just when you are willing and in a quiet and restful situation. And it's more like I can calm your mind and allow you to fall asleep quickly. It's very useful in the field where rest doesn't come easily.

I'm sure it is. Malach considered the offer for a moment and closed his eyes. *Fine, but only because I give you permission. Don't go trying to trick me into sleep whenever you feel like it.*

Of course.

Nothing seemed to happen and Malach started to wonder when he would fall asleep, *How long does this normally take?*

"Open your eyes, Malach," Elzrod's voice came from in front of him. He was startled into obedience. The guards' training grounds were in front of him, but only the training grounds. The walls seemed blurry, and just beyond them, everything was in shadow.

"What have you heard about my father?" Malach demanded.

"Nice to see you, too," Elzrod said sarcastically. "I know. It's impressive that we can construct the training grounds in our minds and train here as if we were really awake. Glad you realized this."

"Elzrod," Malach growled dangerously.

"Not one for small talk," Elzrod noted. "Fine. There's good news and bad, Malach. They weren't able to make it there in time to save your father. The demons had already moved him, and the place had been abandoned for serval days, maybe more."

"And the good news?" Malach asked, his heart sinking in his chest.

"That is two-fold." Elzrod held up one finger. "We found your father is being held at a prison, underground, in Demon Territory. We don't have the exact location yet, but we're working on it." He held up the second finger. "Your father was being held with another prisoner, who we believe might be your mother." Malach's heart skipped a beat. "There is evidence of torture, but no evidence either of the prisoners were killed, so we believe they are still alive. We don't know for how long, but there is hope."

"How can I help?" Malach asked, feeling very helpless even as he said it.

"Training," Elzrod implored.

"I don't see how that will help my parents. I want to help them now," Malach said, determined to be useful in some way. "Maybe I can help sift through information or help scout some areas they think the prison is in."

"Malach," Elzrod held up a hand. "We have our best scholars working on this and angels are scouting those areas already. The best thing for you to do is train with me so that, when the time comes, you can liberate your parents. I know is hard to sit and wait for this, but you are not ready to face a demon. You would be a liability in a fight or even get yourself killed."

"Fine, teach me to fight. I want to kill any demon who has hurt or would hurt my family," Malach said.

A fire seemed to light in him. He was angry, and he wanted revenge on the beings who took his parents from him. He wanted to kill them, but didn't have the skills to.

"Let's start then," came a female voice from the shadows.

A stunning young woman walking out of the shadows to Malach's right joined Elzrod. She was tall and slender but still had a strong build. Malach had no doubt she could handle herself in a fight, but she was probably the most beautiful woman he had ever seen. Her skin was bronzed and her figure perfect. Stunning silver hair flowed down, the ends colored purple. She moved with the grace of a dancer and wore a sword at her side. She walked up to Malach. He was mesmerized.

"You know, if you keep gawking like that, a woman might get a little offended."

Out of nowhere and with blinding speed, she drew her sword, and Malach felt a pain in his neck. The next thing he knew, he was watching his body fall to its knees in front of the lady and then complete its fall to the ground limply. Then everything went black.

The woman had cut off his head!

His mind was still reeling when he was blinded by a white flash and he was back in the training field. His hands went immediately to his neck, and he found he was once again whole. He realized he was breathing rapidly and tried to get it under control. The woman was standing next to Elzrod once again, her sword still drawn but free of gore.

"Wha. . . what just happened?" Malach stammered.

"While you were distracted by my form, I took your head from your shoulders," the young lady said matter-of-factly. "Let that be your first lesson. Don't let a pretty face fool you."

"Storm, is that any way to treat our new apprentice?" Elzrod admonished, but Malach could hear a bit of mirth in his words.

"You're Storm?" Malach asked.

"Who else would I be?" she asked, as if he had just asked the dumbest question.

"Well, I guess that makes sense. I didn't think we could get hurt here. And how am I alive now?" Malach asked again, his hand involuntarily feeling his throat once more.

"You can get hurt in your own mind. If a demon penetrates your mind, you must be ready to fight," Elzrod explained. "But no matter what happens, he can't permanently hurt you unless he breaks your will. He could rend your head from your body, as an example, but if you still have the will to live, it won't do him any good. However, you can still feel pain in your mind, so he may try to torture you to break your will. It's best if you block him out altogether, but that's a lesson for when we are in the real world. Here we will be focusing on physical battle. Since when we are in the real world, I cannot teach you everything you need to know without drawing suspicion. Also, since we are learning everything here, you will have to pretend to be worse than you are when on the training field. As a recruit, it would be suspicious if you progressed faster than you should."

"Fine, but at least give me a chance to defend myself before killing me," Malach protested.

"Your enemies won't give you a chance. Why should I?" Storm asked, and attacked.
Malach threw up his hands and a slender metal bo staff appeared in them. He deflected the overhand swing from Storm and used the other end to hit her in the side. He might have hit her a little harder than he normally would, but he didn't care, since she had just killed him moments before. She took the blow in stride and came at him with a crosscut with such speed Malach didn't have time to deflect it. Her sword bit deeply into his side and pain exploded from the wound.

Storm pulled the sword from his gut where it had stopped, twirled and ended him with a stab to his heart. He again found himself in the blackness and again saw a flash of white. The training ground appeared, and he stood there whole and unharmed. He sighed, turning to face Storm once again, this time with bo staff ready. He had a feeling this was going to happen a lot.

"Hold!" Elzrod called, holding up his hand for them to wait.

"Malach, how do you expect to kill Storm with a bo staff? That weapon is for sparring matches, not for combat."

"Well, I guess it was the first weapon I thought of when I was attacked so suddenly, and rudely, might I add," Malach pointedly glared at Storm when he said the last part.

"You're never going to kill her that way," Elzrod stated. "Let me show you a weapon you might like."

Elzrod lifted his hand to the side of his body, and a staff weapon appeared from nowhere. It appeared to be a bo staff until Malach looked at the end of the staff. On either end, there was a cross guard and a double-edged short sword attached, making it easy to deflect an attack in one motion, like the bo staff, but deadly and dangerous, like a sword. It was the weapon he carried in his dreams all those nights he was killed by the demon. This was the path that would lead him to that dream. It would lead him to a bloody, painful death at the hand of a demon. He wouldn't perform great deeds. He wouldn't rescue his parents. He would simply die in the attempt.

He turned and fled from the training grounds, Elzrod shouting behind him, footsteps of someone chasing him slowly fading. The blackness enveloping him started to change. A forest materialized out of it. He slowed, realizing he was in the demon's forest. The staff weapon Elzrod showed him clutched in his hand, and his bow strung across his back. Something in the forest crashed behind him and instead of running, he turned to face it. The demon, taller than a building, loomed over him and he bared his teeth in defiance. Had it gotten bigger? The demon pulled a blade from nowhere and it grew to Malach's full height before bursting into a dark flame. Then it came at him, swinging his blade wildly. Malach was somehow able to fend the demon's attacks off, though later he wouldn't remember how he had managed it. He pushed the demon back and jumped back himself, giving them some breathing room. He didn't know how to kill this thing, but it could bleed, and that was enough. Swinging the new weapon clumsily, unaccustomed to its weight and balance, he hit the demon's sword. He used the energy created to spin off toward the demon's other side, stabbing the blade in deep. The demon bellowed and swatted at Malach like he was a fly, hitting him square in the chest and sending him flying into the underbrush.

Dazed, Malach sat up, watching the demon walk toward him.

He struggled to get up. Between the entangling brush and his foggy brain, he wasn't able to gain his feet. This was it. This was where he died if he continued fighting against the demons. He lived a little longer this time, but there wasn't anything he could do about it. This would be his fate in the real world, and he knew it. Maybe he would be better off fighting on the demons' side. The demon smiled, its wicked grin looking as if it had won something more than their fight.

That's what it wants! He realized in a sudden moment of clarity.

Storm came out of nowhere. The demon bellowing in agony. It turned and Malach could see Storm was hanging on to one of its shoulders by the hilt of her sword, which was plunged deep into the demon's back. That was what it was shouting about. Elzrod was beside him, helping him up then. The fog in Malach's brain was starting to lift as he gained his feet.

"This is what you're afraid of, isn't it, boy?" Elzrod shook him by his shoulders.

"Yes. If I train with you, I will die by this demon's hand. It has happened almost every night for three years," Malach told him.

"Then let's kill this thing once and for all," Elzrod growled, drawing the same sword Malach had seen Storm holding. He would have to figure out that conundrum later. He lifted his weapon and followed Elzrod onto the battlefield.

The demon was still preoccupied with trying to pull Storm off his back, turning and reaching, but never quite able to get at her. Elzrod ran up to its leg and swung his sword at it. The blade bounced off harmlessly and Elzrod took an involuntary step back.

"Go for the underarms and the side," she called down. "There's less armor there and at the joints."

Malach lunged and stabbed the demon in the back of its knee. It bellowed as its knee collapsed, trapping Malach's weapon between two of the armor plates. Malach tried to pull it free, but before he could, the back of a large clawed hand hit him broadside, launching him across the clearing. His head smacked against something hard, and he saw stars in his vision. He rolled onto his stomach and looked up.

Storm was being dragged off the demon's back by her leg and flung to the side; her sword fell to the ground, point in. The demon turned to face Elzrod.

Malach's vision darkened to the point he could only see vague shadows. He could just make out Elzrod fighting the demon. He forced himself to his feet, vision still hazy, but his knees buckled, and he hit the ground again. When his vision cleared, he saw Elzrod running to him.

"Get up, boy! This is all in your mind!" Elzrod yelled. "Focus Malach. He only has the power you give him!"

Malach could hear what Elzrod was saying, but none of his words made sense to Malach's rattled brain. In his mind? They were in his *mind*. The demon wasn't real. He heard its deafening bellow and felt the sound reverberate through his chest. It *felt* real, though.

"Malach, listen," Elzrod panted. "This demon has infiltrated your mind! The demon is real, but it is still in *your* mind. Your will is all you need to defeat it."

Malach understood what he was saying now. But how does one will a demon out of one's head? Somehow, he didn't think that thinking really hard about it would cut it. Malach realized his weapon was back in his hand. How did that get there? Elzrod and Storm were fighting the demon now. He had to help. Maybe if he defeated the demon in his head, it would drive it out.

Using his weapon to get to his feet, he rushed forward with all his strength and, willing it to happen, he cut clean through the demon's knee. Thick, black blood spurted from the severed limb and the demon collapsed to the side, screaming in agony. It seemed like all the fight went out of it as Malach brought his blade around and severed its head. He watched as the head rolled, coming to a stop in front of him. The red eyes of the demon faded and with the light going out of the demon's eyes, so did the surrounding light. He fell into darkness and hit the sand of the training field.

He laid there for a few seconds, breathing hard, his weapon next to him in the sandy soil. Elzrod and Storm were not far away, just getting up off the ground. Both of them breathing just as hard as Malach. Malach's weapon changed into the young man that he recognized as Reckoning.

"What in the three territories just happened?" Malach asked, sitting up.

Elzrod walked over to him and helped him the rest of the way to his feet. "That demon has been worming its way inside your head for a long time. How long have you had nightmares like that?"

"About three years ago is when they started," Malach said. "Wait, are you telling me that this demon has been in my head for three years?"

"In some way, yes, but it probably hasn't had that much power or say over you since it seems to be just getting into your dreams." Elzrod said. "They can only get in by overpowering you or working their way in slowly, and their power is weakened over distances, since it was too dangerous for a demon to stay in Angel Territory, it would have had to work its way in starting at your weakest point."

"In my sleep? Dishonorable spawn of Hell!" Malach spat. "I've been worried and afraid of sleeping for the last three years!"

"Did the dreams stop when you picked up Reckoning?" Storm asked.

"Right about that time, yeah," Malach confirmed.

"That would make sense. I would be able to boost your normal, innate ability to block out other minds," Reckoning told him.

"Then why could he attack me now?" Malach asked.

"I'm not sure," Reckoning admitted. "Possibly because it's closer, and it's already established the connection so many times in the past. You severed that when you killed it in the dream. We need to spend some time teaching you to block your mind from unwanted attacks."

"A lesson for tomorrow during gate duty," Elzrod replied. "Until then, Storm will block all attacks while we train. We should have been doing that anyway. I just didn't realize they had that big of a foothold in your mind."

"For now, I want to sleep," Malach said. "Actually sleep, without my mind being active," he added as Reckoning opened his mouth to speak. "I haven't gotten a good night's sleep in three years, and now that that thing is out of my head, I want everyone out for the night. I can resume training in the morning."

"Fine," Elzrod conceded. "I can agree to that. Have a good, uneventful night's sleep, Malach."

"Thanks," Malach said and walked out of the training area into the surrounding darkness.

Amara finished her run that day without throwing up at all. She was also getting faster and had more than doubled the distance Demien set that first day. But she hadn't found any evidence that Demien, or anyone else, was the traitor. Borden hadn't talked with Demien after the night in the library, and Amara didn't know how to find out anything more. She could talk with the Master, but she didn't know if she would want to hear speculation instead of cold, hard facts.

Amara's shoulder was healing nicely, and it would only be a couple more weeks until she wouldn't have to go to the healers. Only a week or two after that, and she would be fine to do whatever she wanted. Though, Demien would step up her training at that point, in preparation for her first job. He was only losing money on her until she started stealing again. He didn't seem to mind, though. At first, his off-putting, superior attitude had gotten on her nerves, but after a week of training with him, she could tell he actually cared about those under his charge. He just didn't show it. In fact, she was questioning if he had anything to do with the mole or knew anything about it at all.

Although, there was always that nagging feeling in the back of her head he was keeping secrets. Sometimes he would disappear on their runs, just to show up again later down the tunnel. It could be he simply ran ahead and was just waiting for her to catch up, but she thought he was doing something during those times.

She hadn't seen him wear his cheap suit since the night of the feast, and she thought he was better for it. The suit gave the wrong message, though he didn't seem to care what everyone else thought of him. Now he sat across the table from her, eating breakfast. She realized, for the first time, she didn't *want* him to be the mole. It wasn't that she *liked* him or anything, but she was beginning to not hate him, and that was a start.

"What?" he asked, catching her staring at him.

"I was just thinking that you weren't a complete cretin," Amara said, telling him some of the truth. "But now I can see that was just a trick of the light."

He cocked a half grin at her. "Well, you're turning out to be a mediocre student."

"I'm better than mediocre, and you know it," Amara protested. "I'm probably the best student you have ever had."

"I've had rocks learn faster than you."

"I bet those were the only things that would listen to you. Satan knows you don't have any friends."

Demien's face turned serious instantly. "Don't say that name here," he hissed.

"What? Why?" she asked.

She hadn't taken him for a religious man. She didn't believe in that. Sure, maybe at one-point angels and demons had fought, but that war was long gone. She figured if there were any angels or demons left, they wouldn't want to start any war anytime soon. Then there was the issue of God and Satan. She didn't know if they *ever* existed.

There weren't any reports of them actually fighting any battles, except for that one mention of the man who claimed to be God's son about two thousand years ago, and people said he died in the last battle. Though, people also say the angels won that battle. Again, Amara didn't see any evidence of that. A lot of it was superstition, traditions, and stories people told to manipulate others.

"He is said to be king of the underworld, and you don't get much close to the underworld than here," Demien whispered, as if Satan himself was in the chasm ready to pounce on any who spoke of him. "Many of the men even believe the chasm leads there."

"That's a load of hogwash," Amara said, and Demien jumped at the volume of her voice. Amara pretended she didn't notice. "Besides, if there are any demons left, they wouldn't risk coming out under Newaught. They have a veritable army of guards and would be able to kill them."

"Fine, believe what you want, but I think the war is going to start up again, and I wouldn't be surprised if it happened tomorrow," Demien crossed his arms. "Well, let's get cracking at these books, since you can't do much else."

"That's not fair," Amara protested. "I killed an assassin, one of the best, I might add. One doesn't walk away without a wound or two."

"That's your excuse." Demien barked a laugh. "Well, when I'm done with you, I think you will change your tune."

"We'll see," she said, non-committal.

They got up and walked toward the study room they had been using.

"So why romance?" Amara asked, grinning.

"What?" Demien looked shocked, and a little horrified. "How did you know?"

"Every few nights you go to the library and pick out a new romance novel," Amara said with confidence. "I'm just curious. Why romance?"

"Since you've been spying on me, can't you tell me why?" Demien asked. "Maybe you need a little more training on information gathering."

"I've tried, but the mark keeps that information hidden more than anything else it seems," Amara said, switching to more impersonal terms as if they were talking about a scenario. "It seems like he hides that one thing over any other secret."

"Then it must be important to him over any other thing," Demien stated, as if he were miles away from there. "He won't part with it easily."

"I will just have to keep looking," Amara said, becoming a little embarrassed and wanting the conversation to end.

"Or you could try a different tactic," Demien said, almost as if he wanted to tell someone his secret.

"Like get him drunk and fish for the answer once his tongue is a bit looser?" She didn't know why she continued now, when just a moment ago, she wanted to stop, but it was out there now.

"Why not just ask him?" Demien asked.

They had made it to the study room, and he sat down at the table heavily.

"I did," Amara said.

"So you did," Demien sighed and paused for a moment. "Someone I cared for used to read them. I gave her a hard time about it every day until she didn't come back from a job. Now I read any and all of them in her honor. And I found that I actually enjoy them."

"That's who Borden is planning on avenging," Amara said before she realized it.

"What? How do you know about that?" Demien jumped to his feet.

"Spying, information gathering. You taught me, hello," Amara said, trying to recover, though now he knew she had been spying on him from the beginning and not as a part of her training.

Demien sighed again and sat down. "Yes, he plans to kill the guard who arrested Viessa."

"Viessa?" Amara asked. "Borden called her Runt"

Demien chuckled. "She never liked that nickname, but that never stopped Borden from calling her that. She was small, like you, and Borden called her that from the first time they met. That was before we were officially a chapter of the Shadows."

"I can understand why she wouldn't like that name," Amara said, thinking if Borden ever called her that, she would knock him out cold. If she could.

"Yes, well, you and she are much alike, actually," Demien continued. "The problem is that Borden doesn't see that the guard was just doing his job. It was the mayor who put her to the sword without trial. Without giving us a chance to rescue her."

"Why kill the guard, then?" Amara asked.

"He is mad with grief," Demien said. "You see, he loved her too. Though she didn't reciprocate his feelings. Now he thinks that since I won't kill this guard, he loved her more. He's gotten a group together to pull off this scheme, and I don't think that it will go well for him. Besides the fact that it wasn't the guard's fault."

"But he's going to break one of our laws," Amara said. "Why would he do that for something that's not worth it?"

"He thinks it's worth it. And he thinks he will get away with it." Demien sighed for the third time. "Love makes you do crazy things, Amara, especially if the one you love dies."

Amara thought for a minute and then decide to fish for more information. "If Borden is willing to kill, do you think he would be willing to do more than that?"

"You're talking about the rumors of a traitor," Demien stated, "the one who allowed the assassin in."

"Uh, yeah, I guess," Amara said, non-committal. She was walking a fine line, and she knew it. If she gave up too much, she would out herself as the master's spy, but she had to show she knew something or she would never get anything in return.

"I can't believe the Borden would go that far. I've known him for a long time, and although killing would be something he is capable of, becoming an assassin and betraying all of his friends here? I don't think he would stoop that low," Demien sounded so sure of himself that Amara believed him at his word.

But then he added, so quietly the Amara could barely hear him, "Though someone in his group might."

She pretended like she hadn't heard him and continued, "So why don't you join them? I mean, Viessa loved you and you loved her, so why not join them to get revenge? You could steer them toward who was really responsible for her death."

"One, I've tried to direct his anger already and failed. Borden simple won't see the facts. Two, it's not something she would have wanted." Demien looked like he was starting to get upset over the memories of his lost loved one.

"She wouldn't have wanted us to become murderers and assassins, but to continue living our lives. She wouldn't want revenge. She would want peace and happiness. I believe I would be doing her name a dishonor if I were to let myself become such a monster. Instead, I read what she enjoyed to keep her memory alive in my life."

Amara saw a tear fall from one of his eyes, and he turned away quickly to wipe it. She didn't think Demien was the traitor after listening to his story. In fact, she was pretty certain he wasn't. So she decided to lay all the cards on the table and enlist his help.

"Demien, I'm sorry that this happened to Viessa. From what you said, I believe she would have wanted us to stop what is being planned now, not just stay out of it," Amara said. She took a deep breath, let it out slowly, and then continued. "The master has asked me to find the traitor. I think we need to not only find this traitor, but to stop Borden's plans. And I need your help to do it."

"You mean now that you don't think *I'm* the traitor?" Demien said calmly.

"Uh, well, yeah," Amara admitted, thinking that she'd just made a huge mistake.

Demien laughed. "Don't worry, you haven't offended me." He turned serious again. "I knew the master would have suspected me due to my past with her. But that is behind me. I've turned over a new leaf since Viessa's death. But when she brought me a new apprentice shortly after an attempt on her life, I knew you would be looking for evidence to convict me."

"Oh, so you knew all along?" she asked.

"No, I suspected, but you still were able to find out more information about me than I thought you would," Demien told her, seeming genuinely impressed. "But about your ongoing problem. I think your best bet would be to infiltrate Borden's group to find the traitor. At the least, you would find out who in our organization would kill. Even though finding the traitor might be a little harder, I would bet the traitor would be among that group."

"Why do you think that?" Amara asked.

"The traitor would be wanting to find out who he might be able to recruit or turn against the Shadows," Demien explained. "Getting into that group and acting either like a really nasty person or like a wayward soul is easily swayed would be your best bet. The wayward soul act might be easier, in the long run, to pull off but it would be harder up front to get into the group."

"I can act nasty when I want," Amara responded with confidence.

"No doubt," Demien said, a small smile creeping onto his face. "That may be the easiest way in, but you might have to do things, or let things happen, that you are not comfortable with. Do you think you are ready for that?"

"I think so," Although, she was feeling less confident than a few moments ago. "And my arm is almost healed, so I should be able to be useful to the group soon."

"Great, so at dinner tonight, you need to approach Borden and work on infiltrating his group," Demien said. "Don't be too nasty with him, since he will not want to take you if you throw him off too much. Once you are in the group, then you can start working on building your reputation. When the time is right, you will end training with me and start under someone else. I can help start rumors to build your reputation on my end. Also, we need to talk with the master and bring her in on our plan. I will leave that up to you."

"How quickly you come up with a plan. It's almost like you have been thinking about this for a while," Amara said, grinning at him.

"Only for a few weeks, but I needed someone that few people know to do the dirty work." He grinned at her. "It seems like everyone has been doing that to you as of late."

"Yep, it would seem that way," Amara replied with a sigh. "But let's go for it anyway."

Amara sat down next to Borden with her tray. "I want in on your scheme," she said without any preamble. She started eating as if she had simply greeted him and didn't say anything that would be considered dangerous or out of line.

She was rewarded with a slack-jawed look from Borden. He composed himself and cleared his throat. "I don't know what you are talking about."

"Sure, you do, and that look you gave me told me as much. I will meet you in the library, row ten, after dinner to talk about it. See you then." She got up and started to pick up her tray to walk away, but Borden grabbed her wrist and stopped her.

"Or what?" he asked, a warning clear in his tone.

"I tell the master what you are scheming," she said, and pulled her wrist free. She walked off before he could say anything else. She took her normal spot across from Demien.

"What was that about?" he asked, as if he didn't know.

"Nothing," Amara said.

"Well, I want you to meet me in the study room later. I have a new scenario to give you," he said with just the right mixture of sincerity and boredom to be believed.

Demien got up and walked his tray up to one of the drop off stations and walked out of the room. Amara finished her food in silence. Just before she got up to walk away, Borden walked past her and leaned down.

"Meet us tonight at study room one-zero-three soon as you can get away from Demien." It was his turn to walk off before she could say anything.

She watched him go, but couldn't stop herself from grinning. She thought she might look a little maniacal. When she was finished eating, she put her tray up and walked to the study room where Demien was waiting. She walked in and closed the door behind her. They could talk freely in the study room, as it dampened the sound so no one could overhear them.

"Did he bite?" Demien asked as soon as the door was shut.

"Yep, tonight. Study room one-zero-three," Amara replied.

"Good, did you talk to the master?"

"Yes, she didn't like it, but she trusts my findings. Your name is cleared, and Borden's head is on the chopping block no matter what happens. But she knows we don't suspect him of being a traitor. I made sure of that. She does know, however, he would kill a guard for a personal vendetta," Amara said.

"Good, that's the most we could hope for," Demien said, though he sounded a little sad.

"I know he was a good friend, Demien." She tried to console him. "I'm sorry it's come to this, but you know it has to be done."

"Yes, I'm sorry it's come to this too," Demien agreed. "There's not much to do but wait for tonight."

Chapter 14

Amara walked confidently into the room of would-be murderers, as they all turned to look at her. Their eyes said that they didn't trust her, and that she was still an outsider there. She would have to deceive them and make them think that she was really one of them. She would need to find out their plan and, just before or as they were striking, bring the full weight of the Shadows down on them. But most importantly, she would need to find the traitor and bring him, or her, to the Master to be executed.

"'Bout time you joined us," said a scruffy man hunched in the corner.

She realized it was Grent, the hunchback.

"Couldn't get away from Demien until now," she replied coolly. "That man really likes to study books."
Borden let out his bellowing laughter. "That he does. Please close and lock the door behind you, and we will get started."

Amara did so, a little pang of fear stabbing at her as she did, trapping herself in the room. She took a position to the right of the door, leaning on the wall instead of taking a seat at the table in case things went south. There were only three members, Amara making four. She already knew two of them. Borden quickly introduced her to the others and then, in turn, introduced them to her. Grent, or Hunchback, who she already knew, and a dangerous-looking woman playing with a curved dagger, whose name was Xylissa.

"How do we know we can trust her?" Xylissa eying Amara suspiciously.

Borden started to reply, but Amara cut him off before he could say anything. "I didn't out you to the master, did I?"

"You didn't have proof until now," Xylissa countered.

"Look, I understand losing someone you care about to the guards," Amara said, changing to argue with reason. "I never got revenge for what they did to my parents." That was a lie, of course. "So, if I can help someone else get what I couldn't, I would do it in a heartbeat."

Bringing her parents into the lie would disrespect them, but she never knew them, so she didn't care too much. Also, none of these assassins would be able to catch her in that lie, since there was no record connecting her to her parents.

"Fine, but I'll be watching you, and if you step out of line one time, I will end you," Xylissa warned.

"Well, now that that's settled. Can we get started?" Hunchback asked, walking up to the table and sat down.

"Right. Tonight is the time to strike," Borden said, leaning into the group and lowering his voice to a conspiratorial tone and volume.

"Tonight?" Amara asked, alarm sounding in her voice. All three heads turned to where she was standing.

"Yes, tonight," Borden responded. "Just because you wanted in at the last minute doesn't mean we change our plans. Tonight is still the best chance we have to kill the guard. He and his new trainee are manning the wall tonight as one of their only night watches for the next few weeks. If we miss our chance tonight, it will mean we wait weeks for the next one, and I'm ready to have this over and done with."

Amara didn't know what to do. They were moving sooner than she had anticipated, and she had no time to warn anyone. She could leave now, ousting herself as a spy, or see if she could help foil their plans in some other way. She made a quick decision to stay with the murderous group and stick it out.

"Grent is the lookout," Borden was saying. "Amara, you're new to the plan, so you will help Xylissa with the trainee, and then come to help me if things go south with the guard. Does everyone understand?"

"I don't wanna babysit her," Xylissa retorted, looking disdainfully at Amara. "I can take the trainee on my own. *Some* of us have killed in the past."

Borden looked at her, a little shocked, and Amara caught a grin on Grent's face. Could they both be traitors? Obviously, Borden didn't know Xylissa had killed before, but Grent didn't bat an eye. Actually, he seemed to enjoy the thought of Xylissa killing someone. She didn't get to think about this for long, as the group was gearing up. She had all of her knives on her, just in case things went south. Which was a good thing, since they had. They headed out of the study room, through the tunnels, and into the main chamber.

They all climbed onto the cart, and Borden and Grent used the lever in the center of the cart to move them over the chasm and back up the hill to the tunnel's entrance. It was much slower going out than it was when Amara had come in. What had taken her moments to cross at such a high speed seemed to take hours when they were moving the cart by man power. It also could have been her trepidation and worry about what was to come. How could she stop this before it happened? Maybe she should have left to tell the master? It was too late now. She was committed to the path she was on. When they made it to the top of the track, they all got off as Grent pulled the brake lever. This was it then, what she had been working toward since she got to Newaught.

Malach and Elzrod stood on the wall, watching the sun go down on the horizon. He and Elzrod were taking the night shift tonight. Daziar had said he had night shift on the same nights, but he was on a different part of the wall. They wouldn't cross paths tonight unless something were to go horribly wrong. Soon their training period would be over and they would be full guards. However, Malach's training under Elzrod and Storm would be far from finished.

They had gotten word back from the division of angels sent to find his father and mother. They hadn't found his parents at the second location. They had killed a demon, liberated several prisoners, and found another lead which would take them, of all places, close to Newaught, just inside the border of Demon Territory. They presumed the demons might try to leverage them against Malach or use them to gain something else of greater use to them. No one knew for sure why the demons had taken such an interest in Malach, except that he was the only child born to an angel. He had a large role to play, but no one knew, or at least wouldn't tell him, what that role was. Until then, he would stay in Newaught training with Elzrod.

Elzrod, Storm, and Reckoning had taught him how to shield his mind from any outside attack, including angel blades and demons. They kept him on his toes by attacking his mind at different times unexpectedly. They even tried to catch him off guard and attack his mind in his sleep. Storm was the first to do that, and she had killed him four times before he had realized she was attacking his mind, not his body. Once he had, he kicked her out with little effort. He thought that was a bit unfair, but he did learn to stop mind attacks while sleeping. Though most of the time it would wake him up. He lost a bit of sleep that way. Now he was going to lose the whole night, and for what? To look out on the field of nothing. He *hated* guard duty.

Elzrod was prattling on about something or other, and Malach just didn't have the heart or mind to listen or even act like he was listening. His parents were supposedly so close to him. Just across the border and he could do nothing but look in their general direction.

Sometimes it was hard to believe his parents were still alive after believing for years they were dead. They, of course, kept telling him that there was no evidence of his mother being with his father for sure. Only that there was another prisoner and that they weren't an angel. Somehow, he knew they were both still alive. They had to be. He couldn't lose them twice. He didn't know if his psyche could handle it with all that had happened to him. He already felt like he was going crazy. Malach let out a sigh, long and slow.

"Am I boring you?" Elzrod asked.

"To tell you the truth, I haven't been listening for the last few minutes," Malach admitted. "I've just been thinking about my parents. And I'm not much in the mood for a lecture on some obscure battle only you were alive to see."

"I see," Elzrod said, and Malach could tell he was trying not to be disappointed and not doing a good job of it.

"Elzrod, I'm sorry. I just need time to process. A lot has been thrown at me in such a short time. And my parents are alive but in a demon prison. We just got word they've been moved closer, yet I can't do anything to help them." Malach turned and look at Elzrod. "Instead, I'm stuck up on this wall, learning history."

"I understand," Elzrod said. "It's hard to stand idly by knowing someone you love is in trouble."

"Yeah," Malach agreed halfheartedly.

Perhaps Elzrod *did* understand, but it was hard to believe that at the moment. Skie was sitting by him and he looked at her. She was looking at him with mournful eyes as if to say, "I'm here, but I don't know how to help you."

He ruffled the fur on her head appreciatively, and she seemed to smile at him. The major allowed him to have her on duty and it lifted his spirits. He knew it was an exception, but with a word from Elzrod and the papers he was given, plus a little cooperation from Skie, he had agreed.

Skie's ears perked up, and she turned her head to the stairs. Malach turned to look at what she was seeing. Someone was there in the shadows, and neither Malach nor Elzrod had heard them. Malach leveled Reckoning, who was in the form of the pole weapon, at the intruder.

"Come out of the shadows and keep your hands where I can see them," he called.

Elzrod pulled Storm from her sheath with the rasp of steel on leather, as the stranger came out of the shadows. It was a woman. She had her hand up in front of her. No, it wasn't a woman; it was a girl. She was a little younger than him, maybe born in Newaught? She was certainly too young to have made the Journey yet.

"What do you want, girl?" Elzrod asked harshly, and it made the girl flinch a little, but a hard light came into her eyes.

"I don't have a lot of time. I slipped away from a group of assassins that are intent on killing a guard tonight in retribution for an arrest made a few months ago. That arrest led to the death of a Shadows member," she said quickly. "I must go, or they will know something is wrong."

"Wait, I thought the Shadows had something against killing?" Malach said.

"They do, and you aren't going anywhere, little miss," Elzrod said, never taking his eyes off the young girl. "Which guard are you talking about, and where is he stationed?"

"All I know is that he has a trainee with him, and they are on wall duty not too far from here. I thought you might want to know to stop them." She glanced around, eyes wide. "I would ask that you try not to kill them unless it is necessary, though they have brought this on themselves. But I must go now, or they will know something's wrong and may call it off."

"You're a part of the Shadows?" Malach asked. "Why turn your own members in?"

He could tell by the withering look she gave him that her patience was running out. "They are breaking our laws, and the guard is innocent. I would not see an innocent man die when I could do something to stop it. Now please, I need to go. If you get there in time, I will see you there and will help you, but they think I'm scouting the wall to make sure there are no other guards near their target. If I don't show up soon, they might call off the hit until a later time." With that, she turned and dashed down the stairs.

Malach jumped to go after her, but Elzrod grabbed his arm. "We must find out if there is any merit to her warning. We can't go after her if there is someone in danger."

"What can we do?" Malach asked. "We don't know who is going to be attacked. There could be a bunch of guards with trainees manning the wall tonight, and it's a big wall. We can't just check on each one."

"Well, I think we can safely say it would be a guard on this side of the wall and there are two guards with trainees on this side of the wall." Elzrod mused. "She said the one had made an arrest which led to the death of a shadow member. And of those two guards, I know only one who has made an arrest in the past two months. I think we ought to head that way."

"Great, lead the way," Malach said, eager to move. He picked up his bow he had propped up against the wall and checked his quiver of arrows.

Elzrod began moving toward the north side of the wall, and Malach's heart went to his throat. He followed quickly, attaching Reckoning to the holder on his back.

"Elzrod, who is the guard and trainee?" he asked, already suspecting the answer.

"His name is Jarsar; he's the trainer of the other recruit who came in the same day you did," Elzrod said.
Malach tore into a sprint. Daziar was in danger and didn't know it. He would have to get there before the assassins or possibly lose his best friend.

"Malach!" Elzrod called from behind him.

Malach didn't look back.

Elzrod would chase after him, and he knew it was dangerous to run into a fight without more information. In fact, the information given to them could just as easily be a farce to get him to run into an ambush, but if he didn't hurry and the information was true, his friend would pay the price for his caution. To his surprise, Elzrod caught up with him. No one Malach could remember could match his speed for long. That came with being part demon, or part angel, he supposed. He guessed being blade-bonded came with its own set of benefits.

Elzrod didn't stop him until they were close to the post where Jarsar and Daziar were guarding. When they were in sight of the post, Elzrod grabbed his arm and pulled him to a stop. Malach didn't offer too much resistance. He knew that the old man's actions were the correct ones. They needed to assess the situation, but he couldn't help but want to run in and save his friend. He saw the post, but not Daziar or Jarsar.

This post had a building just for standing watch and they would be inside it. Malach wondered briefly if they were too late, but pushed those thoughts aside. Darkness had almost fully fallen, and the assassins would be choosing their time to strike, but he didn't think they would have already attacked. Malach watched Daziar casually step out of the building. They hadn't been attacked yet. Malach turned to Elzrod.

"We need to warn them of the danger," He pleaded.

"Yes, I agree, but if we make ourselves known now, we will become targets as well or scare off the assassins," Elzrod explained quickly. "If we find the assassin's position before, however, we can stop the attack and not have to worry about future ones."

Malach nodded but looked back at his friend, making his rounds around the wall. Malach knew he would walk away from the building and then walk back. When he got the farthest away, the assassins would strike. Where would they be hiding? He saw a shadow move just below the inside of the wall, about twenty paces in front of Daziar. They were hanging off the side of the wall.

He didn't know how many assassins there were, but he would need to get there before the first one struck. He pointed out the assassin to Elzrod and time seemed to slow.

He realized Storm and Reckoning were standing with them, and he knew they had entered into his mind. "Elzrod, we don't have time for this. We must attack now, before the assassin strike. I can get within bow range and take out that assassin on the wall."

"Yes, we do have time. We are thinking this conversation. It is much faster than talking. We can come up with a well-formulated plan and hopefully make it in time to save both men."

Malach looked back at Daziar and watched as his foot ever so slowly dropped as he took a step. It took several moments before it touched down and a few more moments before he lifted his other foot to start the next step.

He turned back to Elzrod. "Fine, but make it quick."

"The girl told us there were multiple assassins, so if you take out one, the rest will attack, most likely costing Jarsar his life. You might save your friend, but losing one life for another is never a good trade," Storm said.

"So, how do we take out all of them?" Malach asked.

"It would make sense that there are only a few of them, two or three, including the girl who warned us," Reckoning suggested. "They wouldn't want to move with much more since they wouldn't want to draw attention to themselves."

Malach turned back to the assassin hanging from the wall.

Daziar had only moved a few steps closer. He search the wall around where he spotted the first assassin and saw that there was a second assassin on the steps not far from the first. This one looked closer to the size of the girl that had come to warn them, though Malach couldn't be sure.

"They have two ambushing Daziar, so they might have two to attack Jarsar as well." Malach pointed out. "What's the plan, then?"

"Well, they might also have a spotter. That's why I stopped you when I did," Elzrod explained. "I just need time to get to the guard house before you warn Daziar. Once that's done, you are free to do what is necessary to warn him. If you don't give me that time, I fear you are forfeiting Jarsar's life."

"Fine," Malach agreed. "Can we go now?"

"Yes, but stay low so you aren't seen," Elzrod said. "It may already be too late for that, but there's always a chance."

Malach snapped back into real-time instantly. He was a bit slower reacting to the sudden change than Elzrod, and the man was already several paces in front of him crouched low behind the wall.

Malach started off after him. It was slower than running upright, but he could still gain ground quickly.

"Go help Daz." Malach hissed at Skie.

Skie seemed to understand and took off at top speed. She couldn't be seen over the parapets, so she would make it well before either Malach or Elzrod.

Malach chanced a peek over the top of the wall. Daziar was almost upon the assassin and redoubled his efforts. Elzrod reached the building. Malach stood up straight and broke into a full sprint, pulling an arrow from his quiver and notching it. Judging the distance, he took aim then, pausing his run, he lifted the bow, drew the arrow back and let it fly in one smooth motion. "Daziar!" he called after the arrow was loosed. "Assassins!"

Daziar and both assassins turned his way and he could see the surprise on Daziar's face at seeing him. The assassin must have seen the arrow flying at him. He loosened his grip on the rope he was holding, dropping a few feet. The arrow skittered harmlessly off the wall. It took Daziar only moments to register what Malach said and moments more to pull his sword from its scabbard. The second assassin rushed up the stairs with knives already in her hands. It was the girl who had warned them of the other assassins.

Daziar didn't know that, however, and whirled, swing his sword at her. As he did, he aimed only by using the sound of her footfalls as a point of reference. He was good and his sword would have struck true if the girl hadn't already anticipated the swing and slid under it. Malach watched the first assassin as he climbed over the wall and threw two knives toward Daziar. Malach realized that assassin was also a woman.

Amara had heard one of the guards she had warned just moments before, calling to the trainee she and Xylissa were supposed to be assassinating. She leaped into action, readying her knives and running up the stairs. She heard the clatter of an arrow hitting the side of the wall and she saw the massive wolf barreling down the top of the wall. At the sight of the terrible beast, her nerves almost failed her. She wondered briefly if it would recognize her as a friend or kill her outright. She saw the trainee's muscles tense to swing his sword. She hit her knees, sliding under the blade, looking up to watch it pass over her head. She let her momentum carry her past the trainee leaving her back exposed to him. She jumped to her feet knowing that Xylissa would be coming over the wall soon.

She was right.

Xylissa rolled her body over the wall in front of Amara before she threw two knives toward the trainee. She hadn't yet suspected Amara had betrayed them. Amara reached up and pulled one of the knives out of the air as Xylissa turned her back on Amara. She assumed Amara would defend her against the trainee and took up a stance to take on the wolf and other guard's attacks. She took two steps forward to reach Xylissa and brought the hilt of the knife she had just caught down on the back of Xylissa's head. The woman crumpled unceremoniously to the ground. She heard a heavy step behind her and knew the trainee would end her life with one swing from his sword, still assuming she was a threat. She turned to face the trainee, preferring to face her death head on. She brought her hand up that held the knife, hoping to get lucky and fend off the first attack.

She heard something move through the air beside her but instead of the pain of a sword biting into her, she heard the thump of another body hitting the ground. Amara looked up and found the wolf had tackled the trainee, saving her from his sword and was now standing on top of him, pinning him to the ground.

Why would it do that? she wondered, Spinning to see the guard she had warned running up. *Had he given a command to the wolf?*

She looked back at the trainee and then again at the wolf. It might have been easier for them if she had died. How did the wolf know not to kill her?

"She's with us, Daz." She heard the guard say to the trainee. "She warned us of the assassins. That's the only reason we got here to save you and Jarsar. We need to make sure Jarsar and Elzrod are alright."

She peered up into the young guard's eyes again. She remembered his eyes from somewhere. They were black and had a depth to them she fear she would fall into and never find her way out. She broke eye contact before that could happen, looking down at the unconscious woman. She decided to tie Xylissa up in case she came to. Amara felt like she had betrayed a friend. Xylissa had trusted her to have her back in that fight and instead she had put a knife in it, luckily not literally.

The door opened, and the guard and trainee readied themselves. She could see a man's form fill the door and knew at once it was Borden. He must have killed his target, and the old guard, and would now kill the three of them. She readied her knives just as Borden fell forward. She didn't understand until she looked back up and saw the older guard standing over Borden's body with a bloody sword in his hand. He must have bested Borden somehow.

She looked past the old man and spotted the guard they had targeted laying in a pool of blood, his own blood, Borden's knife sticking out of his back. She looked back at Borden. He got his misguided revenge, but in the end, paid for it with his life. He knew she had betrayed them. She could see it in his face as the guards rolled his body over. His face had frozen with the look of shock and betrayal on it. She was the last person he saw, and his face would haunt her dreams for a long time to come.

She turned to the young guard. "Do you have a way to restrain this woman?" She decided not to use Xylissa's real name, since it might be linked back to the Shadows.

"Umm. . . no, I don't think I do," he replied, patting different pockets.

"I do!" The trainee said excitedly. He produced a leather thong from his pocket and held it up. "I've even been practicing my knots in case I needed to tie a criminal up!"

"Uh. . . alright," she replied, looking back at the young guard.

He rolled his eyes at the trainee.

When she turned back, she realized the trainee had already finished tying Xylissa's hands.

The older guard came out of the building, "Jarsar is dead. We need to take these two into custody until we can sort out what happened."

Amara panicked at that comment. Not wanting to be taken into custody of the guard, she slung Xylissa's unconscious body over her shoulders and ran. She ran from Borden's eyes, full of the knowledge of her betrayal. She ran from the blood, from the fruits of her labor. The terrible, poisonous fruit of betrayal.

Her feet lead her to the exit they had used to head out on this mission. Before ducking inside the door, she realized she was being watched. She looked at the large man in the cloak. He was the man from the woods who had strong-armed her into making a deal with him. Fear gripped her, but he simply nodded as if he approved. He turned to walk down the alley. She had no idea what any of it meant.

She quickly ducked inside the door before anyone else noticed her.

She didn't remember feeling fatigued carrying Xylissa back to the exit, but once she was there, Amara couldn't carry her anymore. She laid Xylissa's limp form down on the ground and leaned her back against a wall and slid down to the floor. Tears were still streaming down her face. She looked at her hands. How would she live with herself after this? How would anyone trust her? She was just supposed to find the traitor, not betray and get people killed. Borden, they had been relatively sure, was not the traitor, just misguided in his pursuit of revenge. She might have just as well killed him herself. Her actions had killed him.

She heard a growl that grew to a roar as Grent jumped out of the shadow of the door at her. He wrapped his hands around her throat and slammed her head against the wall, but instead of befuddling her mind, it proved to have the opposite effect. Her mind cleared of the fog of emotions.

The threat of death and pain of the blow sharpened everything around her as her brain went into survival mode. She broke Grent's hold on her throat and threw him bodily off her. He landed hard on his back and she stood to her feet shakily.

"You betrayed us!" he yelled, but it came out as a squeal. "Now, you will pay!" He pulled a knife and lunged at her.

He was slow and Amara easily sidestepped and tripped him, sending him sprawling. He was already off balance because of his hunch, so it didn't take much to knock him over. When he hit the ground, he landed on the knife in his hands and it sunk into his hip.

He screamed.

Amara kicked him in the head, knocking him out and silencing his screams. Now she had to get Grent *and* Xylissa down in the tunnels before someone came to see what all the noise was about.

Maybe she could still salvage this mission. She tried to lift the small man, but he was much heavier than he looked. She dragged him to the hidden door and hit the button that opened the entrance. After Grent and Xylissa were inside, she closed the door. She had to stop and rest a few times along the way down the tunnel, but finally managed to load them onto the cart. She pulled the brake lever, allowing the cart to move.

She rode it down, checking on Grent to make sure he was still breathing. The knife had gone in deep, almost up to the hilt, and she didn't want to try to remove it in case he bled out before they reached help. She was about to check on Xylissa when she heard a gasp and a moan come from her direction.

"What's going on?" Xylissa asked groggily.

"Borden's dead." Amara said without emotion. It was almost like her intensity had run out. She had expended all of her emotions and didn't feel anything anymore. Maybe she never would.

"What happened?" Xylissa asked, sounding more awake. "Why am I tied up?"

"You're tied up because you broke our code," Amara told her.

"What?" Xylissa sounded confused now, but fully aware of what was going on.

"You, Borden, and Grent conspired together to kill a man and I'm taking you and Grent back to be tried for your crimes." Amara explained.

"What?" Now Xylissa was struggling against the knots that held her hands together. "You won't get off without punishment, either. You plotted with us."

"The master already knows about my involvement, and she sanctioned me to stop you." Amara explained.

"No!" Xylissa shouted, realization sinking in. "I have friends in the Dark Hallow! They will get me out, and they will kill you!"

The cart flew down the track and as it approached the plateau on the other side of the chasm, she could see two figures standing there. She recognized them as Demien and the master. When she got closer, she pulled the brake lever, holding onto it as it bucked under the pressure of slowing the cart. She should have pulled the lever sooner, as she went past the two, still going a decent speed. She reached the tunnels and went into them a little way before the cart finally came to a full stop. Demien and the master came rushing up to her.

"Amara, what happened?" Demien asked.

"No time, we need to make sure Grent stays alive," Amara told them.

Without a word, Demien ran to find a healer at her prompting.

"Did you hear what Xylissa shouted?" Amara asked the master.

"Yes, she all but admitted she was the traitor. Where is Borden?" the master asked. "Demien told me you and Borden's group left unexpectedly, and we guessed the hit was planned for tonight, so you didn't have a choice but to go with them. What happened?"

"Borden is dead," Amara said somberly. "He was killed by the guards, I warned." Amara filled the master in and then repeated the tale when Demien returned with a healer.

"You think Xylissa and Grent were working together for the assassins?" Demien asked when she was finished.

"Yes," Amara said. "At least, that's the theory."

"Fast thinking, getting the other guards involved. I guess Borden got what was coming to him," the master said.

"As for Grent, he will have to be questioned once he is stable. We need to get proof he was involved, as well as Xylissa or if she was just working alone. I'm having people search their rooms now. We will know soon. Until then, Demien is going to help you get cleaned up. You did well, Amara."

The numbness spread once again through her head and body, making her thoughts slow, "Thank you, Master."

Demien led her to a washroom and helped her get her armor and knives off. She went into the room and washed the blood off her hands and arms, then stripped and slid into the warm water and let herself cry once again for the things she had done and what it had cost her.

Malach and Daziar heaved the body of the big assassin into the cart at the bottom of the stairs leading up to the wall. For all the work they had done to save Jarsar, in the end, it hadn't mattered. He had been dead before Elzrod opened the door. However, Elzrod had been able to kill the assassin that had done the deed. The girl who had warned them had run off with the other assassin before they could take her into custody and left them with the two bodies to clean up. Malach wished he knew how to find her so he could thank her for the warning. Without that warning, Daziar would most likely be dead. He hadn't even gotten her name.

He and Daziar sat down on the stairs, both letting out long, tired sighs. It was about midnight now, but with all the excitement they hadn't noticed the time as much. They still had most of the night to go, though Daziar would most likely be relieved with another team of guards as his trainer had been killed.

"You going to be alright?" Malach asked him.

"I. . . I don't know," Daziar said. He looked shaken. "I'm. . . I don't know what to think. I don't think it's fully hit me yet. Jarsar was just standing next to me not two hours ago, talking about some of the things he had seen and been a part of in the city. Then the next thing I know, he's lying in a pool of his own blood. If he hadn't told me to leave to walk the wall, maybe. . ."

Daziar's voice trailed off, and Malach broke in before he could linger on the possibilities for too long. "You would most likely be dead with him. There was nothing you could have done to change this, and dwelling on what could have been won't do you any good."

"You're right," Daziar responded, but his heart wasn't in it.

"Check in with the major and go home," Elzrod said, walking up to them. "There wasn't much else you could have done, boy."

"Yeah," Daziar said, absently standing to his feet.

"Daziar," Elzrod put a hand on the boy's shoulder and spun him, locking eyes. "Be careful. I don't think there are any more assassins out there, and they weren't targeting you, but if they are still out there, they might be looking for revenge."

"Skie," Malach called, and the wolf plodded over as if she knew the sadness Daziar was feeling and was bearing the weight of his sorrow. "Go with him and make sure he gets home safely."

She trotted up to him and put her head under his hand. He smiled, and they walked off toward the house together. Malach watched them go and then turned to Elzrod. "Do you think we need to worry about the other two assassins?"

"I'm not sure, but they got their target. Maybe they won't be coming back," Elzrod said, though Malach could tell he didn't believe what he was saying.

"You don't believe that." He dared to voice his thoughts. "You know as well as I do that if any of them survived, they will come after one or all of us. We need to be careful."

"Yes, yes," Elzrod waved his hand at Malach. "It was odd the assassin who warned us knocked out and took the other lady. For an assassin, she seemed oddly against killing, even shocked when we killed the big man. She must have known when she told us we might have to kill the assassins."

"Yeah," Malach agreed. "I guess you're right, but I know I won't be sleeping very well for the next few nights with the two of them still out there."

"Yes, I know the feeling," Elzrod said thoughtfully. "Are you alright to finish our watch, or do you need me to find us a replacement?"

"I'm fine," Malach replied, and with all the excitement, he doubted he could go to sleep even if he wanted to.

He was right. With the excitement and the thought of assassins coming back to get revenge, he was wide awake, even through Elzrod's history lessons. As he walked back to the house, he couldn't help but look down every alley and up at every roof top. He made it to the house without any issues, and when he finally laid down on his mat, he fell asleep just as the sun was peeking in through the windows.

Chapter 15

Amara walked through the tunnels of the Shadows' lair. She could feel the stares of her fellow thieves. In the last few days, Grent had confessed to conspiring with the assassins, but blamed it all on Xylissa.

The master had decided not to execute them, but to imprison them and work on them for information regarding the Assassins' guild. They had to, of course, change all the pass phrases to stop any assassins from getting in. The word had spread quickly that Amara was the one to infiltrate and apprehend Xylissa. The master and Demien had made public statements to the Shadows, letting them know Amara was under their orders and her actions were theirs, but that didn't stop the gossip or the general hate for someone who would betray a fellow Shadow. It seemed no one trusted her anymore, and she couldn't get away from all the stares. Demien had said it would get better after a few months, but Amara didn't know if she could wait that long.

She had continued her training with Demien and was finally able to use her arm, though it still pained her slightly. Demien stepped up her training to include climbing and infiltration. They went to the surface a few times to train, but she was always looking over her shoulder for any assassin to come to get retribution for capturing Grent and Xylissa.

Demien had started training her in a few different weapons, including the knife. Although she knew how to fight with a knife, *he* was a master at it. He was showing her things she had never thought of. She was proficient with a bow, but with his teaching, she made leaps and bounds in how well she could use it. He had taught her the sword, though she was not strong enough for a full-length blade, and the dirk he had her using still felt clumsy in her hands. He had helped her procure a knife set that was almost identical to the set she already had to fill out the rest of the sheaths on her armor. She had a full complement of sixteen daggers, as well as two fighting knives hanging from her hips. When she first put all of her weapons on, they felt very heavy, but after a few days of their normal workout routine while wearing it all, she now felt awkward without them.

She couldn't shake the feeling of being an outsider since the events with Xylissa and Borden, and she saw Borden's face every time she closed her eyes. Thinking of the face of the young guard she had warned helped keep her mind off of them. He had a hard expression on his face, and his hands were calloused. He had lived a hard life, but there was kindness in his eyes. His black eyes were familiar, but she still couldn't place where she had seen him. She couldn't help but want to know more about him and his wolf, but she had no way of finding him that wouldn't get her in trouble and possibly executed. But thinking about him was easier than thinking about Borden's betrayal-ridden face at the end of his life. He had gone to his death knowing she had betrayed him, and she would have to live with the knowledge her actions had gotten him killed. She held onto the thought that her actions had also saved at least one innocent life, and possibly more than that, since she had stopped Xylissa from fully betraying the Shadows.

She walked into the study room they had for the day and sat down across from Demien. He had his head in a book, per usual. When she sat down at the table, he put his finger on the page to mark where he was and looked up at her.

"I don't know how much longer I can take this Demien," she told him.

He put a feather in the book to mark his spot and shut it. "Take what?"

"All the suspicious looks and rumors," she said, as if it was obvious. "I can feel the distrust when I walk down a tunnel or the hushed whispers that go silent when I enter the mess hall."

"Those will die down soon," he said, like he had said twenty times before. He opened his book and went back to his reading. "Within the next month or so, they will have something new to talk about and people will start to forget."

"I still see him," she admitted. She hadn't told anyone, and she needed to.

Demien froze, and then once again looked up from his reading, "I would be worried if you didn't."

"He knew at the end," Amara said. "I looked into Borden's eyes as he died, and he knew I betrayed him. He didn't even know about Xylissa and Grent being assassins. He just thought I betrayed him to the guards, and I think it hurt him worse than the sword."

Demien thought for a few seconds. The silence was heavy. "I know he would have accepted the reasons for your betrayal, and he would have admitted he deserved that fate in the end. I know that doesn't make it any easier for you, but you did your best, and you managed to save the guard's trainee from the fate of his trainer. It is your fault it happened the way it did."

She couldn't believe he had said that.

"But I don't think it could have turned out any better any other way," he continued quickly, seeing the look on her face. "I can't know how hard this was for you, but you did your best, and I think that was enough."

Strangely, that made her feel slightly better, but it didn't take away the ache in her heart. She was still responsible for the deaths.

"Amara, you have to know that you made the best decision out of two extremely hard ones. Both choices had bad outcomes, no matter which one you chose. If you told us what they were up to and not warned the guards, both guards would have died, and we would still have no idea who the traitor was. Grent or Xylissa might have talked, but there was no guarantee," Demien was looking at her now, and she couldn't meet his eyes. "I want to say I would have made the same choice, but I don't know that I would have the strength to do what you did, and that is nothing to be ashamed of."

A tear rolled down her cheek before she even realized she was crying. "Demien, I am sorry that I got your friend killed." She was sobbing now and, speaking through the tears, she said, "I don't know if I can stay here anymore. I don't know if I can face you after what I did."

Demien moved quickly around the table and pulled Amara close to him and held her. It helped and made it worse at the same time. He didn't blame her for Borden's death, but she did. She couldn't bear to look at him, knowing she killed someone he had once counted as a friend. She pulled away from him, and he let her.

"I need to clear my head." She got up and left the room. Demien just stood there and watched her go.

She used a different exit than the one that crossed the chasm. This one was a long hike up and exited into the woods outside of Newaught. She walked through the trees and let her thoughts roam.

She didn't know how long she let herself wander, but she found herself under a large oak tree, watching a colony of ants march to and from their nest. Some brought food, and they even worked together to carry some of the larger pieces into the nest. That's how the Shadows worked, she realized. She saw a lone ant of a different color crawling its way up to the nest. Multiple ants ran out to meet it and killed it quickly. She realized that the different color ant was her. She had betrayed Shadows, and she was not a part of them anymore. Sooner or later, they would turn on her. It was time to leave.

She stood and started walking back toward the city. She would get her few things from her room and leave. Maybe she could find a job and make her own way in the world. As she walked, her thoughts circling back to the young guard and who he was. He had the blackest eyes she had ever seen, but she found they didn't frighten her. Instead, she found them alluring and deep. There was more to this guard than she knew, and she needed to find out for her own peace of mind. She realized with a jolt that she was attracted to him.

The memory hit her. She remembered where she had seen him, and the trainee. They were the same two people who were unloading their cart when she first entered Newaught. They had been unpacking their cart and moving into the temporary houses for those making the Journey. That meant he was a trainee, too. He had moved with confidence and had taken command of the situation so quickly she assumed he was a full guard. He was strong and sure of himself. Now she knew where to find him, and damn the consequences; she needed to know this man.

She looked up at the sky. The sun was going down, and even though she wasn't far from the entrance to the Shadows' lair, she would have to be quick to get down there and get to the guard's house before they went to sleep. She hadn't realized how long she had been out here. Maybe she could pay for lodging there, or if they wouldn't let her stay, maybe she could find an inn. She made it down the stairs and to her room in record time.

All thanks to Demien's training regime, she thought with a pang of guilt. She would miss him, but she couldn't live like this anymore.

Looking over her shoulder, wondering if any would trust her again, walking into a room to have all conversation stop suddenly; she couldn't live like that. He would understand. She finished putting her things into her pack, pulled the leather drawstring shut and slung it over her shoulder. She turned to leave and ran right into the master.

"You're leaving," she said, and it was more of a statement than a question.

"Yes. Maybe one day I can return to the Shadows," Amara said. "And my oath still stands. I will never give up this place, if that's what you are worried about."

"No," she said simply, and then added. "I understand. Amara, you will always have a home here, and I personally owe you a debt, not to mention the Shadows as a whole. If you ever need anything, don't hesitate to call on us."

"Thank you, Master," Amara said, dipping her head in respect.

"I'm not your master anymore," the master said. "You can call me Raza."

Raza turned and walked out of the room, leaving Amara absolutely speechless. No one knew the Masters' names. To give Amara her real name was to have full and complete trust in her. She slung her pack onto her back and walked out of her room for what might be the last time. She didn't look back, but kept walking. Even when she got on the cart with the new doorman, she didn't know his name; she didn't look back.

They made it to the entrance, and the man opened the hidden door at the bottom of the abandoned guard house. She made her way through the almost abandoned streets. She didn't remember exactly which house was the trainee's since all the houses looked the same, but she would find it. Starting at the gate, she retraced her steps back down the street. Not far from the gate, she recognized the alley she had stopped in.

From there, she narrowed it down to three houses. There were lights coming from two of them, but the one between them was already dark. She walked over to one side of the middle house and the windows were shuttered. She climbed silently up to the balcony and peered in the windows that weren't shuttered. People always thought that no one can see them on the second floor. She saw two people walking around. One was a man and the other a woman. This was not the right house.

She climbed down and walked over to the other house that was lit. The first-floor windows had curtains, but they weren't drawn all the way closed. A single person sat on the floor, and she got excited for a second, but then a closer look revealed it was a woman. A quick climb to the second floor confirmed there wasn't anyone else occupying that house.

The dark house it is, she thought and trudged over to it.

This house had curtains just like that last one, and they were fully drawn. She thought about knocking but didn't think the occupants would enjoy being woken up, and she didn't know for sure if this was the correct house. She took a quick look around to make sure the street was still empty. It was, so she climbed to the second floor.

Those windows were also covered by curtains and she couldn't see anything inside. She decided to pop the latch on the door and take a look in the house. If it wasn't the guard's house, she would simply leave.

And if it is? She asked herself, but she didn't have an answer.

Maybe she should just wait until the morning. She shook her head, deciding quickly. If it was his house, she would wait until the morning to talk with him, but if it wasn't, she would continue her search until she found the guard. She popped the latch with her knife and carefully opened the door.

Malach was breathing hard and sweating. Though somewhere in his mind, he knew he wasn't really sweating. He was locked in battle with Storm on the training ground in his head. So far, he had only been killed four times, and they had been at it for what seemed like hours, though Malach thought only an hour had passed in the real world. It was still odd how time moved differently in their mind world. He parried three lightning-quick strikes from Storm and initiated a set of attacks against her as a rebuttal. He was getting faster. And he was getting faster in the real world as well.

Augmented by his superhuman strength and the training he was receiving each night, he was able to best anyone who came against him in the training arena except for Elzrod. The pole weapon did not feel awkward in his hands anymore, and he was able to wield it with more confidence.

"You have improved, Malach!" Elzrod called from the sidelines.

Elzrod and Reckoning were standing there, occasionally throwing out tips or advice to Malach. He had yet to best the woman in a fight, however, and she had killed him too many times to keep track of in their second training session, not to mention all the ones that followed. They hadn't allowed him to augment his strength with his will as he had done with the demon. He had to fight her as if it was real life. He rolled through several strikes quickly without stopping, letting his weapon's momentum carry him through the movements. First attacking one side and then the other, spinning and swinging the weapon in large arcs.

Storm jumped back away from Malach's last swing, just as he had hoped she would. Using the momentum of the swing to propel himself forward, he reached out and hit Storm's ankle. The impact made a cracking noise, and he knew he had broken it. Even before her back hit the ground, he was driving one of his blades through her heart, the look of shock evident on her face. Before she died, she smiled at him. Then her body went limp, and her sword fell from her hand.

Reckoning let out a whoop. "Well done, Malach. You have bested Storm in a fight for the first time!"

Malach pulled the bloody blade from Storm's chest and smiled at him. "Now what?"

"We wait for Storm to get back, then we continue. Next, you will face a demon." Reckoning said it with such excitement Malach thought he had heard wrong.

"A demon?" he asked.

"Well, not a real demon, of course. A demon of our own making. You will fight him just like you fought Storm. No augmentation from your mind, which will give you experience fighting demons without having to be in danger."

"That actually sounds like a good plan. Last time I fought a demon, it just about killed me, and I'm tired of having to run from them," he admitted.

"Great. Now we wait. Storm will want to be here for this," Reckoning said.

"So, where is she?" Malach asked. "I mean, usually it's only moments before I'm back after she kills me."

"For you maybe, but it's a good while for us," Elzrod said. He had sat on the ground he had solidified so he wasn't sitting in the sand. "It's different every time, but she will be back, eventually."

"Really? That's why she was always so ready to go. She was getting time to rest between each bout!" Malach said, realization hitting him. "That's not fair."

"Oh, but it is," Elzrod replied. "She earned the respite by killing her opponent. Just as you have now."

"Fine," Malach conceded. "What do you do while you wait?"

Elzrod pulled out a deck of cards and started shuffling, "Well, we've gotten rather good at cards during this time. Care to wager something?"

"Not against you," Malach laughed.

"Malach!" Reckoning suddenly sat straight up. "Someone is in your house."

"Yeah, I know," Malach said. "If you haven't noticed, I live with Daziar."

"No," Reckoning said urgently. "It's the girl assassin. You must wake up now and deal with her."

Amara crept inside the dark room, pausing to let her eyes adjust to the darkness. It was empty, so she crept to the stairs and descended them silently. She saw two forms sleeping on the ground; one was facing away from her. The guard she had come to see, however, was sleeping on his back on the other side of his friend. She moved carefully around the first guard and contemplated waking the second guard now, instead of waiting for morning. She finally decided against that, but she couldn't help but stare at his face for a bit longer. He was beautiful with his black hair and strong jaw. She knew she would be lucky if he ever saw her as even a friend, much less anything more, but she could still look, right?

His eyes suddenly popped open, and he drew a knife, jumping at her. He tackled her and pinned her hand, which still had her knife in it, to the ground. She felt the cold prick of his knife at her throat and involuntarily swallowed. How could she have been so stupid to think that coming here was a good idea?

"What are you doing here?" The man almost yelled at her, though he was only a few inches away from her.

"What?" the other trainee asked groggily, waking up from all the commotion. "With everything that is holy! What is going on?"

"This assassin crept into our room and was standing over me with a knife," the man told his sleepy companion.

Amara noticed movement in the corner and the enormous wolf lifted its head nonchalantly to see what was happening. After a moment, it lowered its head and curled back up, seemingly uninterested.

"Lazy," the guard pinning her muttered, apparently noticing the wolf's reaction as well. He turned his attention back to her.

Amara finally found her voice. "Wait, it's not what you think. I just used the knife to pop the latch on the door. I mean you no harm. In fact, I was about to leave and wait to talk with you in the morning."

"Sure, you were," the guard that was not pinning her said sarcastically. "It's normal to sneak into someone's house in the dead of night and stand over them with a knife. Most people do that the day before they meet with a stranger."

"She's no stranger," the first man said. "She's the assassin from the wall. The one who warned us and fought with us, Daz."

That's who the other man was. She didn't realize that they lived together. She should have done more information gathering before attempting this.

"Yes, I am," she said quickly. "I can't live with the Shadows anymore. They see me as a traitor." It was mostly true.

"Then why did you come here?" Daz asked. "Why not go to another town or a rival group?"

"I had to find out who you were. I think I was drawn to you." she didn't realize it until she said it, but she really did feel drawn to the man who now had a knife at her throat.

"Why me?" the man asked.

"I. . . I don't know," she said truthfully.

She thought he was attractive, but that wasn't any reason to go to a guard and basically turn herself in. She knew what happened to Shadow members if they were caught by the city guard; somehow, she knew this man wouldn't do that.

"Malach," Daz started.

So that's his name, Amara thought.

"We need to turn her in," Daz continued. "She's part of the Shadows."

"Let's get to the bottom of this first," Malach replied. "Get up."

He was still holding the knife to her throat, but allowed her to, slowly, get to her feet. "Help our guest disarm, Daz."

Daziar came up behind her and unclasped her cloak. He whistled as it fell off her shoulder. And at first, she was incredulous. All men were the same! Why would she think these two would be any different?

"She's carrying an arsenal, Mal," Daz said appreciatively. "And not cheap weapons, either."

Now Amara couldn't help but feel a little rejected. He was admiring her weapons more than her figure.

He took the daggers hanging from her belt and then unclasped the armor that held her throwing knives. As she took it off, she could tell both men were embarrassed. She was only wearing a shirt and shorts, and the hem of the shirt stopped at her midriff; it was rather form fitting.

She noticed that, even though Malach was blushing, he still took a second look.

"Sit," Malach ordered, and she did, putting her back against the wall and crossing her arms in defiance. "Do you have any more weapons on you?"

"Yes," Amara asked, growing tired of this dance. She pulled two knives, one from each boot, and tossed them into the growing pile. She saw, with some satisfaction, both men tensed visibly when she did.

"So why are you here?" Malach asked again, and she could tell that he was a little flustered.

She smiled at him. "I couldn't stay with the Shadows, and you are the only other person in the city I know."

"But you don't know me," Malach said. "I saw you for the first time on the wall a week ago, and you were telling us you and your assassin friends were trying to kill Daz here."

"I wasn't their friend. I was ordered to infiltrate their group and stop them. By the time I got in, they were ready to strike. All I could do was warn you," Amara said, and it was mostly true.

"Why should we trust you?" Daz asked.

"If I was going to kill you, I would have started with you, sleepyhead. Your back was to the door, and you were so fast asleep it took your friend yelling to wake you." She knew that the fiery retort wouldn't help her much, but she couldn't stop herself. "You would have been dead before you even woke up, allowing me to kill your friend over here."

"Mal, we should just kill her now," Daz spat. "She's trouble, and we are well within our right to do so."

Malach. . . was laughing, not very hard but slightly chuckling, "She's right, Daz, she would have killed you first if she was here to kill us. I believe her."

Amara breathed a sigh of relief.

"So, what do you expect us to do with you?" Malach asked.

"Umm... I don't know," Amara said. She truly hadn't thought that far ahead.

"Malach, if you won't kill her, at least turn her in," Daz said. "The guard will get the location of the Shadows' lair from her, and there is a reward for any Shadows members turned in."

"Daziar, she saved your life and was thrown out because of it." Malach frowned. He finally put his knife in its sheath. "I don't think she deserves to die for that."

"She won't necessarily die if you turn her in," Daziar said.

Malach gave him a skeptical look. "You know as well as I do what they will do if we turn her in. They will torture her for the information they want and then hang her as an example."

"Well, maybe," Daziar said reluctantly. "So, what do we do with her?"

Malach shrugged, "Let her go, I guess."

"What?" Daziar just about shouted.

"Look, I already sent a message to Elzrod, and he is on his way. We will wait for him to get here and then go from there," Malach said.

"What?" now it was Amara's turn to be confused. "How did you send a message? There was no pigeon or any messenger around."

"I have my ways," Malach said cryptically. "So, you came here to get help from me?"

"Yeah, I guess," she said. "I didn't know what else to do."

"Maybe we could help you find a job," Malach said.

"Malach!" Daziar chided.

"What?" he asked. "She came here for help. I think we should help her." He sat down in front of her.

"Now that you are not a member of the Shadows, would you give us their location?" Malach asked, looking her in the eye.

She couldn't think clearly, looking into his eyes. They were so deep and mesmerizing.

"Uh…no," she finally said, shaking her head to clear her thoughts. "I won't betray them."

"Alright," he said simply. "Worth a shot."

"That's it?" Amara and Daziar said at the same time, though she sounded more confused and he more incredulous.

"Yeah. I mean, if you aren't gonna tell me, I'm not gonna push," he replied. "So, what skills do you have? What job do you think you would want?"

"I haven't thought much about it," Amara said. "I'm trained in a few weapons and I'm stealthy. I'm not sure what job I would want or be good at, though. I've been a thief all my life."

A knock sounded at the door downstairs.

"That must be Elzrod," Malach said. "Daz, will you get the door?"

Daziar, closest to the entrance, opened the door with a huff, revealing an older guard who had to be Elzrod. He had a uniquely beautiful sword hanging from his belt. Malach and Daziar filled him in while Amara sat quietly. To her surprise, Malach defended her when Daziar accused her of trying to kill them. Elzrod had sat down while they had told him what happened, and he sat cross-armed now, looking thoughtful.

"Storm says she trusts your judgment, Malach," Elzrod said.

"Who's Storm?" Amara asked.

"Really?" Daziar said, ignoring Amara. "Storm is fine with letting the assassin walk free?"

"I'm not an assassin. I'm just a thief," Amara objected and then added. "And who's Storm?"

"Yes, she says if Malach says it's fine, then she thinks it will be fine," Elzrod said, still ignoring Amara. "I tend to agree with her. Besides, the girl warned us of the assassins and saved your life."

"I know she did. Malach already said that. But she was a Shadow member," Daziar pleaded.

"Daziar, I think it's been decided," Malach replied calmly. "Reckoning agrees as well, and we can take precautions to make sure she doesn't try anything."

"Now, who is Reckoning?" Amara asked, getting more confused by the second.

"Fine. But if she kills us in our sleep, I'm going to kill you, Malach," Daziar said. He walked back over to his pallet and sat down with his back to the group.

"Well, I will get our guest settled upstairs," Malach told Elzrod. "Thank you and Storm for coming over and helping."

"Of course," Elzrod said. "I trust I will see you in the morning?"

Malach smiled. "Yes, I will make sure I stay alive that long."

Elzrod turned and closed the door behind him, leaving the three of them alone. After locking the door behind him, Malach turned to Amara sitting on the floor. He smiled at her, and she realized she was smiling back. He had a kind smile. One that was genuine and infectious.

"What's your name?" he asked. "You've no doubt heard all of ours by now, but I'm Malach."

"My name is Amara," she replied. "And I've heard more names than the amount of people I've seen."

"Well, Amara, have you eaten anything tonight?" Malach asked, blatantly ignoring her comment. "I find it's easier to go to sleep with a full stomach."

Daziar huffed over on his pallet, drawing Malach's eyes toward him.

He turned back to Amara. "Don't mind him; he's a sore loser," he said the last bit a little louder and aimed it toward Daziar for effect. "Come on. Let's go get you settled. Do you have bedding?"

"Yes, it's on my pack in the alley, across the street," she replied. "I'll go get it."

"Alright." Malach unlocked the door and pulled it open.

"Will you let me back in after I get it?" Amara asked suspiciously.

Malach laughed, "Yes, besides, if I didn't, you could always come back in the way you did before."

Amara thought for a second and realized he was right, and the only reason he would lock her out of the first floor would be to play a cruel joke on her. She walked out the front door and thought it was a good sign he didn't immediately close it on her. She went and got her pack, pulling it onto her shoulders, and looked back. Malach was still there, holding the door open. She returned, and he let her back in, closing and locking the door. He ushered her upstairs. Daziar didn't even glance at them when they went past where he was laying.

"See, I still let you in. Now, did you say you had eaten or not?" he asked as she set her pack against the wall.

"I didn't, but I haven't, and I'm starving," she replied.

"Well, we don't have much. We need to head to the market and get some more supplies," Malach admitted. "But you are welcome to anything we have left." He pulled out some dried meat and bread.

To Amara's disappointment, there was no cheese. Malach brought the meal over to her and sat down with her.

"So, did you grow up here?" he asked. "You look too young to have made the Journey already."

Amara narrowed her eyes. *What is he getting at?* she thought and then said, "I'm not sure that's your business."

He handed her the bread and meat. "So, I'm not allowed to know anything about the person I'm letting spend the night in my house?" He smiled at her. "I understand. You probably have always been taught that people, especially guards, can't be trusted."

She nodded thoughtfully. She bit into the meat and moaned.

"Something wrong?" Malach asked, looking genuinely worried.

"It's so good," she said, drawing out the words.

Malach smiled again. "Good, I seasoned it myself."

"It's amazing!" she said again. She decided it might not be too bad to tell him the easy things about her past. What could it hurt, anyway? "I grew up in Caister, a city on the western sea. The Shadows raised me."

"No parents then?" Malach asked.

"Maybe my parents were a part of the Shadows," she said defensively, then saw the pain in his eyes and wished she hadn't said it.

"I lost my parents when I was young; grew up most of my life without them." He looked at the front door, lost in memory. "It was hard, but it made me who I am."

"I never knew my parents either," Amara said before she could stop herself. "I was raised by a man in the Shadows' chapter in Caister."

"How did you end up here so young?" Malach asked.

Amara explained what had happened to her and her journey here, leaving out the mysterious man in the woods. Then, without prompting, and for reasons she didn't know, she explained her part in the assassination and her story so far in Newaught. She, of course, left out things like the entrance to the Shadows' lair and other secrets.

When she was done, Malach told her a little more about his life while she ate her meal.

"So, now you're a guard, but you really just want to be a hunter?" She asked.

"Yeah, but I don't think I'll ever be able to do that as a job again," Malach replied sadly.

"How come?" Amara asked, surprising herself with how genuinely curious she was.

"Well, some events are going on right now that I can't really talk about, but safe to say that my life has changed, and I don't think it's going to go back to normal anytime soon," he said and before she could pry further, added,

"I've kept you up long enough, and I've got the day off tomorrow, so I'm going hunting first thing in the morning. I am going to call it a night. If you try anything, I will know, and I won't stay Daziar's hand this time. And thank you for your story. Goodnight, Amara."

"You're welcome," she said, smiling at him. "And goodnight, Malach."

He walked downstairs while she laid out her pallet to sleep on.

He was very nice to her. She didn't trust him. Not yet at least, but she could tell he was a good man. It was still unsettling how attracted she was to him. Maybe she would see if he wanted company on his hunting trip tomorrow and learn more about him. She had never been hunting before.

She laid down and rolled onto her side. The discomfort of the hard floor under her pallet made her miss the plush bed she had in her old room, but there was a familiar comfort to it, too. She fell asleep, thinking about her room in Caister and other childhood memories Malach's stories had pulled to the surface.

Chapter 16

Amara woke up before Malach and was waiting for him when he finally got up. He had sneaked silently upstairs until he saw that she was awake and waiting for him. He seemed to be more at ease with her. She thought he must have at least a little more trust in her, since she hadn't done anything all night. Skie even seemed more comfortable with Amara, but was still a little wary.

"So, when do we leave?" Amara asked quietly, not wanting to wake Daziar.

"We?" Malach asked with a sideways glance at her as he strung his bow.

"Yeah, I thought I might go hunting with you this morning," she replied hopefully.

"Did you now?" Malach asked. "Have you ever been hunting before?"

"No, but I can move quickly and quietly," she said. "I thought you might teach me."

"Did you now?" Malach said again. He thought about it for a moment and then said.

"Fine, but if you slow me down, I'm leaving you behind, and if you are too loud, I'm sending you back to the city."

"That's fair," she said. "What's for breakfast?"

"Whatever we kill," Malach replied. He already had his bow strung, and he attached his belt with his knife and quiver on it and headed out the door, Skie following him out. Amara grabbed her pack and hurried out behind him.

"So, when do I get my weapons back?" she asked as they walked down the road to the gate. The guard wouldn't let them out until after first light, but that wasn't far off.

"When I think you won't stab me in the back first chance you get," Malach replied.

"When will that be?" she asked, trying again for a more straightforward answer.

"When I say so," he answered, even more vaguely.

They arrived at the gate, and Malach gave them his papers. They let him through early. Perks of being a guard, Amara guessed. From there Malach broke into a jog, Skie loping easily beside him. Amara almost had to run full tilt to keep up with his long legs.

Why do tall people do this to me? She thought. *It's as if they take pleasure in seeing me struggle to keep up.*

They made it to the woods just as the first light was showing on the horizon. Malach slowed, and Amara stopped next to him. She normally ran much farther than this, but not at that pace, and she was out of breath.

"Too fast for you?" he asked in a hushed tone.

"No, just your long legs take one step for every two of mine," she replied just as quietly. "Why the rush?"

"All the other hunters get out after first light when the gates open," he explained. "That means if I get to the woods a good distance before them, I get first pick at the tracks."

"Ah," Amara said, still catching her breath. "I understand."

A rustle in the underbrush ahead of them just about made her heart jump out of her chest. Malach held a finger up to his lips for her to be quiet and motioned for her to stay put. He pulled his bow off his back and an arrow out of his quiver, notching it. She froze, remembering the giant monster that had attacked her in the swamps. They were too far from the swamp for another one of those, but she had no idea what else might be out there. Malach moved into the forest and out of her sight. She heard something quickly scurry away from them, then stop suddenly. Silence reigned in the forest, and the snap of a twig to her right made her jump slightly.

"Malach?" she whispered, peering into the darkness. She didn't see or hear anything.

"Got it!" Malach called as he came out of the darkness suddenly, as if he had just materialized out of thin air.

Amara physically jumped with fright at his sudden appearance. "Don't do that!"

"Jumpy, aren't we?" Malach commented with a smile on his face.

He held up a rabbit. Blood ran down its fur, dripping off its nose, staining the ground red wherever it landed. He opened a leather bag which looked to have held many dead animals in its time and stuffed the rabbit inside. He grinned at her, obviously enjoying her fright.

"Last time I was outside of the city, I was attacked by a monster. I'm a bit nervous as to what else might be out there waiting to kill me," she said in her defense.

"Many things, but don't worry." He smirked at her again. "I'll protect you. Come on and keep quiet; I think I found tracks for some much bigger game."

She swallowed involuntarily and followed him into the woods.

Without a sound, Skie broke off from Malach's side. Amara watched her go, feeling a slight stab of fear as the wolf disappeared into the darkness.

"Where is she going?" Amara asked, a little worried that they had lost their escort.

"Don't worry; she doesn't go far," Malach said. "She likes to do her own hunting. Sometimes she even brings it back to me first. Though I think she will keep it this time."

"Why do you say that?" Amara asked.

"She hasn't hunted in a long time," he explained.

"But haven't you trained her to always bring it back?" Amara asked, thinking that it seemed like it would be the smart thing to do.

"Skie follows me and listens to me most of the time, but don't mistake her for a domesticated animal," Malach said, stopping to look at the ground. "She is anything but tame."

"But you have her in the city," Amara said, feeling less and less safe with Malach.

"Mostly because of a nice clerk, or she wouldn't have been allowed in. I have papers for her, but she is still not mine." Malach turned a little and continued walking. "She could leave anytime she wanted, and I would be sad, but she is a wild animal, and there's only so much I can do to keep her."

"How did you get her to follow you in the first place, then?" Amara asked, curiosity getting the best of her.

Malach told her the story of how he saved Skie and in returned she saved him. They fell silent when his story was finished and kept moving. Amara did most of the talking, questioning Malach here and there. He would usually respond, but not always with a straight answer. Several times, he held up his hand to stop her, and once he went ahead, leaving her alone in the dimly lit woods. She had felt another pang of fear, and it seemed like forever before he came back.

"There are a few deer just ahead," he whispered. "How are you with a bow?"

"Umm, decent. Why?" she asked, confused.

He handed her the bow. "Because you are going to take the shot."

"What?" she said, forgetting to stay quiet.

"Shhh," he hushed her. "You'll do fine. Come on."

She followed him up to a clearing and stopped just behind him.

He pointed to a herd of deer that were in the clearing, grazing. There was light enough to see them clearly now, and she had no problem picking out the largest of them. There were several deer without antlers on them, and only one with antlers. Some hunters prized ones with antlers for sport and trophies, though most hunted for the meat. The one with the antlers was by far the largest of the deer in the clearing, and a very impressive sight to behold.

"That's the one we want." Malach pointed to it. "But if you can't get a good shot at it, either of the largest does will do."

"Where do I shoot them?" Amara asked, feeling panic starting to rise in her chest.

"Right behind the front leg. Only fire when they aren't looking at you, or they will see the movement and bolt. Your shot will miss, and you will only wound it," Malach instructed.

Amara nodded, watching the deer graze. The big one with the antlers was behind one of the larger does Malach had pointed out. It didn't seem to be going anywhere in a hurry.

"How long should I wait?" she whispered.

"As long as you think you can," Malach replied. "Sometimes if you wait out the large one, they will catch sight or smell of us and run. Then you won't get anything. Sometimes when you wait it out, you can get the bigger one and feed yourself longer. It's a bit of a gamble."

Amara decided she would wait only a few moments longer and then take what was available. She watched the animals walk around for a while, finding food on the ground. She always thought that deer were smaller and fluffier. These were large and sinuous creatures. One of the smaller does kept looking their way, and she thought it might have caught sight of them. She decided now was the time to take the shot.

Just as she pulled the bow up to fire, the antlered deer stepped out from behind the doe, and she quickly adjusted her aim. She pulled the bowstring back and let the arrow fly. The shot felt good and struck the deer right behind the front leg. The deer stumbled forward, righted itself, and let out a loud snort. The entire herd took off, and the one she'd shot followed, though a bit more sluggishly.

"I don't understand," Amara said. "I hit him just where you said too."

"Yes, you did," Malach said excitedly. "It was a great shot!"

"Then why did it run?" she challenged.

"They do that," Malach responded. "We will have to track the blood trail for a way until we find it, and you might have to finish it off if it's still alive."

"Really?" Amara asked. "This is normal?"

"Yep," Malach said excitedly. "We will see how far we have to go, but it looked like you made a good shot, so I would wager less than a mile."

Malach walked out into the clearing and, to Amara's surprise, was met by another man. He had similar deerskin and fur clothing to Malach. He was obviously a hunter and didn't seem happy.

"You and your girlfriend here cost me my deer!" he shouted.

"Is this your land?" Malach asked without concern.

Amara didn't know how he stayed so calm. Her heart was pounding in her chest. Her first reaction was to make a run for it back to the city.

"No, but I've been tracking those deer for two days now!" The man was still shouting, and his face was turning red.

"Then you need to get better at tracking. I found them within an hour," Malach said. "There's no law that says we can't shoot a deer. Another has been tracking. Besides, the reason they've stayed ahead of you is you're coming from upwind. They would have smelled you from miles away. The reason you caught them now is the wind changed directions this morning."

"But. . . who-" the man sputtered, seemingly too angry to talk. "Don't tell me how to hunt, boy!"

"Well, if you don't let people tell you how to hunt, it would explain why you are so bad at it," Malach said, stretching his arms and then yawning lazily.

"You owe me that deer!" he shouted again, poking Malach roughly in the chest.

Malach moved like lightning. Before Amara knew it, Malach had grabbed the man's collar and pulled him close. He halfway lifted the shorter man to the point he had to stand on his tiptoes.

"Look, friend," he almost spat that last word, "we owe you nothing. Quit trying to swindle this girl out of her first deer." Malach released the man with a push and he fell to the ground. "Go find another hunting ground."

The man nodded, clearly frightened, and scrambled away from Malach, finding his feet and running into the woods, looking back to see if Malach was following.

"Sorry about that." Malach turned back to Amara, a pleasant smile on his face once again.

She realized that beneath the nice man was a fierce fighter who knew what was right and wouldn't stand for anything less. Instead of frightening her, which was her first reaction, the realization comforted her. She understood what she was getting with him.

"I think we ought to track that deer in case that oaf comes back and tries to steal the kill again," Malach said.

Amara still just nodded, not trusting her voice to speak without cracking or sounding tiny. She followed Malach, and he showed her how to track the deer. It was pretty easy with the blood trail, but he also showed her the prints in the dirt and other signs that the deer had passed that way. They found the deer she had shot. It was lying on its side with the arrow sticking up in the air. It was breathing hard and was letting out a rasp with every breath.

"Sounds like you might have just gotten one lung with the first shot," Malach whispered.

He showed her where to place the next arrow to kill the deer quickly. She stood, drew, and shot, all in one motion. The second arrow struck the deer, and it tried to jump up to run, but the second arrow got in its way and it fell again. Malach rushed forward, sliding to a stop in front of it, putting one hand on its neck to hold its head down and deftly sliding his knife into the animal's chest. It let out one more shuddering breath and lay still. Malach let out a sigh and pulled his knife out.

"Sorry," Amara said, thinking she must have gotten the shot wrong.

"It's fine. The arrow bounced off a rib bone, and I knew it wouldn't kill it right away, so I stepped in to finish it quickly," Malach said with a sad smile. "I don't like to let them suffer long."

He's kind, Amara thought. Not just to her, but even to the animals he hunted. He respected them and didn't let them suffer any more than was necessary. She liked that about him; she decided. He pulled the arrows out of the deer as she walked. The first arrow came out without a head.

"Well, that's unfortunate," Malach said, frowning at the shaft. "We will have to find where that went."

He pulled a rope out of a pocket in the bag he had put the rabbit into and tied one end to the deer. The other end, he tossed over a thick limb and hauled the deer up, hanging it. It was rather morbid, seeing the deer hanging like that.

"Why are you doing that?" Amara asked.

"Well, I don't particularly want to carry out the whole carcass," he said over his shoulder, "So I take the pieces I want and leave the rest for the wild animals."

He walked over to her and handed her his knife. His only knife.

It left him weaponless. *She* knew she wasn't going to attack him, but he didn't. He was trusting her with all of his weapons, and she suspected, testing her to see what she would do. She walked past him and could tell he was tense and ready for any attack. She kept walking until she was right in front of the deer. He followed and showed her what to do.

It didn't take long, and the deer was skinned and cut up. To Amara's surprise, they didn't even have to touch the guts. Malach untied the rope from the tree and let the deer down.

"Now for the heart," Malach said, taking the bloody knife from her hands. He cut the chest open and stuck his hands in almost up to his elbow. He pulled the heart out of the deer and there was the other part of the arrow sticking out of it.

"Well, we found the arrowhead," Amara commented.

"Yeah, and it was a great shot!" Malach praised. "An inch more and we wouldn't have been chasing it quite as far."

They packed everything away and just as they were finishing up, Skie walked into the clearing. The evidence of her kills still on her snout. She sniffed what was left of the deer and started to pick it over.

Amara turned away. She didn't want to see that.

"Come on," Malach said, seeing her discomfort. "Let's head back. She will catch up when she's done."

They headed back the way they had come, tracing their steps back to the clearing and then the winding path back through the trees and out to the fields outside of Newaught. Even from this distance, the city walls seemed to loom above them. Malach sat down and cleaned the rabbit that he had killed earlier and started a fire. Once it was going, he made a spit and stuck the rabbit on it and started cooking, sprinkling some seasoning on it as it cooked. When it was done, he put the fire out, and they sat, eating the rabbit.

"You're a good cook," Amara commented, enjoying her part of the rabbit. "Who taught you?"

"My mom taught me a little," he said, looking at the city walls. "My dad taught me to hunt. Those skills and the cottage back home are the only things I have left of them."

"I have an amulet I think my mother gave me, but I'm not sure where it actually came from. They found it when Lawdel found me," Amara said.

"Is that who raised you? Lawdel?" Malach asked.

"Yeah. I probably won't see him for a long time," she said sadly. "Especially now that I'm staying with a member of the guard."

"I can understand that," Malach said. He opened his mouth and closed it a couple time before saying. "I've recently learned my parents are still alive. But I don't know if I will ever see them."

"What?" Amara asked. "You just said they were dead."

"Yeah, I can't really say anything to people yet. I've just told my close friends so far." Malach shrugged.

"So, are you going to go find them?" She asked. Why wouldn't he just go find them? And why was it such a big secret?

"I hope I can. There are other people out looking now but..." his voice trailed off.

"If it was me, I wouldn't let anything stand in my way to find my parents," Amara said confidently.

"I know, but they are being held in a prison not far from here." He looked at her.

She didn't know why he was telling her after he had said he wasn't supposed to. For some reason, he was trusting her. "Then let's go break them out!" Amara said, jumping to her feet. "I know a place they can stay and be safe. What city are they in? I have access to a large number of thieves."

"They are being held by demons, Amara," Malach said, somewhat defeated.

"Oh, I didn't think there were any of those left," Amara said, deflating. She took her seat again on the ground next to him. "Who's looking for them, then?"

"I can't say," Malach said, looking away from her. "Thanks for the offer, though. It means a lot."

"Well, if there is anything I can help with, let me know," Amara said, and she really did want to help him. His pain was so familiar to her. She didn't know if her parents were still alive or not.

She didn't really even know her parents, but they must have loved her even a little to leave her with an amulet and wrapped up against the chill of the night. Sometimes, she hoped she would find them someday, but that was a false hope.

Malach got up and brushed himself off, and stamped out the remainder of the fire. "Ready to go?" He proffered a hand to help her up.

"Yep," she said, taking the hand and then brushing herself off. "Malach. . ."

"Yes?" Malach looked at her.

"I think. . ." she almost told him how she was feeling but stopped herself. "Thanks for giving me a chance. And thanks for teaching me to hunt."

"You're welcome, Amara," he said and started toward the city.

The sun was just reaching its highest point in the day when they made it back to the gate. Skie had caught up to them about halfway across the field and plodded beside Malach now. They showed their papers as they entered the city and walked toward Malach's house. As they got close, they could see a group of guards standing outside the house. Panic rose in Amara's chest, making it feel tight.

Malach walked up to Daziar, who seemed to be leading the group.

Amara held back but stayed within earshot.

"What is this, Daziar?" Malach asked.

"She's a member of the Shadows," Daziar hissed. "We need to arrest her to find out what she knows."

"Daz, she left that life when she saved you," Malach argued. "You heard her last night; she couldn't stay there anymore."

"That's what she says, but she still won't give up their hideout," he countered.

"So, she still cares about people there. I'm not going to fault her for that." Malach was getting a little upset.

"It doesn't matter now. The major knows about her. If we don't catch her, we will all get in trouble for it," Daziar said so quietly the Amara had a hard time making out the words.

Once she realized what was happening, she turned to flee but ran right into another group of guards who had been working their way up behind her. They grabbed her and held her fast. She tried to get away but couldn't get loose.

"Daziar!" Malach shouted, seeing what was happening. "This is wrong, and you know it!"

"That's not for you to decide," Daziar countered again. "The law will decide her innocence or guilt."

Malach slugged Daziar, put him on his butt, and three of the guards grabbed Malach, holding him back.

The irons placed on her wrists were uncomfortably tight, pinching them painfully. The guards picked her up and just walked away with her.

Daziar stood but didn't return the

Malach caught her eyes. "Amara, don't worry. I'll get this all sorted out. Just be patient. Elzrod is already on his way!" He called as they took her away.

Two days.

Amara had sat in the cell for two days with no visitors. Even the guards who brought her food didn't say a word to her. They just slid the tray under the cell door and came back for it about an hour later. She was starting to wonder if she would die in the cell without ever talking to anyone ever again. Did the master know she was here? Did Raza even care? Was Malach going to sweep in and take her away from this place, or was he just saying he would, so she wouldn't worry? Was he really her friend or just pretending to be until they could capture her?

The door opened to the hall and someone walked in. "A bit early for lunch," she called, not looking up at the guard.

"Amara Westbay," a voice called hard and deep, with no feeling in the tone.

She looked up and saw Elzrod. "You're Elzrod right?"

"Yes, I'm glad you recognize me," he said, a warm smile spreading across his face. "I've been sent to bring you to the hearing."

"Hearing?" she asked, heart sinking a little that he wasn't here to release her.

"Yes, the judge is here to find out all the facts," Elzrod said and then leaned close to the bars. "I have taken steps to make sure justice is carried out. Just stay quiet unless you're asked a question directly. And if things go badly, use this."

He unlocked the bars and gently put the shackles on her wrist. Something small and medallic slid into her hand and she quickly hid it away. The old man winked at her. He led her out of the cell and through the door to the hallway.

They walked down the hall and out to a cart. Elzrod helped her into the cart next to Malach.

"How are you holding up?" He smiled at her, and she couldn't help but smile back.

"Making new friends," she replied. "Though they weren't the most talkative."

He chuckled, "I can imagine."

"Where are we going?" She asked.

"Your hearing at the main council room," he said, turning serious. "We are going to plead your case, but if it doesn't go according to plan, I'm afraid they will sentence you to death."

"Ah," she said soberly. "That's what Elzrod was talking about."

"Yeah," Malach said. "But you are shackled, so you can't knock us out and escape." He said the last part as if suggesting something.

"I understand," Amara said calmly, though she still felt the panic bubbling in her chest.

They rode the rest of the way in silence. When they made it to the council building, Elzrod and Malach helped her out of the cart and walked with her inside. The council room was circular and had seats all around the room with a stand in the middle. Elzrod and Malach walked her up to the stand and hooked her shackles to a chain connected to a podium. She studied the people that were sitting in the surrounding seats. There were a lot of guards present, but there were just as many people in rich civilian clothing.

"Amara Westbay, we are here today to see if you are guilty of being a member of the Shadows, a group of thieves that have been plaguing this city almost since its founding." A man directly in front of her said. "Once we have established that, we will decide your punishment."

"Amara, do you admit to being a member of the Shadows?" a man standing between the seating area and the stand asked.

"Yes," she said proudly. There was a collective gasp around the room.

As if that was ever in question, she thought bitterly.

"Then will you tell us where the Shadows are hiding?" the man asked.

"No," Amara said flatly.

"Amara," he said, his tone softening. "If you tell us where they are hiding, we can let you go with no penalties. We can let you out now. Nothing else needs to be asked or said. So, I ask again, will you tell us where they are hiding?"

"No," Amara said again. "I will not turn on my friends."

"You admit that you are a member of the Shadows but won't tell us where they are hiding?" the man asked again, as if hoping that the repetition of the question would yield the answer he wanted.

"That is correct," Amara replied solemnly.

"Why?" the man asked, and it took Amara by surprise, but he continued before she could answer. "From what I'm told, they kicked you out after you betrayed some of them to save the life of one of our city guards, but you still call them friends. Why protect someone who turned their back on you?"

"The people I 'betrayed,' as you put it, were traitors to the Shadows and what they stood for. I was tasked with infiltrating and weeding out those traitors. Unfortunately, by the time that I had done that, they were ready to strike, so I was forced to betray and kill them in an attempt to save the guards of this city," she recounted briefly.

"The Master of the chapter here in Newaught did not and never would authorize an assassination of anyone. I will not betray the Master or the people I still count as friends."

"I see," the man said. "I will leave it to the judge, then."

"I believe I have heard enough," the man seated in front of her said. He must be the judge. "I find Amara Westbay guilt-"

"Wait!" Amara heard Malach's voice shout to her left, and she turned her head to find him rushing down from his seat.

"Yes, trainee?" the judge asked, perturbed.

"I think that her actions in saving Daziar and her attempt at saving Jarsar should be considered more than it is," Malach pleaded. "She even fought one of the assassins in the attempt to save them."

The judge sighed as if bored, wanting to get the trial over with. "Fine, tell us your recollection of the events."

Malach did and told them of the time he had spent with Amara getting to know her. To her relief, he left out a few of the more sensitive things that she had told him. When he was finished, the judge was looking at him with the same hard eyes unmoved by his testimony.

"And what, Trainee Tresch, would you have me do with her?" the judge asked.

"Put her under a guard and watch her. If she has turned over a new leaf and no longer steals, let her live her life," he replied. He had obviously been planning to ask for this from the beginning.

"And who would I put with this troublemaker?" the judge asked. "No guard would want to watch her all day, every day."

"I would take the assignment," Elzrod stood. "She has proven to be honorable to me, and I would take her as a trainee in the guard."

"What?" the judge almost fell out of his chair. "But you already have a trainee."

"Malach is a week away from being a full guard. He is to be my partner since Jarsar was killed," Elzrod explained. "I can easily take her as a trainee."

The judge thought about this. "You would have me put a former Shadows member in the guard? I don't know if that is wise."

"With respect," Elzrod started, "she was a member only because that was all she knew. Now, she has a chance at a new life. And I believe she shouldn't be faulted for her loyalty to her friends, even if they are thieves."

The judge took another moment to think about Elzrod's words and finally nodded. "Fine, I find Amara Westbay guilt-"

"What?" Malach shouted, and Amara put the key in the shackles, readying herself for the fight that would come.

The judge continued shouting over Malach's objection. "Guilty of living under the Shadows' oppression. She is to be kept under guard day and night and will be trained as a guard until she is deemed safe to live her own life.

Hopefully, at that point, she will be reformed enough to tell us where the thieves are hiding."

"What?" the man that had been asking her questions asked. "She was a member of the Shadows, and she admits it! That should be enough to hang her!"

"She has no prior charges, and I don't have any real accusations against her. Besides, we are in need of guards right now." He turned to Amara. "If you step one foot out of line, I will see you back here, and I won't be so lenient, understand?"

She nodded.

Malach and Elzrod came over and unlocked her shackles from the chain. Malach slipped his hand into hers, and her heart skipped a beat at his touch. Then she realized he was taking the key Elzrod had slipped her, so he could unlock the shackles. Her heart fell a little.

Why are you feeling this way? She questioned herself. *You just met him and barely know him. Why are you so attached already?* However, she could find no answer withing herself other than she was attracted to the honorable and strong young man.

They walked outside and turned in the direction of Malach's home when Daziar ran up. "Malach."

"What do you want, Daziar?" Malach said, and she could tell he was annoyed.

"I wanted to say congratulations on the win at the hearing," Daziar said and then, a little softer, added, "And I'm sorry for bringing the guard."

Amara could see the black and blue bruise on Daziar's cheek where Malach had hit him. He hadn't pulled his punch at all from the looks of it.

Malach turned on his friend. "Your actions nearly cost an innocent woman her life! Not only that, but you did it after she saved you! You shouldn't be telling me you're sorry. You should be talking to her. I can't believe you. I thought you were an honorable man. Turns out, you think more of your job than you do an innocent life."

"Malach, I. . ." his voice trailed off, and Amara could tell that he was hurt. "I didn't think-"

"No, you didn't," Malach barked, cutting him off. "That was your problem."

Daziar turned to Amara. "I am sorry. I hope you can forgive me someday." He turned back to Malach. "You were right, and I should have listened to you. As soon as I saw the guard take her away, I knew I had made a mistake and betrayed you. Betrayed you both. I am sorry." Daziar turned without another word and walked away from them.

Malach and Elzrod took Amara back to their assigned barracks and helped her get fitted for a uniform and the equipment she needed. Elzrod took her to the major, and he put her through all the tests to find out where she was in her training and education. She excelled at combat, but was found lacking in the more formal education.

Malach took his guard test early and aced it with all the extra training he had been receiving at night. He had to hold back for fear or calling suspicion onto himself. The rest of the day and the night they had wall duty to make up the time that they had spent getting Amara out of prison. Elzrod said goodbye to Malach and Amara at the end of their shift and they started walking back to the house.

"I think since Daziar is working today, you ought to sleep at our friend Honora's for the day," Malach suggested.

"You don't want to be alone in the house with me?" Amara asked jokingly.

"It's not that." Malach's face turned red.

Amara laughed loudly at his plight.

"Not funny," he said, realizing she was giving him a hard time.

"I thought it was. That's fine. Do you think your friend will mind?" Amara asked.

"I don't think so, as long as you keep your sticky fingers to yourself." He gave her a playful shove.

"Fine, I promise." She smiled up at him.

They walked up to Honora's house, and Malach knocked. When no answer came, he knocked a second time. Again, there was no answer.

"She must have already left for work," Malach said. "I guess you *will* be staying at my place. But we can't do this too much longer."

"Yeah, cause you're worried about what people think," Amara said, elbowing him and slipping inside the house.

Malach shook his head, smiling, and walked in after her. As he walked in, she was already taking her uniform off, and Malach's heart jumped to his throat. He turned his head away quickly.

"Relax. I have clothing on under this," she said, watching him awkwardly, trying not to look at her.

"Umm, well, umm, I'm going to go upstairs," Malach said and moved past her quickly, heading up the stairs.

"Goodnight, Amara."

"Don't you mean good morning?" she called up playfully, but didn't get a response.

She *did* have clothes on under the uniform. She still had her cut-off shirt on from two days ago. *That* would need a wash right away, and under her leather pants, she had a pair of form-fitting shorts. It covered everything important. She didn't know what the big deal was and decided to go up and talk to him about it. She slid out of her leather pants and mounted the stairs in her bare feet, not making a sound as she climbed.

Her head was just above the landing when she caught sight of Malach's back. He had taken off his shirt, and the muscles rippled under his skin. There were too many scars to count marring the flesh of his back, and she imagined there were more on his chest as well. He was lean and fit, and all the muscles on his arms and back were well defined.

He walked over to a bowl of water and splashed his face with some of it. She decided he was the most beautiful man she had ever met. He turned her direction, and she ducked below the landing quickly. Had he seen her? She ran back down the stairs and decided the conversation could wait until they had slept. She still wondered why he had acted the way he did. Most of the women in the Shadows in Caister dressed like that. None of the men ever acted strangely. She fell asleep thinking about Malach without his shirt on.

Chapter 17

Amara was settling into her new home with Honora, though she thought the other girl didn't like her too much for some reason. It had been a few weeks since the hearing and the start of her training, and things were going well. She had received a messenger from Raza inquiring about what had happened, and Amara had sent back a message with him, explaining everything and letting her know she hadn't revealed the Shadows' location. There would be, no doubt, a collective sigh on receipt of her message and a large amount of discussion on whether they could trust her word, but eventually, they would believe her.

Malach and Elzrod were definitely hiding something, though, and she had started to piece some things together. Elzrod still believed the war was going on. Crazy old man. He was training Malach under him as something called a Blade Bearer. She heard them arguing one day about whether to tell her all of it, but Elzrod had won that argument and nothing was said to her. Every once in a while, the names Storm and Reckoning came up as if they were there listening or even a part of the conversation, but she never saw anyone else.

Honora and Amara were over at Malach's house. Daziar had decided to sleep at the barracks as of late. Their relationship was a little strained. They were all eating and talking when a loud knock came at the door.

"Malach?" Elzrod's muffled voice came from the other side of the door. "Malach, we've found him. Open up!"

Malach jumped to his feet and ran to the door, throwing it wide. Three men stood there, the two newcomers towering above Elzrod. Malach stood to the side of the door and allowed the three men to walk in.

"Malach, this is Camael and Cathetel," Elzrod introduced the two men, quickly pointing to each one.

"Great, I'll never get those names mixed up," Malach said sarcastically.

Elzrod gave him a withering look and introduced the two men to everyone else. "We've found your father. We need to move now to break him out before they move him again."

"And my mother?" Malach asked.

"We don't know where she is, but she might be with him," Elzrod said.

"What is going on?" Amara asked, still in the dark about most of what was going on.

"We might need her skills," Malach told Elzrod. "You know I trust her, and you should, too."

"Fine, I don't have time to argue the point." Elzrod agreed reluctantly. He quickly filled Amara in on the situation and about the blades Malach and he held.

She was silent for the explanation, but when he was done said, "Wait, let me get this straight. Malach's dad is an Angel, and he has a blade that can talk to him. That's insane. You're insane."

"Storm is the name of my blade," Elzrod told her, putting a hand on Storm's hilt.

"You're all insane!" Amara cried.

She looked from Honora to the two towering men that had walked in with Elzrod. As her gaze fell on the two men, they shed their traveling cloaks and sprouted wings.

Amara fell back, landing hard on her butt.

They obviously couldn't open them to their full length in the small room, but those were angel wings, nonetheless. The wings looked as if they were armored, but there was no mistaking them for anything else. Malach, Honora, and Amara wore expressions that ranged from shock to awe.

Elzrod chuckled. "Did I forget to tell you that Camael and Cathetel are angels?" He turned serious then. "Now we need to go before the changing of the guard. Can you get a message to Daziar?"

"No, he made his choice," Malach replied coldly, snapping out of his stupor.

"Malach," Honora chided. "You know, he was doing what he thought was right."

"Fine. Tell him if you want, but I doubt he will come," Malach conceded.

"Honora," Elzrod turned to her. "Can you get us horses for the Journey? I have requested them from the guard, but they are at the stables."

"Yes, I will go now." Honora grabbed her cloak and headed out the door.

"Honora," Amara called before she was gone. "My horse Shasta is stable at the guard's stables. Could you get him for me?"

"I will," and with that, Honora disappeared out the door.

Malach and Amara started packing the things they would need for the road while Elzrod filled them in. His father was being held at a prison just inside Demon Territory, a little more than a day's ride from Newaught. It was disguised as a farmhouse not too far off the road. Most of the prison was underground, and there was only one way in or out. They would need Amara to sneak in and do reconnaissance to know what they were walking into, and then they would act swiftly. Hopefully, they would be able to overpower any human or demon defense and liberate the prisoners, including Malach's father and possibly his mother.

Malach and Amara followed the three men outside and into the cold. It had been slowly getting colder over the last few weeks, although the temperature hadn't dropped as far as it would have in the mountains, and the sky had been threatening to storm all day. So far, the rain had held off, and Malach hoped that their luck would hold. He could see their breath in the air, though, and knew it would get colder before it got warmer.

They started toward the gate and were halfway there when Honora and Daziar caught up with them. Malach was a little surprised to see Daziar, but couldn't help feeling relieved that his old friend would be coming with them.

"Thank you, Honora," Elzrod said. "I need you to stay here in case we don't return."

"But I can help," she protested.

"I know you can," Elzrod said gently. "But I need you here. If we don't return in a few days, go to the city center to the Black Bear Inn and find Anauel. Tell him we have failed; he will know what to do."

"Fine," Honora crossed her arms. Malach knew she would do as she was told, but he also knew she wouldn't be happy about it.

Daziar rode up beside Malach. "Hey."

"Hey," Malach said a little awkwardly

"Are we good?" he asked.

"Are we?" Malach raised an eyebrow.

"Yeah," Daziar nodded and grinned. "Let's go get your parents."

"Good to have you back," Malach smiled back .

As they mounted up and galloped quickly toward the gate, Amara started putting the pieces of this new revelation together. The man who pressed her into his service in the woods all that time ago before she entered Newaught. He was either a demon or an angel in disguise. The size of the man was the giveaway. He wanted her to do something for him, and she doubted it would end with simple information gathering. The fact that he hadn't appeared since she sided with Malach and Elzrod made her feel like he wanted her to go along with them. Either that or he had forgotten all about her. She hoped it was the latter.

Maybe the man was an angel. He sure didn't act like what she thought an angel would act like, though. Either way, this was the path she was on; if that meant betraying the demons, then she would do that.

She owed Malach for saving her, and if she was honest with herself, she would follow him into much worse for much less. They slowed to a trot as they reached the gate. Elzrod nodded to one of the guards, and the guard waved them through without any questions. They galloped out, down the road, and into the forest. They were headed toward the swamp Amara traveled through. She galloped past Malach and Daziar and up to Elzrod.

"Elzrod!" she called to him, the wind almost taking her voice.

"Elzrod!" She tried again.

He slowed the pace a little. "What?"

"There is a swamp ahead and there are some pretty big monsters in there," she warned. "We may want to avoid that."

"If we go around, that will add an extra day on the trip," he replied. "We can't delay that long."

"We could be killed going through!" she called back.

Elzrod called for a halt and reined in his horse. Amara explained what had happened on the way through and the monster that attacked her. She pulled the tooth out of her pack that she had taken from the monster.

Daziar whistled at the size of it. "I don't think I want to tangle with that thing."

"Elzrod's right, if we go around, we lose a day," Malach reasoned, siding with Elzrod. "What are the chances of us running into another one of those things?"

"I don't know, but I don't want to find out," Daziar said.

"I think we will be alright," Amara said, now regretting that she had said anything.

"Everyone but you is in agreement," Elzrod replied, looking at Daziar. "If you don't want to come, then go back, but we go through."

"Fine," Daziar agreed reluctantly. "But if we get attacked, I want everyone to remember that I was against this."

"Come on, then. Amara, I want you up with me," Elzrod said.

"You let me know if you see anything."

The group pulled their horses around, and Amara guided hers beside Malach. "Sorry," she said as she passed.

"It's fine," Malach said. "I'd rather know about the danger than go into it unaware."

They kicked their horses into a gallop again. Amara moved to the front of the group next to Elzrod. As they entered the swamp, they slowed to a trot. Everyone was sitting straight, head swiveling, watching for any movement. The stars and moon were not out, so they had a hard time seeing through the inky blackness. A large shape loomed in front of them, and Elzrod put a hand up for the group to stop. The smell hit them about that time. Something was rotting ahead of them.

Elzrod moved forward, flanked by Camael and Cathetel. They hadn't said anything, but Malach knew they were in constant mental communication. Malach, Daziar, and Amara waited and watched for the signal that it was safe to move forward. Elzrod waved them forward, so they kicked their mounts into movement.

When they got close, they could see the shape was the monster Amara had killed. There were large bite marks on the hard scales, like something had tried to take a bite out of it. The soft underbelly had been eaten away, but there wasn't much left other than scales and bones.

"Well, there is definitely something else out there that tried to eat this thing, but *it* couldn't even get through the scales," Elzrod said, a little awe in his voice. "How in the world did you manage to kill this?"

"There's a weak spot at the top of their head just behind the eyes," Amara explained. "I got lucky and found it."

The creature was longer than the two angels and Elzrod's combined height and about twice the size around as a large oak tree. It would have just swallowed Amara whole, without a problem. Daziar whistled again.

"These teeth marks are in the same shape as the mouth of this monster," Malach observed. "There is another thing out there that is almost this size. We need to move before it comes around."

"Good idea," Elzrod agreed. "Mount up. Let's get out of here."

Just then Daziar fell back and landed hard on the ground, shouting with triumph, "Got it!"

Everyone turned to look at him and he looked a little embarrassed.

"I just wanted one of the teeth." He explained, holding up the tooth that he had pulled from the creature's mouth.

"Mount up," Elzrod repeated himself, and without another word, mounted and kicked his horse into motion.

Malach helped Daziar to his feet, and he gave Malach a sheepish look.

The rest of the group mounted up and galloped away after Elzrod. Luckily, they didn't meet the creature that made the bite marks on their way through the swamp, though none of them would forget there was another monster out there which would eventually grow just as big as or bigger than the one Amara killed. They came out of the trees of the forest not far after they left the swamp. The road forked, and Malach could see the sun coming up over the trees.

"That road will lead you to Caister," Amara said, pointing to their right.

"Right, but this road will lead us to Kargod," Elzrod said, pointing at the road on the left. "It's a little farming town. Just before we reach the town, there is a farmhouse, and that's the prison. Camael and Cathetel will tell us when we are getting close."

A few hours before first light, the party got off the road and out of sight to set up camp. They would rest themselves and the horses for a few hours and be off once again, just after first light. There were still storm clouds overhead, and just as they were preparing to settle down and sleep, the first drops fell. They scrambled to set up cover for themselves, and only a few minutes later, they were somewhat dry under their shelters. The horses, having been left out in the rain, steamed as their bodies cooled. Malach didn't remember falling asleep, but he woke after a while to find Camael standing over him.

"Come," was all the angel said.

It was still drizzling, and Malach found his boots were soaked when the wind changed direction, driving the rain in under his shelter. They quickly broke camp and set off again toward the farmhouse. They traveled for several hours and Malach kept thinking the farmhouse would be just over the next hill or just around the next bend. He was getting tired, and he could tell his friends were, too.

Just when Malach was going to ask for a break, Camael and Cathetel headed off the road. The rest of the group followed them for a way until the two angels dismounted.

"We will camp here," Elzrod declared. "Get a few hours of sleep. We move at dusk."

It was midday, and they made camp as quickly as they could. No one wanted to wait any longer than was necessary to get some sleep. Once they had rolled out their bedding, Daziar grabbed some sticks to start a fire, but Camael stopped him with a hand on his shoulder and a shake of his head. Amara wondered if those two ever spoke, even to each other.

Malach laid down on his bed next to hers. Daziar was on the other side of him.

"Hey, no mischief, you two," Daziar said jokingly, just loud enough that the three of them would hear it.

"What do you mean?" Amara asked innocently. "We've already had plenty of time since you haven't been at the house."

Both the boy's faces turned bright red and Malach looked at her in shock. She laughed so loudly that one of the angels shushed her.

"We haven't," Malach told Daziar seriously.

"No, but it was worth saying just to see the look on both your faces," Amara said, still giggling softly.

"Go to sleep, you three," Elzrod said from his bedroll on the other side of camp, and that was that.

Malach tried for a while to go to sleep and couldn't. A mixture of excitement, fear of what was coming, and his still wet boots kept him awake. He might have his father back by tomorrow. But he and his friends could also be dead within the same amount of time. One mistake was all it took to change the outcome of the fight.

He turned to Amara, but she was asleep. She was a pretty young woman. She looked peaceful as she slept there, and he was glad she had come into his life. Although it had made things difficult for a bit. In the short time she had been around, she had become a good friend. They had gone hunting a few times, and she was a good shot too, though tracking was taking a bit longer for her to learn.

He didn't have to look to see if Daziar was awake. He could hear his oldest friend snoring behind him. Daziar could sleep through a battle without waking up, and he could do it anywhere he wanted to.

Malach sighed and got up. The two angel's gazes snapped to him, drawn by his movement. Elzrod slept soundly on his bed, not too far from where they sat. Malach walked carefully over to the angels and sat down.
Silence hung in the air between the three.

"So, where are your wings?" Malach asked, trying to fill the silence.

"Hidden," Cathetel grunted.

"You hide them?" Malach asked.

"Of course," Camael replied. "If you haven't noticed, most humans don't have wings. We would draw too much attention to ourselves if we flew around everywhere."

"But you can change your appearance?" Malach asked. "Can demons do that same thing?"

"Yes," Camael replied. "But you already knew that. I was told a demon approached you masquerading as a human."

"Yeah, I was," Malach affirmed.

"But I would guess he was covered in a heavy cloak, correct?"

"Yes, how did you know?" Malach asked, surprised.

"Demons and angels can change some of their appearance, like our wings. However, they, like us, cannot change their nature. Since their fall from grace, their bodies were disfigured into the monstrous form you have witnessed. They cannot change *that* form."

"But this demon was much smaller than the one that attacked me in Brightwood," Malach said, confused.

"Changing size is easy, but there are limits to that too," Camael told him. "We cannot go much smaller than we are now."

"Did you know my father well?" Malach asked suddenly.

"Yes," Camael admitted reluctantly.

"I barely remember him," Malach said. "I just remember the time we spent hunting.

"He was a good fighter," Cathetel said simply.

"He was a good commander," Camael said.

"Commander?" Malach asked.

"He was our commander in hundreds of battles," Cathetel told him. "Your mother quickly became his hidden right hand."

"Hidden right hand?" Malach asked.

"Assassin," Camael said simply.

"Mom?" Malach asked, chuckling. "She barely wanted to kill a chicken for dinner."

"She always did have a soft spot for animals," Camael said, and Malach thought he saw a hint of a smile for a split second. "But she was the most ruthless of the Blade Bearers. Michael always worried she would fall to her darker side."

"The Michael?" Malach asked. "The Archangel Michael? He thought my mom would fall to the demons?"

Cathetel nodded. "She did turn in the end, just not to the demons."

"She and my father loved each other and me. They didn't turn against you. They just wanted a life outside of the war." Malach said angrily. "Is that so much to ask?"

"They betrayed those who were counting on them," Camael shot back. "Many people died because of their actions. They were selfish."

"They were in love!" Malach barely kept his voice under control. "You know nothing about my parents."

He stormed off into the woods. He couldn't believe they blamed his parents for leaving the war to start a family. They probably didn't know what love was, let alone ever felt it. Amara must have woken up with his outburst because, only after a few moments, she appeared out of the darkness.

"You alright?" she asked.

"No, those angels think my parents are traitors." He said through gritted teeth.

"I heard," she said. "I woke up when you went to sit with them."

"They just wanted to live their lives peacefully together," he said. "Instead, the demons found them and took them."

"I'm not sure what to believe, but I know they loved you," she said. "You always talk about them fondly, and they taught you a lot. Things you've turned into your passions."

"Thanks," he said, feeling a little better. "Hopefully, you will get to meet them in a few hours."

"I will," she said confidently. "Things are going to go well tonight, and we are going to spring your father."

"I hope you're right," Malach said.

"I'm a woman," Amara said, winking at him. "I'm always right."

"Is that so?" A grin spread across his face. "Well, let's go back to the camp. It's going to be a long night."

They walked back, and Amara lay down on her mat. Malach laid down too, but waited just long enough to make sure she was asleep. He got up again, this time being very careful not to wake her, and sat on the other side of the camp from the angels. There he waited for night to fall.

Elzrod awoke first, just as dusk was falling. Malach watched him roll his mat up and strap it to its spot on his pack. He took out some food and had a small meal, then strapped his pack to his horse. He talked with the angels and then walked over to Malach.

"Are you ready?" he asked.

"Have been for a few hours now," Malach replied.

Elzrod let out a grunt of understanding. He went over to the other two and woke Amara, but left Daziar to sleep. They talked for a minute and then came over to where Malach was standing.

"Amara is going to go scout out a good point of entry and where their troops are. After that, we should be able to make a good plan of attack." Elzrod told him. "Hopefully, we can make it all the way to your father's cell and most of the way out before we are spotted. Camael and Cathetel tell me that there is a demon outpost in the town, and it won't take them long to come to the aid of the prison. I want to have a good start on them before they know what's going on. If all goes well, we should be able to stay ahead of them long enough to take refuge in Newaught."

"Sounds good," Malach said, and then to Amara. "Be careful, this is not like facing a guard patrolled building. If they catch you, they will kill you. I've seen first-hand what a demon can do."

"I know, Malach, I'll be careful." Amara winked. "Besides, no one sees me coming."

With that, she disappeared into the shadows of the trees. Night would be fully upon them soon and Amara would be hidden from view in the darkness, but Malach still worried. He couldn't do anything but wait, and there was no point in letting his mind wander. He laid down on his mat again, and his exhaustion finally allowed him to fall asleep.

Malach woke with a start; Amara was kneeling over him. She was still dressed in her black armor and cloak. She had dulled her throwing knives with something so they wouldn't glint in the darkness. Malach looked her up and down, but there were no wounds that he could see. He was relieved.

"Like what you see?" she asked with a smirk on her face.

"I was checking to see if you were alright," Malach tried hard not to blush but failed miserably.

"Sure," Amara said, still smirking at him and held out a hand to help him up, so he took it.

"I assume your scouting mission went well," Malach said.

"Yeah, and Elzrod has a plan together, so I came to get you," Amara said.

Malach nodded.

They made their way over to the rest of the group, and Malach could see an impromptu map drawn in the dirt. There was an approximation of the grounds and the main level of the farmhouse on the right, and a larger map of rooms that must have been the underground portion of the prison. Xs were marked in various different places, noting the guards' locations, and several paths were drawn as well. Most of those paths converged on one room in the underground portion of the map. Two of them, however, stayed on the ground level.

"This is your path in Malach," Elzrod explained, pointing at the start of one of the lines. "Cathetel and Camael will follow and once the guards on the first floor are taken care of. They will stand watch for any sign of backup arriving. Amara will stay with the horses and ride in when signaled for our getaway. Daziar will take this guard,"

He pointed to one of the Xs. "Malach, you will take this guard." He pointed again. "And I will deal with anyone coming up from underground. From there, we are blind to positions. Amara could not get in any farther without tipping our hand. I believe your father would be in this cell. It's not a large compound, so he shouldn't be hard to find. Any questions?"

"No," Malach answered, assuming the question was directed at him.

"Good. Let's go before we lose the cover of night," Elzrod said.

Malach peered up through the inky blackness but couldn't tell how far off dawn was. It couldn't be long until the light would appear on the horizon, though. Malach wished Skie was here with them, but she wouldn't have been able to help with this. She was safe with Honora, and she would be waiting for them to return.

He followed Elzrod and Daziar out of the camp and Cathetel and Camael followed him. They split up not far out. Each of them would move to flank the farmhouse from their respective positions.

Malach broke from the cover of the trees almost at the same time he saw Daziar make a break for the house. Malach would deal with the guard patrolling the perimeter, and he needed to get there faster than Daziar. He picked up his pace as much as he could without making undue noise.

He reached the corner of the house and peeked around the corner. The guard was walking the other way about halfway down the wall. Malach pulled Reckoning quietly from his sheath. He ran the distance that separated him and the guard. The guard heard Malach coming but too late, and he turned just in time to catch Malach's blade across his throat. The man gurgled as he fell, clutching his throat. Malach left him writhing on the ground and turned the next corner to see Daziar and Elzrod entering the front of the house. So far, there was no sign of demons.

By the time Malach went in, the two guards inside had been killed and a third was coming up through a trapdoor to see what the commotion was about. Malach threw Reckoning with a flick of his wrist, and the blade killed his second guard of the night. Malach was just a few feet behind the blade, and he pulled Reckoning out of the man's neck before the guard fell.

"What happened to 'taking care of' anyone who came up?" Malach asked Elzrod.

"Quit, you're whining," Elzrod said with a grim grin. "You should know no plan survives first contact."

"What's this?" Daziar asked, holding up a relatively small object.

It was a small pipe looking object with a handle and trigger. It almost looked like a crossbow handle and trigger, but there were no strings or limbs.

"Not sure," Elzrod responded. "Bring it with us, and we will look at it later."

Malach started to open the trapdoor to descend to the prison level, and a roar deafened him. The trap door exploded outward and Malach fell back in surprise, some of the splinters embedding themselves in his sword hand.

"There's a demon down there!" Daziar was shouting, but Malach's ears were ringing so badly he could barely hear him.

"That's no demon!" Elzrod shouted back.

A man appeared through the opening holding a sword and one of the pipe-crossbow things. He hung the odd weapon on his belt and put both hands on the sword. He continued to climb out of the opening, focusing on Elzrod.

Malach, Malach could hear Reckoning in his head just fine. *Storm informs me that Elzrod is in no condition to fight at this moment. You need to get up and help him!*

Malach looked at his hand. He had somehow held onto Reckoning, and he willed him to change to his pole weapon. He staggered to his feet, shouting at the top of his lungs to draw the man's attention away from Elzrod. It worked. The man turned toward him, and Malach charged. however, their swords never met. Cathetel barreled into him from the side, slamming him into the far back wall. The man slumped down, broken and bleeding in many places. Malach's knees gave out, and he hit the ground unceremoniously.

Malach, you and Daziar stay here and look after Elzrod, Camael told him through a mind link. *We will find your father.*

"Camael!" Daziar shouted, though he still sounded muffled to Malach's ears. "They have a new weapon! Watch yourself down there!"

Camael nodded and, putting one hand on the floor, vaulted down through the opening. Malach was just getting back to his knees when sudden nausea hit him, and he threw up. It must have been from whatever weapon they had used against them. Malach knew it had to do more than just deafen them, though he still didn't know what. He pulled himself to the window, looking for any sign of reinforcements.

"How's Elzrod?" Malach asked, not looking behind him.

"What?" Daziar shouted back.

"How's Elzrod?" Malach asked again, much louder this time.

"He's hurt!" Daziar shouted. "But I don't think any of his wounds are serious. He has a nasty bump on his head, though."

"I'm fine, boy!" Elzrod shouted, annoyed. "I've had worse!"

Malach must have regained his hearing much faster than the other two because of his healing ability. He looked both ways down the road and in the sky. The storm clouds had cleared, and he didn't see anything in the darkness yet. The demons most likely would have been in mental contact with someone here, and they probably knew about the prison break by now. Hopefully, they would get a good enough head start that they would make it back to Newaught without seeing a demon at all.

Malach heard someone coming up the ladder from the underground prison. He turned quickly to see Cathetel's head appear in the opening. He was carrying someone.

"Did you find him?" Malach asked, rushing over to help the angel with his burden.

It was not his father. Even through the cuts, bruises, and lacerations, Malach could see that. The man was too small to be his father anyway, and his heart sank in his chest. He took all that in within a moment and he looked up at Cathetel.

"Don't worry, son; your father is coming up behind me," Cathetel said, smiling at Malach. "Now help me move him out of the way."

Malach quickly did as he was bidden. And soon a second person was climbing the stairs. His father appeared beaming from ear to ear, looking directly at Malach. His smile instantly was replaced by a frown when he saw Reckoning in Malach's hand.

"You've become a Blade Bearer," were the first words out of his father's mouth. "Your mother and I had hoped to keep you from this life."

"Good to see you too, Dad," Malach said with more than a little bitterness in his voice.

Ariel's features softened. "We can talk about that another time. It's good to see you, son. And you have grown so much." He pulled Malach into an embrace, and Malach hugged him back awkwardly.

A flood of memories came to him at that moment. His first deer his father had carried back for him, a comforting hug when the local boys had knocked him down on purpose, a strong, fair hand when he had done something he'd been told not to do. His father was here, now, back from the dead, and it felt good.

"Malach, we have to go," Ariel said. "Your friend is here with the horses."

Malach snapped back to the present. His father was right. They had a long journey ahead of them, and the demons would be at their back. He willed Reckoning back to a knife and sheathed him. Daziar and Elzrod seemed to be getting their hearing back, and Amara had indeed arrived with the horses for their getaway. The angels were just waking up the other prisoner.

"Can you ride?" Cathetel asked.

The man nodded groggily and stood up. He had to have help to get up on the horse, but once he was up there, he seemed well seated.

They hadn't brought enough horses for the extra man, and Amara would need to double up with someone. Malach gave his horse to his father and hopped on behind Amara after she motioned for him to do so. He put his arms around her and realized he enjoyed the feeling of closeness. He decided was a matter for another time, though. They needed to move now.

Elzrod kicked his horse, and the rest followed. There was no sign of the demons yet, but everyone was well aware they would be coming.

They Started at a gallop to maximize the distance between them and any pursuit, but the horse would not be able to keep that pace for the distance back to Newaught. Honora always told him that horses could cover more ground faster at a trot than a gallop over multiple days of travel. It kind of made sense, since he knew when he ran he could cover a lot more distance if he paced himself.

Elzrod slowed his horse and lead them just off the road under the cover of the trees. He motioned for them to stay quiet. Most likely, he was hoping any demons flying overhead would miss them under the cover of the trees. Malach caught sight of Ariel's bare back and just about threw up again. Two large scars ran down his father's back where his wings would have been. The demons must have cut them off so his father couldn't escape. It must have been excruciating for him.

They reached the crossroad with no signs of demons yet, but the road was a long curve. Since the demons could fly, it would make sense for the demons to cut them off somewhere up ahead rather than chase them along the road.

A few hours later, they entered the swamps, and Malach's suspicions were proved right. Ahead were two huge demons. Their black wings keeping them a few feet above the ground. Malach and Amara turned and saw two more demons following them at a distance.

They were trapped.

When they got within earshot, the demon on the left in front of them held up his hand.

The company pulled up their horses.

"Give us the prisoners and we will let you go free!" the demon called.

"You mean freely into death, snake!" Elzrod spat back.

"I know what the angels want with Ariel, but these children you have with you. What stake do they hold in this?" The demon asked.

"Ariel is my fath-" Malach started to say, but was cut off by a hiss from Elzrod. "It's not like they don't know. They've sent demons after me already."

Ariel whirled, looking wide-eyed at Malach, then seem to look at him with new appreciation. He turned back to the demons in front of them without a word.

"So, the mighty angel Ariel truly has conceived a weak human son," the demon mused, an evil glint in its red eyes.

"We knew the boy was important, but we didn't know he was your son, Ariel. How is your family reunion?"

"Silence your poisoned tongue, devil!" Ariel shouted back. "You will never have him as long as I draw breath."

"Well, Elzrod," the demon mused. "My demands have changed. Turn over the prisoners *and* the boy, and we will let you go free."

"That's still not happening," Elzrod said.

Malach looked behind them and the two demons had stopped not far from them. As he turned back, he caught movement out in the swamp waters. It was just a ripple at first and then an island appeared as if from nowhere. It started moving toward them slowly, and as it got closer, Malach realized the island was made up of the same scaly hide as the monster Amara had killed.

Reckoning! Malach nearly shouted out loud in panic.

Malach, how many times do I have to say it, you don't have to. . . oh. . . oh dear, Reckoning must have noticed and come to the same conclusion as him. *I'll warn the others. Be ready to ride.*

Amara sat straighter in front of him, and he knew she had gotten the message. Elzrod flinched as if he wanted to look toward the water, he but didn't. Malach continued to watch the island grow and come closer. It was almost to land, and it was headed straight for them.

"You will never have these men nor that boy," Elzrod said, suddenly cutting off whatever the demon had been saying. "Go!"

They all kicked their horses into a gallop as the beast rose out of the water to attack. The demons pulled their dark swords out of their sheaths and readied them. The two angels outpaced Elzrod and, pulling their swords, caught the demons' blades, pushing them back and letting the group pass. Cathetel fought with the leader and took a gash on his arm from the demon's claws. Camael fared better against his demon and ended up cutting a large gash in its wing, causing it to have to land. The two angels disengaged simultaneously following the group as the beast, forgotten about by the two demons, chomped its large maw down on the demon who had been grounded. The bottom half of the demon disappeared into the beast's mouth as the top half bellowed in pain and agony.

Malach looked forward to make sure that they weren't about to run into anything, and Amara kicked the horse to go faster. They couldn't keep up this pace long enough to make it to Newaught.

Apparently, Elzrod had the same idea. He slowed his horse and turned it around. Malach and Amara flew past him. As Malach looked behind them, he could see the demon who had been talking with them had broken off and was following. The other two demons seemed to have their hands busy, at the moment, with the monster.

Elzrod drew Storm, readying himself to meet the demon head-on. Their swords clashed, but Elzrod was not strong enough to stop the blow, and it knocked him from the horse. That was the last Malach saw of Elzrod as they went around a bend in the road. The two angels sprouted wings, at the same time lifting off their frightened horses and turning to go to Elzrod's aid. Malach Noticed the armor once again coating their wings and briefly wondered how they would be able to fly. The two angels quickly flew out of sight, and Malach was forced to focus his attention on what was in front of them.

Keep going! Camael's voice boomed in his head.

Amara must have gotten the same message because she kept the horse moving, even kicking him a little harder to speed up.

Shasta started to slow after another ten minutes of galloping, and Amara allowed him to do so but kept him moving at a decent speed. Ariel and the other man followed her lead and slowed their mounts as well. Amara looked behind them, and her heart just about stopped. One of the demons was flying over the trees, headed straight for them.

"Malach!" she nearly screamed in panic. *How in the world were they going to fight that thing?*

"Just keep the horse moving," Malach said calmly.

Ariel looked at his son. "Malach, don't."

He had drawn Reckoning, and the knife had changed into a hook-like weapon. She glanced back at the demon; it had made significant progress. She turned back to Malach, still confused as to what he was planning.

"Keep moving, and make for the city as quickly as you can!" he called to the group that had grown much smaller in the last few moments.

He made his way up until he was standing on the back of the saddle. Amara finally saw what he was planning.

He's insane! She thought.

The demon bearing down on them, only a few horse lengths away. It was headed for Ariel, who was directly in front of Malach and Amara now. She felt Malach prepare himself and then jump just as the demon went overhead. Reckoning's hook found purchase in the demon's shoulder.

It bellowed and broke off from attacking Ariel. Malach had used the momentum of the turn to swing up onto the demon's back. Amara saw it carry Malach up until the clouds swallowed them.

Chapter 18

Malach held on to the wing bones protruding from the demon's back. He had taken Reckoning out of the demon's shoulder once he had gotten a good grip, but now it was carrying him high into the sky. It was all Malach could do to just hang on. If he lost his grip, he would fall to his death, but he needed to do something soon. It was getting colder and harder to breathe.

He could see the sun on the horizon now, and from its position he could tell they were facing Newaught. Maybe he could force the demon down toward the city and get help from the guards on duty. No doubt they would fire on the fearsome sight. He made certain his grip was sure on the demon's wing with his free hand and then he slammed Reckoning, still in hook form, into the demon's left wing. It was just a flesh wound, but the blade was wedged in a way that made the wing useless until it was removed. He had learned that trick in one of the many sessions with Elzrod. Although, the maneuver was to make sure the demon didn't take off; it wasn't meant to be used once the demon was already airborne.

The monster bellowed, and they stopped their upward climb. Moments later, however, they started falling with only one wing flapping, desperately trying to keep them in the air. As they tumbled, the demon tried to grab Malach and pull him bodily from its back, but Malach was just out of reach. Its armor blocking its arms.

Once they had fallen far enough that the cold was bearable again, Malach pulled Reckoning from the wing, allowing the demon to gain control of it again. Their descent slowed, but the demon didn't stop trying to get at Malach. It pulled at its black breastplate and it came free, falling down until it was lost in the clouds. Malach deflected a clawed hand that swiped at him, and then the one with the sword came at him. He ducked and the demon's sword hit its own wing. It cut deep into the bone and stuck fast. They started dropping again. Malach sheathed Reckoning and pulled at the sword stuck in the wing.

As soon as he touched it, a tortured scream sounded in his head. It was an angel blade. Malach mentally shouted at it to change to a smaller blade, hoping to pry it free before they hit the ground. It didn't listen, just kept screaming incoherently in agony. Malach yanked with all his strength and it came loose. He just about fell off the demon's back, but the wing started moving again. It was sluggish and moved with a jerking motion, but they slowed again. They had fallen back through the clouds, and Malach could see they were over the fields outside of Newaught, but nowhere near the walls. He still would have no help from the city.

The screaming in his head continued as he still held the blade in his hands. The demon had started trying to reach him again and Malach swung the newly acquired, too large blade at one of the clawed hands. It cut through at the wrist, almost as if it was paper, and he watched as the hand fell away. Malach lost his balance again and had to grab the injured wing again to stabilize himself. He noticed that both the wound on the wing and the demon's wrist were cauterized and not bleeding. That was good for him, as it didn't make things so slick.

His throat was raw, and he realized he had joined the blade's screams in his head with his own in some strange duet. Anger overtook him and he turned to the blade around before he could think about what he was doing and plunged the point into the base of the demon's neck, letting go of the blade. The screaming in his head stopped, and so did the demon's movement. They started to plummet again.

Malach! Reckoning shouted.

"I can hear you!" Malach shouted aloud over the wind that was picking up as they sped toward the ground.

Open the demon's wings! Reckoning shouted in his head. *It will slow our descent, and you may have a chance of living.*

Malach hooked an arm under each of the bones that had folded back as they plummeted head first and hauled up on them. One snapped open, filling with air and spinning them violently. He held onto the open wing, trying to stabilize it, and pulled with all his might on the one that hadn't. the wing not open was the one that had been injured. It slowly painstakingly opened until there was a popping noise and it too filled with air. The spinning slowed until they were upright and straight again. The wings, although now open, wanted to move in the wind and he had to continuously adjust them to keep the body from spiraling out of control.

Their descent slowed marginally, but not enough to where he would survive the landing. With the wings out, they weren't going straight down, but they weren't really gliding either. They were headed for the base of the wall, which wasn't much better than just hitting the ground. Malach put an arm under each wing and pulled back again. They started leveling out more, but still not enough. He hauled even harder, planting his feet under him and using all of his muscles to angle the wings up. He roared as his muscle burned with the strain.

They slammed into the top of the wall; the impact making Malach crumple onto the demon's back, belly first. The small spikes lining its back pierced into his chest in multiple places, rock shards pelting his face and arms, stinging him like bees. Then they were off the top of the wall, still moving too fast for Malach to chance jumping off. He lost count of how many buildings they impacted, but each one pushed him into the back of the demon. Several times, his head bounced off the hard, leathery skin.

After a few moments, he realized they had stopped. He managed to roll off the demon into the dust of a street. As his vision started to darken, he took in his surroundings. Several guards pointing spears at the demon. He rolled over to look at the brightening sky and laughed. He knew he sounded insane, but he had survived something that no one he knew of had ever thought of doing. He laughed until he didn't have any breath left, and as he breathed in, the darkness took him.

It took Malach only a week to heal from everything that had happened with the demon. Although he had to wear the bandages for two more weeks, so he didn't draw any suspicion. The city officials couldn't deny that the demons were back this time, as he had literally dropped one on their doorstep. The demon and Malach had finally come to a stop on the street in front of the council building. He found that to be a bit of poetic justice, even if it wasn't the council building in Brightwood.

Malach learned from the angels they made it just in time to save Elzrod. They had blocked a killing blow from the demon, and it hadn't wanted to stay and fight two angels, so it left to pursue Malach and the others. Elzrod only had a few bruises and some small cuts on him, surprisingly minor injuries for what they had gone through.

Ariel and the other prisoner were treated for their wounds as well, though Ariel was up and about the same day due to his healing powers. He had told them that about a week before they liberated the prison; the demon had moved Malach's mother. He didn't know where, but he had promised Malach and they would look for her as soon as they were both healthy enough to do so.

The angels left the sword Malach recovered from the demon with Ariel. It had calmed down enough since Malach rescued it they could speak with it now without it screaming incoherently. Its name was Fury and had been in the demon's clutches for more than two thousand years. Malach could only image the horrors it had seen. Though it was on the road to mental stability, Malach still thought something was strange about that blade.

The city had allowed Malach to continue Amara's training as a guard, but they weren't happy that he had killed a demon on neutral ground. Malach and Amara both now trained under Elzrod. They would be ready for the demons the next time they faced them.

Finally, the day came. Malach, Ariel, and Elzrod would leave first thing in the morning to go find Malach's mother in Demon Territory. They had gotten packs together for the both of them, and though Daziar had asked to come,

Malach had told him to stay and live his dream of being a city guard while he could. Amara, however, hadn't asked. She just told him she was going and when he told her no, she simply got a pack together and said she would follow them no matter what he said. Malach had finally given in.

Amara, Malach, and Skie were standing on the wall. It would be their last guard duty in Newaught, and Malach was actually going to miss the city. It was crazy to think just a few months before. All he could think about was leaving this city to go back to his home in the woods. The air had finally grown cold, and he was feeling a bit homesick for the mountains.

"How long do you think we'll be gone?" Amara asked.

"Don't know," he responded. "As long as it takes, I guess."

"You know it will be dangerous, traveling in Demon Territory with an angel." She warned.

"We've thought of that," he replied, still looking out at the field.

"The people there have been told stories of angels similar to what you have been told about demons." she warned. "That they are evil monsters. If he is discovered as an angel, we will be hunted by more than the demons."

"I understand, Amara," Malach said, as gently as he could. "We have to do this. If you don't want to come anymore, no one will fault you."

"That's not it, Malach, and you know it," she said, turning to look at him for the first time since the conversation started.

"Then what?" he asked, turning to look back at her.

"I like you, Malach. I don't want to see you hurt." She looked down at her feet then back up into his eyes. "I think. . ." her voice trailed off, and she turned away.

"You think what?" Malach asked.

"Nothing," she said, waving a dismissive hand.

"No, what were you going to say?"

"Is that smoke?" she asked, shielding her eyes from the setting sun and looking hard over the wall.

"Oh no," Malach said, grabbing her wrist. "You're not changing the subject on me now."

Skie growled a warning, and Malach realized Amara wasn't just changing the subject.

"No, really," Amara said, looking at him again. "There is a lot of smoke out there. I think it might be a fire in the forest."

Malach looked where she was indicating, and he saw it. There was smoke rising from the forest. He looked closer, shielding his own eyes from the sun. He realized it wasn't a solid wall of smoke, but hundreds of small tendrils combining as they rose.

Then he saw the first column of troops coming down the path. It looked to be a large force of armed guards. Maybe an official from another city or a wealthy man that could afford armed transport was coming to Newaught. He watched for the carriage that should hold the person of importance to appear, but it never did; instead, two mules pulled some kind of large metal pipe on wheels out of the forest pass. Then more troops appeared. Most were on foot, but the commanding officers were on horseback. They were marching in lines, but as they emerged from the woods, they formed into larger columns. He didn't understand. He had never seen so many men marching at once, and there were more coming. If the columns of smoke were any indication, they would be a whole army.

It finally clicked in his head. This was an army. Coming from the Demon Territory. This was the demon army Elzrod said was forming. They had no idea the demons were ready to march yet.

Elzrod had said they were a few years away from being ready. Yet here stood the army. Malach watched, still dumbfounded, as the first demon flew out of the forest and landed in front of all the troops. Malach jumped to run for the alarm bell, but another guard had put it together before him and was already ringing it.

Soon the wall was full of guards and officials watching as the army continued to file out and form up. They had a lot of those metal pipes on wheels and they strangely reminded Malach of the weapon the man had had at the prison. They hadn't figured out what it was, other than really loud. There was a residue inside the pipe, but no one knew what it was. If these things were the same as that weapon, only on a bigger scale, he was going to need something to cover his ears with.

The end of the column finally came out of the woods and formed up. All in all, there were only a few thousand troops, not near enough to take the city with its wall. Malach wasn't the only one to think that. He heard a few guards mumbling about how few troops they had.

One of the five demons came forward to stand front and center of the army. He raised his hand, and a man carried something forward, some sort of metal ball. He placed it in one of the pipes and pushed it in with a stick. Another soldier, with a torch beside the pipe, lit something on it as the demon lowered his hand.

"Cover your ears!" Malach shouted to any that would listen and covered his own ears. Amara followed suit.

The thing the man had lit sparked and sputtered and then went out with no sound. Malach was confused. Several of the men who had covered their ears at Malach's shout put their hands down, looking sheepishly around them. Malach almost put his own hands down, feeling a little foolish.

BOOM!

A whole section of the wall to the right of Malach shuttered as the ball they had loaded slammed into it. A small section cracked and started to fall. Men screamed and tried to escape the falling section. Only about half of them managed to make it to safety. The rest fell, screaming with the crumbling wall, to their deaths.

The demon flew up until he was level with the wall but just out of bow range and bellowed. "Bring me the men responsible for my brothers' deaths, and we will destroy your city last!"

Appendix A

Amara: uh - m AH r - uh

Anauel: AH n - oo - eh l

Angelcross: AY n - g eh l - cr ah s

Ariel: Ah r - ee - uh l

Arjun: uh r - j UU n

Auron: AW - r ah n

Barclay: b AH r - k l AI

Bartholemu: b ah r - th AH L - uh - m oo

Borden: b OH R - d uh n

Bray: b r AI

Brightwood: b r IY t - w uu d

Broak: b r OH k

Caister: c AY - s t eh r

Camael: c AA m - ay eh l

Cathetel: c AA th - eh - t eh l

Celewen: s EH l - eh - w eh n

Daniel: d AA - n ih - y uh l

Darhian: d AH r - ee - eh n

Daziar: d ah - Z EE - ah r

Deadpost: d EH d - p oh st

Demien: d eh m - EE - eh n

Dros: d r AH s

Durvain: d R - v ay n

Dyeling: d IY - l ih n g

Elzrod: EH l - z r - ah d

Emmiline: eh m - ee - l EE n

Enziarel: eh n - z IY - ah r - eh l

Fairdenn: f AY r - d eh n

Fury: f UU ry

Grent: g r EH n t

Honora: h aw - N OH - r ah

Jarsar: j AH r - s AH r

Jecrym: j EH - c r ih m

Jennari: j eh n - ah r - ee

Johm: j AH m

Kargod: k AH r - g ah d

Kath: k AA th

Lanifair: l AA n - ih - f ay r

Lawdel: l AW - d eh l

Lindow: l IH n - d ow

Malach: M AH L - ah k

Marena: m ah - r EE - n uh

Maria: m ah - r EE - uh

Marletta: m AH r - l eh t - uh

Newaught: n OO - aw t

Pangor: p AY n g - oi r

Prinna: p r EE - n uh

Ragewood: r AY j - w oo d

Ravenbard: r AY - v uh n - b AH r d

Raza: r AH - z AH

Reckoning: r EH - k uh - n ih n g

Reybella: r ay - B EH L - uh

Reymold: r AY - m oh ld

Shasta: sh AA - s t uh

Skie: s k IY

Storm: s t OH r m

Tresch: t r EH sh

Togan: T OH - g eh n

Viessa: v EE - eh s - uh

Wervine: w R - v IY n

Westbay: W EH - st b ay

Whiteshade: w IY t - sh ay d

Xylissa: z ih l - IH s - uh

Yargate: y AH r - g ay t

Zahra: z AH - r uh

<u>Acknowledgments</u>

First, I would like to thank God, since he has given me the dream and ability to write this book. It has always been a dream of mine to write and publish a book. I have written several starts to several different ideas over the years; I even had a terrible red dawn type scenario that I wrote about two hundred pages on in high school. Luckily, that manuscript will never see the light of day again.

The idea for this book came to me while I was sitting through a Sunday morning sermon. My pastor mentioned what it might be like if we had to physically fight the spiritual battle that is waged every day. As the idea for this book blossomed in my mind I have to admit I didn't listen to a word he said after that. This book has been a three-year journey for me and I want to thank all the people in my life that have encouraged me through this process, whether it was just listening to an idea that I was working on or simply an encouraging word. Also, I would like to thank my parents for instilling in me the love for a good story. There are three people that have really done a lot to help me through the writing, editing, and publishing process. First, I need to thank my editor, Jonie. She has single handedly turned this book from simply good, to excellent. She did an excellent job editing and she was so easy to work with. There were a few places in the book that would have made no sense without her help. The second person I need to thank is my good friend and fellow author Cole Fox. I met him early on when I was writing this story and he has been there to answer all of my endless questions. He even dropped everything to "talk me off the ledge" so to speak during the publishing process when I texted him out of the blue. If you enjoy SciFi look him up. I am so very much a fan of his works. The final and probably most important person would be my wife. She has done so much for my writing career. She has listened to my endless rantings about ideas for this and many books to come. She has patiently, and sometimes not so patiently, endured me waking her up in the middle of the night as I write down things that have come to me mid-dream. She has encouraged me throughout the process of writing, editing and publishing and many, many more things. I love her more and more each day and I know that she will continue to be there for me as I continue my writing career.

About the Author

H. L. Walsh lives in Kansas City, MO with his wife and two kids. They enjoy camping, hiking, and spending time together as a family.

H. L. has been writing since he was fifteen but only published his first book in 2019. He is a self-employed author and enjoys reading multiple genres including fantasy, science fiction, the classics, etc.

Follow H. L. Walsh on his website at www.hlwalshbooks.com, on Facebook at www.facebook.com/hlwalshbooks, on Twitter @hlwalshauthor, and on Instagram @hlwalshauthor to catch all the updates!

www.ingramcontent.com/pod-product-compliance
Lightning Source LLC
Chambersburg PA
CBHW051603100726
47898CB00001B/207